I0825302

CLIVE CUSSLER

COLD FIRE

TITLES BY CLIVE CUSSLER

DIRK PITT ADVENTURES

Clive Cussler The Corsican Shadow (by Dirk Cussler)
Clive Cussler's The Devil's Sea (by Dirk Cussler)
Celtic Empire (with Dirk Cussler)
Odessa Sea (with Dirk Cussler)
Havana Storm (with Dirk Cussler)
Poseidon's Arrow (with Dirk Cussler)
Crescent Dawn (with Dirk Cussler)
Arctic Drift (with Dirk Cussler)
Treasure of Khan (with Dirk Cussler)
Black Wind (with Dirk Cussler)
Trojan Odyssey
Valhalla Rising
Atlantis Found
Flood Tide
Shock Wave
Inca Gold
Sahara
Dragon
Treasure
Cyclops
Deep Six
Pacific Vortex!
Night Probe!
Vixen 03
Raise the Titanic!
Iceberg
The Mediterranean Caper

SAM AND REMI FARGO ADVENTURES®

Wrath of Poseidon (with Robin Burcell)
The Oracle (with Robin Burcell)
The Gray Ghost (with Robin Burcell)
The Romanov Ransom (with Robin Burcell)
Pirate (with Robin Burcell)
The Solomon Curse (with Russell Blake)
The Eye of Heaven (with Russell Blake)
The Mayan Secrets (with Thomas Perry)
The Tombs (with Thomas Perry)
The Kingdom (with Grant Blackwood)
Lost Empire (with Grant Blackwood)
Spartan Gold (with Grant Blackwood)

ISAAC BELL ADVENTURES®

Clive Cussler The Iron Storm (by Jack Du Brul)
Clive Cussler The Heist (by Jack Du Brul)
Clive Cussler The Sea Wolves (by Jack Du Brul)
The Saboteurs (with Jack Du Brul)
The Titanic Secret (with Jack Du Brul)
The Cutthroat (with Justin Scott)
The Gangster (with Justin Scott)
The Assassin (with Justin Scott)
The Bootlegger (with Justin Scott)
The Striker (with Justin Scott)
The Thief (with Justin Scott)
The Race (with Justin Scott)
The Spy (with Justin Scott)
The Wrecker (with Justin Scott)
The Chase

KURT AUSTIN ADVENTURES®

Novels from the NUMA Files®

Clive Cussler Cold Fire (by Graham Brown)

Clive Cussler Desolation Code (by Graham Brown)

Clive Cussler Condor's Fury (by Graham Brown)

Clive Cussler's Dark Vector (by Graham Brown)

Fast Ice (with Graham Brown)

Journey of the Pharaohs (with Graham Brown)

Sea of Greed (with Graham Brown)

The Rising Sea (with Graham Brown)

Nighthawk (with Graham Brown)

The Pharaoh's Secret (with Graham Brown)

Ghost Ship (with Graham Brown)

Zero Hour (with Graham Brown)

The Storm (with Graham Brown)

Devil's Gate (with Graham Brown)

Medusa (with Paul Kemprecos)

The Navigator (with Paul Kemprecos)

Polar Shift (with Paul Kemprecos)

Lost City (with Paul Kemprecos)

White Death (with Paul Kemprecos)

Fire Ice (with Paul Kemprecos)

Blue Gold (with Paul Kemprecos)

Serpent (with Paul Kemprecos)

***OREGON* FILES®**

Clive Cussler Quantum Tempest (by Mike Maden)

Clive Cussler Ghost Soldier (by Mike Maden)

Clive Cussler Fire Strike (by Mike Maden)

Clive Cussler's Hellburner (by Mike Maden)

Marauder (with Boyd Morrison)

Final Option (with Boyd Morrison)

Shadow Tyrants (with Boyd Morrison)

Typhoon Fury (with Boyd Morrison)

The Emperor's Revenge (with Boyd Morrison)

Piranha (with Boyd Morrison)

Mirage (with Jack Du Brul)

The Jungle (with Jack Du Brul)

The Silent Sea (with Jack Du Brul)

Corsair (with Jack Du Brul)

Plague Ship (with Jack Du Brul)

Skeleton Coast (with Jack Du Brul)

Dark Watch (with Jack Du Brul)

Sacred Stone (with Craig Dirgo)

Golden Buddha (with Craig Dirgo)

NONFICTION

Built for Adventure: The Classic Automobiles of Clive Cussler and Dirk Pitt

Built to Thrill: More Classic Automobiles from Clive Cussler and Dirk Pitt

The Sea Hunters (with Craig Dirgo)

The Sea Hunters II (with Craig Dirgo)

Clive Cussler and Dirk Pitt Revealed (with Craig Dirgo)

CHILDREN'S BOOKS

The Adventures of Vin Fiz

The Adventures of Hotsy Totsy

CLIVE CUSSLER

COLD FIRE

A Novel from the NUMA Files®

GRAHAM BROWN

G. P. Putnam's Sons

New York

PUTNAM
— EST. 1838 —

G. P. Putnam's Sons
Publishers Since 1838
An imprint of Penguin Random House LLC
1745 Broadway, New York, NY 10019
penguinrandomhouse.com

Book design by Kathleen Soriano-Taylor

LIBRARY OF CONGRESS CATALOGING-IN-PUBLICATION DATA

Names: Brown, Graham, 1969–, author | Cussler, Clive, contributor
Title: Cold fire / Graham Brown.
Other titles: At head of title Clive Cussler
Description: New York : G. P. Putnam's Sons, 2026. | Series: Kurt Austin adventures
Identifiers: LCCN 2026003649 (print) | LCCN 2026003650 (ebook) |
ISBN 9798217184972 hardcover | ISBN 9798217185009 ebook
Subjects: LCSH: Austin, Kurt (Fictitious character) |
National Underwater and Marine Agency | LCGFT: Thrillers (Fiction) | Novels
Classification: LCC PS3602.R69768 C65 2026 (print) | LCC PS3602.R69768 (ebook)
LC record available at https://lccn.loc.gov/2026003649
LC ebook record available at https://lccn.loc.gov/2026003650

Printed in the United States of America
1st Printing

The authorized representative in the EU for product safety and compliance is
Penguin Random House Ireland, Morrison Chambers, 32 Nassau Street,
Dublin D02 YH68, Ireland, https://eu-contact.penguin.ie.

CAST OF CHARACTERS

NATIONAL UNDERWATER AND MARINE AGENCY (NUMA)

KURT AUSTIN—Director of Special Projects, salvage expert and boating enthusiast, leads the mission to recover the EAGL

JOE ZAVALA—Assistant Director of Special Projects, helicopter pilot and mechanical genius, Kurt's right-hand man

RUDI GUNN—Assistant Director of NUMA, runs most of the day-to-day operations, graduate of the Naval Academy

VICE PRESIDENT SANDECKER—Former head of NUMA, now Vice President of the United States

PAUL TROUT—NUMA's chief geologist, graduate of Scripps University, married to Gamay

GAMAY TROUT—NUMA's leading marine biologist, also graduated from Scripps

GIGI CABRERA—Member of the *Lyra*'s crew during the Arctic mission

PLAN (PEOPLE'S LIBERATION ARMY NAVY)

MAJOR GUSHAN—Revered operative of the Chinese military, counterterrorist specialist, chosen for the Arctic recovery mission

REAR ADMIRAL YANG LI—Politically astute flag officer, eager to join the high command, in charge of the Arctic mission

RUSSIAN MILITARY

GENERAL BORISOV—Ranking commander in Russian military intelligence

MISHIN—Civilian executive working with Borisov, member of the special committee

EAGL PROJECT TEAM AND C-17 CREW

DAN CALDWELL—Senior test engineer for the Enhanced Aerial Gunnery Laser (EAGL)

RIDLEY WILES—Targeting and control programmer for the EAGL prototype

GENERAL OFFERMAN—Head of the EAGL project

CONTRABAND SMUGGLERS

AHAB—Leader of a smuggling ring, shot while dumping radioactive waste into the sea between China and Japan

RAND—Colorful South African expat who smuggles rare earths and computer chips, sometime associate of Ahab's

PRUDENCE—Rand's sister, mechanical genius and calm counter-presence to his flamboyant personality

CLIVE CUSSLER

COLD FIRE

PROLOGUE
THE BURNING SHIP

The thudding sound of the Chinese helicopter's rotor shook the cabin from nose to tail. Flying the overloaded craft low and slow on a hot and humid afternoon put a tremendous strain on the engine. The temperature gauges were creeping up. The pilot didn't like that. Under different circumstances he would suggest they dump some fuel or perhaps a little cargo, but they were a long way out to sea, and the cargo . . .

He glanced back into the main cabin. Fifteen heavily armed commandos from the People's Liberation Army Navy. Some of them wearing scuba gear. Others strapped up in so much body armor he wondered how they could move. All of them looked ready to assault some well-defended objective.

"We should climb and add some speed," the pilot advised. "Engine heat is rising. We need cooler air and more of it. Otherwise, we risk a system failure."

He was addressing the combat team's leader, a hard-faced lieutenant from a special unit of the Chinese army. The lieutenant ignored him, his eyes locked onto a growing cloud of dark, oily smoke that was drifting across from the shimmering sea. The smoke concealed a burning freighter known to be hauling stolen weapons and barrels of radioactive waste. Somewhere on that freighter a ruthless cabal of smugglers awaited their arrival, no doubt ready to use the stolen weapons against them. He expected the flare of a missile to burst forth at any moment. Climbing would only make them an easier target.

"Keep us on the deck," the lieutenant ordered bluntly. "Circle the freighter. We need to assess our options."

The pilot did as ordered, manipulating the controls with the smooth precision of a veteran. His flying skills were the main reason he'd been chosen for this mission. He was known for his pinpoint control. But he couldn't do the impossible. The freighter was engulfed in smoke, it was listing and sinking, its masts and cranes had broken loose and could be seen swinging unpredictably through the fumes with every wallowing movement of the ship.

Metal cables dangling from the cranes had been strung up across the ship like anti-bird wires near an outside dining area. Landing, or even getting close enough to deploy the commandos, would be almost impossible.

They rounded the stern to find smoke billowing from every gap. Flames could be seen through open hatches. The engine room had to be ablaze at this point, diesel slurry burning and pumping out black clouds. Other parts of the ship burning with secondary fires suggested a deliberate act.

"They're trying to scuttle the ship," the pilot guessed.

"Any sign of the Americans?" the lieutenant asked.

The pilot shook his head. He saw no flares or flashing lights. He saw no one standing on the deck waving for help. "They can't possibly be on the ship. Not in that condition."

The lieutenant knew better. He'd studied the files of the men they were speaking about. He knew they would not abandon the mission until the ship went down and perhaps not even then.

He reached for the radio controls, checked that he was on the right frequency, and spoke in well-studied English. "NUMA, this is Dragon Lima," he announced. "Landing impossible. Freighter is burning from the stern to the number two mast. Aft of the main hold is an inferno. We recommend you abandon the assault. Escape may be possible from the bow. We will pick you up. Do you copy?"

As he waited for an answer, the lieutenant played with the volume, listening to static and silence. He was angry. For the first time in years a joint operation between an American agency and a Chinese one had proven fruitful. A ring of smugglers who had been dumping toxic waste into the seas between China and Japan had been tracked and cornered. Now it was all falling apart.

Political meddling had delayed their departure from Shanghai. A mechanical problem had forced a second helicopter to turn back, and the lieutenant's squad had pressed on alone.

With help coming late, the Americans had gone for the ship on their own. They were now trapped in a hellish firestorm if they even remained alive. Not the result anyone wanted out of this rare moment of cooperation.

"NUMA, do you read?" the lieutenant called out again. "Freighter is ablaze and sinking. If you can get into the water, we will pick you up."

This time a voice cut through the static. It asked only a single question. "Any word from Gushan?"

Gushan was the Chinese team's point man. He'd boarded the freighter covertly to confirm the presence of the stolen weapons and waste.

"Negative," the lieutenant said. "The major has not reported in since confirming the presence of the radioactive samples."

"We'll find him," the American insisted. "Just watch for anyone attempting to escape. They wouldn't be scuttling the ship if they didn't have a plan to get away."

The lieutenant acknowledged the request, glanced at the pilot, and made a whirling motion with his hand. They would circle the freighter until they were needed one way or another, though the lieutenant feared it would only be to recover bodies. Between the burning ship, the brutal reputation of the smugglers, and the unexpected radio silence from the major, he assumed Gushan was already dead. And if the Americans kept looking for him, they would only end up joining him in the world beyond.

Kurt Austin had no doubt he would end up in Valhalla or somewhere similar one day, but he had no intention of having today be that day. He moved along the deck on the upwind side of the ship, carrying a short-barreled assault rifle designed for combat in close quarters. He moved in the quick spurts of a soldier transiting hostile territory: darting from cover to cover, clearing the rigging above as he went, swinging the barrel of the rifle quickly as he passed blind spots and stacks of equipment on the deck. So far, he'd encountered no sign of the smugglers. In fact, he hadn't found a living soul.

He paused in a sheltered nook beside a bulkhead wall and covered the approach of his partner, Joe Zavala. Though they weren't soldiers, Marines, or military operatives of any kind, the two men had been through plenty of scrapes and firefights together. They formed a tight unit. Each man knowing what the other was thinking.

The thickening smoke wafted past them, the fumes burning their lungs, throats, and eyes. They'd stuck to the outer edge of the ship on the windward side, but it was not enough to keep them in the clear. Touching the bulkhead behind him, Kurt could feel the heat. Looking up at the sun, he found only a fading disk drifting in clouds of thickening brown smoke. It had been robbed of its brilliance and glare. It seemed almost ready to go out.

Considering their next move, he put a hand through the tangled locks of his unruly and prematurely silver hair, brushing it back and off his forehead. He was a taller man of almost forty. He stood six foot two, with broad shoulders but an otherwise lanky frame. His silver-gray hair often gave him away, but his most striking feature was a pair of intense blue eyes, which were now bathed in a sea of red as the fumes irritated their corneas.

As Zavala ducked into the protected nook, he turned sideways to Kurt, covering the area behind them. Joe was shorter than Kurt, and had dark eyes and dark hair, which was buzzed down to a layer of stubble at the moment. He had the compact muscular body of a boxer and moved with the quick grace of someone who'd spent his youth training to throw and avoid punches.

As Joe settled in, he noticed a dead crewman on the deck ahead of them. "That makes five," he said to Kurt.

Kurt had seen the man. It did indeed make five. All shot in the back. "Ahab and the other smugglers are trying to cover their tracks. Eliminating anyone who can identify them."

"He's nothing if not ruthless," Joe said.

They'd been looking for the man who called himself Ahab for months, since information revealed that Ahab was taking toxic waste off the hands of unprincipled companies and dumping it in the sea for a hefty price, but one that was much lower than the true cost of dealing with such materials. The Chinese government had become involved when they learned he was smuggling weapons and siphoning radioactive material out of the waste he trafficked in for use in a "dirty bomb." A bomb he would almost certainly sell to the highest bidder.

It had been a good collaboration, but each time they got close, Ahab slipped away. Informants turned up dead. An Interpol agent had gone missing, and several members of the Chinese federal police had been blown up by a rocket-propelled grenade when they stopped a truck believed to be carrying one of Ahab's shipments. If the man left this ship in anything but chains or a coffin, plenty of other deaths would certainly follow.

"They have to be up near the bow," Kurt said. "They started these fires in the stern for a reason."

"Why set them at all?" Joe asked.

"To slow us and the Chinese down," Kurt said. "To cover their tracks. They might even think the fires and smoke will help them escape."

"They may have abandoned ship already," Joe suggested as a counterpoint. "I would have."

Kurt probably would have left by now as well, but he wasn't a smuggler trying to salvage a large payday. "The Chinese would have seen them if they'd taken a boat out," he said. "Ahab's waiting for something. Help, maybe. Or just hoping to hold out until the Chinese helicopter has to go back to the coast. It can't loiter for too long."

Joe was a pilot. He knew the numbers better than Kurt. "Twenty minutes tops. Less if they had to fight a headwind coming out."

"That's when Ahab will go," Kurt said. "We need to find him and stop him before the timer runs out."

"What about Major Gushan?"

"He's either being held hostage or he's dead. If he's alive, he'll be with Ahab."

Joe looked around at the smoke. "If the safe place is ahead of us—and they still want to bring some of their cache with them—then there's only one spot left to hide. The forward cargo hold."

Kurt agreed. The forward hold was smaller and could be sealed off from the rest of the ship. That kept the smoke and fire at bay while the smugglers waited for their chance to escape. It also had side hatches down close to the waterline for taking on provisions in port. They would make it easy for Ahab and his men to get off the ship and onto a boat.

"That means we have to go inside," Kurt said.

Joe nodded. From their packs they pulled small hoods that went over their heads and shoulders. The hoods had acrylic lenses and filters that would remove the smoke and particulates, allowing them to breathe. The hoods wouldn't protect them from an inferno, but they'd make it possible to run through a corridor or two. That was all they needed.

In the forward hold, nine men waited nervously, while one man bravely faced his death. The ship was burning. The smoke had begun drifting through the ventilation system. The bulkheads themselves were growing warm to the touch. The sound of a helicopter thundering past every minute or so added to the tension.

They had a boat prepared. Stacks of weapons and metal drums carrying the radioactive materials lay strapped into place. The boat itself sat on a conveyor belt designed to move cargo in and out of the hold. The belt ended beside a roller-equipped ramp that would be deployed and extended to the water once the side door was opened. This was their path to freedom. But with the helicopter outside they couldn't risk a move.

"You can't get away now," a battered and beaten Chinese man said. "You're trapped."

Gushan was down on his knees, his hands tied behind his back. His face was bruised from kicks and punches. A gash just beneath his right eye streamed blood like red war paint.

"They will run out of fuel and crash before I have to make any move at all," an entirely average-looking man said. About the only thing that stood out on Ahab was a jutting jaw, hidden now by a grimy beard.

"They won't come alone," Gushan said. He wore a crewman's overalls, having infiltrated the ship to search for the radioactive materials that Ahab intended to use in the dirty bomb.

"Alone is exactly what they are," Ahab insisted. "The other helicopter never left Shanghai. My associates saw to that. There won't be any rescue. They cannot possibly land on the burning deck. And by the time your ships get here I will be long gone, this freighter will be on the bottom, and your body will be food for the crabs and fish of the South China Sea. But before that happens you will tell me how you learned that I was aboard this ship."

Major Gushan stared up at the man who'd been beating him. "The high command has a source in your organization," he said.

"Who?" Ahab demanded.

Gushan shrugged. "They don't share the name of a source with someone like me."

Ahab grew irritated. He knew it was a lie. Just a way to put doubt into his mind. But he was tired and angry. His face was itchy from the salt and the heat. His eyes had begun to sting from the traces of smoke.

The helicopter rumbled by again. Another pass or two and it would have to leave. Ahab was certain of this. He would wring the information out of the major or end his life before then.

He picked up a length of metal from the deck, examining its jagged end. "I'll ask you one more time," he said. "But first . . ."

He lunged forward with the staff, thrusting it downward and through the major's gut. It stuck out through his back, the jagged tip grinding into the metal deck behind him.

Gushan howled in pain and writhed around the stave like a fish impaled with a spear. Ahab used the leverage it gave him to make

Gushan bow down before him. "Assuming you can speak, I will take that answer now."

Gushan coughed and choked and drooled a string of blood. Then bravely shook his head.

Enraged, Ahab grabbed the metal shaft with both hands, intending to rip the major apart. But a rifle crack sounded, his leg exploded in a spray of blood and bone, and it was Ahab who went to the ground.

His men raced for cover. Some of them diving to the deck, others hiding behind the stacks of machinery and equipment in the hold. A firefight erupted as shots rang out from all sides. Ahab watched several of his men go down.

"Throw your weapons away," a voice demanded from the rafters.

Crawling desperately for cover, Ahab was stunned by the timbre of the voice, it was loud and deep and cut through the clamor circulating in the hold.

"The Chinese navy is surrounding the ship," the voice added. "It's over."

Almost poetically the helicopter raced by once again. But Ahab heard the pitch of the rotors change. It was headed out, going back to the mainland at last. They still had a chance.

Removing his belt, he cinched it around his leg, pulling it tight and stemming some of the blood loss. With his leg stable and numbness already setting in, Ahab drew a long-barreled pistol from his chest pack. The weapon was oddly shaped, fitted with attachments. It almost looked like a homemade weapon, but was actually a modified competition pistol.

Ahab was so accurate with the weapon, he'd once shot a man dead by firing a bullet down a sixty-foot length of pipe no wider than a tennis ball. The shell had flown dead center down the pipe, striking its target on the far end without ever grazing the sides.

If he could spot the intruder, even just part of him, he would not miss.

"Open the hatch," he ordered.

One of his men had been standing near the controls. The man threw the switch, and the huge cargo door cracked open and slid backward. Orange sunlight poured into the vast compartment, filtering through the smoke.

"Anyone who makes a move for that door is a dead man," the voice shouted in warning.

Ahab had heard only one voice. Even in the brief gunfight the attackers had fired only a few shots. Through the intense pain he calculated the reality. A large group would have opened fire en masse, taking out most of the smugglers in a single volley. There could be only one or two men stalking them now.

"They're up in the rigging above the cranes," he said to his men. "Pin them down."

His men took potshots at the catwalks and ladders that ran across the top of the hold. Ricochets rebounded, but neither Ahab nor his men faced any return fire.

Ahab crawled to a new position, spotting a man slithering along the yellow steel I-beam rail that supported one of the mobile cranes. He raised his weapon and fired.

The first shot plunked the beam dead center. He cursed himself for missing, but he was unsteady and losing blood.

He aimed again, exhaled, and squeezed the trigger. This shot missed the steel rail and grazed the man's arm. Not a fatal wound, but one that drew a reaction. The target rolled off the I-beam and dropped onto a catwalk.

Ahab fired again, but the man leapt down onto a cargo container and out of sight.

"Get the boat ready!" Ahab yelled.

One of his men activated the conveyor belt. The ribbed inflatable boat began to move.

While another one of his men engaged the second attacker, Ahab saw his chance. “Help me,” he shouted. “Get me up!”

The man who’d started the conveyor rushed to Ahab’s side, lifting him up and assisting him across the deck. They reached the boat and tumbled inside.

As the boat neared the open hatch, gunfire burst forth from beside the cargo container. Bullets ripped into the inflated sections of the boat. They plugged the control column and the engine, but hit neither Ahab nor the other smuggler.

Ahab fired back, forcing the attacker to take cover once more. The ribbed boat neared the top of the ramp. Two more of his men ran forward, jumping into the boat. They fired their weapons in all directions, trying to keep the attackers pinned down.

The front end of the boat tipped over onto the slope. Just then the American who’d hidden behind the cargo container reappeared. The outside light lit upon him as he stepped forward.

Ahab saw him fully now. Tall and lanky. Silver-gray hair. Weathered face streaked with sweat and grime but marked by intense blue eyes.

Ahab raised his pistol, intending to put those eyes out, but the rifle in the other man’s hands chattered first.

Another spread of shells hit the boat, but this time they ripped into the metal cases. Gobs of contaminated radioactive liquid erupted outward. The fluid doused Ahab and his men. It burned with a cold fire as if some infernal curse were being conjured upon them.

One of the men screamed. Another dove off the boat, hitting the ramp and tumbling into the water below. Ahab focused only on his enemy, pulling the trigger one last time, firing his final bullet as the boat went over the ramp and raced down into the sea.

He never saw the outcome of that shot. The boat had sped downward too quickly. It hit the ocean, nearly throwing him out. Its momentum carried it away from the freighter.

It drifted aft, moving into the thick smoke and deflating slowly. It vanished in the clouds of burning diesel near the stern.

The boat would be found a mile from the freighter, adrift, swamped, and floating on its side; buoyancy provided by two compartments that still contained air. It was discovered empty, the smugglers, the weapons, and the radioactive materials it had once held long since spilled into the sea.

Inside the cargo hold, Kurt and Joe took three men prisoner, covered the others' bodies with tarps, and gave aid to the grievously wounded major. They didn't dare remove the metallic spear that had punctured his gut, but they cut the ends off and did their best to staunch the bleeding.

The major grunted as they laid him on a makeshift stretcher. "Thank you," he said. "I would like to see the sun again before I die."

They carried him toward the open cargo door and placed him on the deck, where he could see the sun through the smoke. Kurt looked him over. "Don't worry. You're not going to die from a flesh wound like this."

The major offered a half smile, then he looked up at the sun and closed his eyes.

CHAPTER 1

Fifty thousand feet above the Arctic Circle the air temperature was a frigid one hundred nineteen degrees below zero. A heavily modified C-17 transport cut through this bitterly cold air with two F-35 fighters trailing a mile behind. At this temperature, the atmosphere held nothing in the way of moisture and offered crystal clear views of the stars above and the moon, which oddly appeared below the aircraft, as it had just emerged on the far horizon.

Inside the C-17, in a comfortably heated compartment just aft of the cockpit, a group of engineers and technicians sat at various computer consoles watching different systems and analyzing incoming data.

"Target spotted," a voice announced across the compartment.

Senior test engineer Dan Caldwell looked up from his screen. There wasn't supposed to be a target for them to shoot at yet. He glanced around to see who'd spoken. He was not surprised to see Ridley Wiles, one of the systems analysts, standing at the window. Ridley was twenty-three, a civilian contractor, and not all that big on discipline. But he understood the laser system they were using like no one else.

"What target are you talking about?" Caldwell asked sharply. "Nothing on my scope."

"It's big and round . . . and allegedly made of cream cheese," Ridley replied. "We can hit it from here. Then it's bagels for everyone."

Groans and mild laughter wafted through the cabin as Ridley stepped back from the window and pointed at the moon.

Caldwell was not amused. "Get in your seat, Ridley. The punishment for failed attempts at humor is washing the plane by hand once we get back to Greenland. No gloves allowed."

Ridley took his seat and strapped himself in like he was supposed to. Caldwell let it go at that. He didn't mind the break in tension that a few well-placed groaners could bring on, but it was time to get serious.

The aircraft and laser system they were about to test was known as the EAGL, Enhanced Aerial Gunnery Laser. Caldwell had always wondered why someone hadn't added another word to the name so they could call it the EAGLE proper, but that was above his pay grade.

The laser in question was the most powerful laser in the world by a wide margin. It was far too heavy to be mounted in a fighter or attack craft. But placed aboard the modified C-17 and lifted to a high altitude, it could do things that would alter the rules of war. Assuming, of course, that it worked as planned.

Time to find out, Caldwell thought.

He pressed the intercom switch and spoke to the captain. "All systems go," he reported. "Cryogenics functioning at optimal levels. Laser waveguides are tuned. Change course to two-four-zero. We're entering the firing window now. Test protocol commencing."

The pilot replied affirmatively, and the big aircraft banked into a turn. For the next few minutes, they would watch their screens and wait, while an extremely powerful radar system mounted below the craft scanned the ocean's surface out to the edge of the curvature of the earth.

Several hundred miles away, an American submarine was about to launch an unarmed ballistic missile. It would burst from the surface in a spray of mist and foam, linger for an instant, and then rocket skyward on a pillar of flame.

As it climbed above the horizon, the radar system mounted on the underside of the C-17 would find it, lock on, and track it. Seconds ticked by. Then several tense minutes. They knew roughly when and where the missile would be launched, but to make the test realistic they hadn't been given the exact data.

Finally, something appeared on the scope. "Target acquired," a radar technician said. "Altitude three thousand feet and climbing. Range, speed, and acceleration computing now."

"Bring the laser to ready," Caldwell ordered.

Ridley moved a trio of switches from standby to active. The system, which had been tested before at lower settings, would be operating at the maximum power level for this final test. The high-pitched whine of rapidly spinning generators could be heard emanating from the aft section of the aircraft.

"Energy storage at full," another of the techs announced. "All systems green."

"Targeting solution confirmed," Ridley reported. "We're locked on."

"Activate laser," Caldwell said calmly.

Ridley reached forward, flipped open a protective plastic cover, and pressed a square, red button. A soft click was heard, but nothing else. There was no pulse, no recoil, no crash of thunder. There was no bright beam of a death ray to be seen, as the laser operated in the X-ray part of the spectrum.

Four hundred miles away, the submarine-launched ballistic

missile was at ten thousand feet and streaking skyward at five thousand miles an hour; three times the speed of a rifle bullet. To the laser, which traveled at the speed of light, it might as well have been standing still.

The laser hit the target squarely, melting through the exterior in a hundredth of a second and detonating the rocket propellant. The explosion in the night sky over the Atlantic was visible for a hundred miles. Confirmation came to the C-17 via radar.

"Target separating," the radar tech announced as the green dot on the scope spread out and faded. In seconds, the rapidly expanding ball of fire and fragments had diffused past the point of radar detection. The blip vanished from the screen. "Target eliminated."

A small round of applause and congratulatory shouts erupted. Caldwell cut them short. "We still have work to do, gentlemen."

He heard the grumbling behind his back, but didn't turn around lest the team see the broad smile on his face.

As he ran through a systems check, a loud pop sounded behind him. Now he was angry. He spun in his chair, shouting as he turned. "That better not be champagne, Ridley!"

As he spoke the last word, Caldwell's mouth hung open in shock. Ridley held a gun and was firing it into the backs of the other technicians. Blood was splattering across the computer screens and consoles. They slumped forward or recoiled backward as the bullets hit. One of them managed to undo his seat belt and get up, only to get hit at point-blank range in the chest.

Caldwell freed himself from his harness and launched himself at Ridley, tackling him before he could swing the pistol around. The two men slammed to the floor of the aircraft, with Caldwell trying to drive his shoulder downward into the traitor's neck.

The gun discharged beneath him. It felt like a small explosion. A burning fire flared in Caldwell's gut.

Caldwell knew he'd been hit, but sensed it wasn't a mortal wound. He kept his weight on Ridley, rising up and slugging him in the jaw with a right hook. Ridley's head snapped to the side and blood splattered from his lips. It was a solid blow, but not a knockout punch. And it left Caldwell off balance. His core muscles, torn by the first shot, were too weak to keep him upright as Ridley bucked him off.

He fell to the side, put his hands on the deck, and spun back toward his opponent.

Ridley fired a second shot. This time the gun was pointed upward not sideways. Caldwell felt as if he'd been kicked in the chest. He reeled from the impact, rocking backward and then toppling over as his vision blurred. He slumped to the deck gasping for air.

Ridley got to one knee, leaning over him, trying to determine if he needed another bullet.

"Why?" Caldwell asked, his voice a raspy whisper.

"Why not," Ridley replied nastily, as if that explained everything.

Caldwell barely heard the words; he'd lost too much blood. He lay his head on the deck and closed his eyes.

Ridley looked around the compartment. The first part of the job was done. The test crew were dead. The compartment secure. Now for the more difficult disappearing act.

He stood up, put a hand to his bruised mouth, and wiggled a tooth free. He looked at it for a second and then tossed it aside. He'd get implants, and anything else he wanted once he had money to burn.

Ahead of him the cockpit door opened. Ridley raised the gun as the copilot came out. Instead of firing, he lowered the pistol.

The copilot held a bloody knife, which had been used to good effect on the aircraft's captain. "I assume we're flying on autopilot," Ridley said.

"For the moment," the copilot said. "I came back to see if you needed any help."

"Good work," Ridley told him. "Time for the second act. Turn toward Murmansk and shut down all the data relays. It's time for this plane to disappear."

"What about the F-35s?"

Ridley tried to smile, but his bruised face wouldn't allow it. "I'll take care of them."

Eight hundred miles away in a high-tech conference room a group of senior military officers watched the successful test and cheered. They pumped their fists and slapped each other on the back. They spoke enthusiastically about controlling the twenty-first-century battlefield with fleets of EAGL aircraft circling high above.

"The EAGL can shoot down a hundred ballistic missiles before they leave enemy territory," an Air Force general named Offerman boasted. "It can stand two hundred miles from a battlefield and take out a thousand drones in an hour's work."

"We could park one over every major city," the Assistant Secretary of Defense added. "And office workers can take their lunch at sidewalk cafés in the middle of a war."

A representative from Scion, the company that had built the laser, grinned and shrugged as if that was a little far-fetched in his mind. But his smile suggested it wasn't too far off. The main idea behind the EAGL was not to shoot down drones, but to make ballistic missiles obsolete. The plan was to build a fleet of the aircraft and have them patrol the Arctic, where all the ballistic missiles from Russia or China would have to travel to reach the United States. It was conservatively estimated that nine such aircraft could eradicate the entire Russian ballistic missile force even if it were launched simultaneously. Half the missiles would be destroyed before they reached the upper atmosphere. The other half would be wiped out as they raced directly overhead through the dark limits of space.

The Israelis had built an Iron Dome to protect their country. The United States would have one made of X-rays and invisible light.

Amid the celebration, one of the technicians noticed a problem. After confirming it wasn't on the receiving end, he alerted Offerman. "General, we're losing telemetry on the EAGL."

The celebration hit a wall. The laughter died. Everyone turned back to the screens they'd been watching earlier. Video from the chase planes showed the aircraft flying straight and level. It appeared fine.

"What data blocks are dropping out?" Offerman asked.

"We've lost navigation," the technician said. "Speed, altitude, heading, temperature."

On another screen, which showed a virtual mock-up of the cockpit, the indicators went from accurate numbers to a series of question marks. Seconds later they became dashed lines. Engine readouts failed next.

"Were losing laser telemetry now," a technician from Scion reported.

Offerman wavered as he felt a sudden numbness in his knees. If not for the view from the chase plane they would have no way of knowing if the C-17 was still flying or had exploded midair.

"Contact the pilot," Offerman said calmly.

The Air Force communication specialist put in several calls, but to no avail. "No response."

"Aircraft is turning and descending," someone called out.

"Contact the chase planes," Offerman ordered. "Find out what the hell is going on."

The communications specialist made the calls. "Blue Shadow Leader, this is Bullfrog. We've lost communications and telemetry with the EAGL. Track shows it changing course and descending. Can you confirm?"

The fighter pilot's steely voice came back an instant later. "Confirmed. EAGL is departing approved course. Aircraft is not responding to radio calls."

"Look at this," the Scion representative said. He'd pulled up a low-resolution feed from the cameras inside the aircraft. The video wasn't watched live because it was really only useful to review the crew performance after the fact. It showed the laser technicians slumped in their chairs. Caldwell's body could be seen on the floor, a swath of dark liquid seeping out from underneath him.

"Damn," someone blurted out. "It's a hijacking."

Offerman wasted no more time. "Send the self-destruct signal. Take it down."

Keys were turned. A switch guarded by plastic glass was revealed. The keys were turned again, arming the system. The Air Force staff sergeant in charge of the self-destruct system looked up for confirmation.

"Do it," Offerman snapped.

The switch was pressed and held. The signal went out via satellite. A sickening delay followed during which Offerman wondered what his next career would be after blowing up a billion-dollar aircraft. At least he'd go out with a bang.

Every eye focused on the view from the chase plane, awaiting a series of explosions that would start in the center of the fuselage, rupture the fuel lines, and quickly produce a massive fireball.

But nothing happened.

The sergeant reset the system and sent the signal again. "No response," he announced.

Curses filled the room. The assembled officers couldn't believe what they were seeing and hearing.

Offerman grabbed the microphone and spoke to the F-35 pilots. "Chase team, this is Bullfrog actual. The EAGL has been hijacked. I repeat, the EAGL has been hijacked. I'm giving you a direct order: Shoot down that plane."

The lead pilot responded in a businesslike tone, asking for a code word only they and Offerman knew.

"Confirmation code Red Whistle Falcon," Offerman said.

"Red Whistle confirmed," the fighter pilot replied. "Stand by."

General Offerman turned to the screen in time to see a missile launched from one of the F-35s. It raced forward in a trail of smoke, exploding long before it reached the EAGL. A second missile met the same fate.

"They're using the laser," someone shouted.

The screen flared once more as the first F-35 exploded in a ball of flame. Offerman pressed the talk switch, communicating with the second chase plane. "Shadow Two, switch to guns," he snapped. "Fire immediately! Fire imm—"

It was too late. This time there was no explosion, only a flare on the lens, followed by static. A moment later, the screen went dark, and the words **SIGNAL LOSS** appeared at the top.

Offerman froze, stunned into silence while staring at the dark screen. Somewhere over the Arctic, the second fireball in the sky was dimming. It marked the end of Falcon Two and the beginning of a new danger, the true depths of which Offerman struggled to fathom. They'd built a machine that could rule the sky, proven its worth in a difficult test, and now lost it to parties unknown.

Reality began to sink in. Offerman felt his hands trembling. He tucked them in his pockets and tried to slow his breathing. "Give me the EAGL's last known position and heading."

The technician gave a position report and then announced a heading. "One-five-five degrees."

The men in the room didn't need a map to tell them where that heading would take the plane. They'd spent their lives preparing for combat with the Russian bear. A heading of one-five-five would take the EAGL to Russia, directly to the sprawling military complex in the port city of Murmansk.

"Get me the Pentagon," Offerman said grimly. "We need to deliver the bad news."

CHAPTER 2

Kurt Austin stood in the Blue Room of the White House thinking he'd been tricked. A grand state dinner had been planned. Dignitaries and celebrities were expected to attend. Ambassadors and staff from two dozen countries would be there to mix and mingle. A fine time was to be had by all. So said the headlines.

As part of this dinner, agencies around Washington had been directed to send important representatives. The National Underwater and Marine Agency was no exception. Only, the director of the agency, Mr. Dirk Pitt, was on an expedition that had taken him into the jungles of South America and couldn't be reached, even by satellite phone, which seemed rather suspicious.

With Dirk off the grid, NUMA's assistant director, Rudi Gunn, had been next up to attend. But at the last minute he'd been called out to the West Coast, where some vague and mysterious ecological disaster was allegedly unfolding. Based on Rudi's GPS coordinates, that disaster was happening at a winery in Napa Valley. All of which left Kurt to carry the banner as the honored guest, or sacrificial lamb.

As he smiled benignly and made endless small talk, it dawned on Kurt why both Dirk and Rudi had suddenly been needed elsewhere.

After what seemed like fifty insipid conversations of little consequence, he was certain he would soon lose his mind.

Refreshing his drink, he retreated to an alcove where he'd be less likely to be spotted. Scanning the room from this spot, he finally noticed someone he hoped to talk with on a more personal level. The beautiful blond woman was standing alone and smiling at him. She was perhaps thirty, dressed like a model, and sipping a drink that left her pink lips glistening.

Kurt offered a slight nod of recognition. His senses came alive once again and he started toward her. He was wearing a fitted tuxedo and a French cuffed shirt held together with studs made of cobalt that had been mined from the bottom of the sea. His shoes were polished, and his notoriously unruly hair had been tamed nicely. He figured he was dressed to get a date.

He'd made three steps in her direction when a strong hand landed on his shoulder. "Don't bother," a stern voice warned him. "She doesn't speak a word of English."

Kurt turned to see the Vice President of the United States, James Sandecker, standing right behind him. The men shook hands heartily.

Sandecker was a man of endless energy and vigor. He'd founded NUMA and built the agency up over a period of decades, guiding it to a position of prominence if not outright fame among those in the know in Washington. A few years back, he'd accepted the President's request to join the administration as the Vice President.

Not a large man, Sandecker was bristly and intense, and he stood out with wiry red hair and a well-trimmed Van Dyke beard, which many people mistakenly called a goatee. He reminded some of a bulldog, others considered him like the honey badger, a small but fearless animal known to be relentless at getting what it wanted.

In conversations, Sandecker liked to present his thoughts first and then challenge others to change his opinion—if they dared. It was a quality that irritated many, but endeared him to the President, who appreciated a man who spoke his mind regardless of the consequences.

Kurt considered Sandecker a friend and a mentor. He'd thanked him on more than one occasion for personally recruiting him off a CIA salvage unit and bringing him over to NUMA. And as friends they could talk plainly.

"Are all these parties so boring?" Kurt asked.

"Almost all of them," Sandecker admitted. "But eighty years ago, in this very room, a giant chandelier almost fell on Bess Truman and the Daughters of the American Revolution."

"Any chance something like that will happen tonight?"

"Not likely," Sandecker said. "Harry had the entire White House rebuilt afterward."

Kurt figured that was probably a good thing. He glanced back at the blond woman, who was still watching him. "You obviously know her. At least tell me her name and where she's from."

"Her name is Katja," Sandecker obliged. "She's from a small town, in a mountainous part of Sweden. Near the ski slopes, I think. Her accent is so thick, my interpreter could barely understand what she was telling us."

Kurt found himself imagining a chalet in the frozen hills, with cords of wood stacked up beside an outdoor hot tub, which the two of them could share while the snow drifted down and the drinks flowed. He didn't see the need for much in the way of conversation.

"Why would the Swedes send someone to Washington who can't speak English?"

"I'm not sure," Sandecker admitted. "We send you all over the world and you don't speak anything but."

"Good point," Kurt said. "I'm going to remedy that and start learning the world's great languages immediately."

"Swedish first?"

"Have to start somewhere," Kurt replied.

The two men laughed, and the conversation turned to other matters, nothing political, just old friends catching up. It came to an abrupt halt when several members of the President's staff rushed into the room in a way that attracted significant attention.

They moved quickly through the crowd, checking with each other and whispering into small radios that were all but concealed in their hands.

Sandecker saw them pick out the Secretary of Defense and then the Secretary of State, quite a pair. "I'd better go see what this is all about."

The Vice President left, and to Kurt's surprise, the Swedish woman came over to take his place. She moved into the alcove beside Kurt and took another sip from the champagne glass without ever taking her eyes off him. All of which had Kurt wondering how fast one could actually learn a foreign language.

"Hello," he said. Then, pointing to himself, "I'm Kurt."

She smiled coyly and nodded.

"To international relations," he added, raising his glass. *Everyone*, he thought, *knew a toast when they saw it.*

She raised her glass and clinked it softly against his. Another sip. Another smile. Before Kurt could come up with anything else to do or say, she spoke.

"I've been wondering," she began in accented but perfectly understandable English, "why do you stand over here in the corner? Are you a spy? Or perhaps a detective, watching someone and waiting for them to steal the silverware?"

Kurt laughed softly and shook his head. First Pitt and Gunn had gotten him, and now Sandecker. These scores would have to be settled, Kurt thought. And soon. But first to say something to the beautiful blond woman, who'd been brave enough to make the first move.

Before he could think of anything witty, the buzz kicked up in the room again. The President was leaving without explanation. Several members of the cabinet were following. Sandecker came striding back over to Kurt with a scowl on his face.

"Bad news?" Kurt asked.

"Did anyone ever leave a party because they got good news?" Sandecker said. He exhaled sharply. "You'd better come with me," he added. "I have a feeling we might need you on this."

Kurt turned to the woman, intending to tell her duty calls or something similar and then offering to meet her later, but Sandecker preempted him once again, this time addressing the woman.

"Don't waste your time on this one," he told her. "He's been married to Thalassa for years, and she'll never let him go."

The woman's eyes widened almost as far as Kurt's did. She offered a withering look, glancing at his unadorned ring finger.

Kurt looked at Sandecker as if to say, *What are you doing?* He started to protest, but words failed him. At this point, what was the use? He turned back to the woman and shrugged as she scowled and walked away. Another Washington cad crossed off her list.

"Thalassa?" Kurt asked, focusing on Sandecker. "Really? What kind of name is that?"

"Goddess of the sea," Sandecker replied. "I thought you might appreciate my poetry."

Kurt could do nothing but shake his head. "You're literally the worst wingman of all time."

"Maybe, but we're trying to close a deal with her boss," Sandecker told him. "Who also happens to be her father. I don't need you mucking it up by causing an international and highly emotional incident. Regardless, we have more important matters to attend to."

He turned for the exit, Kurt followed.

"What's going on?" Kurt asked, his attention fully on the here and now.

Sandecker spoke the same way he walked: briskly. "The Air Force lost a couple of planes over the Arctic. One of them is a billion-dollar prototype that shouldn't be allowed to fall into enemy hands."

"If it crashed into the sea, there won't be much left of it," Kurt said.

"*If*," Sandecker agreed. "From the sound of it, hitting the ocean would be the best-case scenario at this point."

CHAPTER 3

The world-famous Situation Room at the White House was actually a collection of several conference rooms, all connected to the world through high-tech communication nodes and guarded by security stations that were manned twenty-four hours a day.

Kurt had been in the room before, but never during a rushed gathering like this one. He was cleared into the main room at Sandecker's insistence and given a place against the wall to stand. The seats were already taken by important members of the administration and enough military brass to form a marching band.

As Kurt leaned against the wall, Sandecker made his way over to the President, who was speaking with a three-star Air Force general and the Secretary of Defense. All three men looked positively ill.

Turning his attention to the late arrivals streaming in, Kurt noticed a distinct difference in clothing. Unlike the first group, who had come from the party in tuxedos and thousand-dollar suits, this crew was showing up in casual clothing. Khakis and polos. Jeans and sweaters. Whatever they'd been wearing at home or could throw on quickly.

The President's chief of staff—who was no friend of Sandecker's, as Kurt recalled—rushed in wearing a tracksuit. He'd been jogging on a treadmill at the White House gym when the call came in.

All things considered, Kurt figured it was time to get rid of the bow tie. He pulled it off and unbuttoned his collar. A feeling of relief swept over him.

The doors closed and the lights went down. Everyone fell silent as the three-star general from the Air Force stepped to the front.

"This is the Eagle," he said, pointing to the image of the modified C-17 that had appeared on screens around the room. "E-A-G-L," he continued, breaking the acronym down. "The Enhanced Aerial Gunnery Laser. It's the most powerful directed-energy system in the world by a factor of ten. Each pulse it generates carries enough energy to burn through a panel of aircraft-grade aluminum in less than a hundredth of a second. Linked with the AQX-9 radar, which is mounted below the C-17's airframe, it can hit a target the size of a refrigerator at a range of five hundred miles. It was in the process of being tested over the Arctic when something went wrong."

"A failure?" someone asked.

"Unfortunately not," the general explained. "The aircraft has been hijacked."

Very few statements elicited shock in this room. The people in it were no storm-shy greenhorns, and they understood that a rushed meeting in the Situation Room would only happen if something had gone terribly wrong, but the audience was startled to hear the term *hijacking* used in conjunction with a top secret project.

"How?" someone asked. "By whom?"

"We're looking into that now," the general admitted. "The more pressing issue is figuring out where the plane went and where it might be now."

"Weren't you tracking it?" someone else asked.

"Of course," the general said. "But the hijackers knew this and immediately disabled the onboard tracking systems. They then used the active laser to shoot down both F-35 chase planes and an E-6 AWACS radar plane that was monitoring the test from approximately a hundred miles away. When the E-6 went down our primary coverage was lost. Shortly thereafter they descended to the deck, dropping below our land-based radar coverage. We managed to follow it for a short time by monitoring emissions from the AN/APN 241, which stood out like a man carrying a flashlight in a dark and empty field. But when the hijackers turned the radar off, they disappeared."

"Where were they at that moment?"

"Out over the Arctic Sea, on a heading that would take it directly to Murmansk, Russia."

"Russia?" the President's chief of staff exclaimed. "Good gravy, man. Why the hell didn't you intercept it?"

"With all due respect," the general insisted, "the attempt would have been futile or worse."

The chief of staff didn't back down. "We have hundreds of frontline aircraft based in northern Europe, do we not?"

"And we could have launched them all," the general insisted, "only to see them shot out of the sky long before a single plane got within miles of firing a missile."

"You can't be serious," a member of the National Security Council suggested.

"I'm deadly serious," the general grunted. "Taking out large numbers of fast-moving targets at long range is exactly what this aircraft was designed for. The laser can destroy any mechanical object in a line of sight. It can hit low-flying aircraft down across the horizon at incredible range. It can hit high-flying aircraft at even greater distances. It can hit ballistic missiles traveling twenty-five thousand miles an hour from half a continent away."

Kurt noticed a newfound silence in the crowd. A showing of respect. He himself was surprised to hear about such a weapon.

"At the time of the hijacking," the general continued, "we had approximately three hundred fighter aircraft available for launch in the theater. The best of which can reach a top speed of fifteen hundred miles per hour. That means with afterburners full open and traveling in a straight line, the nearest squadron would have been exposed to laser fire for a full thirty minutes before they brought the EAGL in range of their longest-legged missiles. Thirty minutes of exposure to a weapon that can obliterate an aircraft in a fraction of a second is an absolute eternity. It would be nothing but suicide for the pilots."

"What about encircling it, coming at it from all sides at the same time?" someone asked.

"The laser is aimed using mirrors," the general explained. "There are no moving turrets, no shells to load, no delays in triggering the next burst. It can be trained on one target, fired, and then refocused on another target in a fraction of a second. It can discharge ninety pulses per minute without overheating or overdrawing its onboard power source. And unlike physical weapons, which are limited by the number of rounds carried in their magazines, the laser on board the EAGL *never* runs out of ammunition. Once powered up, it can destroy an almost unlimited number of targets during a single mission."

The general turned back to the chief of staff. "A mad scramble to intercept the aircraft might have cost us our entire fighter capacity in northern Europe, while almost certainly proving futile and quite possibly provoking a war. I ask you to imagine the Russian response when we scramble all our frontline aircraft and send them toward Russian airspace at maximum speed with no explanation."

The news was sobering. No one liked what they were hearing,

but it was hard to argue with the logic. Silence descended over the room.

Finally, the President spoke. The EAGL had been his pet project for three solid years. For it to end like this was almost too much to take. "Is there anything to suggest the EAGL isn't in Russia at this point?"

The question was addressed to the general and more broadly to the room. The general deferred and the rest of the room became a sea of murmurs, filled with eyes and faces looking anywhere but at the President.

The head of the National Security Council sighed and shook his head, the director of the Central Intelligence Agency looked down at the computer in front of him as if he'd find the truth somewhere on the screen. But no one met the President's gaze to offer an answer.

Kurt found that surprising. He thought the answer was obvious. And he felt the President deserved a reply.

He stepped forward. "Based on what's been presented here," he began, "I'd say there's less than a five percent chance the aircraft is in Russia. And then only if the pilot got lost and wound up there by mistake."

A smattering of laughter and surprise emerged in the wake of Kurt's statement. A few derisive comments came from dark corners of the room, but the President silenced everyone by raising his hand.

The President was a tall man who loomed over others, even sitting down. As he looked up over the crowd trying to find the voice crying in the wilderness, the defeated aura around him seemed to vanish.

"And you are?" the President asked.

"Kurt Austin. NUMA special projects."

Hearing this, the chief of staff turned to Sandecker. There was an undeclared war between them regarding who was the President's most important advisor. It usually presented itself in a cordial manner but occasionally flared into snide comments from the chief and gruff bluster from Sandecker. "One of your people," the chief said. "Care to tell us what he's doing here and what he's talking about?"

Sandecker offered an unflinching poker face; he looked composed, even though he'd never expected Kurt to jump into the fray, certainly not with a comment like the one he'd just offered.

"Considering the possibility that the EAGL or the wrecked F-35s would need to be recovered from frigid Arctic waters, I thought it would behoove us to have a salvage expert here. One who has actually pulled things off the bottom of the ocean. As for what he's talking about"—Sandecker paused and looked Kurt's way—"I've always believed in letting my people elaborate on their own thoughts. Kurt," he said, using a tone that suggested *This better be good*, "Why don't you enlighten us?"

"It's simple," Kurt said. "These men hijacked the EAGL only after they were fully convinced it was operational. They killed the crew, shot down the F-35s, and took out the E-6 radar plane to clear their path. They did all that as a warning to the Air Force: *Come up and challenge us and we'll turn your squadrons into heaps of molten metal.* A warning the general took to heart. They then turned toward Murmansk, while switching off every system in the plane that would allow you to track them, including the APX-9 radar, which as you said stood out like a man in a dark field wielding a bright flashlight. It's the last act that gives them away."

"How so?" the President asked.

"As long as the targeting radar is operational, they're invulnerable," Kurt said. "Turning it off gives us the chance to mount up and scramble a few squadrons or at the very least attack them with surface-to-air missiles. It also leaves them in the dark as to our actions, creating a guessing game they don't need. If they truly wanted to reach Russia, they'd leave the radar on until they entered Russian airspace, at which point going after them would bring about World War Three. Which means the only reason to turn the APX-9 off is so they could run and hide somewhere else."

"So, the turn toward Murmansk is designed to throw us off the trail," the President said, following Kurt's line of reasoning. "Tap into our greatest fear and get us looking in the wrong place. Is that what you're saying?"

"Exactly," Kurt said. "They wanted you to think they were headed to Russia. Otherwise, they'd have switched the radar off before they made the turn."

Kurt left it at that. He expected there would be those in the crowd who scoffed at his analysis, but he knew the logic was sound and he wasn't there to score points with anyone.

Low-level discussions broke out around the room. The chief of staff leaned toward the President and whispered something in his ear. They seemed to argue. Eventually the President shook him off and turned his attention back to Kurt. "Austin . . . is it?"

"That's right," Kurt said.

"The same Austin who stopped some mad airship tycoon from dusting Guantánamo Bay with toxic gas a few years ago, and who was instrumental in destroying a rogue artificial intelligence entity that had come to life in the Indian Ocean this time last year?"

Kurt nodded. It seemed that the President knew of his adventures. Briefings from Sandecker probably helped in that regard, although both incidents involved the type of world-altering events that any sitting President would have been aware of.

"I had something to do with preventing the attack on Guantánamo," Kurt admitted. "As for the artificial intelligence incident . . . I've always been hard on computers. Can't keep a laptop working for more than six months at a time."

The President allowed himself a modest grin, which was significant considering the circumstances. "All right, Austin," he said, growing stern once again. "I'm listening. Tell me more. If the EAGL isn't in Russia, then where do you suggest it went?"

Kurt glanced at the map. The Arctic Ocean and Barents Sea didn't offer much in the way of safe landing spots. Bear Island was an uninhabited spot of land right in the middle of the search zone, but it was a rugged, rocky place that jutted from the ocean like a mountain poking up through the clouds. It would be all but impossible to put down there without a disaster. The Svalbard archipelago was farther north. Its various islands offered plenty of snow-covered terrain to choose from, but a couple thousand Norwegians lived there, along with scientists from a dozen countries whose stations dotted the far reaches of the place.

Greenland was out of range. Iceland was closer. But the tiny island was a hub of activity and not the type of place one could sneak a missing military transport into without being spotted. Not with NATO forces on the lookout for it.

Kurt shrugged. "It's a lot easier to say where a missing thing *isn't*, than guessing where it *actually is*. But I expect you'll find it on some flat piece of land in the middle of nowhere, covered in nets and foliage in an attempt to hide it from view."

At this the Air Force general redirected the conversation. "With all due respect to Mr. Austin's theory, we've had satellites scanning every square inch of open terrain in the aircraft's range. Every island. Every field. Every empty highway and abandoned air base. We've found no sign of it. No heat plumes from the engines, no smoking craters to suggest it crashed. No sign of it whatsoever. If the aircraft is on the ground, then it's hidden in a hangar somewhere. And that brings us back to Russia."

The President nodded thoughtfully before turning to the CIA director. "Carson," the President said, using the DCI's first name. "What do you have?"

The DCI cleared his throat and then spoke up. "I would have to agree with Austin," he said reluctantly. "We don't think the plane is in Russia. There's no sign of increased signals to and from Moscow. Nothing to suggest any sense of celebration or glee within the higher levels of their command structure. On the ground floor, we've seen no unusual activity at any Russian air base. A large American aircraft coming in from the northwest at low altitude would set off all kinds of alarm bells once it got close enough to appear on radar."

"Not if they knew it was coming," someone suggested.

"In which case they would send up fighters to escort the hijackers in. Both to keep us from attempting to shoot the plane down and to keep the hijackers from changing their minds."

The President concurred. "Standard procedure, but it didn't occur."

"No, it didn't, Mr. President. Furthermore, we've seen nothing in Murmansk to indicate any hangar large enough to hide the C-17 has been put into special use. No signs of increased vehicle and foot traffic—which we would expect to see as Russian experts and intelligence personnel gathered at an airport to study the newly arrived plane. No signs of other planes being pushed out onto the ramp to make room for a larger aircraft. What we do see is business as usual. The Russians are busy winterizing their fleet this time of year. Buttoning things up. Putting things away. Packing the hangars to the gills with vulnerable aircraft and locking the doors and windows. There's nothing to indicate them doing anything special to make room for the EAGL."

The President was feeling more confident as the meeting went on. Perhaps his worst fears had been avoided. "So, it's not in a Russian hangar, and not anywhere out on open terrain. That leaves only one possibility. The aircraft went down over the ocean. Do we have anything to support this?"

At this the director of the National Reconnaissance Office chimed in. The NRO was in charge of America's spy satellites, collecting and disseminating information to the various military branches and intelligence agencies.

"There is one thing," he began slowly, "one *possible* piece of evidence to suggest the aircraft hit the sea. Though I'm not sure we should fully rely on it."

"Give it to us," the President ordered.

"Approximately two hours after the hijacking, one of our satellites picked up an unusual radio signal in the Barents Sea. It was a continuous burst on multiple frequencies at the same instant. It lasted only three-quarters of a second and then vanished. No intelligible data was recovered, but the recorded frequencies match up precisely with systems used on the C-17."

"What are you trying to tell us?" the President asked.

"It might be nothing," the NRO's director said. "It could be a fisherman thumbing his radio switches in the middle of the night or a malfunction on some nearby container ship. But it's possible that we picked up what's known as an 'impact jam signal.' An erroneous radio burst triggered during a crash when radios and other equipment are exposed to powerful destructive forces. It's thought to occur as the impact shatters equipment, causing the remaining standby energy in the circuits to be channeled through the transmitters. Think of it as an electronic shout from a dying machine."

The President nodded. "And this 'jam signal' would suggest the plane crashed?"

"Possibly," the NRO's director said. "But—and I cannot stress this enough—I would not label this a high-reliability indicator."

Kurt saw the President's face change even as the NRO's director warned him not to put too much stock in what they'd picked up. The President wanted to believe it, he needed to believe it. In his mind it was the proverbial smoking gun.

"Where did this transmission occur?" the President asked.

"Only one station picked it up," the director admitted, "which prevents us from triangulating its exact location. And that gives us a line to draw on the map, instead of a single point."

The mild-mannered director tapped on the computer terminal in front of him and the line appeared on the map for everyone to see. It ran diagonally from a spot in the middle of the Barents Sea, up to the northwest, terminating twelve miles short of an island chain known as Franz Josef Land. To everyone's dismay, a red flag labeled the islands as Russian possessions. At no point however did the signal cross the land.

The President turned back to the Air Force general, who'd conducted the briefing. "Could the aircraft survive intact if it hit the sea?"

"Doubtful," the general told him.

"Why not?" the President said, pressing him. "A few years ago, someone landed a plane on the Hudson River. It came down in one piece."

"A river is child's play in comparison to the ocean," the general said. "The Barents Sea sports large waves, floating chunks of ice, and swaths of fog that stretch for miles. Landing safely on its surface would be extremely unlikely. Hitting it and flipping or breaking apart is a much more plausible result."

"Would that destroy the plane?" the President asked hopefully.

"It would be rendered inoperative," the general said, "but it's possible that the top secret components would remain intact and retrievable."

Exactly what no one wanted.

The President turned back to Kurt. "NUMA," he said, "what kind of depth are we talking about here?"

Kurt knew what the President wanted to hear, but it wasn't in the cards. "Unfortunately, Mr. President, the waters of the Barents Sea are relatively shallow. It can be described as a tabletop between the deeper waters of the Arctic and the Atlantic Ocean. Depths probably average no more than seven hundred feet along the route indicated by the signal line. In some places less."

"So not deep enough?"

"No," Kurt said bluntly. "Not deep enough at all."

The President had heard enough. He turned to the ranking Navy officials. "Okay, gentlemen," he said. "I don't have to tell you how important this aircraft is to the future security of this nation. It's the one weapon that can protect us from a nuclear onslaught without having to retaliate by frying the rest of the world. It's the first brick in a wall that will keep us safer than we've been in a hundred years. If the Russians or Chinese or any other enemies of ours get ahold of it, we'll have lost an advantage that should last us ten years. If Russia had such a weapon they might be inclined to attack Europe knowing they were safe from retaliation. If the Chinese had a fleet of these planes, Taiwan, Japan, and South Korea would be swept into their clutches while we stood by unable to get enough weapons onto their targets to make much of a difference. This EAGL is *our* strategic advantage, and I want it found or destroyed beyond recognition."

The Navy's assistant chief of staff was present. He cleared his throat. "Mr. President, we have oceangoing salvage assets in Norfolk that could sail within twenty-four hours."

"How long would it take them to reach the search area?"

The reply was disheartening. "These are not fast ships, Mr. President. We're looking at eight, maybe nine days until they're in the on-site."

At this the CIA director interjected. "Mr. President, may I suggest *not sending* the Navy's main salvage team to the area. At least not toward the signal line. All it would do is telegraph what we know to the Russians, who at this point seem to be aware that something has happened, but are currently focused on missing F-35s."

The President grasped the logic. A secret operation would be preferable. He turned slowly back to the man who'd given him some hope in the matter. He almost seemed pleased that the options had presented themselves in this manner. "Sandecker is always telling me that you NUMA guys have ships everywhere. Is this true?"

"Not everywhere, Mr. President," Kurt said. "But as fate would have it, there's a NUMA vessel looking for the wreck of a World War Two U-boat off the coast of Norway right now. Several good friends of mine are on board."

"Perfect," the President said. "In fact, it couldn't be more perfect. I want you to get yourself to Norway and start looking for that aircraft."

"And when we find it?"

The President grinned at Austin's confident nature. "We'll let you know. But I would plan on being able to recover it or blow it to a thousand pieces."

Kurt nodded his understanding and stepped back. As he did, Sandecker shot him a look that said, *Well done.* He remained eminently proud of the organization he'd built, having instilled an unflinching attitude into NUMA's core.

Kurt couldn't have agreed more. The fact was he'd rather take on a high-stakes mission than attend a boring party any day. To that end, he made a mental note: the next time Pitt and Gunn left the office together, he was going to get as far away from Washington as fast as he possibly could.

CHAPTER 4

The NUMA vessel *Lyra* had an odd profile for a seagoing ship. She had been built with a wave-piercing bow, which was smooth and enclosed, like the front end of a Japanese bullet train or, more nautically, the hydrodynamic head of a large shark. This design had been chosen over the traditional V-shaped bow with the flat open deck behind it in order to give the *Lyra* great stability in a storm. Instead of pitching upward as the waves rolled in and then downward as it crashed into the troughs, the *Lyra* cut through the largest waves, puncturing them and allowing the water to slide upward along the enclosed front of the ship. A central peak in the hull divided oncoming water, shedding it equally to port and starboard. This allowed it to face storms head-on and kept the vertical movement to a minimum.

Behind the smoothly curved shape of the bow stood a tall superstructure, which had been pushed forward in a bulldog-like stance. Behind that lay a long flat deck, perfect for landing helicopters and storing submersibles, ROVs, underwater drones—all the equipment that made searching for sunken objects possible. Viewed from the side, the ship looked as if it had come to a sudden halt, causing everything above the main deck to slide forward in the process.

While the aesthetics weren't all that pleasing, the design balanced the ship. Keeping weight forward helped hold the bow down, enhancing its ability to push through the sea. The effect was a silky, smooth ride, smooth enough that some of the crew complained that it didn't feel like being on a ship at all.

Standing in front of the bridge, at the vertex of the arrow-shaped wall a few decks below the towering superstructure, Kurt Austin understood the complaint. With a bitterly cold wind coming in from the north, ten-foot waves were rolling by. He watched them ride upward on the hull and then peel away, vanishing long before they reached him. Only a soft hint of vertical motion suggested he was standing on a ship rather than a concrete pier.

At least he could feel the wind.

With each passing wave, the breeze whipped a cloud of fine spray across the ship, coating the hull, the deck, and the lone madman standing afoul of the weather in tiny crystals of frost and salt.

As Kurt stared at the waves, he thought of the ancient mariners who sailed these waters in small wooden boats powered by sails and oars. Kurt's ancestors were mostly central European, but his mother was descended from English stock and insisted that Nordic blood ran in their veins, left over from the Viking conquest of Northumbria in 865 CE. That ancestry, she insisted, was the source of Kurt's intense blue eyes and his love of the sea.

True or not, Kurt could feel the kinship with those ancient Vikings. He was never more alive than when he was out at sea. He felt the ocean calling, and the louder and fiercer that voice, the better. At the moment, the sea was just whispering, but it was still trying to tell him something. He was sure of that.

Kurt had flown out of Washington on a NUMA jet, taking off less than an hour after the White House briefing. With Joe Zavala at his side, they'd traveled to a tiny enclave called Hammerfest three hundred miles north of the Arctic Circle, near the upper reaches of Norway.

From there, they'd taken a helicopter out to the *Lyra*, which was already searching for a lost vessel: a World War II U-boat that had been hit with depth charges in the closing month of the war. Some people believed it had gone down with a cache of gold, stolen artwork, or even secret Nazi plans for a Fourth Reich. If they ever found it, Kurt suspected they'd find nothing but the bodies of scared young submariners, most of whom would have been teenagers, as that was all the Germans had left to fight with by the end of the war.

Needless to say, they hadn't found the submarine. Nor had hours of trolling along the path of the so-called signal line revealed any trace of the missing C-17. Something told Kurt that wasn't about to change.

Maybe it was a lack of patience, maybe it was those ancient Viking instincts, but as he stared at the black water rolling by and the whitecaps blowing off the top, he became convinced that they were looking in the wrong place.

As the *Lyra* sliced cleanly through another incoming wave, the heavy watertight door creaked behind him as it was shoved open against the wind. Kurt glanced over his shoulder to see Joe Zavala stepping out into the elements, bundled up from head to toe. He wore a jacket that would have made the Michelin Man proud. A balaclava covered his mouth and nose, while a thick toboggan hat was pulled down tight over his head and ears. His hands were covered by large fingerless gloves that looked like oven mitts.

By contrast Kurt wore only basic winter gear; a heavy jacket, a NUMA-issued wool hat that didn't quite contain his unruly silver hair, and a set of round sunglasses with gold lenses and leather side shields to protect his eyes. He didn't even have gloves on—which he would have admitted was a mistake had he been under oath.

"Is that you, amigo?" he said to Joe. "I can't quite tell."

Joe pushed the door shut and lumbered toward Kurt. "I drew the short straw, so I had to come out here to see if you'd frozen in place like the hood ornament for the ship. If you want, we can boil some water and unstick your feet from the deck."

There was a heated track in the middle of the deck that maintained an ice-free path for anyone that had to use it, but Kurt was standing in front of that. He lifted one foot. It came off the metal plate with a firm click, suggesting the spray had indeed created a bond between his boots and the ship. He cleared the other one as well. "Less likely to go overboard if you're frozen to the deck."

Joe nodded as if that was accepted maritime logic. "Even less likely if you're inside, where it's not fifteen below with the windchill."

Kurt laughed. "At a certain point it's so cold you don't feel it anymore."

"That's the beginnings of frostbite."

The truth was, Kurt needed space to think. The crowded, screen-filled sonar room was not a place that allowed the mind to wander. It required focus, even if it was just to ward off the monotony of finding nothing.

Kurt figured Joe knew that. After years of working together Joe knew him better than anyone. He knew Kurt preferred solitude to chaos, quiet contemplation to loud, chatty rooms. He knew the look that suggested Kurt's feet might be frozen to the deck of the *Lyra*, but his mind was a thousand miles away.

"You're a pilot," Kurt said to Joe. "How low would you take a C-17 across these waters?"

Joe cocked his head, thinking about the question. "Having never flown a C-17, that's a little tough to answer, but I hear it's a pretty agile aircraft for such a big bird. It has to be to get in and out of short fields in dangerous places around the globe. A competent pilot would probably be confident with fifty feet between the bottom of the plane and the top of the waves. Why do you ask?"

"What if there was fog?" Kurt asked, ignoring Joe's question for the moment.

"Not really a problem," Joe said. "The plane would be equipped with plenty of terrain-avoidance features to tell the pilot exactly how close to the water he was. Radar altimeters, infrared sensors, even night vision."

Joe sounded confident. It helped make Kurt's case. "Which makes a crash unlikely."

"Unless they ditched it on purpose," Joe suggested.

Kurt had been thinking the same thing. But that idea begged another question. "Would you want to land in these waters, in the middle of the night, in conditions that suggested ice, fog, and snow flurries?"

Joe shivered at the thought. "Kurt, I grew up in the hottest part of New Mexico, where any temperature below ninety degrees calls for a light jacket. I wouldn't land here on a calm, sunny day. You can be sure I wouldn't ditch an airliner-sized aircraft here in the dark. But then again," he added, "I wouldn't steal a billion-dollar prototype and kill my fellow crewmates to do it, so there's no telling what the hijackers might be willing to try."

Kurt thought that made sense. He asked his next question. "What are the odds of a safe landing? Conditions last night were smoother, but there was fog."

"The plane is going to sink either way," Joe said. "But if the swells were small, I think you could get the odds of landing without breaking off major components like the wing and tail down to about fifty-fifty. Maybe sixty-forty."

That was better than Kurt would have thought, but it didn't

change his mind. "Even if you did land without a mishap, you still have to get out," he said. "The water around us is already three degrees below freezing. The only reason it's not a solid block of ice is the salt content. But if you get in that water, you suffer instant cold shock in all your extremities that makes functioning nearly impossible. Hypothermia follows. Leading to death in less than fifteen minutes."

Joe paused, looking out at the water. "Operating over the Arctic, the Air Force would make sure the plane is stocked with life rafts and survival gear."

"All of which carry emergency beacons that activate when deployed," Kurt pointed out.

"But the hijackers would know that," Joe replied. "They might be able to disable them beforehand."

Kurt didn't think so. "That stuff is all in sealed containers. Most of it's designed to self-inflate when put to use. None of it would be easy to access and mess around with in the middle of a flight."

"Maybe they brought their own rafts."

"On a top secret test flight?"

The *Lyra* pierced another wave, this time nosing down a bit, which allowed the wave to slide almost up to the platform. Joe turned his face as the spray flew by, catching the sunlight and hitting the ship's superstructure with a sound like sleet against a car window.

Joe stamped his feet and then adjusted his hat with the oven mitts. "Before my lips freeze shut, how about you tell me what you're getting at?"

Kurt figured it was obvious. "The hijackers didn't wake up yesterday and decide to steal the plane over coffee and donuts. They would obviously have spent months planning this. But if they can't bring their own survival gear, and they can't use what the Air Force provided, they'd have to have another way off the plane. Unless they planned to swim for it, they'd have someone here waiting to pick them up."

Joe looked out to sea and then back at Kurt. His eyes lit up. He got it. "We're looking for the wrong thing."

Kurt grinned through the cold, which was numbing his face at this point. "We need to know if there was a ship out here last night. Anywhere along this line."

"And if there wasn't?"

"Then the EAGL isn't here."

Kurt noticed Joe nodding, or perhaps it was an involuntary muscular response to keep his core temperature up. Either way it was time to get back inside. "Let's get to the operations room and see if anyone was out here."

CHAPTER 5

Gamay Trout sat at a computer station with three flat-screen monitors arranged around her like a bay window into an electronic world. The setup was similar to those used by day traders on Wall Street, or video game players immersing themselves in a virtual world. Activities that were far more intense than watching the slowly unfolding display of a sonar scan as it swept across the featureless plane of the seabed below.

Knowing she was going to be staring at screens for hours on end, Gamay had made sure to dress comfortably. She wore a NUMA hoodie, fleece sweatpants, and thick wool socks—she'd long since kicked off her shoes. A ball cap kept the light out of her eyes and kept her red wine-colored hair in place.

Sitting in a club chair with her legs crossed—no easy feat, as she was five foot ten—she watched the screens with a look of disinterest, a coffee mug the size of a soup bowl cradled in both hands. She'd only taken a few sips so far, preferring to absorb the warmth of its contents through her palms while breathing in the satisfying aroma with its hints of caramel and vanilla.

An icon on the central screen flashed as a tiny speaker chirped for her attention. Gamay pressed a key on the keyboard in front of her, silencing it.

The central screen displayed the readout from the *Lyra*'s powerful towed array sonar. The screens to either side of her were broken into multiple boxes showing the similar data that was coming in from a small fleet of underwater autonomous vehicles, or UAVs, that were currently plowing along the same path, spread out on both sides of the *Lyra*. All together this underwater fleet was covering a strip ten miles wide; five miles on either side of the signal line. The images were flat, featureless, and dull: a digital rendition of the smooth, sedimentary bottom six hundred feet below.

The alarm on the main screen chirped again. Gamay tapped the computer key once more. But this time an image appeared: a large object and its elongated shadow on the bottom. The shadow wasn't cast by sunlight—it was completely dark at that depth—but by sound, as the object blocked the sonar signal the way a wall would block the light.

Gamay squinted, studying the object as she typed a note to mark its size, shape, and location.

"You find something?" a voice called from across the compartment.

Gamay glanced at her husband, Paul, who crouched in front of a similar set of screens. At six foot eight, he looked out of place in the cramped compartment.

"A sunken fishing boat," she told him. "Judging by the sediment that's piled up against the hull, it's been there for a while."

"So not a U-boat or giant airplane," Paul said.

"Neither one," she said, returning the screen to its multi-box format and leaning back in her chair once again. "Not even close."

Paul and Gamay were a team in every sense of the word, husband and wife, close friends, coworkers at NUMA. She had degrees in microbiology, while he was a chemist and geologist. If it was a living thing, she could classify it, describe it, and discuss its life cycle in detail. If it wasn't imbued with the spark of life, that made it Paul's territory.

Over the years at NUMA, they'd become skilled members of the Special Projects Team, which meant they had to be familiar with all types of nautical equipment. They'd driven submersibles, raced on hydroplanes, and had used every type of search and scanning device known to man.

Gamay had become an expert on underwater systems like the towed array sonar and the UAVs they were currently using, while Paul had become interested in drone technology, even building a few from scratch. On the other side of the compartment, he was managing a small squadron of the machines. They flew an interlocking search pattern scanning the sea for floating debris, fuel slicks, or anything else that might have come from the missing plane.

"Any luck on your side?" Gamay asked.

The drones covered a hundred square miles every fifteen minutes. Their sensors could pick up something as small as a life jacket from a thousand feet up. They'd found nothing of interest so far. "Just waves and whitecaps," Paul said. "Haven't even seen a flying fish."

"As they prefer tropical waters, that would be quite a surprise," Gamay informed him.

"Good to know," Paul said. He leaned back in his chair, yawning and stretching while tipping the chair back to its absolute limit. He nearly toppled over when the compartment door swung open and Kurt and Joe barged in.

Gamay lifted the coffee mug to her mouth to hide the smile and the laugh that almost escaped. She loved her husband endlessly, and the fact that he was comically uncoordinated at times only made her love him more.

As Paul righted himself, Gamay looked at the intruders. "To what do we owe this glorious interruption?"

"We're looking for a ship," Kurt said.

"This explains our lack of success," Gamay replied. "We were told to look for an airplane."

"And before that a submarine," Paul added, having righted himself.

A grin on Kurt's face suggested his appreciation of the joke. Other than that, it didn't faze him a bit. "It's the fact that we haven't found an airplane—or any parts of one—that has me thinking we need to switch it up."

Gamay looked at Joe. "Do you know what he's talking about?"

"Don't be too hard on him," Joe said. "His brain is still thawing out."

Kurt pulled up a chair, swinging it around so he could sit with his arms resting on the back. He explained his theory, insisting that the hijackers crashing into the sea by accident was unlikely and that even ditching the plane on purpose was a stretch, unless they had a ship in the area to pick them up.

Gamay took a sip of the coffee, surprised at how fast it was cooling down. "Did you check the AIS database?"

She was referring to the automatic identification system that tracked the movements of most commercial ships and anything carrying a reporting transponder or beacon.

"Of course," Kurt said. "Aside from our ship, nothing has come through this stretch of water in the last forty-eight hours. But if you were planning to pick up hijackers from a ditched aircraft, you wouldn't be broadcasting your position."

Joe chimed in, looking Paul's way. "Your drones are covering a pretty wide swath. Have you seen any traffic?"

Paul shook his head. "No ships, no boats, not even a periscope. No wreckage, no rafts, no flotsam or even jetsam of any kind. Not even a flying fish, but as we all know, they prefer tropical waters, so I wouldn't expect to find many of them this far north."

Paul winked at Gamay as he finished the statement, and she hid behind the oversized cup once more.

"Can you get them out a little farther and up a little higher? I'd like to use them for recon instead of a lower-altitude search and rescue pattern."

"I can," Paul said. "But there's no need to. Gamay has satellite data going back to a few hours before the plane went missing. We were looking at it earlier."

Gamay put the mug down as Kurt and Joe turned their focus in her direction. "We weren't looking for ships," she said while tapping at the computer keyboard. "Just infrared signatures that might indicate a fuel slick on the surface, which could theoretically be spotted using changes in reflected sunlight. We can delve deeper and have the computer look for smaller features. How small do you want to go?"

"Can it resolve down to fifty feet?" Kurt asked.

Gamay typed a command code and the computer began looking for odd features in the satellite data fifty feet or larger. It was a slow process, and it resulted in dozens of false readings where frothing whitecaps covering more than fifty feet in length were reported as boats, only to be dismissed after human eyes studied the images.

"Bump the size up to seventy-five feet," Kurt said, "and add an infrared. Say . . . at least ten degrees warmer than background."

This time the program ran faster. It found nothing in the overnight data and only four possibilities in the daytime images, but they all turned out to be artifacts caused by concentrated solar reflections.

"Zip, zilch, zero," Gamay said.

She looked at Kurt. His eyes were focused, his face impassive. She couldn't tell if he was disappointed or pleased. Most likely he was just busy calculating what this new data meant.

"Widen the search field," he said calmly.

"How far?"

"A hundred miles to either side."

She made the adjustment and ran the program again. Once more, only a few solar reflections, but no ships.

"Widen the search," Kurt said again.

This time they picked up a dozen ships, but all of them were proudly broadcasting their AIS information, and back-tracing their courses revealed that none of them had been anywhere near the search area during the night.

"Widen it again," Kurt said. "As far as you can go."

"That'll cover halfway to the North Pole," she replied.

"Do it. Use all the data."

Gamay wasn't sure what good that would do. The infrared data suggested the search line was clear of traffic the night of the incident. Finding a ship several hundred miles away wouldn't change that. "Whatever we find will be too far away from the line to have been here the night before," she told Kurt.

"Maybe the line is not *the line*," he said.

"You think the signal is a red herring?"

"Maybe," he said. "Or even something less sinister like a data error at the receiving station or an atmospheric event. Either way we're putting a lot of stock in a one-second burst of radio static."

"It occurred an hour after the plane was taken," Joe reminded him. "Be quite a coincidence to have a data glitch at that exact time and place."

"So back to the red herring, then," Kurt said. "No better way to throw your pursuers off than letting them think they've discovered something you overlooked."

Gamay wondered what it would take to fake this particular kind of signal. She decided she didn't have enough expertise to really know. It might have been difficult, or as easy as squeezing a bunch of transmit buttons on different radios at the same time.

As she considered this, the computer finished compiling and sorting the data. This new batch brought up hundreds of vessels both small and large, most of them plowing the Norwegian coast. Checking their beacons and back-tracing their overnight positions quickly ruled them out as being available to help the hijackers. Just as she suspected.

She turned to Kurt, but found him staring intently enough at the screen that she didn't want to break his concentration. She noticed he wasn't looking at the center, near the signal line, or the area to the south, where the ships were. He was locked in on the northern half of the image.

She looked at the screen. There was nothing on it. No ships, no boats, nothing but a great wall of white, where the sea ice began its unbroken stretch across the ocean. From there it ran all the way back up over the top of the globe and then down into the Bering Strait between Alaska and Russia.

The satellite images didn't cover that distance, in fact they cut off two hundred miles shy of the pole. It didn't matter really; there weren't going to be any ships in the ice pack.

"What's this?" Kurt asked, pointing to a thin black mark cutting through the ice field on an impossibly straight line.

The line ran downward from the top of the screen, keeping true right up until just before it stopped. At that point, a ninety-degree jag to the right followed and then nothing.

"Don't know," Gamay said.

"Zoom in on that," Kurt requested.

Gamay found her curiosity piqued as well. After centering the image, she tapped the zoom key several times.

The image blurred and resolved over and over again until it

brought out a colorful slash in the middle of the white ice. Two more clicks revealed that slash to be a red-hulled ship with green decks, parked in the heart of the ice pack.

Gamay clicked zoom once more. The angle of the satellite image allowed them to see some of the ship's profile and even its markings. While the numbers were unreadable, the design was obvious. As was the huge red five-pointed star in the center of the foredeck.

"Icebreaker," Gamay said.

"Chinese," Joe added.

Kurt leaned back and crossed his arms. "What's it doing out there, I wonder?"

Gamay detected plenty of sarcasm in Kurt's voice. He obviously thought he knew exactly what it was the Chinese were doing out there.

"What's that off to the east?" Paul asked, pointing to a discolored area that ran straight for about three-quarters of a mile.

Gamay zoomed once more. The grayish smudge in the surface looked like a road . . . or a runway.

"Paul," she said turning, "do you have the C-17's range data handy?"

"Nine hundred sixty miles from the point where it went dark," Paul said. "If we're assuming low-altitude flight, that distance compresses to about seven hundred miles, adjusted for wind."

Gamay typed a few things into the computer. The Chinese icebreaker was parked five hundred miles from where the military lost track of the EAGL. And yet, it was only a tantalizing hundred and twenty miles from where they were now.

"Well within range," Joe said.

Gamay sat back and exhaled deep and slow as if she'd been holding her breath for a long time. She knew what was coming next.

"We need to get up there," Kurt said.

"We're under orders to scan the signal line," she reminded him. "Not our regular kind of orders—the ones that you and Joe seem to think of as suggestions, but *real* orders directly from the White House."

"She's right," Joe said. "This is not a normal situation."

Kurt looked hurt. "Relax," he said. "I'm not going to ask Captain Akers to take his ship off the line. But we don't need four people to watch a sonar readout or wait for a drone's AI system to spot a flying fish. You two can handle that."

Gamay frowned with obvious disdain. She didn't like being the voice of reason or sounding like the mother hen, but Kurt's bravado often forced her to act that way. As far as she could tell, he'd never met a risk he didn't think was worth taking. In her armchair psychology review of him she would say his decision-making process was based on an overriding belief in his own ability, a sense that luck was always going to be riding by his side and a default mechanism that told him that *even if* things did go horribly wrong, he would figure a way to get himself out of the mess somehow.

As long as she'd known him, he hadn't been wrong. But it only had to happen once.

"And just how do you plan on approaching this ship?" she asked.

"Very carefully," he replied.

"Not funny," she said.

"It's an icebreaker," Kurt said. "Not a ship of war. It probably has a weather radar and short-range collision-avoidance set designed for navigating traffic near congested harbors. It's not going to be bristling with antiaircraft missiles and fifty-caliber machine guns."

She gave a shrug, imagining how Kurt must have driven his mother crazy as a child. Before she could offer more reasons to be cautious Joe spoke up.

"I'm all in for the adventure," he said, "but aren't we ignoring the obvious?"

He pointed to the screen. The bright red hull of the Chinese ship stood out against the endless expanse of white ice. The gray swath of a runway was easy to make out, but there was nothing else around. "I don't see a plane."

"Joe makes a good point," Gamay said, grinning.

"What's at the end of that runway?" Kurt asked.

All eyes focused on the screen. Off one end of the "runway" lay a hundred miles of jumbled ice. Not far from the other end lay the gap of dark water formed where the icebreaker had plowed its way south and made the ninety-degree turn.

"You think it went into the water?" Gamay asked.

"Not sure," Kurt said. "But I can't imagine a better way to hide a salvage effort from prying eyes."

Even Gamay had to agree there was logic to Kurt's line of reasoning. She kept it to herself. "So, you're just going to fly up there and knock on the side of the hull with a hammer and ask the Chinese if they've seen our missing plane?"

"That's not a bad idea," Kurt joked. "We should bring a housewarming gift as a pretext for looking around. Just like you do when someone new moves into your neighborhood."

Joe and Paul laughed at this. *The boys*, she thought. "I'm sure a houseplant would do wonders for international relations. But then what?"

"We'll see," Kurt said. He was already up and sliding the chair back into place.

"And what are we supposed to do while you're gone?"

"Keep watching those screens," he said, heading for the door. "Just in case I've got it wrong."

CHAPTER 6

The Chinese ship rose up from the ice like a red castle in a field of white. The *Xue Hong* had boxy lines and a towering rectangular superstructure that looked like someone had plucked a ten-story building from the middle of a crowded city and placed it onto the ship. The monolithic block contained the crew quarters and the ship's main operating spaces. The bridge at the top was covered in a forest of antennas, satellite dishes, and radar housings. Its broad windows were canted downward. As the ship was designed to cruise through endless floes of ice, these windows were heated, polarized, and tinted a reflective bronze like a set of giant ski goggles designed to keep the crew from going snow blind.

A long deck ran out behind the main structure, extending toward the stern. An octagonal crown at the far end was painted green, with a gigantic yellow circle around the edge. Planted squarely in the middle of this circle was a midsize helicopter, its windows, engine intakes, and rotor blades covered with removable plastic shields to keep the snow and ice from accumulating on them. At the stern, a pair of red cranes had been swung outboard, where they acted as elevators, transporting vehicles, men, and equipment down to the ice and back up again as needed.

Inside the warm bridge, a trio of uniformed officers waited pensively. At various times they gazed through binoculars at the men on the ice or the empty sky. But there was nothing to see, not on radar or with the human eye. Nothing but endless frozen water and a cobalt-blue sky.

Two of the men wore the naval uniforms of the People's Liberation Army Navy, PLAN. The third wore winter camouflage fatigues in a white and gray pattern.

"I don't like this," the first man said, lowering his binoculars. He was a stocky man in his late fifties with a broad, square face and steel-gray hair. He wore the uniform of a senior captain. The icebreaker was his ship. But the mission was being run by another. "We shouldn't be waiting like this."

Beside the captain stood a willowy man with long arms and legs. Rear Admiral Yang Li was elegant and composed. His rank was impressive for his age, as he was only forty-five, almost ten years younger than the captain, but his ambition was to reach even more important positions. "Our orders from the high command are to remain on station," he said calmly. "We shall do so until otherwise directed."

By stating it this way, he took none of the blame for those orders. He gave no hint what he thought of them.

"What is the high command waiting for?" the captain grumbled. "It's been twenty-eight hours. The American aircraft couldn't have remained aloft for more than three. It's not coming."

Admiral Li didn't appreciate the captain's tone, though he actually agreed with the sentiment. They had come here to meet the American C-17, creating a runway on the ice. The men had worked without stopping for the better part of two days, taking chainsaws and flamethrowers to the uneven parts of the ice, cutting it away or melting it flat. They'd laid fifty tons of steel mats down and then used snowmaking equipment and melted ice water to cover it and seal it in place. Their work had produced five thousand feet of smooth, reenforced ice, lined with low-intensity lights to help the American pilot see it and make a safe landing.

As a precaution, Li had ordered a gigantic berm built up at the far end, in case the American overshot the runway or proved unable to stop. The sixty-foot pile of snow and ice loomed in the distance. But all of it was for naught. Aside from a few of the ship's crew climbing the hill and sliding down it on their backs, none of the handiwork had been put to use.

After a certain period of time, it had become obvious to everyone that the aircraft was not coming. A few hours later it became a mathematical impossibility. The plane simply could no longer be airborne. But the men above Li, those in the highest levels of command, which he hoped to join one day, felt otherwise. They insisted, nonsensically, that the plane would still arrive. When Li pressed them, they offered information from a source who advised that the plane had landed elsewhere to refuel and was waiting for nightfall to make the trip out to the ice.

The admiral considered the likelihood of that happening to be slim. They might as well have been hoping for sea nymphs to bring it to them. But as he hoped to join the high command one day, he'd chosen not to argue. He decided to share what he'd been told.

"Our superiors believe the American jet put down at a remote airfield, where it has been hangared and refueled. We only have to wait for nightfall to see it arrive."

The captain shook his head in disbelief. "Where could such drivel possibly come from?" he asked, failing to hide his exasperation. "The most wishful of wishful thinking."

"The high command hasn't chosen to share the source of their information with me," the admiral said truthfully. "Wherever it came from our orders are the same. We wait until they tell us otherwise. We keep the runway in working condition."

The captain scowled, failing to hide his irritation. "Every minute we stay here we risk being discovered."

Before the admiral could answer, the third man in the trio came over to join the conversation. "Discovered doing what, exactly?"

Gushan was a large figure with thick, black hair and a roundish face. He was slightly overweight, and had the look of a soft-living, mid-forties male who'd spent too much time on his couch and not enough time in a gymnasium.

Nothing could have been further from the truth. Gushan was a hardened warrior, a black belt in several martial arts disciplines, a marksman, and a former wrestling champion who chose the military rather than a life training for Olympic glory. Over the last twenty years, he'd led several different Special Forces groups. He'd personally swum to and scouted beaches in Taiwan for an inevitable invasion. He'd traced down traitors and terrorists. He'd led missions into the disputed border region of India.

His reputation alone was enough to make both Li and the captain listen. But if they thought twice about hearing him out, the fact that his father sat in the upper echelons of power in Beijing kept them on their toes.

"Until the American plane appears out of the mist," Gushan continued in a soothing voice, "we're merely a group of scientists, setting up various experiments before the winter sets in."

"And how do you explain a half mile of metal grating to reenforce and smooth the ice?" the captain asked.

"We won't have to explain it to anyone," Gushan replied. "No one owns this ice. But if anyone should ask, it's merely an experiment to see if this type of grating can be used to keep the sea ice from breaking up. A method to reduce the damage caused by global warming."

For a man known to be ferocious and lethal, Gushan's voice was surprisingly pleasant. The captain was quickly soothed by his words.

"I suppose you're right," the captain said. "Either way, I need to get our men back out on the ice. The wind is causing the pack to shift. If this plane does arrive, we don't want it tearing itself apart on a jagged ridge."

The captain posed the question to Gushan as if he could give the order, but Gushan chose not to answer, instead he diplomatically pivoted toward Admiral Li.

Li appreciated that. "Have them check the runway and the nets," he ordered. "Just in case."

As the captain moved off to discuss the work detail with his executive officer, Li turned to Gushan. "Your father's political finesse did not skip a generation," he began. "But the captain is worrying for nothing. At best the Americans would protest our presence here, rattle on about more sanctions."

It was a scoffing boast; the admiral was grinning as he made it.

Gushan's face reflected nothing of the admiral's bluster. "With all due respect, you should not kid yourself, Admiral. Nine Americans are dead aboard that plane—wherever it is. Their military is embarrassed and angry."

"We're not responsible for those deaths," Li said. "We're merely playing the hand that was dealt."

"Of course," Gushan said. "But the Americans won't see it that way. This plane is the most important military project they've undertaken in decades. It means supremacy to them. *Or to us.* It is a prize that will reshape the entire world. The Americans will not react with restraint if they find us with it."

The admiral found the words sobering. But he showed no weakness. “Neither will we. Should the Americans attempt to interfere with us, you and your men will kill them. There will be no quarter given in this game. Not until the prize is safely brought to Beijing.”

CHAPTER 7

A mile from the Chinese ship, two men in white winter gear lay flat, hiding behind a jumbled ridge of ice. The taller of the two gazed at the Chinese ship through a powerful spotting scope, following its blocky lines to the wide rounded stern, where the cranes were in motion, lowering vehicles to the ice. Forward of the cranes, a cargo hatch gaped open. A long metal gangplank descended from it to the ice. A few men could be seen coming down the ramp. Others were already out on the ice. From this range, they looked like tiny red dots on the field of white.

"See anything interesting?" Joe Zavala asked.

Kurt thought all of it was interesting, but it was difficult to tell what might be going on. The men were spreading out across the frosty white plain. They carried or towed various kinds of equipment, stopping here and there to perform various tasks. In one area they'd set up a couple of tents. Nearby, a stream of ice particles could be seen blasting up into the air.

Pulling the hood of his jacket back and inclining his ear correctly, Kurt could just make out the buzz of a chainsaw. "Is it the Chinese New Year?"

"Not even close," Joe said. "Why do you ask?"

"Someone's carving an ice sculpture," Kurt said. "Looks like they're setting up for a party."

He panned slowly across the scene. To the left of the ice-carving station, he saw men using a small, tracked vehicle with a robotic arm to lift something off the ice. The mystery object twisted slightly as it rose, revealing itself to be a flexible grid of metal links. It reminded Kurt of the runway matting used on dirt airstrips to keep them from developing potholes during the rainy season.

The Chinese crew cleared some debris from the metal grating and then lowered it back down. Once it was lying flat, the small truck rolled over it slowly, pressing it into the surface.

Having seen enough, Kurt handed the scope over to Joe. "See for yourself."

Pulling off an outer glove so he could better handle the device, Joe wiped some condensation from the lens and then put it to his eye. After scanning the scene for a moment, he spoke. "The equipment coming off the ship is heavy stuff. Most of it would be right at home at a construction site."

Kurt nodded. "What do you think they're up to?"

"I'd say they're smoothing out the runway," Joe said. "Getting rid of pressure ridges like the one we're hiding behind."

From the air, or any appreciable distance, the sea ice looked like a flat surface, an endless unbroken plain that stretched to the horizon. In reality, it was a mosaic, made up of countless small tiles. Some covered acres, others grew to the size of small towns and cities, many were much smaller.

The wind and currents moved them about the way tectonic forces moved the continents around the globe. Pushing them together. Pulling them apart.

They tended to stick together, where they rubbed shoulders, much like ice cubes floating in one's drink. Sloshing water froze them together, but those connections were tenuous and could be broken if the wind shifted.

Where they pushed up against each other they formed pressure ridges, much like how the continents formed mountain ranges when they crashed into each other.

The ridge Kurt and Joe were hiding behind was typical, five to six feet in height, running across the ice in a zigzag-like pattern. In some places the ridges were larger, rising twenty to thirty feet. The higher the ridge protruded above the ice, the thicker the ice grew below it. A ten-foot ridge jutting upward was supported by a fifteen-foot keel of ice underneath.

When the wind or current pulled instead of pushed, sections of this great field were drawn apart. This created gaps and lengthy crevices, called leads, or irregular-shaped openings known as polynya or skylights, as they led back up from under the ice to the outside world.

It seemed logical that the Chinese runway would sustain some damage from these processes over time, especially since the wind had shifted overnight. What didn't make sense was bothering to repair it at all.

"They can't still be waiting for the plane," Kurt asked.

"I wouldn't think so," Joe said. "But they might be waiting for another plane."

"Another plane?"

"I'm just guessing," Joe said. "But if they do have the EAGL—and they pushed it into the water to do the salvage work far from prying eyes—they might want to send the parts home by airmail instead of taking them on a literal slow boat to China."

Kurt appreciated the reasoning. "One that our Navy might stop and inspect," he said. "Regardless of the international repercussions."

"Submitting to an inspection is easy peasy when you have nothing to hide," Joe added.

Joe's logic was sound. But they were just guessing at this point. "We need to get closer," Kurt said. "If they do have the EAGL sitting on the bottom, we need to confirm it and let Washington know."

Joe handed the scope back to Kurt. They were wearing white snow gear, but it didn't make them invisible. "I wouldn't do it on foot."

They'd already come a long way on foot, having landed three miles to the southwest. But they hadn't come alone.

Kurt turned around. Behind them, a torpedo-shaped object rested on a sled beside a circular polynya filled with black water. "That's why we brought the Otter."

"And I thought we dragged that thing all this way so we could work up a sweat," Joe said.

"I noticed you'd stopped complaining about the cold," Kurt replied.

"Hauling a five-hundred-pound tub across miles of ice like a sled dog will do that to you."

Kurt laughed. Joe's complaints were not well-founded. Like a self-propelled lawn mower, the sled had powered wheels underneath it that handled most of the load. He and Joe were really only guiding the thing. In most cases they got a free ride, having to put their backs into it only when the wheels spun or got stuck.

"You or me?" Joe asked. The Otter was a one-man sub.

"Since I can't fly the helicopter out of here if you get lost, I'll go," Kurt said. He had no intention of letting Joe take the risk anyway, but using this logic, Joe couldn't fight him over it.

"And what am I supposed to do while you're down there?"

"Get back to the helicopter, check your email, take a nap," Kurt said. "And run the engine every hour or so to make sure it's warm enough to start when we're ready to leave town."

They backed away from the pressure ridge and moved to the waiting sled. Removing the tarp revealed a tube-shaped device about twelve feet in length. It had a rounded nose and a slightly flattened profile, wider than it was tall. Aside from several vents and an impeller exhaust nozzle, it sported a completely smooth exterior.

At the touch of a button the cockpit opened on hydraulic arms. Kurt pulled off his bulky jacket, content to wear the mid- and base layers he had on underneath. He handed it to Joe.

"You might want to put this on, you look a little blue."

"You really must be a Viking. In case you forgot, we designed this thing to do salvage work in harbors and rivers. A heater is not standard equipment."

It didn't matter. There was simply no way he could operate in the cramped space with the bulky jacket on. "The impeller motor will keep things warm enough."

The Otter was designed to work in small spaces; it was controlled completely by water jets. It had no external dive planes, propellers, or appendages that could snag on wreckage, debris, or submerged trees. It maneuvered by opening and closing various vents through which high-pressure water could be directed. It couldn't dive much past three hundred feet, but its portability and minimal weight had made it a favorite on NUMA expeditions.

Kurt climbed in, folding his six-foot-two frame into the space. He ended up in a position similar to a man riding a high-speed motorcycle with his arms extended, his chest resting against a padded support, and his legs bent and stretched out behind him. Reaching forward, he gripped a pair of handlebar-like controls.

Flicking a single switch brought power to the systems. A quick check of the battery and oxygen readings showed them both close to a hundred percent.

"You have six hours of battery power and about four hours of oxygen," Joe said, looking over Kurt's shoulder.

"With a little luck I'll be back here in two," Kurt said.

"I'll try to time my nap accordingly," Joe said. He tossed a beacon into the dark water in the gap between the ice floes. A leash connecting it to the sled would keep it from drifting away. "You should be able to pick this up from a half mile out. The internal navigation system will easily get you within that range." He handed Kurt a radio. "Call me when you surface."

The radio was a compact device, no bigger than a cell phone. Kurt slid it into a breast pocket, gave Joe a quick salute, and pressed the button to close the cockpit.

"Watch out for angry whales," Joe said as the acrylic hatch lowered.

"You too," Kurt said. "Not to mention polar bears. I'm told they're particularly hungry this time of year."

"Polar bears?" Joe said. "Up here?"

Kurt shrugged as the canopy met the Otter's frame and locked itself down. When the pressure light turned solid green, confirming that he was sealed in, Kurt gave Joe the thumbs-up signal.

Out on the ice, Joe hiked to the rear of the sled and began cranking a lever around in circles, like a man raising the sails on an America's Cup yacht.

Each winding lifted the tail end of the Otter a few inches higher, tipping the nose downward. At a fifteen-degree angle, the submersible slid forward into the frigid water, knifing under and then bobbing back to the surface.

A rush of air escaped the vents, and the Otter went under for a second time, vanishing as the black waters closed over the top.

Joe stood transfixed by the churning water for a moment. It was impossibly black in contrast to the pristine white ice, more like printer's ink or crude oil. Not a hint of the small, gray submersible could be seen once it dropped below the surface.

That could be a good thing. Especially if Kurt got too near the Chinese ship. But it left Joe with an uneasy feeling that he struggled to explain or shake off.

Though he'd built and operated at least fifty different submersibles over the years, Joe had never liked climbing into the Otter. It was too tight and too dark. It triggered a vague sense of claustrophobia that he'd never felt before. It made him think of the old submariners who called their boats iron coffins. He hoped it wouldn't prove to be Kurt's.

Standing there he began to feel the chill. He'd been still for too long. He got back to work, lowering the rails on the sled and then pulling the white tarp over the top and lashing it down with bungee cords.

With the sled hidden and the hydrophone clicking, his work was done for the moment. With Kurt's jacket pulled over his own, Joe turned toward the west, heading for the relative warmth and shelter of the helicopter.

It would be no more than a few hours before Kurt returned. But time, he sensed, was already slowing down.

CHAPTER 8

Kurt took the Otter down to a depth of seventy feet to make sure he wouldn't bump his head on anything, but even at that depth, the view above remained alien and extraordinary.

It was strangely disorienting gliding under the ice. Light penetrating the ice made it appear to be glowing, mostly white, but in places blue and green hues could be seen. Bubbles skated along the underside of the ice, moving here and there with the current in an endless attempt to escape to the atmosphere, where they belonged. Downward spikes of the frozen water jutted at him in places. Some were long and thin—like stalactites in a cave—but most resembled upside-down mountain ranges in miniature, while the seawater below him swallowed the light so quickly that it resembled the depths of outer space.

Feeling his neck stiffen from looking upward for too long, Kurt switched his attention to the small screens in front of him. Like a modern car, the Otter had a plethora of screens and cameras all over the place. They looked upward, downward, sideways, and backward. The system was designed to allow the Otter and its occupant to see everything around it at all times.

Kurt could bring up the view from any camera, at any time, by toggling a thumb switch. He could click on a button and see a three-dimensional representation of the Otter and its surrounds, a useful feature when navigating in and around wrecks and dangerous debris. For now, he kept the forward view on the right-hand screen and the artificially created overall view on the left.

Because it was designed to work in murky lake water and sediment-filled rivers, the Otter also possessed tools that allowed it to swim blind. It had sonar to scan the bottom and sides along with a top-notch internal navigation system.

Kurt wasn't entirely sure what made the nav system so accurate—high-speed gyros, lasers, and accelerometers had been mentioned in the briefing—but he was impressed with its precision. Once the onboard computer completed its analysis of the currents surrounding the sub it placed it on a map and gave him an ETA to the satellite-confirmed position of the Chinese ship.

Twenty minutes into the journey it told him he was approaching the destination. Kurt saw little evidence of that through the window or on the screen. But a minute later he found the water brightening. He was nearing the open channel in the ice. Almost directly ahead he spotted the hull of the Chinese ship, jutting down through the ice.

He took the Otter deeper and passed underneath the ship and made for the bow.

Kurt had seen countless ships from below. Some up close while chipping barnacles from the hull, most from a deeper depth with sunlight filtering down around them. He always found it a view worth lingering on. One never really appreciated the concept of buoyancy until he looked up at a hundred-thousand-ton hunk of iron floating above his head with nothing but sinuous water to keep it there. Even with all those images locked away in Kurt's memory, the view of the Chinese ship was unique. Surrounded by the ice, it looked more like a fossil or an ancient artifact embedded in the rock.

Moving slowly underneath it, Kurt saw no sign of divers, ROVs, or submersibles. Studying the view from the upward-pointing camera, he saw nothing to indicate the ship had vast doors that could open up and gobble a wreck whole, as the *Glomar Explorer* had done with a Russian submarine all those years ago. The hull was solid, red, steel, marked only by a tangled pattern of scrapes and gouges from crushing its way through thousands of miles of ice over the years.

With nothing to see above him, Kurt checked the Otter's downward-pointing sonar. The submersible was small enough that he could feel the clicks reverberating through the hull with a dull *thud, thud, thud*, like he was driving a car with a square tire.

The seafloor was six hundred feet below, giving Kurt enough depth between himself and the bottom for the sonar beam to spread out like the cone of light from a streetlamp. The returns covered a mile-wide swath. It was nothing but flat, featureless ooze.

"If they do have it," he said to himself, "they didn't park directly over the top of it." He decided to angle for the open cut in the ice in case they'd pushed it off the far-edge runway and into the abyss.

The Otter passed beneath the breaker's stern and moved beyond the collar of ice that had formed around the ship. The water slowly brightened until he emerged from the overhang and was bathed in the sunlight coming in from above.

The brightening effect made him feel a bit exposed, but there was little chance anyone was standing on the edge of the broken ice staring down into the abyss. Especially not when they were all busy out on the ice trying to repair the makeshift runway.

He found the area behind the ship was clear, the bottom remained nothing but sediment. He continued along beneath the opening, skirting the edge.

He kept his eyes on the sonar readout, too closely perhaps, as the Otter hit something and twisted to the right. The jarring impact took Kurt by surprise. He looked up as something scraped loudly across the acrylic canopy above him.

Flipping the throttle to a stop, he studied the damage to the clear acrylic panel. It had been scratched and gouged, not unlike the underside of the Chinese ship's hull, but he was far too deep for it to be ice.

Drifting a bit, he cycled through the camera views looking for what he had hit. A second lesser impact got his attention. It made a slow grinding sound as the Otter slipped past something in the water.

Kurt knew the sound well. It was metal on metal. Steel scratching across the titanium hull. He saw a blurred image on the port camera. Whatever he'd encountered was too close for the lens to resolve. He bumped the thruster, moving the Otter to the right.

After flipping on an exterior light, Kurt craned his neck around to see what he'd found. He had run into a braided steel cable, several inches thick, but nearly invisible in the dark water.

Taking on some more ballast, he allowed the Otter to sink to a greater depth. At a hundred twenty feet he went back to neutral buoyancy.

With the Otter hanging suspended in the water and tiny sedimentary particles around it catching the light that was filtering down, Kurt looked up. He found the cable again and followed its length back to a point where it intersected a second cable. Farther on there was a third and a fourth and possibly more.

He took the submersible lower. The farther down he went, the more he could see against the light from above. At two hundred feet he stopped the descent. The view above him was clear now. There were dozens of cables suspended in the water. At their far edges they appeared to be connected to huge yellow bags, which in turn appeared to be anchored to the ice. The bags were inflated lifting bags, each one the size of a house. The cables stretched out between them, crisscrossing and interlocked.

It's a web.

With the whole structure in sight, it became clear what the Chinese had done. They'd built a massive, submerged net out of braided steel cable, then anchored it to the ice and supported it by connecting large numbers of the giant flotation devices.

It was indeed a web, designed to catch a very large fly. But the net, Kurt noted, was empty.

"It's not here," he said aloud.

A grin appeared on Kurt's face, partly from the satisfaction of being proved right in his analysis, but mostly from the knowledge that the Chinese hadn't succeeded in stealing such an important example of American technology.

Using the Otter's cameras, he took photos and videos of the vast metal net. He got in close enough to get good shots of the connectors and the lifting bags. He estimated the size.

With that done, he checked the navigation system, the power levels, and the oxygen supply. He had plenty to spare, but decided it was time to head home.

He tapped the thruster controls, pivoted away from the net, and then nudged the throttle ahead. He'd just begun to turn back when a new impact shook the sub, shoving it forward and pushing it end over end.

The Otter had been rammed by something. The whirring sound of a rapidly spinning propeller gave the attacker's presence away. It radiated through the water as the Otter tumbled.

Getting control of the sub, Kurt looked out through the canopy. He spotted a bulky, industrial-sized ROV silhouetted by the light above. It was traveling away from him, but slowing and turning. As he watched, it came around and charged back at him once again.

"Damn," Kurt said, gunning the throttle. He'd overstayed his welcome by the thinnest of margins.

CHAPTER 9

Up on the bridge of the icebreaker, the dull tension of waiting for something to happen was shattered when a door flew open and the leader of the salvage team burst in. His group had strung the braided metal cables below the surface.

He raced over to Li, breathless and carrying a printed image. “Excuse the interruption, Admiral,” he began, “but I have something you should see.”

Li took the photo. It was grainy and dark; anything but impressive. “What am I supposed to see here?”

“It’s an American submersible,” the man said. “One of the ROVs hit it while checking the cables. It’s operating below the net.”

Li’s eyes widened. “Are you certain?”

“We have video,” the man said, stepping to a console. Switching it on without waiting for permission, he brought up the navigation screen from the ROV in question.

At first all anyone could see was a trail of bubbles and occasional specks of sediment as the machine sped through the dark water. Then, as it turned, Li saw the target: a cigar-shaped machine. It was compact and sleek, all the things the construction ROVs weren’t.

"Are we sure it's an American craft?"

"Who else could it be?" the salvage specialist said.

It could have been Russian or Norwegian perhaps. But one look at the sleek lines, the style over substance, and Li agreed there was little chance of it being owned by any nation other than the United States.

Gushan and the icebreaker's captain joined the conversation.

"Some of their nuclear submarines carry teams of commandos and submersibles to deploy them," the captain said.

"You're referring to their Navy's SEAL teams," Li said. "They could cause us great trouble out here on the ice." He turned to Gushan. "You will deal with them if they appear."

Gushan wasn't concerned. "If I have to," he said.

Like any combat specialist he believed he and his men were the best. Part of him longed to prove it, and testing them against America's famed warriors would give him just that chance. But as he studied the American craft, he didn't think it was carrying SEALs or commandos of any other type. For one thing, it was too small. It couldn't possibly hold more than two men.

"How many ROVs have been deployed?" Li asked.

"Two."

"Give them orders to track the American sub. Ram it once they get in range," he ordered. "Hit it repeatedly until it cracks open and sinks to the bottom."

The ROVs operated on an artificial intelligence system. They didn't require connected cables like a traditional submersible robot. Once an order was given, it would be followed until achieved or new orders were received.

The admiral felt a surge of adrenaline as he gave the order. Despite his rank, his combat experience was mostly limited to training and war games. He found the wave of energy to be a rush, but also accompanied by anxiety. He looked at Gushan for confirmation. He hated himself for feeling this slight weakness, but this was the commando's field of expertise.

Gushan nodded calmly. "They must not report what they have found. Sink them before they get the chance."

CHAPTER 10

Kurt knew he had a problem when the ROV turned back toward him. By accelerating away and moving back under the ice, he hoped to shake off the pursuit. This water was dark; he'd shut off all his lights and made a hard right turn. Without sonar to track him, a few hundred yards would be enough to make him invisible.

Running at full speed for a couple of minutes, he thought he might have slipped free. But as the water around him brightened unnaturally, he knew he'd been found.

Switching to the rearward-facing camera, he saw a set of powerful lights blazing away in the dark behind him. The submersible following him had brought its own illumination to the party. Its high-intensity work lights sat out wide on a pair of posts, like the eyes or antennas of some giant insect.

To Kurt's dismay the ROV was gaining on his sleek craft. It closed in on him slowly, pulled even beside him, and then swung toward him, aiming for the stern and the thruster exhaust port.

Kurt pushed the controls downward, dropping the Otter below the attacker's depth.

The attacker crossed directly above the canopy, close enough for Kurt to see the Chinese flag painted on the bottom.

The machine was bulky and square with several robotic arms that looked like claws. It was larger than the Otter, but what it gave away in streamlining, it made up for in power. Without the need to carry an occupant, it carried larger batteries, a more powerful motor, and instead of an impeller, used a pair of adjustable propellers.

As Kurt watched, the submersible moved ahead of him and then swung back at him, charging like a bull.

This time Kurt was able to escape it by rising above it. He waited until the last second and angled to the right, snapping off one of the ROV's extended arms and the portside lighting pod.

The shattering bulbs sent an electric blue flash through the water as they failed, and Kurt allowed himself to grin. One more attack and the giant insect would be blind in the dark. He chose a course away from it, watching on the screen as it turned to follow once more.

At first it seemed to be dropping back, but soon gathered steam and began closing the gap once more.

Kurt figured he could swing to the right and then back around to the left and clip that last lighting pod, then go on his merry way. He set up the move. "Just a little closer."

Once again Kurt found his eyes in the wrong place. As he watched, the first ROV come at him, a second one hit him from the side. It had approached with its own light off in a coordinated attack.

Kurt was thrown against the bulkhead of the submersible, banging his head and shoulder. He would have been tossed to the deck if there was any room in the Otter to fall. As it was, he found himself disoriented, wedged between the pedestal and the curved hull plating.

He struggled in the cramped, dark space to get back onto the pedestal. As soon as his hands reached the controls, he put the Otter into a steep climb. It was an old submariner's instinct. Anytime you hit something, head for the surface as fast as you can.

Traveling upward toward the ice, Kurt had a second to assess the damage. The second ROV had rammed him in the side, like a dolphin attacking a shark by slamming into its gills. Warning lights flickered and a pressure alarm sounded, indicating a leak somewhere. A second warning chirped, indicating the battery pack had been damaged.

Kurt looked around for water coming in, but found none in the cockpit. He checked the damage-control screen and learned that the number two battery pack had gone instantly to zero percent power. That pack was on the left side, directly behind him. Precisely where the attack had hit home.

He'd lost half his power and was taking on water. The tiny sub was compartmentalized, but there was no guarantee the bulkhead dividing the two battery packs would hold.

Flicking through the camera views, he could see the two ROVs positioning themselves for the kill. His only chance was to lose them in the ice. He continued up, getting as close to the ice as he dared, and then leveling off. Now he raced along beneath it, heading for one of the inverted ridges.

The ROVs came up after him, closing in until Kurt weaved behind a jumbled downward thrust of ice.

He ran along beside the jagged arrangement, remaining close, and scraping it several times. A gap appeared and he darted through it and continued to run.

He quickly found another pressure ridge and ducked behind that one. Moments later he was able to drop down and pop up behind a third ridge.

It was like flying across and through upside-down hedgerows. Kurt grew quickly used to it; he even sensed a rhythm to the way the ridges were arranged.

He felt he had an advantage in the ice. Human reactions to the constantly changing surface would have to be quick. The ROVs would have to process the situation with limited experience. And they would have to be cautious. It only took one bad move for them to slam into an outcropping of ice, and perhaps one wrong turn for them to lose track of him.

With growing confidence Kurt checked behind him. To his great irritation, the ROVs were right there, following at a distance, stalking him. Up ahead an inverted pyramid-shaped jumble of ice loomed. Kurt went right for it. He cut close to it and then looped all the way around the obstruction before continuing on his way.

Only now did Kurt realize how the ROVs were tracking him. He was trailing a long stream of bubbles from the rupture in the side. It might as well have been blood in the water or smoke from a damaged aircraft. He would never get away with that stream of air trailing out behind him.

Wondering how much air was left, he double-checked the damage-control screen. The computer told him he had twenty minutes of air and power for about thirty minutes of high-speed travel. Neither one of those would be enough to make it back to the pickup point. Not with the ROVs tracking his every move. All he'd end up doing was leading the Chinese to Joe and the helicopter.

Kurt had always been the type of man to face facts quickly. In this case there was no way home, but word still had to get out. And that meant he had to surface and send Joe on his way.

He considered looking around for a skylight, but that would be relying on a stroke of good fortune that had so far been missing. Instead, he glanced at the internal navigation system and turned back toward the Chinese icebreaker and the only place he could possibly reach that would allow him to surface.

On board the Chinese ship, the change in direction took everyone by surprise. The salvage leader figured out the new heading first. "The exhaust trail leads back toward us now."

"It has to be a ruse," Li said. "No one in their right mind would come back toward the danger."

"Have the ROVs follow the trail," Gushan ordered. "Don't guess."

Li glared at him, but said nothing.

The ROVs turned and followed the steady stream of bubbles collecting under the ice. Before long they caught sight of their quarry again.

"It's heading directly at us," the captain said.

"Why?" the admiral asked. "Could it be armed?"

Gushan said nothing. He wasn't sure, but they would soon find out.

As Kurt closed in on the Chinese ship, he figured he needed to do two things at roughly the same time. First, he needed to send a message to Joe, ordering him to get off the ice and fly back to the *Lyra* and alerting him to the Chinese plan and their empty net. Second, he needed to get out of the Otter without the Chinese spotting him. He'd make the radio call first, in case he didn't have time for a second move.

As he raced along at full speed, the navigation console began warning of excessive battery drain. This course was taking him back into the current. It was a major strain on the remaining battery pack, but it played to the Otter's one true advantage.

The big, squarish ROVs—which had been assisted along by the current as they chased Kurt—were slowed far more than the streamlined NUMA sub as they drove straight into it.

Kurt watched their lights fade as they fell back. Soon there was just a dim glow. And then nothing. But he was still trailing those damned bubbles.

As he approached the opening, daylight poured in. He cruised out from under the ice, realizing he would be easier to spot directly, but harder to follow now that the bubbles had a chance to escape through the open water into the air above. Kurt hoped he'd be able to do the same thing. He turned away from the Chinese ship and followed the cut northward toward the pole. At the same time, he brought the Otter up to the surface. Free-floating ice drifted above him here and there. He could use that to his advantage.

He cruised beneath a small wolf pack of growlers surfacing on the other side. He continued north, raising the Otter's antenna to make the call.

"Base, this is Otter," he said. "Contact with the Chinese confirmed. High probability they were waiting for the EAGL. Runway and subsurface netting suggest they intended to land it and then push it off the ice into the water, where it could be taken apart at a shallow depth and then disposed of. Additional investigation unnecessary. Aircraft is not present. All scout teams return to the boat and await further orders. I repeat, all scout teams return to boat."

The message had been sent. Kurt hoped both Joe and the Chinese had heard it. He doubted it would do much, but if the Chinese happened to think the Americans were here in numbers, they might be less aggressive. And if they believed the Americans were backing off and returning to their boat, they might just decide to leave him alone.

He figured that last hope was a long shot. And that meant he had to roll the dice one more time.

CHAPTER 11

The helicopter sat on the ice rocking back and forth in the wind. Joe had been a stoic passenger, waiting patiently and watching time tick away, checking and rechecking the radio.

The sun was heading down, having spent five short hours above the horizon. As the light became flatter, the wind picked up. Before long, it was whipping flurries of ice crystals past the cockpit windows. Studying the fading horizon, Joe wondered whether they'd get a whiteout and nightfall all at the same time.

Inside the cockpit the air was a crisp twenty-nine degrees. Joe had to keep it cold to prevent the blowing ice from melting and refreezing on every available surface. He could see his breath. He could feel his fingers growing numb.

Checking the oil temps, he decided it was time to run the engine again. He went through the start procedure, omitting the use of lights, which drew a lot of juice from the batteries.

With the starter engaged, the helicopter's engine roared to life. Joe released the starter switch and scanned the gauges as the engine settled into a confident howl. A few minutes later Kurt's voice came through the radio, marred slightly by static.

Joe listened to the message intently, thrilled to hear from Kurt, and then deeply puzzled by what he was saying.

"All scout teams return to the boat."

Joe scratched his head for a minute. The first part made sense: the Chinese had been waiting to rendezvous with the hijacked EAGL. The second part of the message was also clear: the missing plane had never arrived. Joe figured Kurt had used the word *boat* to suggest the imaginary teams had come off an American submarine, as submariners called their vessels boats instead of ships or subs. The last part was meant for him. Joe was the only other "scout team member" out there. Kurt was telling Joe to get back to the *Lyra*.

Now Joe found himself annoyed. As if he would actually leave his best friend behind.

He glanced at the gauges in front of him. Satisfied that enough heat had built up in the engine compartment he shut the system down. He was about to broadcast, but didn't need it to sound like he was in a helicopter at the time.

As the turbine wound down, he thought about what he'd say. Kurt wouldn't order him to leave unless he'd run into trouble. He wouldn't suggest that Joe abandon him unless he couldn't get back to the skylight where they'd parked the sled. Joe figured Kurt was most likely surrounded or being pursued.

Visualizing all of this in his mind, Joe knew exactly what to say. He thumbed the transmitter.

"Otter, this is *Goblin Shark*," Joe began. "Message received. Scout teams being recalled. Proceed to extraction point Bravo. Combat team one will cover your approach to the boat. We will set up green and red flares upon surfacing."

Joe listened closely, pressing the headset to his ear in hopes of getting a response. He picked up a couple bursts of static, but nothing more. He looked outside. The light was fading, the sun a tiny glow on the horizon like a candle about to go out. And then it was gone.

In a few minutes, the Arctic ice plain would drop another fifteen degrees in temperature. Joe exhaled and waited. He could only hope Kurt had received and understood the message.

CHAPTER 12

The wind died as soon as the sun went down. In its absence, the entire frozen venue grew still and silent, while pinpricks of starlight, too brilliant to be believed, appeared in the cloudless night sky.

In this overriding quiet, the crunch of snow underfoot and the voices of men shouting carried with surprising strength. Several groups of Chinese crewmen were now out on the ice, lumbering in their cold-weather gear, searching here and there, flashlight beams playing across the frozen white surface in all directions.

What looked like an unorganized gaggle from one perspective was actually a long picket line of humans spread out in an echelon formation. They were scanning the ice and the water along the cut, looking for any sign of the American or his submersible.

Gushan walked behind them, ignoring the cold. If anything, he appreciated its bite, it kept the men sharp, and it made the American's life more difficult. They would find the American soon. He was certain of that.

The headset he wore under his fur-lined hood crackled. It was Li, calling from the cozy warmth of the icebreaker's bridge. "I need a report."

"We're still searching," Gushan said. "Nothing yet."

"The ROVs have searched up and down the cut to a range of seven miles," Li said. "The American sub is nowhere to be found. Surely this means the American has made his way back to his mother ship."

"His craft was damaged," Gushan countered. "It was leaking air. He didn't come back this way to harass us. He needed to surface. The cut we made in the ice was the only open water for miles around. He's here somewhere."

"Then find him and eliminate him," Li said. "No traces."

Gushan could hear the concern in his superior's voice. In Gushan's opinion, Li was not cut out for this command. He was too mercurial, too emotional. He continued to oscillate between fear of failure and discovery, and the possible glory of success. One minute he wanted to crush his enemies, the next he was gripped by doubt. But then, Li was worried about his reputation and the future of his career, while Gushan was concerned only with the job at hand.

The captain was another problem. He continued to worry about an American nuclear submarine putting a torpedo into the side of the icebreaker.

Gushan didn't believe there was an American boat out there. He didn't believe the back-and-forth communications to be legitimate. They wouldn't have been sent on an open channel if they were. But he knew there were at least two Americans in the area, maybe more. In either case, the best way to protect the icebreaker was to have a hostage on board. Not kill the American on sight.

"We need information from this man," Gushan said calmly. "He can disappear after we've gotten it from him."

The admiral did not reply immediately, but Gushan had calculated the exchange correctly. Li would see the value of this approach and yet still get his way.

"Assuming you can find him," the admiral countered.

Gushan had hoped to find the submersible trapped amid the loosely jumbled ice around the edges of the cut—that's where he would have hidden it had the roles been reversed. But it depended how far the American had run. An hour of searching in the frigid darkness had revealed nothing and Gushan began to wonder if the American had ridden his damaged craft to the bottom.

A voice split the night.

"Over here!" one of the men called. "Look at this."

Beams of light converged on their comrade from different parts of the frozen plain. They soon focused on a frost-covered hump wedged between two chunks of ice. The hump looked nothing like the dark submersible in color because it was now covered in a layer of ice crystals and precipitated salt. But the shape gave it away.

Gushan stepped forward, commending the man who'd found it. It would have been easy to miss.

"Stay back," he ordered. "If you fall in, you stay in. No one is diving in to rescue you."

That was enough of a warning to stop the approaching men in their tracks.

As they stood by, Gushan stepped ahead of them, approaching the craft himself. He found the footing to be treacherous near the machine. Even though the slabs of ice holding the craft in place were the size of tennis courts, they were only tenuously connected to the main shelf by a thin layer of frozen water.

Using a ski pole he jabbed at the ice, looking for weak spots. He found a thin area, stepped over it, and moved even more cautiously until he reached the frozen machine.

Through what he could only imagine was extraordinary piloting skills or incredible luck, the sleek submersible had been driven into a V-shaped gap and up onto the ice itself, like a seal leaving the water to escape a pursuing killer whale. No wonder the ROVs couldn't find it.

It lay on the ice fully exposed and leaning slightly to one side. Encrusted in the salt and frost, the machine looked dead, like a discarded relic from some bygone era.

Gushan paused beside the hull, listening. He heard no sound coming from the cockpit. Nothing to indicate it was occupied or that any of its systems were functioning. Using his gloved hand he rubbed the frost from the acrylic glass canopy in a circular motion. Placing his flashlight against the glass he looked inside. The interior was cramped, dark, and completely empty.

"No one home," he told the men.

He looked around. The ice offered nothing in the way of footprints, but there was little chance the American had gone for a swim.

He gave orders for a snowcat to be brought out and lines secured to the sub. They would drag this American machine back to the icebreaker like a prize captured in battle. It wouldn't make up for the missing aircraft, but it was better than nothing. In the meantime, he would order the men to disperse and continue the search on foot.

Waiting for the tow, Gushan studied the machine. It was sleek and streamlined in every way. Clearing the frost, he counted the thruster vents in various places. He examined the damaged hull plating where the ROV had rammed it. The material grade was very high. The craft itself was absolutely unique. It had obviously been built with significant investment and effort, as opposed to being cobbled together with off-the-shelf parts. Perhaps it was a military craft after all.

The snowcat arrived and a line was thrown out. Gushan caught the rope and stepped to the nose of the submersible, where he attached it to an exposed ring that was clearly designed as a towing point. Beneath it, partially covered by the frost, he could see a vague outline of the American flag and a set of letters and numbers. He scraped the frost from the hull, revealing the flag, the registration number, and a logo he'd seen somewhere before. He rubbed some more of the frost from the machine and discovered four capitalized letters in the Western alphabet. They read NUMA.

Gushan stared at the letters with an angry expression on his frozen face.

"Damn," he whispered to the night. "Damn."

CHAPTER 13

Sometime in his mid-twenties, Kurt had been caught in a blizzard while cross-country skiing in the backwoods of Colorado. A storm that was supposed to whip by, dropping a couple inches of snow, stalled over the area, becoming a three-day storm that dropped several feet of powder onto the Rockies.

Walking, even in the ski boots, became impossible. Cross-country skis were useless because of the depth of the powder. Facing the choice between a superhuman hike back to civilization that was all but impossible and staying put, Kurt decided to settle down and wait for the spring thaw. He trudged to a flatter section of the pass, where an avalanche was less likely to crush him in his sleep, and built a cave in the snow.

His memories of time in that cave were mostly boredom, listening to the wind, listening to the shortwave, rationing his food. The one thing that stood out was the surprising level of heat. After several hours in the igloo-like cavern, he had to start shedding layers. Despite the snowstorm outside and temperatures in the single digits it was simply too warm in the cave for all his winter clothing.

Now, out on the polar ice pack, north of the Arctic Circle, Kurt had found a similar hiding place. After driving the Otter up onto the ice, he managed to get out, close the cockpit, and run across the frozen surface. He made his way to the nearest ridge, found a section of ice that had been thrust upward and toppled over, and ducked underneath it. The large slab acted as a natural lean-to of sorts, propping itself up against a neighbor. Kurt had found and wedged smaller chunks into the gaps on either side, scraping snow together and using it to seal the gaps to the best extent possible.

It wasn't exactly the Ritz, and it didn't even live up to the performance of the snow cave in Colorado, but it kept some of the chill off and hid him from view. From the outside, his hiding spot looked no different than a thousand other jumbled spots formed by the pressure ridges. The Chinese would have to walk right up to it and kick the smaller ice chunks out of the way to see that it was hollow.

There, Kurt waited. Watching through a tiny gap in the opening and wishing he'd taken Joe's advice and brought the heavy parka with him.

He saw the darkness fall; watched the oncoming lights as the Chinese crewmen walked the ice looking for him; heard their excited shouts when they discovered the Otter. He saw the Otter towed away and endured a growing tension as the men spread out across the ice to search for him once again.

Only after they passed him by, their voices growing more distant and the dim glow of their lights fading, did Kurt relax. Human nature would soon take over. While he was sheltered and somewhat insulated from the cold, they were out in it and had been for hours. Where he had no choice but to stay put, they had a warm ship and a comfortable mess hall waiting for them. Soon enough, even the leaders would suggest there was no point in searching any further.

The bitter night dragged on. Kurt glanced at his watch. The time ticked by. Eventually it was one hour till midnight, when the goblin sharks surfaced.

CHAPTER 14

Gushan stepped into his private compartment in the accommodations block of the icebreaker. The cramped compartment was spartan and squared away. After closing the door behind him, he tossed his heavy coat onto a chair and threw his gloves aside in frustration.

He was angry at their inability to find the American, irritated by Li's odd combination of nervousness and arrogance, and incensed that the high command insisted that they remain on station when it was clear to everyone that the American plane wasn't coming. But most of all he was pained to learn that the submersible they'd attempted to destroy had come from the American organization NUMA.

He went to a small metal sink tucked into a corner of the compartment and ran cold water over his numb hands, rubbing them together until they began coming back to life. Grabbing a towel, he dried them, and then looked in the mirror.

Today he looked old and worn-out. The lines on his face were deeper, the scar beneath his eye appearing stark white against the flushing color in his warming cheeks.

He threw the towel aside and looked elsewhere, settling his gaze on a decorative bottle of baijiu on the shelf beside the mirror. The twenty-year-old bottle—purchased from one of the more ancient makers of the spirit—was meant to be opened upon celebrating their success. Preferably on the way home to China with the primary parts of the American laser system secured on board.

He opened the bottle. Baijiu wasn't meant to be consumed alone or during moments of anger, but at this point he knew there would be nothing to celebrate, only more trouble and pain.

He poured himself a shot, studied the liquid through the glass, and then knocked it down. His swirling thoughts took a short vacation as the alcohol singed his throat and the nutmeg and licorice flavors emerged on his palate.

Calmer now, and warming rapidly, he put the glass down and pulled off his other layers. He got down to a T-shirt saturated with sweat. Strange, he thought, how the body could be so cold and hot at the same time.

He pulled the shirt over his head and tossed it with the other clothes. As he reached for a clean shirt, he caught sight of a second scar, this one was jagged and angry. It had been inflicted on him by a smuggler named Ahab, who'd captured him, tortured him, and then stabbed him and left him for dead.

If it hadn't been for the bravery of two men from NUMA, Gushan would have died there, impaled on a burning ship. And now he was being asked to hunt and kill someone from that very same agency.

He poured another shot and, after cursing the fates, slugged the second drink down as quickly as the first.

A knock at the door interrupted his rage. It was a bold knock, an insistent one. It didn't come from some middling crewman sent to give him a message.

As he turned, the door swung open prior to any permission being given.

Li barged in as Gushan pulled on the fresh T-shirt.

"I expected you to come to the bridge and give a report."

"I needed a change of clothes," Gushan said.

"And more than that, I'd say." The admiral's gaze had settled on the bottle of liquor.

"Tell the captain I need more men," Gushan said, ignoring the barb. "My men are frozen stiff. They need to eat and warm their bones. Have him detail a search party. I will lead them out myself."

"You sound as if you're giving orders, Major."

Li sounded edgy. He stepped past Gushan, studying the compartment. He focused on the clothes strewn about and then picked up the bottle and sniffed the aroma. "Warming your own bones?"

"It's very effective," Gushan insisted. He figured there was no point in pretending. "See for yourself."

He poured the admiral a shot and handed it over.

Li drank it swiftly. His face betrayed neither pleasure nor disdain. He put the glass down without commenting on its quality. "You don't seem quite yourself, Major. What's bothering you?"

"It's pointless for us to sit here," Gushan said. "Waiting for a plane that isn't coming."

"The high command—"

"The high command is wrong," Gushan snapped, dangerously interrupting his superior.

Li took this dereliction with a surprising level of calm. "They have information that says otherwise."

"From whom?" Gushan demanded. "Where is this story coming from? Who is this mysterious source?"

"An emissary of the hijackers," Li said.

This was the first time Li had shared that bit of data. It moved the needle enough for Gushan to pause. Sadly, he doubted its veracity.

"The plane isn't coming," he repeated. "Nightfall has come and gone. It's nearly midnight."

"It may remain hidden."

"There are only so many places to hide an aircraft that large," Gushan said. "By now the Americans will have checked them all. The plane has obviously crashed. Whoever this mouthpiece for the hijackers is, he or she is playing a game. Probably trying to get something for nothing. Mark my words, they will soon ask for money—as a show of good faith or an entry fee of some sort. They will tell us there are other bidders. It's a stalling tactic at best. Or a con."

"Perhaps," Li said with a groan. "But that's not our concern. We have our orders. Maintain the runway, and find and eliminate the American. We will accomplish both."

The runway was useless at this point, Gushan thought. The Americans had obviously spotted it. They would be watching it. If the EAGL somehow materialized and attempted to reach them it would be shot out of the sky, and the runway and the icebreaker would be hit with a barrage of cruise missiles.

Gushan let that point go. Li would never go against the high command. "I'll look for the American using the helicopter. We can rig up an infrared camera. If he's out there, it will be easier to spot his heat."

Li considered this. "Very well," he said. "The captain wants to move the ship before the ice at our stern gets any thicker. We're going to turn and move back up the cut and clear things out a bit to keep the channel from closing. I'll have him wait until you're airborne. Be quick about it."

Gushan had no intention of delaying. He nodded his understanding and put the cork back in the bottle. Celebrations would have to wait.

Joe sat in the helicopter drumming his fingers on his knee. He'd had to run the engine three times since Kurt's radio message and was wary about going through the start procedure a fourth time without actually taking off. Each start was a significant draw on the battery. But to conserve fuel for the ride home he could only run the engine for five minutes before shutting it back down, which was not enough time to recharge the power pack.

He watched the oil temps dropping, allowing them to go lower than he had before, attempting to squeeze every last second out of his delay. Finally, he'd waited as long as he dared.

Time to go.

He started the engine once more. It came to life without protest and Joe made a mental note to commend the mechanics and write a letter to the company that made the batteries, thanking them for the quality of their product.

As the helicopter powered up, he turned on the plethora of deice equipment it carried. Heated cockpit windows, heated control surfaces, heated rotors. The window cleared slowly, and the darkness of the night poured in.

It was a quarter to midnight. He would wait a couple minutes before attempting to take off. Then he'd fly across the ice, listening for a call from Kurt and looking for a light in the darkness.

He only hoped Kurt understood his mention of the goblin shark. The strange-looking creatures spent most of their time dwelling in the cold, dark depths of the ocean, but on rare occasions they came to the surface late at night.

On an expedition to the Indian Ocean, Kurt and Joe had been visited by one of the mysterious beasts on three successive evenings, each time almost precisely at midnight.

With the engine humming and the deicing equipment glowing red-hot, Joe decided to get the helicopter up into the sky. He put his hands on the controls, brought the power up slowly, and tested the lift. The blades were clawing the air as they should, with no ice buildup to prevent them from generating lift.

"It's showtime," he said, speaking as if Kurt could hear him. "Ready or not, here I come."

CHAPTER 15

As midnight crept near, Kurt's ice cave became less and less hospitable. Cold air seeped through the cracks no matter how he tried to seal them. With no method of heating the place, Kurt's joints stiffened, while his extremities grew numb. At one point the floor shifted beneath him, a reminder that fathoms of bitterly cold water lay below him, not rock and soil and other forms of terra firma.

He recognized this as his one real mistake. He was only a few hundred yards from the channel cut by the Chinese icebreaker. It made the ice floor beneath him more susceptible to the currents and small waves, causing it to flex and react to the water's push and pull.

As the push-pull of the current returned, one of the larger slabs in his ice wall shifted. Its footing slid back with a grating sound, but it caught on something and stopped before falling completely down. This opened a gap to the outside world. The bitter air seeped in, and Kurt began to shiver.

If there was ever a time for his Viking blood to thicken up, he thought, now would be the moment.

He checked his watch, tapping the dial to make sure the hands hadn't frozen in place. In the pitch-black of the cave, it was easy to see the dimly glowing dots marking the hands and the cardinal hours.

Ten minutes till midnight. Ten minutes until he could broadcast the signal and light a flare to help Joe spot him. It seemed like an eternity.

And then, as Kurt watched the second hand sweep around in the dark, a sound reached him through the triangular gap in his fortress wall. He listened closely, allowing a grin to crack his frozen face. It was the glorious sound of helicopter blades approaching from a distance.

We have something on the infrared," a voice called out, shouting over the din of the helicopter's engine and rotors.

Gushan pointed at the intercom button. They were all wearing headsets for a reason.

The man pressed it and repeated his statement. He showed Gushan the image. It was a smudge on the flickering screen, a vague heat source two miles out and slightly behind them.

It was a dim reading, nothing so bright as a man or beast. The shape was oddly triangular. Like something warm that had been left on the ice.

From the bearing, Gushan determined that they'd actually flown past it and were only picking it up by looking back. "How did we miss it?"

"It must have been shielded by something."

"What do you make of it?"

"Temperature is too elevated to be an error. There's something down there. It's over near the channel. Could be a seal or sea lion." They'd seen several pods of the animals on their journey from the other side of the world. The large seagoing creatures rested on the pack ice when they were tired of hunting fish or hiding from killer whales.

“Show me on the map,” Gushan demanded.

The lieutenant brought up an overhead mapping system with the positions of the helicopter and the infrared signal overlaid on it. The target was not far from where the NUMA submersible had been abandoned. They’d been so close. Some of the men might have walked right by him.

“That’s it,” Gushan said. He radioed Li and shared the good news. “Send out a squad of my men. I’ll turn back and land to complete the capture.”

There was a long delay before Li came on the line. “How confident are you that this target is the American?”

“Ninety percent,” Gushan replied. “Trust me, it’s him.”

“Continue on your course,” Li ordered bluntly. “Make no effort to approach the target. I don’t want him to know he’s been spotted.”

Gushan found the order nonsensical. “I want to be there when we capture him.”

“That won’t be necessary, Major,” Li said. “We’ll take it from here.”

The pilot glanced at him, awaiting a command. Gushan raised a hand and pointed forward. “Stay on course. Follow orders.”

The pilot turned back to the controls and the helicopter continued its slow path northward. Gushan looked out the side window. He saw nothing but darkness, and then a couple of miles behind that the lights of the icebreaker.

It had pulled free from its moorings, turned around, and begun a run up the channel. He couldn’t be sure, but it seemed to be angling toward the location of the heat source.

The admiral didn't want a hostage, a prisoner, or an insurance policy. He wanted the American gone. And he intended to run him down using the great ship itself.

Kurt listened intently to the sound of the helicopter and quickly realized something was off. The machine sounded bigger and heavier than the nimble craft he and Joe had flown up in. And it was lumbering through the night sky, in a lazy, unhurried manner.

Joe would come in faster, screaming across the ice at low altitude, broadcasting as he got in close and demanding Kurt light a flare or use his flashlight to reveal his exact location. Low and fast meant a rescue. High and slow meant someone was searching or loitering. Either way, the aircraft he heard was not his friend.

Kurt pulled the radio from under his armpit, where he'd kept it to help the batteries remain warm. He checked it, heard some static in the earbud that had made a home in his right ear, and determined that the device was functioning perfectly. He resisted the temptation to break the silence, instead slipping the radio into a zippered pocket, which would keep it handy but secure.

Outside the noise of the other helicopter faded as it continued on. This allowed a new sound to make its presence known: a slow churning, a deeper thrum. It came through the ice. Transmitted by the water beneath it.

A veil of light grew outside the cave. The world was no longer black, but turning a dim gray and brightening more with every passing moment. The ice cave swayed and rocked as waves surged beneath the floor. The blocks slid, some of them tumbled. A thunderous crashing sound shook everything to the core.

Kurt dove out through the opening as the ice cave collapsed. He scrambled forward on his hands and knees as the footing buckled and shuddered. A monstrous cracking sound, like great trees snapping in half, echoed from behind him. It was followed by echoing booms as if massive boulders had been dropped from some great height into empty dump trucks.

Kurt ran from the sound, sprinting the best he could on stiff legs.

The ice field around him grew brighter with every moment. It was soon blindingly white, lit up by powerful spotlights converging on his position.

Glancing back, he saw a vision of enormity and destruction. The towering red bow of the Chinese ship was surging up onto the ice, crushing the thick slabs into hundreds of smaller blocks, and spitting them out to the sides as it plowed toward him.

The mammoth proportions of the ship made it impossible to see the bridge or the sides or the length, as if all that existed was that enormous bow, chewing through the ice toward a tiny, fleeing human.

Kurt continued to sprint, thankful for the spikes in his shoes that gave him traction. He cut to the right to get out of the ship's path, but was blocked by a jagged crack that appeared like the San Andreas Fault as the two sections of ice broke apart.

Kurt might have tried to leap over it, but fountains of dark water surged up between the gap and across the ice. He was forced back in front of the ship, which was rapidly gaining ground.

Knowing he couldn't stay ahead of the ship for long, he raced to the left, taking a forty-five-degree angle across the path and hurdling a low-pressure ridge like an Olympic champion.

It was all for naught. The moment he passed the ship's centerline, a trail of glowing red lines cut the night in front of him, tracer fire from a pair of Chinese heavy machine guns.

The fireworks display was impressive. The line of bullets jack-hammering the ice ahead and to the left would have cut him to shreds. He pulled back instinctively. Kurt found himself trapped.

Behind him the ship rose up on a thick section of ice and then plunged downward as the weight of the ship overcame the bonds of the frozen water.

The downward thrust sent a powerful wave surging forward. It lifted the terrain beneath Kurt's feet, tilting it sharply, and propelling Kurt through the air as if he'd been thrown from a trampoline. Kurt's arms windmilled as he flew. He hit the ice hard, sliding across it and then springing to his feet almost instantly.

The propulsion from the launch actually helped him put some distance between himself and the ship, but it would change nothing in the long term.

To the right was a flooding canyon that he couldn't leap, to the left was a death trap of heavy gunfire that would leave his body riddled with bullets, while the path forward wouldn't keep him safe for long.

As his legs started to ache, Kurt wondered what on earth he was going to do.

Joe flew with lights out at an altitude of fifty feet. High enough to avoid the jumbled heaps of the upward-thrust ice, but low enough to keep him off the Chinese ship's radar. He was closing in on the search area when he spotted the Chinese ship running with full lights on and grinding its way into the ice. Moments later he saw strings of tracer fire lighting up the night.

"Well, that makes things easier," he joked to himself.

All the way over here, he'd been wondering how he'd find Kurt in the dark without being noticed by the Chinese. That was no longer a concern. He knew exactly where Kurt was, even though he couldn't see him. And he doubted that anyone on the Chinese bridge was paying attention to anything other than the man they were trying to run down.

He pushed the helicopter to its limits, aimed for the stern of the icebreaker, and pressed the radio transmit switch. "Inbound fast. I'll come up from where you least expect it. Look for me in the blinding light. Remember, it's always best to be POSH when you fly Zavala airways."

Joe hoped Kurt had a bud in his ear because there was no way he was going to have time to pull out the walkie-talkie and listen to the speaker.

Sweeping in behind the Chinese ship, Joe had to reduce speed. He couldn't stop on a dime or pick Kurt up while moving a hundred miles an hour.

He pulled to the right, passing the icebreaker on its starboard flank. He was below the beltline of the ship, well below the elevated bridge. By the time he passed the forward anchor, he was only moving at thirty knots, still more than three times the speed of the ship and the man sprinting in front of it.

Surging out ahead of the vessel, Joe saw Kurt running to the right just as he'd hoped. He pivoted the helicopter's nose to the left, tilting the craft and slowing further as he flew sideways toward Kurt. From above, the maneuver would resemble a car hitting the brakes and skidding sideways to a stop.

Nearing Kurt, Joe dropped toward the surface, leveling off for no more than a second or two. The skids actually scraped the ice as Kurt leapt in through the open side door, grabbing at a cargo net and pulling himself up.

As Kurt clambered inside, Joe banked to the right, swinging the nose around and pivoting away from the oncoming hulk of the red ship. At full throttle with its nose slightly down, the helicopter thundered out of the ship's path.

From there, it raced off into the darkness, leaving the huge ship to chew on nothing but empty ice.

Joe glanced back to see spotlights swinging uselessly through the air in a desperate attempt to reacquire them. Tracers came up looking like tiny fountains of lava shot from hoses that had broken loose. They swung around as uselessly as the spotlights, punching the night in futile bursts.

Joe turned back to the instrument panel.

Behind him, Kurt slammed the cargo door shut. With that secured, he moved up to the cockpit and dropped into the empty chair beside Joe.

"Thanks for the lift," he said. "That was some incredible flying."

"I aim to please," Joe said. "Unless you're the bad guys, in which case I aim to irritate to the maximum of my ability."

Kurt laughed. "Port out, starboard home," he said. "Thanks for the heads-up."

"So, you did hear me," Joe said. "I wondered if it was just a lucky guess."

Kurt removed the tiny speaker and rubbed his aching ear. "I heard you loud and clear."

Joe put them on a heading back toward the *Lyra*, keeping them low for a few miles and then climbing to a higher altitude when he figured they were well clear of any weapon the Chinese might have on board.

With the course laid in, he glanced Kurt's way. He could see the exhaustion on his face. A rare sight indeed. He figured the main debriefing would have to wait, but a quick question wouldn't hurt. "No airplane?"

"Nope," Kurt said, his voice a combination of weariness, satisfaction, and puzzlement. "As they say, nothing but net."

"So, the Chinese don't have it. The Russians don't have it. And the *Lyra* hasn't found it yet. Where does that leave us?"

"Damned if I know," Kurt said. "It's like the plane vanished off the face of the earth."

CHAPTER 16

Fifteen hundred miles from the search area in the Barents Sea, a man in a heavy overcoat and boots walked along a snow-covered sidewalk in the heart of Moscow. There was no sign of hurry in his step, in fact he used a pearl-handled cane to balance a visible but manageable limp.

The snow fell around him in large soft flakes. Perhaps two inches would accumulate. In Moscow that was nothing. The cars and buses raced along the streets, grinding the slush into the gutters, and the trains ran without delay. Even the pedestrians seemed unaffected. Half of them hadn't bothered to wear gloves or even button their coats all the way to the top.

The limping man felt differently about the temperature. He was used to humidity and warmer climates. The chill made his leg ache and dried his skin painfully where burn marks had accumulated. But he'd be warm soon enough.

He was on his way to a meeting that would take place in the labyrinth-like system of underground tunnels that made up Moscow's Metro system. The temperatures down there hovered at a near-constant seventy-five degrees.

He crossed a busy street, continued on past storefront windows filled with merchandise and holiday sale signs and past the impossibly long, concrete facade of an unadorned and unmarked government building. He was late, but then his counterparts knew he was late. He was being watched every step of the way.

He came to a stairwell that descended from the sidewalk. The Metro signage was covered with placards indicating that the station was closed for repairs. The signs were collecting some snow and the caution tape across the stairs was sagging and frayed.

The limping man ducked under the tape, stepped down the stairway, and arrived at a temporary metal barricade that blocked his path. A gate in the barricade was secured by a heavy chain and a formidable padlock.

From his pocket, the man produced a key that had been sent to him. Inserting it into the slot, he jiggled it back and forth, trying to get the tumblers to fall. It was easier said than done. The key was new, but the lock was old. The well-worn tumblers weren't initially accepting what was obviously a recently made duplicate.

On the third try it popped open, allowing the man to slide the chain noisily through the bars, open the gate, and step through. He closed the gate behind him, arranged the chain to look secure, but consciously chose not to close the padlock. It would have felt like locking oneself in a jail cell, something he had no intention of doing.

As he entered the labyrinth of tunnels, the air grew warmer and soon smelled of electrical sparks and oils. He followed the direction he'd been given precisely. Left, right, straight for a hundred feet, and then left again and down another flight of steps.

Like any maze it was easy to navigate when one knew where they were going, but impossible to decipher if a wrong turn or two were made. As he followed the given directions, it occurred to him that a maze was only a maze to the those walking inside it. They could see only the walls and branching tunnels, never really understanding the full picture, or even grasping how vast and complicated the network might be. But to those looking down from above, the entire scene was obvious. The satisfaction came from watching others struggle to figure out what the builder alone could see.

If the limping man had set things up correctly, then the nations of the world were now stepping into a labyrinth of his creation. America from one side, the Chinese from the other. If this meeting went as planned, he would ensnare the third great power in his trap, and from there he could sit back and watch history unfold.

He reached the end of a tunnel, emerging into a dark, abandoned station. A lone subway car waited on the tracks ahead of him, doors propped open, warm light emanating from inside.

He walked to it and stepped aboard. Two men waited for him. One in a suit and tie, the other in a military uniform. The suited man had a hard, narrow face and wore rimless glasses. The military man appeared to be the more jovial of the two, with a heavy build, a jowly face, and gray stubble for hair. He wore a pistol on a leather belt.

The two men stood up as he walked their way. He offered a greeting in Russian and then switched to English. "Gentlemen," he said. "It's good to see you after all this time."

The narrow-faced man offered only a slight nod, gazing at him suspiciously over the rimless glasses. The military man, a general by rank, stepped forward, studying him. Cold eyes took in the pearl-handled cane and the burn marks that crept up the side of the limping man's neck, mostly hidden at this point by the collar of his coat.

"I must say it is surprising to see you, Comrade Ahab," the general said. "I was told you'd been killed. Drowned like your namesake. But you seem to have survived with only scars to prove your pain."

The limping man grinned at the use of his old moniker. He'd been using a different alias for the last two years, but it felt good to hear his old name again. "Radiation burns," Ahab replied. "An unfortunate incident."

"And the leg?"

"An American bullet shattered my femur."

The general nodded. "Perhaps that explains why you're here. I'm told you have something for us. Something the Americans want back very badly. It would be a grand act of revenge to give it to us."

Ahab offered nothing that could be called a reaction. "I'm not into acts, General Borisov. And I don't possess what I'm here to offer you. I have only a connection to the men who control it. You may look at me as a highly paid messenger."

The suited man, whose name was Mishin, got right to it. "And who are these men you refer to?"

Ahab didn't answer.

Borisov gave him a look and then asked a better question. "What is it they have? And why should we want it?"

Ahab could feel the suited man leaning in. No doubt they expected and hoped he was about to reference the missing American aircraft. He made them wait, just a moment or two, ensuring he had their full attention. "They claim to know the final resting place of the American C-17 and its lethally powerful laser weapon, which the Americans call the EAGL."

"Then the rumors are true," Borisov said. "The American aircraft went down after all."

"Down," Ahab said, "yes. But not in the way you think. There was no crash. No explosion. No rendering of parts in all directions. The aircraft is in one piece. And the laser compartment and systems are intact, ready for extraction and study."

Ahab could see the men all but salivating at this point. "There are complications," he warned.

This statement both knocked the enthusiasm out of the men and set up the next phase of the transaction. Nothing, Ahab had learned, was more motivating to men of power than to tell them they might not be able to have what they wanted.

"What kind of complications?" Mishin asked. The question was sharp. An attorney's cross exam, or a policeman's interrogation. It had no tact. All the better, Ahab thought. Mishin had already tipped his hand.

"The Chinese were and are involved. They have agents and a command ship looking for the aircraft, and they expect to receive the location from the hijackers very soon."

"With you providing it to them, I assume," Mishin snapped. "Do you really think you can play us against one another?"

"I will provide the Chinese with nothing," Ahab replied. "They are as responsible for my injuries as the Americans. More so, perhaps. Someone in their government betrayed me. But these men have other avenues to get their message through."

Mishin sat back, folding his arms. Whether he accepted the claim or not, Ahab couldn't tell, but that mattered very little at the moment.

"All the more reason to give us the location," Borisov interjected warmly. "We will take the aircraft and keep it from them."

"Something I would be glad to do," Ahab replied, "but I'm not in possession of that information. These men are not fools. It's their only bargaining chip and they will not reveal it until the end."

"Hmm," Borisov replied. "I see."

Ahab didn't expect them to trust or believe him, but if they wanted the EAGL, they would have to pretend. This would keep him safe. It would keep him from disappearing in the labyrinth of tunnels and never emerging. It would keep him from the interrogation rooms and the doctors with their truth serums.

"And then we have the Americans," he added.

"We've seen their satellites changing orbit to scan our borders repeatedly," Borisov admitted. "Do they think we have the plane?"

"Initially, perhaps," Ahab said. "But they've seen enough to convince themselves otherwise. They're busy looking for it in the Barents Sea. And the men involved are well trained, well equipped, and highly resourceful. If the aircraft is findable, they'll discover it soon."

"You're saying it landed in the sea?"

Ahab shrugged. "The Americans seem to think so. If they're right, your chance to recover the laser will not last very long."

The two Russian men looked at each other. This was an opportunity they didn't want to miss.

"How much do the hijackers want?" Mishin asked.

"Two hundred and fifty million dollars in various cryptocurrencies," Ahab said. "Another fifty million in gold certificates."

"That's absurd," Mishin snapped.

"Actually," Ahab insisted, "it's a bargain. The Americans have spent tens of billions developing this weapon. They're a decade in front of you and it would take twice as much money on your part to catch up. When you look at it that way . . ."

Mishin was not moved. "How do we know the man contacting you is really one of the hijackers?"

"He has information you can cross-check. Data about the plane that I can share with you."

Mishin remained aggressive. "And how can we be sure he didn't just eject and parachute to safety while the plane crashed into the sea and obliterated itself?"

Ahab had expected all these questions, he was ready with the answers. "Because that would leave a trail of wreckage, something neither you, the Chinese, or the Americans have been able to find."

Again, Borisov jumped in to smooth out the edges of the conversation. "If the hijacker truly has access to the plane, he would be able to produce . . ." He searched for the right word. "Components. Items specific to that plane."

"There's nothing wrong with demanding a bit of proof before you begin throwing money around," Ahab said.

At this Borisov raised an eyebrow and Mishin nodded subtly. "It would have to be something he couldn't carry around in his pocket. Something that could come only from the American plane and no other."

Ahab nodded. Of course he agreed.

"Have this hijacker secure a part that matches Mishin's request," Borisov said. "We will choose a time and place for its delivery. Assuming we can verify what he brings us, we'll talk."

Ahab silently agreed. While the Russians waited for the proof, they would search frantically for the aircraft themselves, hoping to take it by force and avoid paying. They would find nothing, and their frustration would only increase their need to win the game.

Ahab appeared stoic, but he knew the truth. He had them in the palm of his hand.

CHAPTER 17

The American President was a habitual early riser. After showering and dressing, he would head to the Oval Office, arriving so early that the only people present were the overnight staff and security personnel. He would often take a mug of coffee and spend some time chatting with these men and women. Political topics and international events were strictly avoided. Instead, they spoke about weddings, graduations, and new babies on the way. If it was a Monday in the fall, they would discuss football. If it was summer, baseball was never far from his mind. He was keenly interested in how their children and grandchildren were doing at school and in life. If he ever wrote a memoir, he would call this the hour of normalcy, the brief blip of regular life he had during an endless procession of international news, economic conferences, and high-pressure meetings that would go on throughout the day. He treasured this hour, and for that reason reacted sourly to the arrival of his chief of staff long before the beginning of the normal workday.

"To what do I owe this displeasure?"

"New information," the chief said.

The grim look on the chief's face suggested bad news. The hour of normalcy was cut short, and the two men walked to the Oval Office in silence, shutting the door behind them.

The chief laid a dossier on the President's desk. "The Russians are moving."

The President took the folder, broke the seal, and opened it. He read the first paragraph of the briefing and then skipped directly to the satellite photos. Half the Russian fleet was sailing from Murmansk. Destroyers, patrol boats, coast guard ships. Anything with a sonar array. Another photo showed helicopters streaming from an air base. The next page was a map covered with yellow highlights showing the paths of a dozen reconnaissance flights that had been tracked by a NATO radar.

"Word is obviously out," the President said. "I'd hoped we could hide it a little longer. How far away is the salvage fleet?"

"They left Norfolk in the middle of the night," the chief said. "But it's six days of sailing to Norway."

"Six days of the Russians scouring the sea for our plane with everything they have," the President said grimly. "Any word from NUMA?"

"Some," the chief admitted. "Most of it bad. They've covered seventy percent of the signal line and found nothing. They also took a side trip and got in a tangle with the Chinese."

The President almost laughed. Of course they did. "What did they find?"

"Turns out the Chinese were waiting for the arrival of the plane. They'd carved a runway in the ice. The only good news is, they don't have it, either."

The President found photos of the Chinese icebreaker and runway in the back half of the dossier. He studied the underwater images of the cables, but wasn't entirely sure what they represented. He put them away. It didn't really matter, they were empty.

The chief waited for him to look up and then spoke again. “It’s possible the NUMA excursion caused the Chinese to alert the Russians. They may be working together now. This is why I didn’t want NUMA up there. They’re always doing the unexpected.”

“Considering it’s them against the Chinese and the whole Russian navy, they’d damned well better do the unexpected,” the President snapped. “They can’t win—meaning we can’t win—if they follow the standard playbook.”

The chief took this reprimand with surprising humility. “I understand, Mr. President. We might as well get whatever help Norway and Finland can provide into the search area.”

The President thought that sounded reasonable, but he had misgivings. “What for? No point in finding the plane if we can’t get down to it for six days.”

“We should still increase our presence.”

The President looked back at the map with the highlighted courses on it. He noticed the planes were hugging the coastline. He asked if that was the case or just a false impression.

“They are,” the chief said. “So are the Russian ships.”

“Why?”

“Shallow waters,” the chief said. “They must think that’s where the plane went down.”

“So, they have information we don’t have,” the President realized. “From where?”

“Unknown,” the chief said. “The CIA is looking into it. But they’ve developed no intel yet. Should I have NUMA move their search toward the coast?”

The President continued staring at the map, trying to take it all in at once. “No,” he said. “NUMA’s our best hope to actually find the plane. Keep them on the signal line until they’ve cleared it. We can best help them by distracting the Russians.”

The chief looked uneasy. “How do you intend to do that?”

“Shallow waters,” the President said, repeating what the chief had said earlier. He leaned forward to share his view of the map. “Find a shallow area around one of these islands,” he began, pointing out Bear Island and then Spitsbergen. “Send a couple of recon flights over it, have them fly a search pattern and drop sonar buoys. Make it look good. And then ask the Norwegians to send out a ship or two in support. I want the Russians and Chinese to think we know something they don’t. I want them to consider that shallow waters can be found somewhere other than the Norwegian or Russian coasts.”

The chief gave an approving grunt. “And if NUMA clears the signal line without finding the plane?”

“Then send them anywhere on earth they want to look next.”

CHAPTER 18

Had the President asked Kurt where to look next, he wouldn't have been able to answer. He was out of ideas. Joe might have said the Bahamas or Hawaii or anywhere near the equator. At this point, they seemed about as likely to find the EAGL in the tropics as in the Arctic.

Having been briefed about the Russian deployment and given an update on the Chinese icebreaker, Kurt found the icebreaker a more pressing concern. Not surprisingly it had finally abandoned the crumbling runway and left its icehouse station behind. But the ship wasn't heading back to China, instead it had come grinding southward through the ice and out into the Barents Sea.

"Where is she now?" Kurt asked.

He was standing on the bridge with Joe and the *Lyra*'s captain. A radar specialist, helmsman, and a couple of other crewmen stood by.

"Ahead of us," the captain said, taking over the radar console. "About thirty miles out. They're basically matching our course, but at a slower speed. In a few hours, we'll be close enough to shake hands."

"Front-running us," Joe said. "Hoping to come across the plane before we do."

"Makes more sense than looking behind us," the captain said.

Kurt had to agree with that. Truthfully, there wasn't all that much left of the signal line to search. They'd covered seventy percent of it now. By using the drones and the towed array sonar, they'd cleared a ten-mile-wide swath without finding any sign of the plane. By noon the next day they'd have covered the whole area. Although, at this point the Chinese would have covered it before them.

Racking his brain for an answer, Kurt looked over the chart. Just beyond the end of the signal line lay a group of desolate islands named Franz Josef Land, the largest and closest of these being Zemlya Georga.

At first blush, Kurt could imagine the hijackers making for the shallow waters of the island. If they didn't have a ship to pick them up, ditching the plane close to shore was the next best option. With a little luck they could put it down close to the beach and then swim—or row a lifeboat—ashore.

But there were still problems with that plan. For one, the signal line ended ten miles from Zemlya Georga, not a thousand yards from the beach. More important, the only people on those islands were Russian military personnel. If the plane had landed near the islands, it would have been seen on radar. In which case the Russians wouldn't be scouring the Norwegian coast for it. He asked the others for their opinions.

Joe put it like this. "If the hijackers wanted to go to Russia, they could have just gone to Russia."

No matter how many times he thought it through, Kurt was certain they were missing something. Somehow, it seemed, all three nations were missing something.

"Let's get a message off to Washington," he said. "Have the NSA, or whomever picked up this crash signal, confirm that it couldn't possibly extend all the way to Zemlya Georga."

The captain nodded. He'd get it sent through NUMA's comm network. "In the meantime, stay the course?"

Kurt thought that made the most sense. "Might as well. And when we catch up to the Chinese, we can ask them to give us the Otter back."

As the captain spoke with the helmsman, the intercom chirped loudly. "Sonar room to bridge," Gamay Trout's strident voice announced. "I think we have a visitor."

The captain deferred to Kurt, who responded quickly. "What makes you say that?"

"We've been picking up stray images," Gamay said. "We thought they were glitches in the side scan, but a diagnostic check ruled out any malfunction. Something has been crossing the beam close to the sonar sled, blocking it for a second and then vanishing. It's happened three times. The screen is clear now, but I doubt it will be that way for long."

"Reel the sled back in," Kurt said. "We'll search using the underwater drones."

Joe used a console on the bridge to tap into what Paul and Gamay were seeing. The sled had cameras on board, but running dark, there was little to see in the water. Still, as they watched, something appeared in front of the lens and grew rapidly larger.

"Get it back on board."

"I'm trying, but it's a half mile behind us."

Kurt looked at Joe, wondering how long that would take to reel in. "Three or four minutes," Joe said. "We're pulling against the ship's wake."

Kurt pressed the intercom button. "Get the lights on," he told Gamay. "We need to see what's out there."

Down in the sonar room Gamay was working feverishly. She was maneuvering the sled in a back-and-forth motion while drawing it in on the cable. She put the lights on and panned the cameras.

"There," Paul pointed out. Something gray cut through the frame from right to left. It moved too quickly to see.

Gamay swung the camera around hoping to follow it. She caught a brief glimpse of it before it vanished into the darkness. A freeze-frame showed it to be an arrow-shaped metallic object, more like a stealth fighter than any submersible she'd ever seen.

"What the heck is that?" she asked.

"Definitely not a flying fish," Paul said.

As the camera searched for a target, another flash went by, and then a second and a third, the last two almost beyond the range of the lights.

"Three against one," Paul said.

"Not good," Gamay replied.

At Gamay's touch the camera continued to swing, sweeping back and forth and ultimately detecting something directly ahead. A shape appeared out of the darkness, speeding directly at the sonar array. She pushed the controls to the side, but the towed array was designed to be stable, not maneuver like a speedboat. It turned late and slow. The approaching shape closed in. It was visible for a second before the image glitched and went blank.

"What happened?" Kurt asked over the intercom.

"Impact," she said dejectedly. "Collision."

"Is the sled still functioning?"

She tried a couple of commands, got no response. There was no data coming through. "The sled is down," she announced, spitting the words in disgust. "I'm sorry. I tried to bring it in."

"Nothing you could do," Kurt told her. "Is it still on the line or did they break the cable?"

"We're still pulling it in."

"Cut it loose," Kurt said. There was great urgency in his voice. "Cut it loose now."

Without questioning Kurt, Gamay released the towed array into the depths. "Bye-bye, sonar system. We hardly knew you."

Up on the bridge, Kurt spoke to the captain. His voice was filled with urgency. "Get the ship to full speed, turn hard south, then run flat out."

"Why?"

"Those are military drones," Kurt said, recalling a briefing he'd attended months ago in Washington. "They're called penetrators. They're designed to puncture a ship's hull without an explosion. The Chinese use them to attack ships crossing their so-called nine-dash line. Then claim the sinking vessels ran aground on rocks and reefs that don't exist."

The captain snapped his fingers at the helmsman, who pushed the wheel over to the right while moving the engine handle to full forward.

The ship began to throb as its powerful gas turbine engine revved and the propellers churned the sea. It had only just begun to turn when a slight impact reverberated through the ship and up through the bridge.

Alarms went off almost instantaneously. Lights flashed on the damage-control panel.

One of the crewmen scanned the screen in front of him tensely. "We're detecting water in compartments three and four," he announced. Those compartments were almost directly under the bridge.

Another thud followed. Duller and farther back. And then a third that was barely detectable. By now half the control panel was flashing red and yellow lights.

"Flooding in compartment ten," the crewman added. His voice was noticeably more tense. "Additional flooding in the engine room."

Klaxons sounded throughout the ship. The captain rushed to the damage-control station. He looked stricken at what he saw.

"How bad is it?" Kurt asked.

"We've got flooding in four compartments, all on the port side. Including the engine room, which is a large space." The captain's eyes darted back and forth as he scanned the data and came to a conclusion, then looked up. "If we don't stop it quickly, the ship will roll."

CHAPTER 19

Kurt and Joe stood by as the captain and the executive officer huddled with a damage-control specialist in front of a computer screen. A couple taps of the keyboard brought up a 3D model of the ship, showing the compartments, passageways, and bulkheads. Sensors spread throughout the ship revealed the current conditions in each area.

The damage was extensive. Four compartments on the waterline were flashing blue, which indicated flooding. A fifth compartment was blinking yellow, indicating water had been detected but only in smaller quantities. The power was out in the forward section of the ship and one of the watertight doors appeared to be stuck in a partially open position. Numbers on the side of each compartment showed the rate at which the ship was taking on water. A list could already be felt taking hold.

"Run a simulation," the captain ordered. "I need to know how much time we have."

The damage-control specialist tapped a few keys. A small clock in the upper right-hand corner began to spin rapidly, making a complete revolution every two seconds. In accelerated time, the damaged compartments turned dark blue. The ship's lights went out as the engine room filled and the list increased until it became unstable. The simulation ended when the *Lyra* capsized. Only eighteen imaginary minutes had passed.

Joe glanced over at Kurt with a grim look on his face. Things did not look good. The flooding was too widespread, and the ship's odd profile was working against it. The bulbous X-shaped bow and the piled-up superstructure made her top-heavy to begin with, which would cause her to flip over rapidly when the lean passed thirty-five degrees.

"Run it again, with ballast taken on the starboard side," the captain said. "Keep us upright."

An age-old defense against capsizing was to flood compartments on the opposite side of the ship. But that approach had limits, too. Take on too much and all you'd managed to do was sink the ship in a more controlled manner.

The specialist ran the test, but with only moderate ballast. The ship still capsized, though it took an additional ten minutes to do so.

"Max it out," the captain ordered. "I need to know if we can stay up or not."

With full ballast added, the on-screen version of the *Lyra* settled on a more even keel. But she settled too far and was soon swamped and foundering. With the seas running six to eight feet, that would never do. "We either sink upright, or we sink inverted," the captain groused.

He was moving closer to giving the order no officer ever wanted to give: abandon ship. His dilemma was a particularly cruel one. He didn't want to issue the command at all, and certainly not if there was any other legitimate option, but if he was going to give that order, the sooner the better. Even for a highly trained crew like the *Lyra*'s, getting off a sinking ship at night, in bad weather, would be dangerous. It was unwise to leave such a task to the last possible minute.

From Kurt's perspective the die had been cast. A steel-hulled ship filling with so much water simply could not remain afloat. Not by any normal means, at least. But Kurt had spent half his life bringing ships and other objects that had lost their battles with the sea back to the surface. Viewed as a salvage operation, Kurt was convinced they could keep the *Lyra* on the surface.

"I think we can keep her afloat," Kurt said.

"How?"

"By doing some things you can't simulate on this computer."

The captain stared at Kurt long and hard. "What do you have in mind?"

"Flood the starboard compartments slowly," Kurt said. "Allow as much list as the ship can safely handle. Believe it or not that'll slow down the flooding by trapping some air. It might even keep the compartments from flooding to the top. In the meantime, Joe and I will take the salvage gear we brought to lift the EAGL and wrap it around the ship like a giant life preserver."

"That gear is designed to lift about five hundred tons," the captain said. "We'll take on three times that weight in seawater."

"We don't have to counteract every drop," Kurt said. "Just enough to keep the deck above the waves until we can do some repairs."

The icy stare returned. If it had been anyone else making the suggestion, he would have thrown the man off the bridge. But the captain knew Kurt's reputation and had even worked with him once before when Kurt had managed to rig up a water jet to blast his way through a sandbar and free a tanker that was stuck in the Bahamas. It would cut into their time to safely evacuate, but there was no point hedging their bets now. He looked Kurt straight in the eye, effectively turning the ship's fate over to him. "Whatever you're going to do, do it quickly."

CHAPTER 20

With the captain's blessing in hand, Kurt and Joe raced to the midships cargo bay, where the salvage gear had been stowed. They discussed the plan as they ran the corridors. It came as no surprise to Kurt that Joe understood most of the idea instinctively.

"We secure the lifting bags on the port side, run the straps across the bottom of the hull, and then pull them tight with the onboard cranes," Kurt said.

Joe nodded. "If we swing the cranes outboard, we'll add some counterweight to the starboard side of the ship at the same time," he said. "That will act like an outrigger and help us stay upright without taking on too much water."

"Great idea," Kurt said. "With the cranes extended it'll be like trying to lift something with a long lever instead of a short one."

"This might just work," Joe said. "Let's hope we have enough time."

As they reached the storage hold, the captain's voice sounded over the intercom, directing the crew to give full and immediate assistance to Austin and Zavala as they attempted to save the ship. Within seconds there were a dozen crewmen helping them haul the equipment topside.

The crewmen, knowing their ship's survival depended on the scheme's success, followed every one of Kurt's instructions with speed and purpose. In minutes, the bales containing the uninflated lifting bags were hauled into position beside the portside rail of the ship. Sets of broad, flat straps—used to cradle sunken objects—were bundled up tight and attached to the hard points on the bags. At the same time, common ropes and lines were attached to the bales so they could be lowered and held out of the water until they were ready to be inflated.

"Drop them down," Kurt shouted, waving his arm forward in the first-down motion familiar to anyone who had ever watched American football.

The crewmen heaved the bales up onto the ship's rail and then pushed them over, lowering them with ropes until they were just out of reach of the waves. Kurt didn't want them in the water yet, where the swells would push them back and forth, causing them to rub against the side of the ship, which might damage them.

Joe looked at a phone-sized screen strapped to his forearm; the waterproof dive computer was glowing brightly as a timer he'd set on it counted down. "Based on the last simulation, we have about twelve minutes before the ship goes wrong side up."

Kurt grimaced at the number. He suspected they had a bit more time to play with.

"Unless the damage goes all the way up past the top of A-deck, there should be some trapped air in each compartment. That'll give us a little wiggle room, but let's try to get this done without tapping into it. Ready?"

Joe nodded. Both men pulled on harnesses holding air cylinders and small propulsion units, donned their gloves and helmets, and then stepped to separate gaps in the rail. Kurt went first, grabbing the nylon rope from one of the crew, turning around backward, and then rappelling down the line with his feet on the side of the ship.

He didn't have to go far. The ship had settled so that the lifting bag was only twenty feet below him. Holding on to the rope, he planted his feet firmly. In their folded and uninflated states, the bales were solid blocks about the size of a compact car. The footing was respectable, which was a good thing, as the bale was swaying back and forth with the ship's motion like a giant pendulum.

Thirty feet away, Joe landed on the second bag. He looked Kurt's way and offered a thumbs-up.

Speaking into the tiny microphone in the radio-equipped helmet, Kurt gave a progress report. "We're on the bags. Crane operators stand by. We'll be on your side in no time."

The plan from here on out was simple. He and Joe would connect the broad lifting straps to their dive harnesses and swim under the ship, towing the straps with them. After surfacing on the far side, they'd attach the straps to the dangling hooks of the recently deployed cranes. From there it would be rinse and repeat until all the bags were connected, at which point they would be inflated remotely by a crewman on the deck.

It was a simple plan, but that didn't make it easy. A hundred things could go wrong.

Kurt hooked the lifting straps to his belt, released the binding that held them in a folded loop, and jumped into the water, pulling the straps with him.

He plunged downward for several feet and then felt a rapid reversal of direction as the buoyancy of the drysuit took over and pulled him up to the surface.

Being on the surface was a miserable experience. The waves

knocked him about, slamming him into the side of the ship not once but twice.

Venting air from the suit, he sank once again, descending until he was far enough down that he was beyond the reach of the wave action. The only issue now was the current. To protect the *Lyra*'s damaged side, the captain had swung the ship around, which meant Kurt and Joe were going into the current. It made for slow going and a lot of exertion, even with the propulsion unit giving Kurt a boost.

He kicked long and hard, crossing under the ship with the lights on his helmet illuminating a small section of hull above him.

A quick glance to the side revealed Joe's lights trailing him by only a few yards. So far so good.

The hull began to peel away from him, curving upward. Kurt rose with it and kept swimming as he cleared the side of the ship. When he'd put thirty feet between himself and the hull, he pumped some air into his suit and bobbed to the surface like a cork.

Looking up, he spied the dangling hook. The crewman had made it easy to spot by wrapping a reflective life jacket around the cable and shining several portable lights at it. A brilliant touch, Kurt thought, considering how dark the crane's parts were and how they otherwise blended in with the black water and the night sky.

Kurt swam to it, grabbing it as a passing wave lifted him, and quickly connected the straps. Joe arrived as he was finishing the job and hooked a second batch of straps on as well. It had all gone incredibly smoothly.

"Bags one and two are connected," he called out over the radio. "We're going back for numbers three and four."

"Roger that," the captain replied.

"That took two minutes," Joe noted, checking the chronometer on his arm. "At this rate we'll be done and sipping whiskey in no time."

"Save that thought," Kurt replied. "The easy part is over."

Joe pushed away from the hook and vanished beneath the waves. Kurt followed him, diving back under and swimming beneath the ship. With the current pushing them, the return trip went quickly. It was only after they surfaced that the difficulties Kurt had foreseen revealed themselves.

Surfacing a few feet from the ship, Kurt watched as Joe swam toward inflation block three. He approached it with ease, reached for it, and was pushed away by the arrival of an oncoming swell.

Kurt had known getting back on the lifting bags from the sea would be harder than rappelling down to them in the first place, but he'd come up with a solution. Attached to each bale was a length of knotted rope that hung from the edge and could be used to pull oneself into position. Divers called it a granny line.

It should have been easy to grasp, but each time Joe reached for it he was washed out of the way by the passing waves. In one case he was slammed up against the side of the ship. The next time, the wave lifted him close, but the following trough pulled him down before he could grab the line, causing him to drop a full six feet lower in the water.

From Joe's perspective it seemed as if the bale had suddenly been pulled up out of his reach, as if the crewmen were playing some practical joke on him, yanking it upward just as he reached for it.

A fourth try ended in failure as well.

Kurt really should have been attacking his own bale, but he was concerned with Joe's difficulties. He'd seen men in lifeboats spend shocking amounts of time trying to grasp cargo nets dropped over the side of a rescue ship in similar conditions. Those men were often suffering from hypothermia and injuries as they made the attempt, but they had the advantage of not wearing bulky suits and carrying heavy air tanks.

Kurt swam over to Joe. "I'll give you a boost."

He dropped down under the surface, grabbed Joe's kicking feet, and pulled them to his chest. As the next swell came through, Joe's legs flexed and then extended. Kurt pushed them upward and then watched as they vanished above him.

Popping up to the surface he spotted Joe climbing up onto the bale.

"Thanks for the help," Joe's voice crackled over the headset speaker. "Now who's going to give you a boost?"

"I'm sure there's a friendly mermaid around here somewhere," Kurt replied.

"With your luck, two or three," Joe said. "But in case they're not interested in helping, let me hook the straps on and then I'll come help you."

"Negative," Kurt said. "I don't want us messing about with those straps floating in the water around us. Too easy to get tangled up. Get them hooked to your belt and get over to the other side. I'll make this work somehow."

Joe grunted a disappointed reply, but followed the order. As he jumped back into the water, Kurt reached the fourth bale.

Having watched Joe's travails, he figured the best thing to do was to ride the swell up onto the side of the lifting bag and grab the line as he got there.

He positioned himself appropriately, kicking hard as the wave pushed in, but the churning eddies of water around the bale swung him sideways. What looked like an easy catch became hands scraping uselessly along the side of the folded bag.

Swept away and dropped down, he circled back under it and tried again. This time he was slammed into the hull of the ship, and though he managed to get ahold of the rope, it was like trying to grab on to a car that had just run into you. He was knocked back and then pulled under the bale. His helmet banged into something and was jarred upward like he'd just been hit in the jaw with an uppercut from some invisible boxer. It didn't come off, but the blow briefly let a surge of water in past the neck seal.

The frigid blast shocked Kurt as it washed around his neck and face. He shook it off. "Well, at least I'm wide awake now," he muttered, fixing his helmet and kicking away from the bag.

He tried again from a different angle, grabbing the line with both hands and balling himself up tight against the inevitable push and pull of the water. His arms burned as the waves tried to pull him off, but he held on tight. He knew that a moment of calm followed shortly after the maximum strain, and feeling the pull of the waves decrease just a bit, he began climbing. He pulled himself up using the knots in the granny line like handholds.

Pulling himself over the top, he paused for only a second before scooping up the straps, linking them to his belt, and dropping back into the sea.

Kicking hard into the current, he raced for the other side of the ship, where he surfaced and swam to the waiting hook. After connecting the straps Kurt hung on to the hook for a moment.

A creeping sense of fatigue was building in his arms and legs. It came from the constant exertion and the slowly deepening cold. For a diver in a drysuit, activity was a double-edged sword. It helped generate heat, but also increased respiration and blood flow to the extremities. In Kurt's case he was both sweating and freezing. The sluggish way his muscles were responding told him that his body was fighting to keep its core temperature up. Fighting and losing. The harder he and Joe worked, the worse this problem would become, but they had little choice in the matter.

He dropped away from the hook and swam back under the ship

to the damaged side. They were halfway done. They needed to finish before the fatigue took over.

Up on the bridge, the captain stood with his arms crossed and his jaw clenched. The ship was wallowing now, the inclinometer swinging back and forth as the ship rocked side to side. With each passing moment the list was getting worse. He looked at the damage-control specialist, who had continued to run scenarios. The specialist just shook his head. All their eggs were in one basket at this point.

Stepping away from the station, the captain opened a weatherproof door and walked out onto the bridge wing in the bitter cold. He looked aft, along the side of the ship. He could see the deployed cranes and the roiling waves and circles of illumination from the ship's lights on the surface of the sea. For a brief instant he thought he'd spied Austin and Zavala in a trough between the swells, but whatever it was vanished behind a passing wave and didn't reappear.

He couldn't imagine being in the water in these conditions, let alone trying to work in them. He marveled at the fortitude of the two men. "Keep going," he whispered to them under his breath. "Finish this."

CHAPTER 21

Four decks below the bridge, Paul and Gamay had ended up in darkness. They'd been working in the sonar room when the penetrators hit the ship. This close to the waterline, they'd felt the impact of the first iron fish like the thud of a sledgehammer against the wall. The second and third strikes were more distant, but they still reverberated through the lower decks in a manner that would not be detected above.

Gamay was thankful for the lack of a follow-on explosion complete with fire, shrapnel, and flying debris. But the sense of calm vanished when the alarms went off and the power went out.

First, the lights went off in a strange pattern of succession. Mains in the overhead, followed by wall lights and then a few desk lamps. The computer screens went dark a few seconds later, along with the LEDs that had been blinking and glowing all around them. The final bastion of electricity resided in the computer towers, but they held only a few seconds of charge and once their constantly whirring fans wound down, the compartment ended up in darkness and relative silence.

Gamay spoke in Paul's general direction. "Tell me you have a flashlight in that desk of yours."

"Um . . ."

Before Paul could produce one, the battery-powered emergency light mounted high in one corner of the room blinked to life.

Across from her, Paul had been looking for a flashlight. He stopped. "It's not exactly mood lighting," he said, "but it's better than nothing."

Gamay laughed at the joke, but the laugh was hollow. The sonar room was right on the waterline, with very little freeboard between it and the sea. "Something tells me we'd better get out of here."

They made their way to the compartment door, pushing it open and realizing instantly that the ship was already leaning. Stepping into the passageway brought on the additional sense that the ship was settling at the stern. It made sense, as two of the three impacts had occurred behind them.

"We'd better go forward," Paul said.

They turned toward the bow, looking for the stairwell or ladder, but ran into a watertight bulkhead. Turning back, they moved past the sonar room and through an open hatch to compartment four, which was almost amidships. They closed the hatch behind them and dogged it down tight. Here they found power, lighting, and the sound of air hissing. As the water flooded inward and the ship's weight pushed deeper into the sea, the air was being forced out through tiny cracks and other gaps in the fittings. Continuing aft, they picked up the sound of rushing water.

"Do you hear that?" Gamay asked.

"Unfortunately," Paul said.

They were obviously walking toward the low end of the ship. "Should we turn around?"

He shook his head. "The next ladder up is between four and five. With the forward bulkhead sealed, it's the nearest way off this deck."

They soon reached the ladder well, finding a crew member whom

Gamay recognized as Gigi Cabrera standing beside it on one foot. Her raised foot was turned at an odd angle and visibly swollen.

"Are you okay?" Gamay asked.

"I think it's broken," Gigi said of her ankle.

"We can help you climb," Gamay offered, pointing up the ladder.

"The hatch is sealed up above us," Gigi told her. "Right now, it's acting like a pressure cap. It can't be opened, or the flooding will get worse."

She pointed downward and then moved out of the way.

Gamay leaned forward to look down the ladder well. Water was surging along the deck below them like it was blasting from a fire hydrant.

"Anyone else down there?" Gamay asked.

"No," Gigi said. "I was the only one. I came up as soon as the water started to come in. But if we don't get that door closed, this section will flood as well."

Gamay looked up. The hatch above would let them escape this deck, but with the water coming in and the air being forced out, this part of the ship would flood to the top, all but dooming the vessel.

She looked at Paul, who nodded. They had little choice. "How can we help?"

Gigi took a breath. "We have to go down into the water and re-boot the door or shut it manually."

"I'll go," Paul said.

"This is no time for heroics," Gamay replied.

"Which one of us does the polar bear plunge every year?"

"That has nothing to do with it," she replied.

"The water is freezing," he said. "I'm larger and heavier. My body will retain heat better and I'll be better able to keep my footing against the current."

Not only was Paul a longtime participant in the insane winter ritual of plunging into the sea when it was at its coldest, he regularly swam in the Cape Cod waters during the fall and spring, when the water temps were in the fifties. That was still twenty degrees warmer than what they'd find down below, but he was certainly more accustomed to it.

"Not a fan of you being so logical," she said. "But I admit that you're right."

Paul could hardly believe he'd actually won an argument with Gamay. Thinking about the rushing frigid water he would face down below he wondered if he could really call it winning.

He stepped onto the ladder and began to descend. Gamay followed a few rungs above him.

Gigi lay flat on the deck so she could keep an eye on them and call out instructions. "The door is just aft of the ladder," she told them. "Ten paces or so."

Paul climbed down another couple of rungs. The rushing water hit his legs. Frigid did not do it justice.

Gritting his teeth, he ducked his head to look beneath the bundle of pipes and electrical conduits that ran along the ceiling of the corridor.

The watertight door appeared to be closed. He saw no gap between its sides and the bulkhead. Studying the churning water, he noticed it was erupting upward from underneath. "I think the bottom half of the door is off the track."

"It's a vertical door," Gigi said. "It comes down from above. There must be something blocking it."

"I'll check," Paul said. He stepped down to the deck, grunting audibly as the water surged up to mid-thigh. The shock hit instantly, as if spears made of ice were plunging into his legs. He exhaled and let out a loud cry to help shake it off.

The secret of a late fall swim, or even the polar bear plunge, he remembered, was walking around on the beach in nothing but your swim trunks until the chilly air had cooled your skin to the point that the water didn't feel so bad. This was not that.

"Okay, okay," he called out, the painful sensation retreating. "I'm good. Frozen, but good."

"I hear ice baths reduce inflammation," Gamay replied.

"Then I'm going to be critically low on inflammation," Paul said. With his mind clear and a decided lack of feeling in his feet, he waded carefully to the door.

"Can you see anything?" Gamay shouted.

The water was too frothy and dark, the corridor too poorly lit. Paul couldn't see through it. Steeling himself for the next ice bath, he dropped down on one knee, pushed himself forward into the churning water, and stretched his long arm out while turning his head away.

His hand found the door. He slid it downward and discovered the edge. Moving his rapidly numbing fingers along the bottom of the door, he soon hit something. With no real sensation in his fingers, he couldn't tell what it was, but the shape was jagged and uneven. Like a small tree. He guessed it was a piece of the hull, or part of an inner support structure torn off by the penetrator. He couldn't identify it with any confidence, nor could he tell if it remained attached to anything on the far side.

He found a place to grip the object and pulled hard. It didn't move. He tried pushing it the other way, but without any success.

Letting go, he pulled back from the door and stood.

"Paul, your hand," Gamay shouted.

He looked down. Blood was streaming from a gash in his palm. The numbness was so instant and complete, he would never have suspected. With his other hand, he removed a flattened piece of metal as sharp as a razor blade.

"There's a hunk of bent metal jammed in there," Paul said, tossing the offending shard into the water behind him. "I can't work it free without raising the door. Where are the controls?"

"Right side of the door," Gigi told him. "Push the yellow button to reset and hold for three seconds. Then you'll be able to use the red lever to raise or lower the door."

Grabbing a notch on the bulkhead to provide stability against the rushing water, Paul pulled himself toward the controls. The yellow reset button was the size of a baseball; it couldn't be missed. He pressed and held it. After three long seconds the lights on the panel began blinking.

He grabbed the sturdy red control lever and pushed it upward.

The door rose a few inches. The water flow surged through the gap with increased fury and force.

He gave it another second and then moved the lever to the middle, stopping the door in its tracks. Dropping down into the swirling liquid, he found the intruding length of steel and shoved at it again. It rocked backward several inches, but as soon as he released it the obstruction returned to its original position.

"I can't move it," he shouted, standing once again and holding on to the bulkhead.

"I'll come down," Gamay insisted.

"No," Paul said. "We need more than another set of hands. Anything down here I could use to give it a shove?" They were smack-dab in the middle of the engineering space. There had to be tools available. He looked up at the injured crewperson. She would know what might be handy.

"You could use the lifter," she replied, shouting down to him. "It's a small forklift we use to carry around heavy equipment. It's in the forward part of the compartment."

Paul left the door and waded back into the engineering compartment. It was easy moving this way, the flow of the water pushed him along. He found the lifter parked beside a wall. It was smaller than Paul had expected, narrow and long like an airline drink cart, but like all forklifts it was heavily weighted. It had four large rubber-clad wheels, a power pack, and a set of hydraulic struts that allowed it to raise and lower heavy items. Paul climbed onto the tiny platform at the back, started it up, and brought it into the corridor.

On its own, the lifter weighed perhaps three hundred pounds, but with Paul on board the weight was over five hundred. Enough to keep it firmly planted on the deck even as he drove it into the onrushing water.

Pushing through the deluge he brought it up against the door, lowered the lifting forks, and brought them together into a single ram. Pushing the controls forward once more he bumped into the object that was blocking the door, backed up, and then went forward at full power.

The motor whined, the wheels moved an inch or two and then spun against the deck. Paul pulled back farther and came at it once again, this time from an angle. The forks hit the blockage, shoved it sideways and out of the way.

The lifter backed against the half-closed door. The impact jarred Paul's numb hands off the controls. He fell forward, one foot slipping off the platform. The surging water grabbed his leg and dragged him back, pulling him off his perch. Unprepared for the sudden force of the current, Paul crashed face-first into the surging water and was swept down the corridor like a man caught in a raging river.

Gamay shouted Paul's name as he vanished into the rushing water. But it was no use. She scurried down the ladder into the flood and was almost washed away herself.

"Close the door," Gigi shouted from above.

She was right, Gamay thought. Wading forward against the current she realized how dangerous the rushing water was, and how right Paul had been to go instead of her. Shorter and lighter, she could barely keep her feet. She grabbed the wall and used an insulated conduit to help pull herself forward. She slid her feet instead of lifting them, keeping both boots in contact with the deck. The closer she got to the door the more powerful the current. It knocked her legs out from under her, but she held on to the conduit like a lifeline. She hauled herself through the water, then up and out of it, wedging her feet onto a small shelf in the bulkhead. From here she could just reach the door.

She lunged for the yellow button. Hitting it and holding it down. Three agonizing seconds went by before the activation lights began blinking.

Pulling the red lever down, she had to wait an additional ten seconds as warning chirps warned any crew in the area to get away from the closing door.

Finally, the slab of reenforced steel began to descend. The power of the hydraulics and the door's own massive weight were enough to force it down through the water. It passed its previous sticking point, closing tighter and tighter.

The water turned into a furious spray, becoming pressurized as it was forced through an ever-smaller gap. And then suddenly it dwindled and ceased as the door hit bottom and locked into place.

Green lights appeared on the panel. White froth spread out along the corridor, heading to the front of the ship and diminishing as it slowed. The dark water went still.

Convinced that the door was sealed, Gamay jumped into the water and headed down the corridor looking for Paul. She found him making his way back. He was limping a bit, his hand was still bleeding, and he had a knot over his right eye where he'd hit his head on something.

"Thanks for shutting off the flood," he said.

"You did the hard part," she said. "Now let's get topside so we can put our life jackets on in time to abandon ship."

Paul groaned at the thought. But it was a distinct possibility.

CHAPTER 22

Out in the sea, Kurt and Joe were racing to finish the salvage operation. They'd linked six uninflated lifting bags to the crane hooks on the other side of the ship; they had just one set to go before they could inflate them. Engaging their propulsion units and using their legs, they moved forward along the side of the *Lyra*.

By now, she was leaning over them awkwardly, wallowing with each passing swell. She was sitting low, having lost a significant amount of freeboard, and her main deck was no more than eight feet above the tops of the swells.

She was also down at the bow—which was to be expected, as the first impact had hit forward—with the waves washing over the NUMA logo, which normally sat ten feet above the water.

"Looks worse than I thought," Joe's voice called out over the radio. "At least the lights are still on."

"We'll take the wins where we can get them," Kurt replied.

With the help of the lights from the crew above, he and Joe zeroed in on the forward set of the folded bales. Shutting down the backpack thrusters, they swam the last twenty yards the old-fashioned way.

Kurt went toward the one nearest the bow. Paddling close, he found the fluorescent tag at the end of the granny line. He grasped it, wrapping his hands around the rope tightly, with each palm just above one of the knots. Kicking and pulling hard, he hoisted himself upward, but as soon as half his weight was out of the water, the rope began to slip through his hands.

Starting over, he regripped, but the result was the same.

Kurt recognized the problem. The line was coated with a thin layer of ice. Thirty-degree water and spray had been covering it as the waves hit and rushed past, but the air around the ship was only nine degrees. The spray had frozen in place, hardening into a slick surface as it dripped down the line.

Joe was encountering the same thing. "We have a problem here," he called out.

"Big mistake on my part," Kurt said.

"You can't think of everything," Joe said. "Especially when you only have two minutes to come up with a plan."

Kurt appreciated the sentiment, but was irritated with himself for not recognizing the danger beforehand. He grabbed the line and banged it repeatedly against the hull, whipping it back and forth. Small bits of ice flaked off and vanished in the sea, but it was not enough. Another attempt to pull free of the water ended just like the first two.

With all the gear he was just too heavy. Treading water, he reached a hand to his chest, found the release latch for the propulsion pack, and pulled it. It unbuckled and the heavy motor and battery pack slid free from his harness.

Forty pounds lighter, he tried again. This time he got halfway up before slipping back down. Using his anger to create renewed strength, he mounted another effort right away. This time he wrapped the nylon line around his forearm, locking it in place. The rubber of the drysuit helped and he climbed inch by inch up onto the bale.

Reaching the top, he pulled his arm free. "I'm up," Kurt said. "But it wasn't fun."

"How'd you do it?"

Kurt explained, but then recommended against it. "One of us needs thruster power. Head my way and grab the lines. I'll go climb up on the second bale and get the straps."

"So, I'm the shuttle service."

"Division of labor," Kurt said. "You go back and forth under the ship. I climb the ropes."

Joe swam over, took the lines as Kurt tossed them down, and went under the waves with a stream of bubbles trailing from his thruster.

With Joe on his way, Kurt focused on the next bag. He jumped in and swam over to it, repeating the procedures he'd just invented; grab the line, knock the ice off, wrap his arm, and pull himself up.

Climbing the last bale was going smoothly until a larger than normal swell came in. It shoved the bale upward and away from the ship. As it passed, the bale fell back toward the hull, slamming Kurt against the ship and unhorsing him as a wrenching sensation ripped through his forearm where the rope was tightly wrapped.

Crashing into the water, Kurt found himself in instant danger. The wrenching sensation had been the rope pulling tight and then being torn free. In the process it had injured Kurt's forearm and ripped through the rubbery fabric of the suit like a knife.

Ice water rushed in, numbing his arm and shoulder. It flooded downward in the suit, chilling his abdomen and pooling around his legs and feet.

Kurt pushed upward, raising his arm like the Statue of Liberty in an attempt to keep the ripped section of the suit above the water. It was no use. With each passing wave, more water entered the suit. As more water entered, he sank lower and lower.

In rapid succession, his legs, stomach, and chest were chilled beyond belief. Contractions in his midriff made it difficult to expand and suck in air.

Whatever worries he had about his core temperature should have tripled or more, panic at not being able to breathe should have set in, but in that moment of highest danger, Kurt's mind went stunningly clear.

He focused on his chest, forcing himself to breathe slowly. One deep breath. Then a second. He turned his attention to the final bale and kicked back toward it. It was only ten yards away, but at this point he was moving more like a jellyfish than a shark. The waves pushed him around. They slammed him into the ship once more. He kept his eyes on the fluorescent tags at the end of the granny line. That was salvation—for himself and the ship.

When he finally reached it, he discovered what should have been his first bit of good luck. Seeing the troubles he and Joe were in, the crewmen had lowered the bale to make it easier to climb up on. But what seemed like a way to help only made things worse. Being partially submerged in the water caused all the problems Kurt had been concerned with in the first place. The bale was sliding back and forth with each swell, rubbing against the ship, and proving nearly impossible to mount.

Almost as soon as Kurt grabbed the rope, the bale swung forward, knocking him off the line. As Kurt regained his equilibrium, the bale fell away from him, into the trough.

Kurt slipped down behind it, but saw it reversing direction toward him. He put both arms out to catch it as it surged his way. This time the impact was a solid body blow that knocked him backward. He found himself floating freely, slowly freezing, and no closer to climbing up on the bale than he had been before.

"Raise it up," Kurt called out over the radio. He hoped the crewmen manning the lines were listening. "Pull it up six feet. Hurry."

A spotlight shone down over the rail. A daring crewman leaning his way.

"Raise it up," Kurt shouted.

Ducking beneath the waves, he avoided another haymaker as the bale swung by. He surfaced and looked up to see the men pulling on the lines. Arm over arm, like the winning side in a tug-of-war, they heaved it backward.

Kurt found the granny line and latched onto it once again. The pain in his arm was gone, banished by adrenaline and the chill of the water. He pulled himself halfway up, his arms burning with the strain, as he was carrying at least sixty, maybe seventy pounds of water in the legs of the drysuit.

He grunted as the weight became fully apparent, but he refused to let go. With all the weight on his good arm, he used the injured arm to access a knife in his chest pack. With two quick slashes, he cut the legs of the suit open. The water exploded outward like the flow from a ruptured dam. The weight vanished in seconds, and Kurt dropped the knife, put his arm back up on the line, and heaved with everything he had left.

Pulling himself onto the top of the bale, he grabbed the netting that held it together and collapsed for a moment. The bale swung back and forth almost peacefully. Kurt felt his mind drifting, hypothermia and true exhaustion setting in.

The radio crackled in his ear. "You up there, amigo?" Joe's voice called out. "Don't tell me you've gone down for a nap."

"Just taking a little break," Kurt said. "Union rules."

"Then I must be getting overtime," Joe said.

Kurt looked over the edge. Joe was riding the swells, illuminated by the light from the crewmen up above. He seemed to have a haze around him.

Unbuckling the lifting straps, Kurt tossed them down. "You get these straps to the other side, you'll get triple time and any kind of bonus I can think of."

Joe grabbed the straps, hooked them on, and saluted before vanishing under the waves once again.

Knowing he had to get off the bale before they inflated it, Kurt got to his feet. He grasped the lines that went up to the deck, using them for support and balance. He no longer felt the cold, just a strange numbness and an overwhelming desire to sleep. He wouldn't survive another dip in the frigid water, not with his core temperature so low and the suit ripped to shreds. Even if Joe towed him to the egress platform on the far side of the ship, his overexerted body would be likely to shut down.

The only way out, he decided, was up.

"Throw down another line," he called out over the radio. "I need a lift."

The lights converged on him. An extra line was dropped down, an orange life ring attached to the end. It made Kurt smile. It seemed as if someone were being funny, but the reality was the line needed a weight, or it would flail all over the place.

Kurt grabbed the line, wrapped his battered arm in the rope as he'd done before, and put a foot into the circular ring.

"Haul me up," he said. "And pour me a drink if you've got one."

The line stiffened and then began to rise. Kurt held on tight as it swung with the rocking motion of the ship. Back and forth he went, banging against the side of the hull several times. He no longer thought much of it, it was just another thing to endure.

Reaching the top, he would have liked to have stepped aboard the ship triumphantly, but he was hauled over the rail more like a prize bluefin.

Landing on the deck, he suddenly felt a great fondness for the heated track. He lay on it for a minute, pulling off the helmet, but retaining the headset so he could talk to Joe. "How's the hookup going?"

Joe responded in his normal jovial tone. "If you mean my last date, terrible. If you're talking about the lifting straps . . . they're in place now."

"Fantastic," Kurt said. "Get to the deployment platform and get out of the water."

"Roger that."

Kurt unzipped the ruined drysuit, pulled himself out of it, and managed to stand up. He grabbed instantly for the rail as the fifteen-degree pitch in the deck threatened to send him over the side and back in the water. The sea looked much closer than it should have. If his plan didn't work, there would be very little time for boarding the lifeboats.

Adjusting the headset, Kurt informed the captain and crew that they were ready. "Lifting bags in place," he announced. "Deck teams, begin lowering the bags on my mark. Crane operators, start pulling the straps tight as gently as you can."

At eight stations along the deck, the *Lyra*'s crewmen went into action. They'd been standing by, waiting and watching. Now they had a chance to act. They released the tension on the lines and allowed the ropes to slide between their gloved hands a few inches at a time. As they let out the slack, the crane operators nudged their controls in tiny increments, reeling in the hooks and pulling the straps out of the water.

Uninflated, the bales were heavy enough to sink through the

swells, but they slid back and forth just as Kurt had predicted, and the men fought to control them.

"Keep your grip," Kurt directed, "but let out more line. We have to get them beneath the swells."

The crewmen followed orders, expediting the drop as the bales threatened to break loose or pull someone into the sea. One by one the rectangular yellow bales disappeared from view.

Kurt watched the lines; they were still sliding back and forth. "Five more feet."

More rope was let out and the sideways motion was quickly reduced.

"Hold it there. Tie them off."

The deck crew secured the nylon ropes, pulling them tight like guitar strings. The crane operators reeled in more line with a deft touch, carefully watching the tension gauge on their panels. The bales were now twelve feet down on the side of the hull, but held tight to the ship by the combination of the lines and the tightening straps.

The broad straps were tough and strong and would eventually bear all the weight, but the nylon cords were needed to keep them from slipping free.

As Kurt waited for the deck teams to complete their tasks, the ship's bosun came over. He handed Kurt a square, weatherized device. "I figure you should do the honors."

Kurt took the device, called an initiator, and armed the switches one by one. "Starting inflation," he called out as he pressed the red button. In the water below a series of inaudible pops were triggered. Cylinders attached to the lifting bags opened their valves and began pumping nitrogen into the folded bales.

Nearly simultaneously the bags flipped open, unfolding once, then twice, then two more times. The newfound buoyancy pushed them upward, a move that was resisted and prevented by the straps hooked to the cranes.

Kurt looked over the side. He saw bubbling, and a hint of yellow color as the downward-pointed lights reflected off the expanding bags below the surface.

At each station along the side of the ship, this same view was repeated and soon eight yellow blocks the size of shipping containers grew up around the ship. The upward force added to the ship was calculated at nearly eight hundred tons. The upward force on crew morale was immeasurable.

They could see it was working. They could feel it working. As the bags filled with air, the ship rose in the water and leaned back to the right. Because the port side was being lifted and the starboard side pulled down, the ship nearly reached an even keel. The collective dread of spending a night in a lifeboat in the rough icy waters was replaced by a surge of hope.

On the bridge, the captain watched the inclinometer rise out of the danger zone and come back toward the center line. It moved slowly but steadily. The plan was working better than he'd even dared to hope.

"Hot damn," he shouted. "It's working."

The crew around him cheered.

The damage-control specialist ran a new simulation. According to the computer they would remain afloat indefinitely as long as the bags stayed intact. He added another bit of good news. "Door fifteen is closed and locked. Compartment five is secure."

"How long to pump it dry?"

"About an hour."

"Find some portables," the captain demanded. "I want that compartment dry in thirty minutes."

As the specialist began relaying the commands, the captain

turned to the next dilemma. They couldn't get underway with the bags attached to the sides. They would have to get repair crews down into the damaged compartments to seal the breaches and pump the water out. That, his crew could do on their own.

He found an ensign and gave him a set of keys. "Go to my quarters," he ordered. "Get my finest bottle of brandy and bring it to Austin and Zavala wherever they are on the ship. Tell them they're off duty for the rest of the night. Captain's orders."

CHAPTER 23

Thirty miles away the mood aboard the Chinese icebreaker was positively joyous. Admiral Li had invited Gushan to his quarters. He had determined that they should now drink from the bottle of baijiu in celebration.

"We've struck the Americans a blow from which they will not recover," he insisted.

Gushan was aware of what had been done, he'd been in the control room commanding the crew as it occurred. His own feelings on the matter were much darker. In his opinion the act was so positively reckless it might have been the first step on the road to war.

"Their ship is dead in the water," Gushan said calmly. He would stick to the facts and keep his feelings hidden.

"If their ship is still afloat in the morning, it will be a great surprise to me," the admiral said.

"And yet we're not turning toward them," Gushan noted. "Shouldn't we go to their rescue? It would make us look innocent in the matter. And it would give us a chance to interrogate any survivors."

"A waste of time," the admiral insisted.

"Let me put it another way," Gushan said. "If they go down and we don't lend assistance from such a close proximity, it will appear more than suspicious."

The admiral's mood didn't sour in the slightest. If anything, he seemed quite pleased to rebut Gushan's suggestion. "Under normal circumstances you'd be right, Major. But the Americans—for reasons known only to themselves—have yet to send out a distress signal."

This *did* surprise Gushan. "Perhaps they're not wounded as badly as we suspect."

"Four iron fish hitting the hull will sink any ship that size, no matter how well-trained their crew. I suspect they capsized before anyone could make a call."

"We put three into their side," Gushan corrected the admiral. "The fourth was used to destroy their sonar sled, to prevent them from resuming operations if they somehow escaped the attack. Had they gone to flank speed they would have escaped us."

The admiral cocked his head as if surprised by this, then waved this off as if it were irrelevant. "Three, four. It doesn't matter. I've seen how these things tear the side out of a ship. The Americans are finished one way or another. And now that they've been removed from the equation, we're free to search the rest of this path alone and undisturbed."

Only now did Gushan notice that Li had taken the bottle of baijiu from his cabin. A power play, perhaps meant to remind Gushan that the admiral could take what he wanted from anyone on the ship. Even his vaunted special operations officer.

Noticing Gushan's gaze, the admiral offered an explanation of sorts. "I'm putting it to proper use," he said. "Instead of consuming it in a state of dour anger."

Gushan nodded without complaint. Admirals in the navy did not respond well to being questioned, especially when it came to their personal behavior. "It was always meant for celebrating a victory."

"And so, we shall celebrate tonight," the admiral said. He went to open the bottle, but was prevented from doing so by a knock at the door.

"Enter."

An enlisted man from the communications unit came in. He handed over a coded dispatch, stood until dismissed, and then left without a word.

The admiral opened the communiqué and read it. His jaunty mood vanished. He placed the bottle down without touching the cork.

"Bad news?" Gushan asked.

With a scowl on his face, the admiral handed the message over. He wasn't about to read it out like a secretary.

Gushan scanned the type, skipping the official banter and slowing down when he reached the pertinent parts. He chose to read it aloud.

"'High command in possession of verified intelligence suggesting the American C-17 entered Tromsø fjord at low altitude on the night of its disappearance. Depart current search area and enter the fjord. Be prepared to meet with possible conspirator. Otherwise, continue the operation clandestinely.'"

Gushan raised an eyebrow as he considered what this meant. He handed the communiqué back to the admiral. "It seems we've crippled the American ship for nothing."

"Their interference was reason enough," the admiral snapped, blunt and grim once again. "Who's to say they wouldn't have hounded us wherever we go next."

"And their NATO allies, the Norwegians? Will they be so eager to let us search their fjord?"

The admiral was unfazed. "We'll dock, take on copious amounts of fuel and supplies, and pay everyone handsomely. I'll suggest we'd like the opportunity to demonstrate our ice-breaking capabilities to their government. That should give us ample freedom to move around. The rest will be done in secret."

Gushan nodded. Money had a way of clearing most paths and the Chinese had plenty of it these days. It was half the reason men like Admiral Li had become so bold, as if nothing could stop China's ascendence or their own. Hubris it was called, and it had brought great men down from time immemorial. Gushan suspected it would soon bring the admiral low as well. He seemed to have a backward combination of traits: brash when he should be cautious, faint-hearted when the moment called for courage. It wasn't that the admiral was the wrong man for this job, Gushan thought, it was that he was the wrong man for any job. And that would catch up with them both someday.

CHAPTER 24

The *Lyra* limped into Tromsø fjord twenty-four hours after the attack. The ship's survival was one miracle. Getting her back to port was another. While the oversized life jacket Kurt and Joe had rigged up was enough to keep her afloat, the ship could not make much headway without the danger of ripping the blocky inflation bags off the hull.

With the engine room flooded, the captain used the bow thrusters and a small trolling motor that extended and retracted from the underside of the hull for propulsion. The combination of systems allowed for very precise station keeping. And the captain used them to keep the *Lyra* steady with the bow angled into the waves at roughly fifteen degrees. This allowed the hull to absorb most of the incoming energy from the passing swells, which protected the lifting bags without exposing the ship to a constant back-and-forth rolling motion.

With Kurt, Paul, and Gamay all suffering from hypothermia to one extent or another, the captain restricted them to the sick bay, while allowing Joe to work with the repair crews down below.

The repair process was straightforward, but dangerous. The holes had to be patched up and water had to be pumped out faster than it came in. That meant using divers inside the flooded compartments to clear the debris, cut away the bent, jagged sections of hull plating, and weld temporary patches over the openings.

The damaged compartment below the engine room was handled first. Over a two-hour time frame, the damaged sections were cut away. A patch made of sheet metal, backed by plywood and braced by steel pipes and two-by-fours, created an adequate temporary seal. The pumps would remove half the water over the next hour or so, but some water would be left in the lower half of the compartment to act as additional weight, which would help counteract the outside pressure.

The hole in the forward compartment was repaired in a similar manner. But the massive amount of damage done where the penetrator had torn into the bulkhead between compartments three and four required a different solution. There was no way to adequately shore up the damage on both sides of the hole without putting immense stress on the damaged and weakened bulkhead. If it failed, the hull plating would buckle around it and the ship might break at the bend.

Looking for a solution that would allow them to sail, Joe and the ship's damage-control officer came up with a plan that would push the water out and replace it with something lighter.

Two factors determine how much weight a flooded compartment adds. The volume of the compartment and what engineers call permeability. Flooding in an empty compartment, like a cargo hold, would add maximum weight to the ship as it fills up. A compartment of the same size, filled with incompressible material like solid plastic blocks, would take on much less water and therefore much less weight, because most of the space is already occupied.

While the *Lyra* wasn't hauling a cargo of plastic blocks, it still carried plenty of salvage materials. The lifting bags placed on the outside of the hull had been the primary means to raise the EAGL if they'd found it, but there were dozens of additional bladders and floats of various shapes and sizes, some of which were designed to attach to other surfaces of the aircraft or go inside the fuselage.

Joe decided these could be put to work inside the hull, but pressure was the problem. He explained it this way. "If we inflate those bags inside the hull the water will compress them, raising the pressure in the compartment. The pressure increase might blow open the watertight doors or crack the bulkhead, and then we'll be right back where we started, flooding and sinking."

The captain understood. "I've seen the deck of a flooded barge blown sky-high when someone tried to use high-pressure air to force water out of the hold. Would rather avoid that if we can."

"So would I," Joe said. "What we need is a liquid. As a rule, liquids don't compress. Filling the bladders with a liquid will force the water out without raising the pressure inside the compartment."

"Well, we're surrounded by a liquid," the captain joked, "but seawater is what we're trying to get rid of. I assume you have something else in mind?"

"This ship runs on turbines," Joe said. "They use kerosene. Basically Jet A. The same fuel we put in the helicopter."

The look on the captain's face suggested he didn't like where this was headed. "And . . ."

"High-grade kerosene is twenty-five percent lighter than seawater," Joe said. "If we fill the other bladders with kerosene and secure them to the bottom deck inside the flooded compartments, they'll force the water out while lightening our load at the same time. And as an added benefit, you haven't increased the weight of the ship at all, just moved fuel from one place to another."

The captain frowned. "You want me to fill an entire compartment of my ship with an explosive liquid?"

"Two compartments actually."

The captain shook his head, even though he accepted the idea. "I suppose if we blow ourselves up instead of sinking, at least we go out with a bang."

"We should be fine, liquid kerosene is not explosive," Joe said. "Only the vapors are. They have a flash point around a hundred forty degrees. With the seawater inside that compartment hovering around the freezing point there's little risk of evaporation or vapors building up."

The captain rubbed the stubble on his face, looking thoughtful but also weary. "You and Kurt have been right so far. Check with the chief engineer. If he says it's okay, then you have my blessing. Just don't blow up my ship."

It would take four hours, some ingenuity with the fuel pumps, and multiple dives to complete the task. When the job was finished, the opening partially sealed, the bulkhead was reenforced and the *Lyra* was riding high enough that the tops of the original lifting bags could be seen above the water. It was a remarkable transition.

With some trepidation, the original lifting bags were deflated and hauled back on board. The ship got underway, making a respectable eight knots. By nightfall she was approaching the nearest port. A small fishing village named Kaldfjord, which was dwarfed by the cliffs of the Tromsø fjord surrounding it.

The village had a population of about five thousand people. It had once been much smaller, but after oil was discovered nearby, one of Norway's large energy companies had come in and built out the harbor, installing large modern docks and a breakwater. The docks were barely used now, as a pipeline had replaced most of the ship traffic in and out of the fjord.

Inching its way down the fjord, the *Lyra* eased through the placid waters toward the lighted quay, with Kurt, Joe, and the captain standing on the bridgewing triumphantly.

Spotting a large, red-hulled ship moored directly across the harbor from where they would berth took most of the joy out of the moment. The *Lyra* had made for the nearest port in the storm. It just happened to be Tromsø. But the Chinese had obviously rushed here and beat them to it.

"What do you suppose they're doing here?" Joe asked.

"I don't know," Kurt said. "But something tells me we'd better find out."

From the communications suite, Kurt put a call into Washington. After a brief delay he was connected with Rudi Gunn. He looked tanned and well rested.

"Glad to see you returned safely from the epic dangers of wine country," Kurt joked.

"You don't know the half of it," Rudi replied. "If you mistake a Pinot Grigio for a Gavi, you'll never hear the end of it."

"Wish I had your problems," Kurt said. "We've made it to Tromsø. We're docking now."

Rudi knew that already. He'd been watching every inch of their progress on a computer screen. "Glad you're all safe. I read the captain's report. All four of you are in for commendations. In your case, you may have invented a new industry: preemptive salvage. The Navy is thinking about installing inflation bags on their fleet. It might cost millions, but if it saves one ship, it's worth it."

"Great," Kurt said. "Any chance I'll get some royalties?"

"Better," Rudi said. "You'll get credit on Wikipedia."

Kurt laughed. "I guess it will have to do. In the meantime, we have a job to finish. I figured limping into port was going to put us out of the action. Funny thing, the Chinese beat us to it. They're docked on the other side of the harbor. Any idea why?"

"New information has come to light," Rudi said. "A couple of fishermen claimed they heard a large, invisible aircraft crossing over the fjord at low altitude the night the EAGL disappeared."

"Invisible?"

"They couldn't see it in the dark of night," Rudi explained, "but they could hear it. Assuming the aircraft was real and was traveling in a blacked-out mode without lights, it makes sense."

"Which way did it go?"

"Seems to be some disagreement on that," Rudi said. "But considering the sound would echo off the walls of the fjord, that's understandable. Considering their differing locations, it seems likely that the aircraft was traveling southeast, that is, directly down the mouth of the fjord."

Kurt found himself mildly irritated. "How long have you been sitting on this?"

"A couple of hours," Rudi said. "We knew you were headed to Tromsø already. We didn't want you busting the seals on that ship trying to get there a little quicker. Besides, it gave us time to arrange another satellite pass."

"And?"

"Nothing to report," Rudi said. "No wreckage, no burn scars in the tree line, no plane sitting on a valley road or an abandoned runway somewhere. Our best guess remains a water landing followed by controlled submersion."

Kurt thought that sounded reasonable. The surface of the fjord was placid in comparison to the rolling waves of the Arctic Ocean. It made for an easier landing and simpler, safer egress from the plane. But there were drawbacks. Unlike the flat abyssal plain of the

Arctic, the fjords were cut in deep V-shaped grooves by the glaciers that gouged them out. It made for a more difficult salvage operation. "Get us a good chart of the fjord," Kurt asked. "If there are any shelves or shallows, I want to look into them immediately."

"Working on it now. Should have the most accurate scan available in about an hour," Rudi said. "What are you going to do in the meantime?"

"I'm going to remind the Chinese that we're still in the race."

"Normally, I'd warn you not to go too far," Rudi said. "But having briefed Sandecker and the President on what happened, you may consider anything short of blowing them out of the water to be pre-approved."

CHAPTER 25

Kurt wasn't interested in revenge. But he did want to irritate the Chinese as much as possible. They couldn't have missed the *Lyra* pulling into the harbor, but he wanted to do more.

He approached Paul, addressing him as if he were a used-car salesman. "What can you tell me about these drones?"

Paul had a bandage over the gash on his eye and a bruise around it. But his wit was as sharp as ever. "Are you looking to buy or rent?"

Kurt laughed. "I'm looking to surveil, if that's even a word."

"It is," Paul assured him. "And it's one of our favorites here at Drone Depot. Let me show you some options."

They were standing in a storeroom reserved for electronic equipment. The compartment was the size of a three-car garage and crammed with cabinets, tools, and a pair of worktables. Paul bypassed the work desk and stepped over to a metal cabinet that occupied an entire wall of the compartment. Rolling a garage-style door up to the top, he revealed shelves filled with the insect-like forms of various different drones. Ignoring several of the larger models, he pulled one off the top shelf. It was no larger than a sparrow. Placing it on the desk he unfolded the four rotors. "May I present the Hawkeye Raptor X-5000."

Kurt studied the tiny machine. "Not knocking your nomenclature. But this is a rather delicate-looking machine for such a big name."

Paul smiled. The bandage above his eye wrinkled. "It's actually just called the P5. But I didn't want it to feel less-than surrounded by all these other drones."

"Wise," Kurt said. "And what can the Hawkeye Raptor do for me?"

"For one thing," Paul said, "it's nearly silent. These rotors are so large in comparison to the body that they can move significantly slower than normal drone rotors. They're also covered with a foamy material and dimples like a golf ball, which reduce the turbulent airflow over the blades. A hundred feet above you, the sound is no more than the rustle of the wind."

"Stealthy little thing," Kurt said. "I like that. What can it see?"

"What can't it see?" Paul replied. "It has two cameras, a wide-angle, infrared search unit, and a high-powered sensor that operates in the visible spectrum while using a two-hundred-millimeter zoom lens. With that you can see a cat's whiskers from a thousand feet away."

"Sounds like a perfect spy drone," Kurt said, surprised that NUMA had such a machine on board. "What do we normally use this for? And don't tell me it's for keeping an eye on the Swedish Bikini Team."

"Uh . . ." Paul stammered. "No. We use it to study wildlife. The high-intensity buzz of a regular drone sets most animals on edge. A lot of them will scatter when they hear one coming. I've seen a polar bear run from a ten-pound drone as if it were being chased by a fleet of Apache helicopters. But the P5 could land on a sleeping polar bear and never wake it up."

"Perfect," Kurt said. "I'll take it. Now . . . What do you have that's obnoxiously loud? Like, 'I can't stand the neighbors, and really want to annoy them' loud?"

Paul turned back to the shelves, looking high and low before settling on a full-size model. "This one sounds like a chainsaw and a misfiring engine all at once. It has a slight nick in one of the blades, which makes the sound oscillate in a most pestiferous and irritating style."

"Pestiferous," Kurt repeated. "Exactly what I'm going for. I want to annoy the Chinese with the big drone while spying on them with the little one."

"Sounds logical," Paul said. "There is one problem, though. The big drone can be controlled from here, but the Hawkeye Raptor has a short-range transmitter. The operator has to be close to the action to use it."

"That's okay," Kurt said. "I know a couple of volunteers who might be ready to get off the ship and walk around on dry land for a while."

"Perfect," Paul said. "Cash or credit?"

"Barter," Kurt suggested. "You set up these drones for me and I'll let you and Gamay take my place at the President's next state dinner. Trust me, it's a once-in-a-lifetime experience."

"Really?" Paul said. His face lit up. "That sounds amazing."

Kurt grinned wickedly. "It does sound that way."

CHAPTER 26

Paul and Gamay learned they were the volunteers Kurt had in mind when Joe arrived with their coats and hats. It made sense. Paul had become the resident expert on drone operations and a couple strolling arm in arm along the waterfront was far less likely to draw attention than Kurt and Joe in their NUMA fatigues.

With their civilian clothes on, Paul and Gamay took the gangway down to what was now a crowded dockside. Thirty to forty people were milling around at the side of the ship, half of them the ship's crew, the other half contractors from the harbor town. They were grouped together in front of the damaged sections of the hull, inspecting what they could and talking about repairs.

Upon reaching the dock, the captain had transferred significant ballast to the opposite side of the ship, rolling it off an even keel in the opposite direction. Tilted this way, the damaged hull sections were partially exposed. The wounds were jagged scars. The repairs appearing little more than temporary bandages.

While the holes weren't as large as Paul had imagined, the twisting action of the penetrators entering and then hydraulically forcing their way back out of the ship ripped the hull plating, bending it outward in a four-point, starlike pattern.

The ship would need to find a dry dock for permanent repairs, but to reach one they'd need something sturdier than what Joe and the repair teams had been able to cook up on board.

A shiver ran down Gamay's spine and it wasn't the cold air. "I'm glad I didn't know how bad it was. It's a wonder we didn't sink."

Paul nodded his agreement and turned away. He silently thanked the engineers for the strength of the ship and Kurt for his quick thinking. "We probably shouldn't linger here," he said. "In case we're under surveillance, too."

They left the dockside and made their way toward a row of small buildings, passing several taverns and other shops before beginning the long walk around the harbor to the far side. It would take nearly thirty minutes to get in position, but the night was mild for a spot north of the Arctic Circle. Cold to be sure, with several inches of fresh snow on the ground and piles of it where it had been plowed from the roads and shoveled from the paths. But there wasn't a breath of wind, and it felt good to be off the crowded ship.

Gamay put her arm through Paul's and pulled him close. "I hate to say it, but Kurt was right again. There were a couple of people ready to get off the ship and walk around on dry land for a while."

"Don't tell him," Paul said. "He'll be volunteering us for things until the end of time."

Back on the ship Kurt and Joe were now ensconced in the control room that had been home to Paul and Gamay for much of the past week.

Looking at a mapping system that was similar to those used on every smartphone, Kurt tracked Paul and Gamay as they made their way around the harbor. After putting on a headset, he made a call to them. "All right, lovebirds, we're ready to launch the big noisemaker. How close are you to the Chinese ship?"

Gamay had the earbud in. She replied in a slightly muffled tone. "We can see it from where we are, but we need to get a little closer. There's a memorial garden for lost sailors up ahead. It has several small monuments that are lit up and a gazebo and some trees. We'll wander that way and launch from there. The Hawkeye Raptor should be airborne in about five minutes."

"Perfect," Kurt said. "We'll make sure they're looking our way by the time your bird is in the air."

Kurt turned to Joe, who had taken over Paul's seat in front of the big screens. He had his own headset on and his hands on the controls. "Ready to launch Broken Mower One," as he was now calling the loud drone.

"Take her up," Kurt said. "Keep it over our deck for about a minute, as if you're testing out the controls. I want the Chinese to know where it came from."

Joe dialed up the controls and activated the rotors. Somewhere up above them the buzzard-sized drone roared to life and jumped off the deck. It rose vertically for a hundred feet, hovering over them as soon as it had cleared the highest point on the ship.

"Let's see how she flies," Joe said.

As he pushed the controls forward, Joe grinned at the instant response. The craft handled like a dream. Modern drones were so light and powerful that they were shockingly quick. There was no lag between throttle and response, no need to control or build energy like one had to in a helicopter or fixed-wing aircraft. It was just point and shoot and the machine seemed to be already there.

Joe fiddled with it for a minute, as Kurt had requested, then moved it slowly forward as if inspecting his own ship. He put it back into hover mode as it reached the bow. "If the Chinese are watching they'll have seen us by now."

"Go rattle their windows and make certain of it."

Joe moved the drone out of hover mode and took it slowly across the harbor. Instead of going right for the Chinese ship, he took it toward a large fishing trawler that was flying a Russian flag. It was the kind of ship the Russians used to gather intelligence, its bridge capped with an inordinate number of antennas and satellite dishes.

"The harbor is a little crowded today," Joe said.

Kurt nodded. He wasn't surprised to see the Russians here. But it wasn't a welcome development. "Any activity on the deck?"

Joe saw nothing on camera. He toggled a few switches and then shook his head. "Just basic heat on the infrared scan. She's running her engines at idle or using an APU. No one on deck."

After a long slow pass over the trawler, Joe was ready to go buzz the icebreaker. He looked at Kurt.

Kurt tapped the radio switch, calling Gamay. "We're about to get their attention. You guys ready?"

"Ready to launch," Gamay said.

Kurt nodded to Joe. "Let's go wake the neighbors."

Joe turned the drone toward the Chinese ship, easing it along and keeping in on the bay side of the icebreaker. As he neared the bow, he turned the drone's spotlight to full power.

At the memorial garden in town, Paul stood near a statue, pretending to admire it. He placed a set of glasses over his eyes and leaned in close to the placard describing the work of art, as if attempting to read what it said.

His right hand remained in the pocket of his overcoat, where it cradled a small controller. At the press of a button, a heads-up display appeared on the glasses in front of him. For now, it was only an artificial horizon and a few numbers showing the drone's altitude at eleven feet above sea level, airspeed at zero, and heading at 090, or due east.

A second button activated the drone, which Gamay had hidden a few yards away behind another statue. A tiny joystick on the controller handled pitch and direction. A two-way rocker switch that his finger rested on controlled the altitude up or down, while squeezing the controller like the sprayer on a garden hose handled the speed.

Paul pushed the rocker switch upward, causing the drone to rise up behind them. Even at this range the machine was quiet. A slight rushing sound, like wind through the leaves, was all they heard.

Studying the drone's view through the glasses, Paul maneuvered it over the garden, catching sight of himself and Gamay.

"What an attractive couple we make," Paul said.

"I'll say," Gamay replied. "I could get used to you in those glasses. You look very studious."

Paul grinned and maneuvered the drone. He took it back across the park, away from the waterfront, and then made it climb over the trees at the edge of the garden. When it was high enough, he turned it toward the Chinese ship, approaching slowly from the dockside.

Back on the *Lyra*, Joe was having so much fun flying the drone, he'd almost forgotten the plan. He made a few passes along the side of the icebreaker and then dropped down almost to the waterline, as if to inspect it closely.

When a group of crewmen appeared on the deck with flashlights and night vision goggles, he buzzed them and then turned back out over the sea. The men ducked and scattered as the flying lawn mower raced at their heads. Two of them turned to run in opposite directions, colliding like two members of the Three Stooges.

Kurt laughed.

"Too much?" Joe asked.

"They put three mechanical torpedoes into our side. No such thing as too much. Buzz them again."

Joe did just that, though the men ducked in a more controlled and less comical style this time. As the drone passed, one man threw something at it, a wrench, or a pipe perhaps. The projectile sailed wide of the mark and vanished when it hit the sea.

"Let's take a look in the bridge windows and see what's happening behind the curtain," Kurt suggested.

Joe took the drone out wide and then brought it back to the bridge, parking it loudly just off the starboard wing and moving it in tiny increments. There was no response.

"I was hoping for angry villagers with pitchforks and torches," Kurt said.

"This is the twenty-first century," Joe said. "For all you know, they might think we're delivering pizza."

Joe maneuvered to the side and brought it right up to the glass. With a deft touch he tapped on the window using the drone's nose. A few baffled sailors stood inside. One took a picture with his phone. The officer of the deck could be seen barking into a microphone, perhaps calling for an anti-drone weapon or some other defensive measure.

"Take it to the helipad next," Kurt said. "Maybe we can make them think twice about flying that thing for a while."

While Joe kept up the distraction, Kurt listened to the chatter from Paul and Gamay. The Hawkeye Raptor was approaching the ship from the land side, moving slowly and silently across the trees. With a flick of a switch, Kurt put the smaller drone's view on his screen. The icebreaker and the quay could be seen clearly in a wide-angle view.

At the same moment, the big drone was approaching the helipad. Joe parked it directly over the first of the two Chinese helicopters, hovering there until a door opened nearby and more angry crewmen came out. This time they carried guns.

Joe moved the controls to the side, peeling off and leaving the angry group behind.

"Good work," Kurt said. "Bring the flying lawn mower home. It's time to see what they do when they think they're no longer being watched."

CHAPTER 27

With the big drone gone, the skies were left to Paul and the tiny Hawkeye Raptor. The quiet little machine moved slowly to a spot above the last group of trees fronting the harbor. From there they had a perfect view of the dock, and the red ship tied up to it.

To Paul's surprise this dock was nearly as crowded as the space beside the *Lyra*. He could see a half dozen trucks parked there. Crates and boxes were being taken off the trucks and put on a conveyor belt that led up and into the ship. "Looks like they're taking on fresh produce and other provisions."

He knew Kurt could see that on the screen back in the *Lyra*, but he figured a little narration wouldn't hurt.

"They didn't come all the way here to pick up nectarines," Kurt replied. "Keep watching."

Paul did just that, but with his eyes focused on what he could see through the drone's camera, he wasn't really paying attention to the surroundings.

He was slightly surprised when Gamay nudged him and pulled close. "We've got some company," she whispered.

Paul knew better than to make a sudden turn. "Trouble?" he whispered back.

"Not sure," Gamay said. "Three men just came through the gate: they're walking our way. This is the main path, but . . ."

"Good point," Paul said. "Let's get off the main path. Surely there's something else to see around here."

Paul took a few steps and quickly realized that walking anywhere while looking at the world through the drone's eye view would be awkward at best. The heads-up display was not too bad, he could see past that, but the flickering images from the drone's camera were more difficult to overcome. He slowed his pace, but when his foot found a pothole in the sidewalk, he lurched to the right unexpectedly and nearly went over.

Gamay caught him and held him up. Then she took his arm in the crook of her own and held it tightly. "Just follow my lead."

He did as requested. When she stepped, he stepped. When she turned, he turned.

"How are we doing?"

"They're still coming," Gamay said. "Let's go up to the gazebo."

She turned and he followed, awkward but without stumbling.

"Crack in the pavement," she said. "Lift your foot."

He stepped over the trouble spot. He could see the outline of the gazebo up ahead.

"Stairs," Gamay whispered.

He tried to move smoothly, but clipped his toe on the top edge of the first step. Stumbling again. She held him up a second time.

The men passed by them a few feet behind, remaining on the original path. He heard a bit of laughter. "Drunks," one of them whispered.

They continued on through the park as he and Gamay made it

into the gazebo, settling into a spot by the railing. With the park quiet again, Paul refocused on the dockside. He zoomed the camera in, checking out the Norwegians who were delivering the supplies and doing what he could to study the delivery. "Considering the volume of supplies they're taking aboard, they seem to be preparing for a long journey. Maybe they're going back to China. Hope that doesn't mean they've found the plane."

"They wouldn't be taking the time to reprovision if they had the laser," Kurt said. "They'd be hightailing it out of here."

Paul thought that made sense. He kept looking. Maneuvering the drone to different spots, changing camera angles. He saw nothing of interest, until a group of Chinese men came down the gangway and walked toward a black van that had just pulled onto the scene.

The leader of the Chinese group spoke to the driver through a half-opened window and then went around to the back, where he opened the rear doors.

Paul maneuvered the drone for a better view. He found no sign of anything inside.

"It's empty," he said.

The three men climbed inside.

"Looks like a pickup instead of a delivery," he added.

Kurt's voice came back with a pleased tone. "The Chinese aren't known for letting their crew out on shore leave."

Paul zoomed in on the back end of the van as the last man to climb in leaned over and pulled the doors shut. The brake lights went off and the van began to move.

"Follow that van," Kurt said in a suddenly serious tone. "I want to know where it's going."

Paul made sure to keep the drone locked onto the van. He and Gamay exchanged glances. Both had noticed the change in Kurt's voice, a shift that was rare and menacing at the same time. Something was definitely wrong.

In the control room on the *Lyra*, Kurt was on the edge of his seat, staring at the screen like a gargoyle perched on the wall looking down over the city. His face was a mask of stone, his eyes taut and squinting like a gunfighter in the hot sun at high noon.

He'd paused the image from the drone, run it back, and zoomed in on the Chinese man who had closed the door. The freeze-frame caught the man in full lean as he reached for the open door. The image was sharp, the zoom lens and the night optics delivering a better photo than Kurt could have taken with an expensive camera in broad daylight.

The Chinese man wore a red woolen hat. A few locks of black hair sprouted from the hat covering the man's ears. A square face, featuring wide cheekbones and a prominently cleft chin, stuck out beneath it. A diagonal scar ran down from a spot near the right eye. It stood out prominently in the illumination from the dockside floodlights.

Kurt knew that face and he knew the scar.

"Gushan."

Joe recognized him, too. "Small world," he said.

Kurt nodded. "It's about to get a lot smaller."

CHAPTER 28

Paul and Gamay had cut through the park diagonally, sprinting through the snow, which got deeper near the trees. Paul had realized he could run with one eye closed and avoid the stumbling motion that made him look and feel intoxicated.

At the west end of the park they'd arrived at the main road, reaching it just as the black windowless van passed by doing thirty miles an hour. There was no way to keep chasing it on foot.

"It's heading toward town," Gamay pointed out.

Tromsø was a fairly large outpost for a harbor town this far north. Fishing was the main industry, but the oil fields to the west had brought more men, women, and industry to the town. There were dozens of commercial buildings and warehouses downtown. Not to mention scores of small shops, restaurants, and bars. Beyond that lay apartment blocks and government buildings.

"We'll never find a single black van once it reaches the village," Gamay added.

"I have an idea," Paul said. Pulling the controller from his pocket, he scrolled a side wheel that brought up a menu. The Hawkeye Raptor had a tracking mode, designed to let it follow an animal moving out of range too fast for a human to catch up. If he could just get the system to acquire the van like it would a snow leopard or wildebeest.

"Got it," he said as a white box appeared around the van on the projected image in the glasses.

"Now what?" Gamay said.

"We can slow down," Paul said, breathing hard. "The drone is on autopilot now. It'll follow the van and broadcast the video back to us and the ship. Kurt and Joe should be able to see where it goes."

CHAPTER 29

Gushan, Admiral Li, and one of the admiral's personal adjutants, a captain by the name of Haifeng, sat in the back of the windowless van on upturned crates like refugees or stowaways. It wasn't much of a hardship for Gushan or Haifeng, but the admiral shifted uncomfortably and complained every time the van hit a bump in the uneven road. As it rounded a turn, he grasped wildly at a hanging strap, nearly falling as his crate tipped over. If not for the quick assistance of Haifeng, the admiral would have gone tumbling across the back of the empty vehicle.

Gushan turned away, barely able to suppress a laugh. Snickering at an admiral's misfortunes in public was not a good career move.

With his face back to its normal stoic mask, he whistled for Haifeng, then nodded at the divider separating them from the driver's compartment. "Get his attention."

Haifeng banged his fist on the metal panel. The driver opened a plastic slider and looked through it.

"Slow it down," Gushan ordered.

He had no authority other than the fierce glare in his eyes, but the scruffy-faced driver nodded and handled the last couple miles with more caution.

As they neared their destination, Gushan considered just how far the situation had diverged from the initial plan. The intended rendezvous on the ice runway was a risky move, but a calculated one. It was supposed to take place at night, immediately after the hijacking, over international waters. The location was admittedly a long way from China, but it was also five hundred miles from the nearest swath of NATO territory. Now they were docked in a Norwegian harbor, riding in windowless van to a clandestine meeting on NATO soil.

And this after trying to sink the NUMA ship to keep it from scouring the rest of the search area.

Gushan shook his head softly. The idea that he'd be ordered to sink an American ship on the high seas, outside of a declared war, was impossible for him to fathom. But it had happened. To follow that aggression by allowing a politically ambitious rear admiral to meet with some unvetted contact in the dark of night was almost as shocking.

The moves smacked of desperation. But the high command wanted its prize, and they would only trust Li to meet with their secret contact, and so the spit-and-polished admiral had donned some ill-fitting civilian clothes and stepped out of his castle. And while Gushan and Haifeng were armed and lethal bodyguards, they could easily be outnumbered and overrun if this meeting turned into a trap.

The van pulled to a stop. Through the slider Gushan could see the lights of a quaint street filled with taverns and other shops.

"This is the place," the driver said. "Go inside. The bartender will show you to a table in the corner."

Gushan opened the door and looked around. The street was lit with illumination from shop fronts, streetlamps, and a crisscrossing set of lights strung overhead in a festive fashion. Snow on the sidewalks and the untraveled sections of the street reflected the illumination and doubled the effect, giving the area a warm glow. It reminded him of the streets in northern provinces during the Chinese New Year.

He saw nothing to suggest danger, but his sixth sense told him they were walking into trouble. The fact that the driver had an American accent hadn't helped.

He stepped out of the van and looked down the road, not for trouble this time, but for help. A short distance away, he spied the white lights of two cars he'd arranged to follow them. The newly built vehicles were made by a Chinese manufacturer. They were sleek and electric. Inside were six of his men. If an ambush occurred, it would help to have backup nearby.

"It's clear," Gushan said.

The admiral and his assistant climbed down. Gushan slammed the door behind them and the van took off. Hiking across the slush in the gutter of the road, they made their way to the entrance and stepped inside. The bartender spotted them immediately, leaving his spot behind the large oak bar and directing them to a back corner table in a section that was relatively quiet in comparison to the otherwise boisterous room.

Gushan guessed there were at least sixty people in the bustling establishment. One group was playing darts; others were watching a World Cup soccer match on a television in the corner. Everyone was drinking and talking. There were advantages and disadvantages to all of that. Crowds created a bit of anonymity, but the swirling nature of the scene would make it hard to detect a threat. All in all, he'd have preferred a dark alley with no one around.

They took their seats. A tray carrying tall glasses filled with golden lager was delivered without a word. The admiral looked at the liquid suspiciously.

"They didn't bring us here to poison us," Gushan said. He reached for a glass and took a sip, quickly disappointed with the taste.

Minutes went by. The admiral fidgeted in his seat. No one came to speak with them. "How long do you think we'll have to wait?" he asked.

As an operative, Gushan had spent plenty of time waiting for clandestine meetings to happen. Sometimes they never did come off. "Until your contact is comfortable. There's nothing we can do to speed that up. Might as well have a drink."

Gushan slid a glass toward the admiral and then one toward Haifeng. They sat untouched.

"Suit yourself." After another sip of the beer, Gushan stood. He had no taste for lager. He wanted something stronger.

"Where are you going?" the admiral asked.

"To the bar," he said, then offered an explanation. "It's of no help for us to sit all together. We have one view. We make a single target. I can better watch for threats if I have a different perspective. And your contact may feel less threatened if you're sitting here alone."

Haifeng moved to stand, but the admiral wasn't having that. He motioned for Haifeng to sit back down. Gushan understood. The admiral would feel naked without his bodyguard. He stepped away, leaving the two of them at the corner table and trying to remember what little he knew about Nordic liquors.

CHAPTER 30

In a darkened attic room two floors above the bar, Ahab stood amid a jumbled mess of boxes, unneeded chairs, and stacks of folding tables. A screen displaying gray-toned images from hidden cameras flickered in front of him as he listened to the feed from a hidden microphone that was picking up most of what the Chinese group was saying.

"You *will* wait," Ahab said to the screen as he overheard Gushan talking. "You will wait until I'm good and ready."

A man emerged from the shadows behind Ahab; he looked sleep-deprived and jumpy. His face had five days of scruff, and he had the remnants of a bruise on his cheek. "Why wait?" he grumbled in an American accent. "The Chinese are here. Let's make a deal and get this over with."

Ahab turned to the American, who had betrayed the others on the fateful flight. Ridley Wiles looked like a hunted man, as if he'd been chased for many miles and hounded every step. This, despite the fact that no one but Ahab knew he was alive.

Like most traitors, Ridley had assumed the betrayal would be the hardest part. As if all he had to do was steel himself to commit the act and everything would be easier on the other side. He was now learning the true nature of his new life. He thought he would be driving fast cars, gambling in Monaco, drinking champagne on yachts with beautiful women around him. Instead, he was hiding in a run-down tavern, sleeping on a dilapidated mattress that had been chewed on by rats.

Even if he got what he was after, the places he dreamed of would remain beyond his grasp. He would live in the shadows, in fear of discovery and with gnawing guilt. Every time he stepped into the sunlight, he would expect a swarm of Interpol cars to surround him or a bullet to take him down.

Ahab knew this misery better than anyone. He'd betrayed more than one country in his time, and many friends. But having spent decades in the shadows, he'd managed to create an alternate reality for himself, one where he was able to enjoy the spoils of his efforts.

Another cough rose up through his chest. Another taste of blood and also bitterness. That alternate reality was gone, or at least it soon would be, thanks to Kurt Austin, Major Gushan, and their respective countries.

Ahab was dying, poisoned by the toxic waste he had been dumping into the South China Sea. While escaping from the burning freighter, Kurt Austin had blasted one of the containers, spreading a witch's brew of heavy elements and contaminated radioactive solvents across Ahab's body. It soaked through his skin and mixed with his bloodstream. By the time he was able to reach a place of detoxification, it had penetrated every bone, muscle, and tissue in his body. It mutated the cells that were supposed to rebuild his bones and turned them into destroyers that were now ravaging him from the inside. It riddled healthy organs with holes or filled them with tumors that were now growing beyond control.

Despite a fortune spent on doctors and radical treatments, Ahab was dying. Dying because of Austin and Gushan. Dying because the two countries they called their own had chosen to work together to stop the illegal dumping operation Ahab was running. Dying because Austin had rewritten his orders and came to rescue Gushan without waiting for anyone's approval.

Had Austin waited thirty minutes, Ahab would have been safely off the freighter and far away from the burning ship as it went down. He would have been healthy. He would have been able to vanish once more and retreat to his own personal Shangri-la, waiting patiently for the next high-paying job.

Instead, he was a man with numbered days. He had maybe a year to live in his collapsing body. In six months, he'd be fighting multiple organ failures. Soon after, he'd be confined to a bed somewhere, doped up on opium until he couldn't see or feel or think. But before then he would have his revenge, on Austin and the Chinese major first, and then on the nations they served and the world of the living—which he now hated—at large.

Suppressing his lingering rage, he turned to Ridley, who knew nothing of this plan. "This is not the time to panic. You'll get what you've earned. Just be patient."

Ridley rocked back and forth as if sitting still was impossible. He shook his head. He seemed ready to explode. "I never should have—"

"But you did."

Ahab glared at the traitor; he'd been waiting for his second thoughts and pangs of regret to come pouring out. He was surprised it had taken this long.

Ridley stood angrily and then grabbed a coat. "I'm going to have a smoke."

As Ridley made his way to the back stairway, Ahab returned his attention to the video screen. To his utter disbelief, Kurt Austin had just walked into the room.

CHAPTER 31

Kurt stepped into the crowded bar feeling far more at home than the Chinese. He'd spent half his life in busy seaports and harbor towns. This was his kind of crowd, even if they mostly spoke another language.

He made a slow pass through the place, just watching and listening. It didn't take long to spot all the players. The Russians were in one corner, blending nicely, but talking a bit too loud. The Chinese sat on the far side of the room, sticking out more obviously despite their civilian clothes. There wasn't a large Asian population in Norway.

Kurt saw only two of them, and not the man he was looking for. Turning, he located Gushan standing at the bar with his back to the crowd.

Kurt went right toward him, noticing a tumbler of whiskey on the counter as he arrived. "Interesting place for the People's Liberation Army Navy to make an unscheduled liberty call," he said, parking himself beside Gushan at the bar.

Gushan didn't budge. He'd seen Kurt approaching in the mirror. He'd been expecting him to show up one way or another ever since the wounded *Lyra* had managed to limp into port. If there was going to be a confrontation, this seemed as good a place as any.

"We've heard good things about the waters," he said, doing his best to borrow a line from the American film *Casablanca*. Kurt had quoted it several times when they'd been hunting the ecoterrorist Ahab. He'd sent Gushan a link to watch it while he recovered from his wounds in the hospital. Gushan had watched it several times, considering it a window into the American mindset and trying his best to keep up with the snappy English dialogue.

"You were misinformed," Kurt said, following along. "The waters here are frozen."

"So it would appear," Gushan replied.

"I saved your life once," Kurt said directly. "How thoughtful of you to repay me by trying to sink my ship and drown my crew."

Gushan's jaw clenched. He refused to look Kurt's way, staring straight ahead. "We saw your ship enter the harbor," he said. "It seems to have had a terrible accident. I must congratulate you on saving it and bringing it safely to port."

"The damage was no accident," Kurt said. "Someone put three iron fish into our side. Fish that were made in China. Know anything about them?"

Gushan stared at his nearly empty glass. "Only that four of them would have done more damage than three."

Kurt considered the information. He hadn't thought about it at the time, but it made little sense to use the first penetrator to take out the sonar sled. Sink the ship and you've dealt with the sled as well. It was a wasted round. A well-placed and purposefully wasted round. One he now assumed had been misaimed by Gushan. Gushan had pulled his punch. The *Lyra* wouldn't have survived if he hadn't.

Kurt nodded slowly. *So now they were even.*

The bartender came into sight. Kurt pointed to Gushan's glass and held up two fingers. The bartender retrieved a bottle and poured the drinks.

"It is fortunate," Kurt said, continuing their conversation. "For both our sakes. Your ship has been tracked by an American Seawolf attack sub since the moment you left the ice field. Had we gone down, they would have blasted you from the sea within a matter of minutes."

Kurt had no idea if this was true. But it made for a good bluff.

Gushan nodded, accepting the dangerous reality stoically. He didn't doubt it for a second. "So the guardrails are off," he said, turning to Kurt at last.

Kurt stared at his old friend. Willing him against all odds to be reasonable. "Let's talk about putting them back on."

As Kurt spoke to Gushan, Joe waited outside in a large orange vehicle outfitted with knobby tires and cold-weather gear. The Big Orange Rig, as the NUMA team called it, was designed to go off-road in the backcountry; handling terrain no regular four-by-four could take.

It was painted the color of a lifeboat, carried the NUMA logo on both the side and the roof, and sprouted no less than four antennas, each for a different radio system or sensor. It was not exactly inconspicuous, but it was the only vehicle available to take off the ship and Kurt was more interested in making an entrance than sneaking up on anyone at this point.

While Joe understood the advantage of being obvious, he was a little wary of lingering in the machine while it sat in the parking lot. He kept his head on a swivel, checking the lot around him, using the mirrors and the vehicle's multiple cameras. It wasn't long before he noticed two people sneaking toward him. They came across the lot and up to the passenger side of the vehicle. One of them banged on the door.

A dark face appeared beyond the tinted glass. A second face huddled next to it, a little lower.

Joe hit a switch lowering the window. "Can I help you?"

"This thing have seat warmers?" Gamay Trout asked.

"Front and back," Joe said. He unlocked the doors. Gamay took the front seat, while Paul stretched out in the back.

As the door closed, Gamay pulled off her gloves, turned up the heater fan, and began rubbing her hands vigorously in front of the nearest vent. In the back seat, Paul pulled off the glasses, took a deep breath, and closed his eyes tightly.

"You all right?" Joe asked.

"Just trying not to throw up," Paul said. "Looking at the world through the drone's-eye view while using your own eyes to see the terrain around you is terribly disorienting."

Joe could imagine. "Doesn't sound fun. But step back outside if you think you're going to toss your cookies. I just had this thing detailed."

"I'm good," Paul said, taking deep slow breaths.

"How long has Kurt been in there?" Gamay asked.

"Only a few minutes," Joe said.

"What exactly does he hope to accomplish?" Paul asked.

"He wanted to put the Chinese on notice. Reminding them that we're still here," Joe said. "While also screwing up whatever meeting they were coming to take part in. We have to assume that whoever their contact is, he or she probably won't show once they spot Kurt walking around."

"We could have just kept an eye on them and followed them when they left," Paul noted.

"I suggested that," Joe said. "Kurt figured this method had some 'additional intangible value.'"

The three of them laughed. They all knew what that meant. Kurt wanted to irritate the Chinese to the greatest extent possible.

Knowing Kurt's plan, they watched the tavern, waiting for a Hollywood-style brawl to kick off. But instead of smashed bottles, patrons running from every exit, and someone getting tossed through the front window, the only activity they witnessed was a back door opening and a scruffy man in an oversized coat stepping outside.

He leaned against the wall, fumbling for something in his coat pocket, and pulling out a pack of cigarettes. Using his bare hands to remove one, he stuck it between his lips. A match flared as he lit the cigarette, and a blue cloud of smoke caught the light as he exhaled.

"It's ten degrees outside," Gamay said. "The guy must really need that smoke."

"Why come outside?" Joe said. "European places let you smoke as much as you want."

"Maybe he's an American," Paul joked.

The words had been tossed out casually, but suddenly the idea took hold. Gamay turned to her husband. "Paul?"

"Already on it," Paul said. He was unfolding the glasses and getting used to them again. The drone was hovering out of sight a half block away, where it could keep an eye on the van. He directed it to move closer and to point its camera at the huddling figure. Once the drone had focused its cameras, Paul neatly broadcast it to the vehicle's navigation screen via Bluetooth so everyone could see it.

The man was young and thin, with short hair and a week of patchy scruff on his face. He wore a withered look, as if he hadn't eaten much. A bruise and abrasion on his cheek stood out.

"That's the guy who was driving the van," Paul said.

Gamay recognized him as someone else. "That's one of the hijackers. Ridley Wiles." They'd all seen the photos and studied them, but Gamay had a knack for recognizing faces.

"So, the Chinese are meeting someone here," Joe said. "But why is this guy sitting out back with the alley cats and the trash cans?"

"Maybe he's waiting for Kurt to leave the building," Paul said.

The cigarette was flicked aside and the man they assumed to be Ridley ducked back into the warmth and shelter of the tavern.

"I have an idea," Gamay said. "Let's grab him and take him into custody."

"How do you propose we do that?" Joe asked.

"The old-fashioned way," she said. "We ambush him and take him by surprise."

CHAPTER 32

Inside the tavern, Gushan wondered what Kurt had in mind. *Guardrails would be a good thing. Rules of engagement had kept the world safe for eighty years.* "What are you suggesting?"

"It's simple," Kurt said. "Tell your people to stand down. That plane is American property. It belongs to us. Let it go."

"The law of the sea and the rules of salvage would say otherwise," Gushan insisted, hiding behind the thinnest of veils.

"Those principles apply to abandoned vessels," Kurt said. "Not hijacked ones."

Gushan found himself irritated. He wasn't interested in being lectured. "Then perhaps a different law applies," he said coldly. "To the victor goes the spoils. One way or another the plane has been lost. We intend to find it. If you and your people find it before us . . . so be it."

"You're risking a war," Kurt said. "One you're not in any position to fight. This isn't the East China Sea. You're in our lake now. Help is a long way from here."

Gushan nodded at the table in the distance. "We have allies," he said.

Kurt was unflinching. "If you were working with the Russians, you'd be sitting with them. Stand down before this turns into a bloodbath."

Gushan found his emotions fighting one another. Austin was correct about who had the advantage of help nearby, and he was correct about the Russians; in fact Gushan had been wondering what they were doing there from the moment he'd overheard their distinctive voices. But none of that changed the facts.

"You act as if I'm the one giving orders here," he said. "I go where they send me. I do what they tell me. If I reject those orders, I'll be gone and another operative will take my place."

The truth was Gushan had envied Kurt's freedom back when they'd worked together. He seemed to have the authority to rewrite his orders whenever needed as long as it served the purpose of catching the terrorists. To change his own commands, Gushan had to go through layers of bureaucracy.

"Find a way to convince them," Kurt insisted. "Otherwise, this is going to end badly."

The drinks arrived. They remained untouched. This was not the time to share a toast.

Gushan looked over at Kurt once more. "Your government should have blown the plane up when they had the chance. It would have been better for everyone."

"They tried," Kurt said. "Now it's our turn. I'll say it once more. Stand down."

Gushan stared back at him, but there was no point in saying anything else. Austin's face suggested he knew this, but had needed to speak his mind anyway. Without another word, Kurt put a few bills down on the bar, tucked them under his glass of whiskey, and walked away without touching it.

Gushan remained where he was, his face a study of grim, repressed anger. Try as he might, he could think of no way to get Admiral Li or the high command to back off. Not even the sudden interest of their Russian allies would accomplish that. The laser system the Americans had built was so effective—so world-changing in its potential—that the rules of engagement had been thrown out the window.

As he looked at the untouched drinks, Gushan felt the walls closing in. Despite his own restraint in the attack on the NUMA ship, despite the Americans holding their own fire and not sinking the icebreaker in response, they were all still inching closer to disaster. In some ways it felt unstoppable, as if some invisible hand was pushing them into a pit of chaos from which no one would escape.

Blood would soon begin to flow. The only questions were whose blood, how much, and what price the inevitable act of vengeance would extract.

In the room above the tavern, Ahab stood frozen in the dark. He could barely believe what he was watching. His Chinese contacts had insisted they'd crippled the NUMA ship. At the very least it was dead in the water, disabled and adrift. It would go down soon enough, they said. And yet here was Austin, appearing as if out of ether, seemingly no worse for the wear.

For Ahab this was more than an annoyance. It was a significant problem. He'd designed this trap for two parties, not three, intending to give equal but differing information to the Chinese and Russian delegations. It would be enough to start a bidding war. One that the Chinese would inevitably win. And then, once the Chinese were given the location of the downed aircraft, he would secretly confer with the Russians, giving them the information they needed to ambush the Chinese.

When all was said and done, he would have used the Chinese to avenge himself against Austin and NUMA, and then used the Russians to get his vengeance on Gushan and the Chinese. But somehow Austin was still alive and still in the game.

Even worse, now he was in the bar discussing something with Gushan. This was an even bigger problem. Both men were smart, intuitive, and resourceful. Their history of working together suggested they would understand one another, even trust each other to a certain degree. There was little chance their nations would allow them to collaborate, but if they shared information, even in an argument, the outlines of Ahab's long con might appear. One or both of them might realize they were being played.

As Ahab's mind whirled, Ridley reappeared. He was still wearing the bulky coat. He'd just come back up the stairs after smoking his cigarette. The smell lingered on him. "I'm not going to play these games anymore."

Ahab turned.

"I'm not going to wait," Ridley snapped, his fight-or-flight reflex switching from fear to anger. "I brought the EAGL to you and you were supposed to cut the deal. All these games are going to end."

"And how would you end them?" Ahab said.

"Make a deal," Ridley demanded. "Choose one of them."

Ridley nodded at the computer screen with its surveillance camera images.

Ahab turned to the screen. "You choose. Russians or Chinese. Who do you want?"

Ridley looked at the screen once more, his eyes darting back and forth as if perusing a menu. In this instant of distraction, Ahab grabbed a snub-nosed pistol that he kept at the ready. He fired two shots at Ridley. The bullets were small caliber, they were fully jacketed, they went right through him.

Ridley stumbled back in disbelief, grasping at his stomach. He crashed through some of the boxes and tumbled to the ground. He pulled his own weapon and fired at Ahab, missing to the right and blasting the video screen.

The room went dark. Ahab seemed to vanish into that darkness.

Expecting another bullet, Ridley scrambled toward the back exit, where he tumbled down the steps. Getting to his feet at the bottom of the stairwell he pushed through the inner door, knocking over a waitress who was carrying a tray filled with glasses back to the bar. They crashed to the ground. The waitress screamed. With a half dozen people looking at him, Ridley took off in the other direction, bursting through the outer door into the frigid night.

CHAPTER 33

Kurt heard the shots, and the crash of glasses, and the scream of the waitress. He rushed to the back side of the tavern, where he found a young woman in a white smock half-covered in blood. Helping her up, Kurt realized it wasn't hers.

"He went out," the waitress said, pointing at the back door.

The door was slightly ajar. Kurt ran to it and stormed out into the frigid night air. He saw a man running near the far side of the parking lot, hopping the curb, and then climbing into the delivery van, where it sat parked out in the street. The lights came on, and the tires spun in the snow as the man put the van in gear and tore out of the parking spot.

Before Kurt could take another step, the Big Orange Rig slid to a stop beside him. He pulled the front door open and hopped in. "That was the driver."

"We know," Joe and Paul replied in unison.

Kurt was surprised to see Paul in the back.

"He was also one of the hijackers," Joe said, getting on the gas and chasing after the van. "A guy named Ridley."

Kurt was astounded.

"Any idea who shot him?" Paul asked from the back seat.

"No," Kurt said. He was surprised to see Paul without his wife. They often seemed inseparable. "Where's Gamay?"

Paul grimaced. "She's, ummm . . ."

"Don't tell me she's in the van."

"We saw Ridley come out for a smoke," Joe said. "We thought we'd set a trap for him."

Kurt offered a withering stare.

"What do you want from me?" Joe said. "I'm the driver. Paul's the eye in the sky. And she's the only black belt among the three of us."

"Plus, she wouldn't take no for an answer," Paul added.

"That part I believe," Kurt said. "Well, we better catch that van before Ridley finds her, crashes, or runs into whoever tried to finish him off."

CHAPTER 34

Kurt held on to a grab bar as Joe ran through the gears, bringing the big vehicle up to speed as he followed the van. Despite Joe's efforts, it was impossible to close the gap. The van was swerving all over the place, making one late turn after another, which was not the big rig's forte.

Before long it found the coast road and sped off with a surprising amount of pep. Joe put the hammer down, but the off-road machine was not optimized for speed, either.

Even as they accelerated, a pair of cars rushed past them. One car sped by on the left, the other zipping by a second later on the right. The cars had closed in unnoticed, driving in the dark with their headlights off. The passes took everyone by surprise.

Now in the lead, the cars turned their lights on and formed up in a staggered position so the lights from the second car wouldn't blind the driver of the first. It took only a second to recognize the distinctive pattern, which gave them away as the latest models from a rapidly expanding Chinese manufacturer.

They were low-profile machines, boasting full-time four-wheel drive and meant to compete with the Audis and BMWs of the world. They had no problem hitting eighty miles per hour on the undulating coastal road.

"Chinese models," Kurt said. "Doesn't prove anything, but . . ."

Joe kept the pace up as best he could, but the uneven road dipped and swerved as it followed the narrow strip of land at the edge of the fjord, forcing him to brake here and there. "We're losing ground."

Kurt turned to Paul, who was still leaning forward, covering his eyes like a man praying or meditating. "How soon will they catch the van?"

"Hard to tell exactly," Paul said. "But it won't be long."

They needed a weapon, something they could use at range. Unbuckling his seat belt, Kurt climbed out of the front seat, squeezed between the captain's chairs, and into the back seat. From there, he went over the seat backs into the cargo compartment that took up the aft end of the vehicle.

Flicking on an overhead light, he studied the options. The rig was set up with all kinds of equipment and gear. He found plenty of items that might make for useful weapons if they got in close. But he needed something more.

The climbing equipment was on the left side. Bundled ropes and safety harnesses. Hammers, spikes, and carabiners. In a large box underneath that gear he found what he was looking for. Pulling it out, he grinned. "I've always thought this might come in handy."

Kurt held on as the rig weaved through a chicane-like section of the road and straightened out. Flipping the lid of the box open, Kurt found a tube-shaped device with a spear-like point sticking out the front end. A warning tag attached to the handle read: Danger—High Explosives.

In the back of the gray van up ahead, Gamay was holding on tight and regretting her insistence on being the one to confront Ridley. She wasn't particularly worried about dealing with him. He had been bleeding and limping and hyperventilating as he climbed into the driver's seat. A few choice kicks would subdue him, if it came to that. But she wasn't sure she'd get the chance. The van was swinging from side to side even on the straight parts of the road. Ridley drove it as if he were drunk and hyped up on energy drinks at the same time. He grunted and cursed, holding the wheel with one hand and using the other to press against his abdomen in hopes of slowing the bleeding.

The next turn came quickly. He grabbed the wheel with both hands, wrenching it to the side. Gamay tumbled over and slammed into the side panel. The bang sounded like an off-key gong. Enough to get Ridley to turn.

He looked back through the partition and turned the interior lights on. Gamay was caught like a deer in the headlights.

"Who the hell are you?" Ridley shouted.

Gamay was stunned by the question. "I'm here to help you," she blurted out.

"What?" he shouted, turning his attention back to the road.

She didn't really know what she meant by that, either. She tried to elaborate. "Someone's obviously trying to kill you. I can protect you."

When he turned around again, he had a pistol in his hand. He pointed it through the opening in the divider and pulled the trigger.

Gamay dove to the deck and out of the way. A second shot hit the sheet metal behind her.

Ridley was dividing his attention between her and the road. Looking in the back, glancing at the road, swerving, and then turning back to her again.

By now Gamay had crawled up to the partition and positioned herself right under it. When he pointed the gun through the gap, she thrust her hands upward, hitting his wrist from below and knocking the gun free. It fell into the back section of the van, rattling around as they flew across a bump.

Gamay went for it, but Ridley smartly doused the lights and swerved hard enough to send her rolling into the side panel once again.

As she grabbed a cargo strap for stability, Ridley turned his attention back to the road.

Gamay spotted the gun and stretched for it, only to be thwarted when something slammed into the van from behind. The van lurched forward, skidded, and threatened to roll.

Gamay gripped the cargo strap as if her life depended on it—which it probably did.

The van straightened, with Ridley somehow managing to keep it on the road. But another impact hit seconds later. This time the back doors flew open.

Gamay hoped to see the Big Orange Rig. Instead she saw the headlights from two smaller cars weaving back and forth as if looking for another chance to attack. One had lost a headlight, presumably from ramming the van, but it seemed undeterred as it raced in again.

The third impact was less jarring, the chase car hitting one of the swinging doors instead of the van's bumper. The door flew off, tumbling away in the dark. The light poured in.

Looking around the cargo compartment, Gamay spotted Ridley's pistol rattling on the metal floor beside the wheel well. Letting go of the strap, she lunged for it as it started sliding toward the open door. Landing on her stomach and stretching full out, she grabbed it before it went over the edge.

Pulling back to a safer spot, she brought the weapon to bear, aiming at the nearest car as it crossed in front of her. She fired several shots into the windshield, hoping to hit the driver. The bullets splattered against the glass, leaving circular impressions, but failing to go through. Still, the car swerved to one side and skidded on the icy shoulder and slid off into the brush. She hoped it might be out of the race, but it didn't roll or crash and was soon bumping its way back toward the road.

Focusing on the second car, Gamay fired another two shots. Once again, the bullets seemed to act more like paintballs than slugs of lead.

Jamming her foot against the wheel well, Gamay wedged herself into the corner of the van and released the magazine. Popping it out, she took a look at the shells. The bullets were blue-capped with a soft rubber covering.

"Safety slugs."

It made sense. This was the weapon Ridley had used aboard the EAGL. Using a frangible round made of tiny pellets instead of a solid slug created a bullet that could still wound and kill a flesh-and-blood mortal, but disintegrated on impact when it hit a hard surface like glass or a metal plate. It was an old air marshal's tactic, meant to allow them to fire at will inside the aircraft while not having to worry about punching holes in the skin of the plane, which would cause an explosive decompression and what some people called a "rapid, unscheduled disassembly." It was certainly something Ridley would have wanted to avoid while the C-17 was traveling at forty-one thousand feet. Unfortunately, that same quality made the bullets virtually useless against the cars behind them.

As Gamay held her fire and considered her options, Ridley swerved to the left and she could see the water dropping below them in the background. They were going uphill.

Any thought that the chase cars wouldn't follow was quickly banished. The closest one slowed and made the turn, then sped up again, closing the gap. Shortly behind it, Gamay saw the single headlight of the padiddle following suit. The situation seemed dire, but just behind that she spied a third set of lights. She could tell from the arrangement that it was the NUMA expedition rig. If she could just stay safe until they got to her, she would have a chance.

CHAPTER 35

He's turning," Paul called out, still watching the van through the drone's lens. "He's taking the switchback road."

Norway was filled with switchback roads that zigzagged up and down the steep hills. The stunning terrain required them.

"Why would he do that?" Paul wondered aloud. "Those cars will handle the turns better than the van."

"It might be smart," Joe offered. "They'll have to brake every time they get to a hairpin. It'll look like one of those Formula One races on a narrow track, where it's impossible to pass and everyone drives in single file. It might even give him a chance to knock one of them off the road and send it tumbling down the mountain. At least that's what I would try."

"They could do the same," Paul pointed out.

"They want to know where the plane is," Kurt shouted. "Can't get that from a dead man. Which should keep Gamay relatively safe."

Joe veered left to enter the mountain road and geared down to keep the speed up, while watching the parade up ahead.

As the cars slowed for the first turn, they bunched up, just as Joe had suggested. All three hugged the mountainside, staying far away from the unguarded drop-off. As the van hit the straightaway, it sped off, putting some distance between itself and the Chinese cars. They raced after it once they got out of the curve, but twenty seconds on the accelerator was rapidly followed by more brake lights and the next tight turn.

For a moment, the van was actually winning. By sticking together, the Chinese cars were getting in each other's way, making the turns slower and more ponderous. By the third turn they'd begun to lose substantial ground.

Joe wheeled the Big Orange Rig into the first hairpin, cutting the corner and dropping the inside tires off the road. They dug into the softer terrain, grinding through the snow and frost and pulling the rig through the turn more tightly than if he'd stayed on the asphalt.

While Joe grinned at the tactic, Kurt and Paul were bouncing around in the back and trying to hold on. Neither one asked Joe to slow down.

The second turn was just as rough. And the third included a slight skid that took them toward the edge before Joe countered it. But the near-reckless driving was having the desired effect. With each hairpin they were closing the gap. By the fourth turn they were in striking range of the rear car.

"What's the plan?" Paul asked. He'd lost the glasses by this point and had given up on seeing the world through the eye of the drone.

"Energy transfer," Joe said, "from us to them. Force equals mass times acceleration."

"Come again?" Paul asked.

"Big car hits small car, small car goes flying."

"Works for me."

The four vehicles had climbed nearly a thousand feet by now. The fjord and the harbor town glittered down below. The idea of something flying was not too far-fetched.

The next turn arrived, but it was a jag to the left and then back to the right, more of a chicane than a hairpin. At this point, the Chinese cars separated, with one speeding ahead and the second one lagging behind to deal with the pursuer.

Joe tried to ram the trailing car as they thundered down the straightaway. It was too quick. Its driver swerved, gunned the engine, and sped away once more.

Another chicane-type jag came at them. The Chinese car handled it well. Joe barreled right through the middle, going off-road and blasting through a snowbank back onto the road on the far side.

The Chinese car remained ahead of them, but only just. A man popped up through the sunroof and opened fire with an automatic weapon of some kind. Flashes could be seen. Bullets peppered the rig.

Joe swerved from side to side, hoping to make them a difficult target. Then he went on the offensive. The Big Orange Rig had more than just headlights. It had spotlights, floodlights, and two racks of overhead lights up on the roof bright enough to illuminate an entire field. Joe found the switches and flipped all of them on simultaneously.

The Chinese gunman raised a hand against a two-thousand-watt glare. Squinting and firing blind, he pulled the trigger again. These shots went wide and low, kicking up dirt and slush, but little else.

The man held on as the car whipped around the next turn. For a second it was broadside to the NUMA vehicle. The man took advantage of a brief respite from the blinding light and fired at the big, orange target.

Slugs plunking the sheet metal made a dull tin-like sound. No one was injured, but a light on the dashboard said they were losing air from a tire. Joe pressed a button, and a self-sealing gel was released inside the tire. It would foam up and fill the gap, but the pressure was still down.

"Took a hit to the right front," Joe said.

"How bad?" Kurt asked.

"The puncture should be sealed, but we've lost some air and we're going to lose some speed. Can't go full out in the turns with a damaged side wall. So much for the energy-transfer plan."

"We have to keep going," Paul said.

"We will," Kurt replied. "But we should take it slower."

"How much slower?" Joe asked.

Kurt didn't hesitate. "Let's just say it would be nice to travel in parallel formation with them for a moment."

Joe looked back. Kurt was opening the observation cupola at the back end of the rig. As the hatch flipped open, a blast of frigid air poured in, and the grinding sound of the tires doubled in intensity. With another quick glance, Joe noticed something in Kurt's hands as he climbed up the ladder that would allow him to look out over the top of the rig.

"I think I know what you have in mind," Joe said.

Joe took the next turn more carefully, dropping back farther. It required some guesswork because they didn't know the exact layout of the road, but Joe made the next turn exactly a half lap behind the Chinese car. They were now traveling in the same direction at the same time, with the Chinese slightly ahead and a hundred feet above them.

Bracing himself against the fiberglass shell of the cupola, Kurt raised the bazooka-like tube he'd pulled from the storage crate. A lethal-looking, diamond-shaped arrowhead stuck out the front. The rocket-propelled spear was designed to be fired into ice from a distance, trailing two hundred yards of lightweight line out behind it.

By Kurt's estimation the distance to the Chinese car was half that. Adjusting for flight time he aimed a few degrees ahead of the car and calmly squeezed the handle.

A six-foot length of flame shot out the back end of the tube. The diamond-shaped arrowhead accelerated outward toward the target. Kurt had detached most of the rope, leaving only a short length to act like the feathers on a dart. The rocket tracked perfectly, the fire and smoke of its path merging with the Chinese car near the end of the next straightaway.

At three hundred miles an hour, it plunged into the sheet metal just ahead of the passenger door, splitting the engine block, rupturing a fuel line, and causing a small explosion. The car was pushed left with the impact. It went into a skid, sliding off the road onto the icy shoulder and then over the side of the hill. It tumbled more than fell; the hill was steep but not a cliff. By chance it ended up on what was left of its wheels and continued rolling downward until it smashed into a boulder and came to a complete stop.

"Great shot," Paul called out. "How many more of those do we have?"

"Unfortunately, that was the only one," Kurt said, dropping back inside the rig and closing the cupola. "It's back to plan A. If Joe can catch them."

Joe pushed the rig as hard as he could, but as the road grew steeper, the weight of the rig became more and more burdensome. There was little they could do as the lights of the van, and the Chinese pursuer, slowly left them behind.

CHAPTER 36

Gamay could see down the hill each time the van turned. She could tell the cavalry was losing ground. She had four bullets left, but they were useless against the pursuing car.

She turned to Ridley. "Pull over!"

"Why?" he called back, sounding sick and exhausted. "What good would that do?"

"If we get them on foot I can shoot them," Gamay told him. "But I can't do anything while they're hiding behind that glass."

"Why are you helping me?" he shouted, nearly swerving off the road as he looked back through the partition.

"Because I need to know where that plane went down. And keeping you alive is the only way that's going to happen. Now pull over."

Ridley didn't respond. He just turned his back on her and kept driving.

"You've lost a lot of blood," Gamay shouted. "This is your only chance."

"I'd rather die," he said.

Rounding the next turn, they were now on a straightaway with a wall of snow and ice to their right.

Gamay turned toward the partition, aimed the gun at the dashboard, and fired. The bullet exploded into a thousand fragments, as it was designed to do, much of the force mushrooming and rebounding back into Ridley's face and eyes.

As Ridley reacted in shock, clutching at his face, Gamay reached through the gap, snagged the wheel, and wrenched it over to the right side. The van pulled hard, hitting the wall of snow and then grinding along it until it stalled out and stopped.

Gamay was tossed around in the back, hitting her head and bruising her knee somehow. Stunned but conscious, she looked up. The airbag had gone off, protecting and trapping Ridley for the moment. She looked out the open back of the van. The lights of the Chinese car were coming around the turn. She jumped out and ducked around to the side. She had a few seconds to run for it, but that would leave Ridley in their clutches.

With nowhere to hide, she dropped down and crawled under the van, pulling her feet in, just as the lights of the Chinese car settled on them.

The pursuit car came to a stop. The doors opened and three men climbed out. They remained behind the open doors for a moment and then spread out in a tactical formation, moving cautiously toward the wrecked van.

Gamay could see only their legs, but she had no doubt they were armed.

Three bullets, three targets, she thought. She would have preferred more of the former or less of the latter, especially as that didn't leave her any way to deal with the driver if he joined the fight, but it was better than nothing.

As the men neared the van, a drop of hot oil dripped on her hand. She stifled a grunt and shoved her hand into the snow.

She inched to the side to avoid any more scalding drips and turned her attention back to the approaching gunmen. She wanted to wait as long as possible. She knew Kurt, Joe, and Paul would get there soon, but she couldn't wait for them to surround her.

Focusing on the leader's boots, she aimed and pulled the trigger. The pistol sounded like a cannon shot beneath the van, and Gamay's ears rang with the blast.

She saw a cloud of red as the man's foot exploded with the impact. She turned to fire at the next target, but the men were running for cover. She saved her ammo.

They dropped in behind the doors of their car and opened fire at the van from both sides.

Gamay cringed at the sound of the automatic weapons in full throat, but so far they hadn't realized where she was.

The wounded man figured it out as he slid himself back toward the car.

"She's under the van."

One of the men dropped down to look. Gamay fired at him, but the bullet hit the bumper and disintegrated. She fired again, hitting his leg. The man tumbled to the ground. He landed in the snow and ice and looked right at her. She pushed backward, trying to get out of the line of fire as he brought his weapon around. She saw the barrel pointing her way and closed her eyes.

A thunderous crash echoed before the gun was discharged. The Big Orange Rig had rammed the Chinese car from behind, pushing it into the ice wall beside it. The impact caused an avalanche as a ten-foot cap of snow slid down from the hill above the road.

It blocked her view instantly, filling the gaps between the cars and then piling onto the roofs of each vehicle.

Gamay had backed toward the hill, but there was no escape that way. She crawled forward now, scrambling to the open side of the van as the weight of the snow compressed its springs and shocks.

Her jacket caught on the underside of the transmission. She wriggled free of it and kept going. Reaching the far side, she tried to squirm out from underneath it, but she'd only made it halfway out when the bodywork pressed into her back.

This time she shouted with everything she had. Snow began piling up around her face. She tried to push it free, but was suddenly buried in darkness.

CHAPTER 37

The return to plan A, energy transfer, had sent the Chinese car into the wall, with the van being an unintended victim of the impact, and the Big Orange Rig getting half buried in the snow.

Joe threw the sturdy vehicle into reverse and backed from the drift.

As soon as they were in the clear, Kurt and Paul jumped out. The Chinese car and the van were buried.

Paul raced forward and began digging in the snow with his hands. Kurt pulled a shovel off the side of the rig and ran over to help.

They went first to the back end of the van, breaking through the snow into the open, and only half-filled, cargo compartment.

Paul dug through some of the snow before stopping. "She's not here."

Kurt raced around to the front, digging with the shovel until he found the driver's compartment. The snow had broken through the passenger side window and poured into the van, but not enough that it had filled up the entire compartment. Kurt pulled Ridley out and dropped him into the snow. "She's not inside."

"What if she was thrown out?" Paul said, looking back down the road.

"She's here somewhere," Kurt said. "These guys were shooting at someone."

They began to dig in the snow around the van. Kurt found one of the Chinese men. He took the man's weapon and then pulled him free, noticing that his foot was a mangled bloody mess. For a second Kurt wondered if he'd shot himself by accident, but the wound was strange, it didn't go through and seemed to have come in from the side.

Gamay, he thought. He tossed the stunned Chinese man aside and shouted to Paul.

"She's under the van. She shot them in the feet."

Paul dropped down and began digging under the bumper. He paused at a muffled sound. Gamay was shouting at them from inside the snowpack, but the sound was closer to the front of the van.

He moved to a spot where he could hear her more clearly and dug once more, soon finding her outstretched arm. "Hold on!" he shouted, grabbing her hand and squeezing it. "We're going to get you out."

He dug ferociously and soon reached her face. Snow and ice had stuck to her hair and eyebrows, making her look like an old woman. He brushed it off. "The van is crushing me," she said. "It's got me pinned."

Kurt reached up and began shoveling the snow off the van, tearing through it like a human snowblower. It poured off the roof in all directions, a huge mass of it sliding down the windshield. The springs creaked and the van rose up an inch or two.

As Kurt cleared the snow off the van, Paul cleared the snow from around and underneath Gamay, creating more space. He was soon pulling her out.

She tried to stand, but had no strength in her legs. Paul helped her up. "Let's get to the rig." She leaned on him as they marched to the orange vehicle. Joe jumped out to help and they eased her into the back seat, where she could lie down.

As Joe and Paul helped Gamay, Kurt returned to Ridley and rolled him over. His blood had marred the snow red, and his face was an ashen mask, but his eyes were open.

"Where's the damn plane?" Kurt asked.

"Get me to a hospital," Ridley managed to grunt. "I'll . . . tell you then."

The man was gasping for air.

"You're not going to make it to a hospital," Kurt said bluntly. "You've been shot in the liver. You've lost a ton of blood. The next voice you hear is going to be your maker's. You want to meet him as a traitor?"

Ridley stared at Kurt. He was so used to lies and deception he doubted everyone and everything. "Go to hell."

"I might one day," Kurt said. "But you're going to get there first. Last chance for redemption. Where's the plane?"

Ridley said nothing.

Kurt began to walk away. "We'll find it ourselves. Enjoy the afterlife."

"Wait," Ridley croaked.

Kurt stopped and turned.

"It's on the lake," Ridley said.

"Which lake?" Kurt said. "There's a hundred lakes around here."

"The fish-head lake," Ridley managed. "Up at the top . . ."

"Top of what?"

Ridley coughed and brought up a load of blood. He was fading fast. "It's in . . . the middle."

Kurt figured that was enough. If Ridley wasn't lying, they'd be able to find it. And if he was lying . . . well, then they were just back where they started.

"Who shot you?" Kurt asked. He assumed the Chinese had tried to grab him instead of paying for the information.

"It was Aaaaa . . ." Ridley whispered.

The faint utterance of a long *a* faded on the wind. It was the last sound Ridley made. Whatever might have followed that syllable died along with him.

Kurt looked at Ridley and wondered briefly where his spirit might have gone. Up or down, or to some spiritual waiting room, where his fate would be adjudicated by powers unknown. Or maybe he'd merely vanished into the fabric of the universe. Ashes to ashes, dust to dust. Whatever the answer was, the man was gone, while the problems he'd set in motion lingered on. Kurt intended to deal with those problems once and for all.

After rifling through Ridley's coat and pockets, looking for anything that might be useful, he walked back to the Chinese man he'd pulled out of the snow. The man hadn't moved. He was in shock, his foot a mangled mess, his leg swelling until the strings of his boot looked like they might snap from the strain.

"Give me your radio," Kurt demanded.

The man complied without protest.

Kurt checked the volume and pressed the talk button three times to get everyone's attention. Pressing and holding it, he spoke. "You're down two cars. One of them is on fire in a ditch and the other one's buried under the snow, halfway up the switchback road. Some of your men are buried with it. I figure they have about fifteen minutes of air left. I suggest you come get them before it runs out."

A burst of static was followed by Gushan's baffled voice. "Austin?"

"I'm giving your lieutenant a shovel in case he wants to start digging. But by the look on his face, he's not going to get much done by himself."

"Austin?" Gushan said again. "What's happening? Austin?"

Kurt dropped a shovel beside the stunned Chinese operative and then made his way back to the Big Orange Rig, tossing the radio and the submachine gun off the cliff as he went. He climbed into the passenger seat as Joe got them moving.

They wheeled around slowly on the narrow mountain road, giving Kurt a view of the fjord that stretched away to the south. If Ridley's dying words were to be believed, the EAGL was out there somewhere parked on a frozen lake.

CHAPTER 38

Comrade Borisov and his men had remained in their seats after the commotion at the tavern. After all, they had nothing to do with it.

The police had come and gone. The place remained open. Half the patrons left, but the others, like the Russians, stayed behind late into the evening.

Borisov had come here for a meeting, and it wasn't with the scruffy man who'd been described by the witnesses as running from the scene with a gunshot wound. And while there was little chance the shooting had anything to do with his meeting, especially considering how the Chinese and Americans had run out the door after the man, it didn't mean his contact wouldn't show. And when he did, Borisov would demand an explanation.

Three rounds later, his patience was rewarded. Limping across the tavern floor was the broad-shouldered man whom he knew as Ahab. "It's about time you graced us with your presence."

Ahab stood at the edge of the table, his fingers wrapped around the silver handle of the cane. "May I sit down?" he said. "My leg aches in this weather."

"Sure," Borisov said. With a wave of his hand, he directed the other men to move off into a shielding position, where they could keep others from looking and listening.

Ahab sat across from him, leaning the cane against the wall.

"I hope you brought us here for more than a box of junk and a show," Borisov began.

The box of "junk" was a small container of parts from the C-17 that had been delivered to their table before the shooting. Some of the items were specifically identified as coming from the EAGL. Borisov had not been impressed.

"I thought you would appreciate a chance to study the material before we met," Ahab said. "Are they not genuine?"

"Some of them appear to come from an American plane," Borisov replied. "But that doesn't mean they came off the missing one. And some of them . . . I'm not sure what they are."

"I was told they come from the guidance unit," Ahab mumbled. "Unfortunately, the only man who could confirm that is now dead."

Borisov was not surprised. "The man who ran out bleeding."

"He was one of the hijackers," Ahab said. "A mission specialist who worked on the laser itself."

"Who shot him?"

"He got careless and allowed the Chinese to see him. They tried to abduct him. He fought and one of them foolishly shot him in the stomach."

"How do you know he's dead?"

"The police radio channel is not scrambled. Ridley crashed the van halfway up the mountain. He bled out."

"How do we know the Chinese didn't get the location from him first?"

"Because the Americans beat them to it."

Borisov didn't need the simple truth explained any further. If anyone had the information, it would be the men from NUMA.

"That's one hijacker," Borisov said. "There must be others."

"All dead," Ahab insisted. "Ridley eliminated the others."

Borisov's face turned sour, but to some extent he was relieved. At least things had fallen apart before he transferred the inordinate sums the hijackers wanted. "It seems our quest is at an end."

"Not quite," Ahab said. "I've had Ridley's phone for the past hour. He was not as careful as he believed. I located the plane on a frozen lake not far from here."

Borisov was not moved. "And how does that help me? If the Americans know where it is they'll surround it with a platoon of NATO soldiers and helicopter gunships."

"I very much doubt that will be the case," Ahab said. "For one thing, the American in charge is a brash and arrogant sort of man. He has a history of acting on instinct and abhors waiting for approval or the marshaling of backup forces. Fearing the Chinese may know where the plane is, he will move the instant he narrows down the location. The overriding desire to reach the prize first—either to collect it or simply deny you and the Chinese access to it by destroying it—will be the rationale for his haste. But more importantly . . . the lake in question is on the border between your country and Norway. Depending on where you draw the line, the EAGL is almost certainly in Russian territory."

A sort of awed silence descended over the table.

"The Americans would never send an army onto the lake," Borisov acknowledged.

"Austin will go for it alone," Ahab insisted. "Or perhaps with a small crew he trusts. With my help, you can meet him at the aircraft."

Borisov warmed to the idea. If the plane was in Russian territory, he would be able to do as he pleased. Encountering Americans on his side of the lake, he would be free to repel them as invaders or simply leave them dead on the ice. "I suppose you'll want the same outrageous payment the hijackers demanded."

To Borisov's surprise Ahab shook his head slowly. "The original deal died with Ridley. I would never have demanded so much. We've worked together before. You know that. My fee in this would have been ten million dollars, but considering this particular American is the reason I walk with this limp, and this damn cane, I'll take half that much, as long as you make sure he dies up there and does so painfully."

Borisov felt his chest swelling with anticipation. Things had turned in his favor. All things. All at once. Not only did he still have a chance to secure the plane and the laser inside it, but he could act under the cover of repelling American spies, and he could do so without risking his career (and life) by dipping into funds best left alone.

He imagined the payoff. If he could return to Moscow with the laser, if he could bring even part of the system home . . . A victory like that would see him rewarded with wealth, prestige, and honor, the likes of which few Russians had ever known.

He would get his men ready. He would draft a few extras from the trawler's crew. He would make all of them understand the need to act with violence and fury, leaving no survivors to tell the tale.

"We'll be ready," he told Ahab. "Give me that location and we'll finish the job."

CHAPTER 39

"We need to go now," Kurt said.

He was in the captain's quarters addressing Joe and the *Lyra*'s captain. Gamay was in the sick bay, having X-rays and MRIs run on her back. Paul was unwilling to leave her side.

"We don't even know if we're looking in the right place," the captain said.

They'd looked over charts and maps and satellite photos, trying to find a body of water called Fish Head Lake. They'd found nothing in the English language or any form of Norwegian. Then Kurt had noticed a curving lake that came to a point near the edge of a cliff while widening in a soft curve as it drew farther back. The lake was symmetrical on the top and bottom. A small island emerged on one side, appearing vaguely like an eye. The lake was fed by a number of streams that met up and joined in the rocks behind it. Because they came in from both sides, they resembled the thin bones of a fish from which the flesh had already been taken.

"If that's not a fish head, I don't know what is," Kurt had suggested.

It turned out the lake had been scanned by a passing satellite twice in the first thirty hours after the EAGL had vanished. The first image was blacked out by thick cloud cover. A foot of snow had fallen in Tromsø that night. Another five inches followed the next day.

The second image was taken after the weather had cleared. It showed a surface blanketed with deep snow, which had been heaped up into drifts by the wind. Kurt motioned toward one of the drifts that appeared much larger and regular than the others.

"That's the plane," Kurt insisted. He pointed to a rise in the snow near the middle of the lake. It was long and straight and compared roughly with the length of the C-17's fuselage.

"Where are the wings?" Joe said. "Where's the tail?"

"Buried under the snow."

"I hate to argue with you," the captain said. "But they got twelve inches of snow that night, not twelve feet. Which means, things should be sticking out."

"Have neither of you guys been to Buffalo in the winter?" Kurt asked. "It's a lake-effect area. If the town got twelve inches they might get twelve feet."

"The C-17 has a fifty-foot tail," Joe countered.

Kurt had no answer to that, but in the end, it was his job to find the plane before anyone else did. And he thought they were looking right at it.

"Look," he said. "Someone shot Ridley. It wasn't the Chinese. It wasn't us. And it wasn't the Russians. It had to be someone else who knew where the plane was and didn't want Ridley spilling the tea. My money's on the pilot who had to land the damn thing. But whoever took Ridley out, they're obviously running hot and scared at this point. They could be making a deal with the Chinese or the Russians at any moment. We have to go now. If there's any chance that the EAGL is hiding there under the snow, we have to reach it before anyone else does."

Both Joe and the captain seemed to be sobered by that point. Joe said no more, but the captain scratched his head and offered one more bit of bad news. "If you're right about that, you have another problem. A bigger one. That plane is a full mile over the border. It's in Russia, after all."

Kurt knew that. It didn't matter. "All the more reason for us to go now."

Joe agreed. "It's forty miles by road and then another ten across the lake. Do you want to take the helicopter or the Big Orange Rig and drive out onto the ice?"

Kurt grinned. "Both options sound good to me."

CHAPTER 40

Paul had spent a solid hour quizzing his wife before agreeing to let her join the expedition. Her official diagnosis had been a stinger, a type of injury football players get from a particularly violent collision. The tons of snow that piled on top of the van had pushed it down on her spine, compressing the nerves, creating swelling and numbness, which went away as the swelling receded.

The doctors said she was fine. Gamay insisted she was fine. But, until she offered a biting comment in response to his fifteenth question, Paul hadn't been entirely sure. Even so he filled her backpack with lightweight items before allowing her to pull it on.

Bundled up, and hauling backpacks full of supplies, she and Paul went down the ramp to the dockside, arriving beside the Big Orange Rig.

A taller figure with silver hair partially tucked under a black wool hat stood there. "Are we ready?"

"Yep," Paul said. "Let's mount up."

As Paul stowed the backpacks and helped Gamay into the back seat, the gray-haired man jumped into the passenger seat. A shorter man with dark hair climbed into the driver's seat. He started the engine, put the vehicle in gear, and drove the rig cautiously along the crowded dockside. He pulled to a stop at the entrance to the harbor. Three roads intersected at the entrance, one to the left, one to the right, and one that would lead them into town.

"Which way?" the driver asked.

Paul looked up, considering the options. He waved his hand like a sultan. "Off that way somewhere," he suggested. "Just drive until something interesting happens."

Aboard the Chinese icebreaker, Gushan had been watching the Americans load up their ostentatious land yacht. He'd seen two figures who looked like Austin and Zavala climb in and then the unmistakable pair of Paul and Gamay Trout. He with the lanky basketball player's build and she with the wine-red hair spilling from her stylish hat.

But the Chinese camera technology was as good as NUMA's. And as Gushan zoomed in on the figures walking dockside he knew something was wrong. Despite the gray hair sticking out from under the cap, he could tell that the leader of the group wasn't Austin at all.

Austin moved with a type of calm confidence, his actions were slow and easy, as if there was not a care in the world that could hurry him along. The man playing his part was a little stiff, a little too earnest in his steps.

As for the man who was supposed to be Joe Zavala, he moved like an athlete, with a bounce in his step much like the man he was imitating, but his look was all wrong. A closer shot of his face showed him to be grim and serious.

In Gushan's time working with NUMA, he couldn't recall a moment when Zavala wasn't cracking a joke, or smiling at life in general. The worse things got, the more he seemed to laugh at the circumstances.

Gushan sat back. "So, we're meant to believe this is an expedition to the downed aircraft. Very well."

He plucked a radio from beside the computer. "Haifeng," he called. "Send one of the cars to follow the NUMA expedition vehicle. Tell them not to get too close unless the Americans get out and start digging in the snow."

Gushan had co-opted Haifeng and several others after the incident at the tavern. With five members of his squad in the hospital after the car chase, he needed all the help he could get.

"Sending one car," Haifeng replied.

He turned to the drone operator on his right. "Show me the American ship again."

A side-angle view from the icebreaker's mast camera was enough to take in the entire NUMA vessel. Their position across the harbor meant they could see only the undamaged side, but drones and a few surreptitiously placed cameras made sure every angle was covered.

The damaged side remained abuzz with activity. Workers on scaffolding could be seen inspecting the damage, planning the repair process. Yellow tarps stretched across the gaping holes. The blue glare of arc-welding equipment and acetylene torches was already flashing here and there. A flatbed truck idled on the dockside. New sections of hull plating were off-loaded and the dismantled wreckage was piled into a jumble on the back in return.

The side facing the water was quiet. Just another ship slumbering at the dock.

"Give me infrared," Gushan demanded.

The ship blushed in a smear of colors when viewed through the heat sensors. The central section of the hull was emitting heat in red, yellow, and tan. The funnel glowed bright white surrounded by shades of pink. Portholes glowed like circular disks of fire.

Up on the top deck, Gushan saw something that caught his eye. A bright pink heat source that was flickering. He changed the settings on the camera, zoomed in, and discovered the unmistakable outline of the NUMA helicopter. Its engines were running as a human-shaped figure walked around it to the far side.

"Regular light," Gushan ordered.

The technician switched to the visual image. Gushan saw no lights on the deck where the helicopter stood. The pad was dark instead of illuminated, as it would normally be during flight operations. The helicopter was dark as well. Even its navigation lights were off.

"Infrared," Gushan now commanded. "Put them on split screen."

The two images flickered side by side. The helicopter was even hotter now. The exhaust trail plainly visible against the cold backdrop.

He reached for the ship's intercom and called the captain. "How soon can the helicopter be ready?"

"Five, maybe ten minutes," the captain replied. "Why?"

That was too long. The Americans would be miles away by then. Gushan didn't bother to explain. "Get it ready. Me and my team will meet the pilots in the hangar."

On-screen the American helicopter began to rise. "Damn," Gushan muttered. He turned to the drone operator. "Follow them. Do not lose sight of the aircraft."

The drone operator took command of his craft and turned it toward the fjord, locating the American helicopter and surging after it. The helicopter was dropping to the deck and flying to the northeast.

With a featherlight touch, the drone pilot turned his craft to follow. The drone accelerated quickly, but would not be able to keep up with the American helicopter if it went to full speed. Still, the cameras on the drone were powerful and the night was dark and cold. The heat from the helicopter's jet engine would be visible for miles and miles. They would not lose track of it while it remained in the air.

With the drone locked onto the Americans, Gushan pressed the intercom button again. "Have my team gear up and meet me in the hangar. If the Americans find anything, we're going to take it from them."

As the American helicopter and the Chinese drone flew off to the northeast, the repair work on the American ship continued unabated. A crane load of debris was lowered toward the flatbed, placed down gently and then covered with a tarp.

Amid that debris—which was mostly lightweight materials, insulation, and the deflated lifting bags—Kurt and Joe huddled under gray blankets.

Joe laughed at their unceremonious method of departing the ship. "I've had a few girlfriends say they wanted to throw me out with the trash, but I never thought I'd choose that option myself."

Kurt grinned in the dark, happy to feel the flatbed kick into gear and lurch forward on its journey. "I like to consider this more along the lines of repurpose, recycle, reuse. As in, we're repurposing this flatbed as a getaway vehicle."

They rumbled across the dock at perhaps five miles per hour. "Slowest getaway ever," Joe quipped.

"It's not speed but stealth that matters," Kurt said.

"How far is the driver going to take us?"

"We get dropped at the dump with the rest of the wreckage. From there, it's snowmobiles. Which is where we'll make up some time."

Kurt looked out from under the blanket. Carefully hidden among the debris were two battery-powered NUMA snowmobiles. The sleek vehicles had a top speed of ninety miles per hour, a two-hundred-mile range, and hard-sided saddlebags filled with tools and explosives.

After checking in with NUMA headquarters and the White House, their orders had been made crystal clear. If they found the EAGL in the middle of the lake, they were to remove a small number of the most advanced parts—to prevent any chance of them being found and reverse engineered—and then blow the rest of the aircraft sky-high.

CHAPTER 41

A pair of snowmobiles racing along an icy road in Norway didn't draw much attention. Tromsø and the rest of the region were staring down the brunt of winter. In a month or so everyone would be using snowcats, powered sleds, and snowmobiles to get around.

Had someone chosen to look more closely they would have noticed that these particular machines were custom-built models, longer, wider, and of a lower profile than most of the commercial models. They used a solid-state battery system instead of a gasoline-powered motor. They raced along almost silently, putting out no exhaust and generating very little heat.

The NUMA crew called them skiffs because they were designed to travel over thick blankets of snow without sinking in. The caterpillar treads on the back end were wider, thicker, and made with deeper treads for better traction, while the skids up front were longer and much wider and more curved than the skids on a standard recreational machine. They helped the skiffs stay on top of the snowpack the same way the wide-body skis that powder hounds used kept them from sinking into the fresh snow after a good winter storm blanketed their favorite trails.

Those traits would come in handy when Kurt and Joe reached the lake at the top of the cliff, but they had to get there first.

Traveling to the south, they made great time. Five miles outside Tromsø the road became pure snow. There were tracks in the middle from studded tires on the few trucks and cars that passed this way, but the shoulder was flat and smooth.

Joe found the ride surprisingly comfortable, with the aerodynamically designed windshield deflecting most of the oncoming air and the heated grips and seat keeping important parts of him warm and toasty. His only complaint was riding single file behind Kurt, where he was navigating in the snowstorm emanating from Kurt's treads. He swung out wide and raced up next to Kurt, until the headlights of their machines were running side by side.

"That's better," he said over the helmet-mounted radio.

"Was wondering when you'd hit the accelerator," Kurt said. He added more throttle and took the lead again.

Joe twisted the throttle on his machine and caught up a second time. "I'd be willing to put a wager on who gets there first, but if I left you behind, you'd probably get lost."

Kurt laughed. "We're about to hit the hard part. As far as I can tell, the route up toward the lake is more of a trail than a road."

The road up to the lake was a dirt path that had been cleared by a logging crew in the summer, but by late November it hadn't been used for months. They found the entrance to it using GPS. They drove around a gate that had been closed to keep cars out and accelerated up toward the higher ground.

The skiffs did their job in the thick snow, digging and turning and staying up on top of a twenty-plus-inch pile of the white stuff. As they neared the rim, they came out into the open. The skies were clear, and the starlight and waning moon were bright enough to make the path glitter. When they finally reached the top, things flattened out. A straight shot to the lake took them to the edge of the frozen surface.

Kurt brought his machine to a halt. Joe pulled up beside him once more and popped his visor. The cold air felt good on his face, refreshing and energizing him as he took a deep breath.

Kurt was getting his bearings. The GPS coordinates had them eight miles from the mound in the snow that might be the plane. "We have three hours till first light. Let's try to be in and out and leave the plane burning like a funeral pyre before dawn."

He slapped his visor down and took off.

Joe followed a hundred feet behind him.

It was a straight shot across the smooth surface. The drifts of snow that were visible on the satellite image were flatter and more spread out than they appeared. The thick snow itself was like a cushion of air beneath them. Joe could feel his mount rising as he picked up speed. The sensation was almost unnerving, as if they were flying and not connected to the ground. A few practice turns told him they couldn't make a tight corner if they wanted to.

Ahead of him, Kurt pressed on, passing the middle of the lake and showing no signs of slowing until the lights from the snowmobiles picked up the rise in the distance. At range, the hill looked like a miniature chalk-white version of Ayers Rock in Australia. It was different enough from the wide snowdrifts that Joe began to think Kurt might be right.

The closer they got, the more he felt that way, but there was still no sign of the wings or tail.

Kurt raced up to it, heading for the south end of the hill. Instead of approaching the hill itself, he stopped a few feet away, next to a second object buried in the snow.

Hopping off his snowmobile, Kurt began clearing the snow away. With a last brush he stepped back.

Joe maneuvered so he could get his light onto whatever Kurt had found. "I guess I'll never doubt you again."

Sticking out of the snow was the unmistakable sight of an aircraft control surface in cross section, painted in standard Air Force gray. Joe parked his machine and walked over to the structure. He could see from the curve of the exterior that it was an airfoil, about sixteen inches thick. The edges were melted and burned. Molten drops of aluminum had run down the side, cooling and hardening back into solid form as they hit the snow.

"This looks like part of the tail," he said to Kurt, admitting defeat. "Which means . . ."

"They cut it off after they landed."

"But how? That's a big job. You'd need a team of—"

"They used the laser," Kurt suggested. "Sliced right through it and let it fall like a tree in the woods."

Kurt had finished clearing enough snow to see part of an identification number. He didn't need it. There weren't any other missing planes out here on the lake.

"How'd you know?" Joe asked.

"I didn't," Kurt admitted. "But they had the laser, which gave them the means. And I remember one of the technical notes from the briefing suggesting that the EAGL's only vulnerability was from behind, since they had to program the targeting system to avoid firing to the rear, so they wouldn't accidentally blast their own tail off. But Ridley was one of the targeting programmers. I figure he could have easily changed the codes."

Scanning the area, they could see other jagged flat shapes. "Looks like they cut it off in sections," Joe said. "But what about the wings and the engines? C-17s have a high-mounted wing."

"This plane isn't just buried in the snow. It's sitting half-submerged in the frozen lake. Either they used the laser to melt the ice as well, or maybe the heat from the engines was sufficient. If we had time to dig, I think we'd find the engines half-embedded in the lake. The snowdrifts are deep enough to cover the rest."

"Getting the engines down on the lake would rapidly cool them down," Joe added. "Hiding any heat signature by the time the satellites passed over a few hours later. These guys had it planned out."

"Or they took the Chinese plan and used it for themselves," Joe suggested. "Either way, they got down safely and vanished in impressive style."

Kurt moved to the back end of the snow hill, digging horizontally through the drift until he hit gray aluminum. He found himself looking at the top half of the tail ramp. The rest of it was icebound.

"No way we're getting that open," Joe said.

"This thing's locked in until the spring thaw," Kurt said.

"The side doors won't be accessible, either," Joe said. "But the plane has escape hatches above the cockpit and the crew compartment. I'm guessing that's how Ridley and the pilot got out."

"Which means we're at the wrong end of the plane," Kurt noted.

Climbing to the top of the plane on the snowdrifts would be difficult, but using the snowmobiles they could race up the side with ease.

"I'll make the first ascent," Joe said, trudging back to his snowmobile. "Call it my penance for doubting you."

CHAPTER 42

Gushan tapped his finger lightly against the side of the carbine he carried across his chest. He and eight similarly armed men were waiting in the hangar along with Admiral Li, who insisted on being there to send them off.

Time ticked by. Reports came in. The orange NUMA transport was still driving along the coast road. The helicopter had turned to the north and was continuing along the length of the fjord. "They're looking for something," the admiral insisted.

Gushan nodded, though he was thinking more than listening. The Americans were traveling at an altitude of fifty feet. They seemed to be following the jagged coastline, but had yet to accelerate past eighty knots.

Why so slow? Gushan wondered. *Safety was not really an issue over the flat waters.* It was an odd velocity to use. Too fast to drag a sonar sled, too slow to cover much ground.

"American helicopter turning," a new report came in.

Perhaps they'd found something after all.

"It's heading back this way," the drone operator said. "New course is the reciprocal of the old course."

"They must have seen the drone," the admiral suggested.

"Impossible," Gushan said, shaking him off.

"The helicopter's navigation lights are coming on," the drone pilot replied. "It's climbing and accelerating. It's transponder beacon just went active."

Gushan's mind spun. The admiral barked questions. A minor state of confusion set in.

"What course is it on?" Gushan demanded.

"Back toward the harbor," the drone pilot told them. "Back toward their ship."

At that moment, Gushan knew they'd lost.

The helicopter was another distraction, much like the bright orange SUV. Its clandestine takeoff had convinced him it carried Austin and Zavala, and he had ordered the drone to follow it, abandoning his best mode of surveilling the NUMA ship.

He had no doubt that Austin and Zavala had slipped out once the drone had left its station. That was nearly an hour ago.

"Bring the drone back to the ship," Gushan ordered. "Tell the pilots to secure the helicopter."

Admiral Li stepped toward him. "What are you doing?"

"I'm standing down," Gushan said, leaning his weapon against the bulkhead and releasing the Velcro strap on his tactical vest before sliding it off.

"Why?"

"Because it's over," Gushan said, admitting defeat. "Austin and Zavala are not on that helicopter. They're elsewhere. They've no doubt found the plane. They've won."

With that, Gushan walked away, trudging slowly and dejectedly across the hangar deck.

The admiral wasn't satisfied. "Explain this to me," he demanded. "How did this happen? How did they trick us?"

Gushan kept walking.

"Major! I want answers."

Gushan left the hangar without responding. There would be plenty of time for explanations once they reached China and the search for a scapegoat began.

CHAPTER 43

Kurt had expected to dig through the drift to the side of the aircraft, find a door, and open it. Upon learning that the plane was partially submerged in the lake—embedded would have been a better term—he assumed they would be digging their way through the drifts and cutting into the side of the aircraft, or perhaps climbing on top of it to find an escape hatch. Joe made the digging and the climbing unnecessary.

Riding his snow machine along the side of the plane, he picked up enough speed to begin floating on the snow once again. With the snowmobile riding high like a speedboat on the flat water, he'd angled toward the fuselage and raced up the side. As he neared the top, he began to fishtail to one side, but with some deft handling of the controls, he added power at just the right moment to keep the machine moving and get it back on track.

Skidding to a stop on top of the plane, Joe straddled his machine triumphantly. Flipping his visor up to reveal his smiling face, he shouted down to Kurt, "Now you try it."

Kurt accepted the challenge, copying Joe's approach run and speed. Near the top he ran into the same problem Joe had encountered: too much slope and not enough traction. He twisted the throttle a bit too hard, and a rooster tail of snow sprayed out behind him.

The sudden burst of power made the nose of the snowmobile pop up. For a second it felt like the machine would flip backward, but Kurt leaned forward, pushing his weight onto the handlebars. The nose came down, the machine surged forward, and quite suddenly he found himself flat and level on top of the aircraft. Cutting to the right to prevent himself from going back down the other side, he managed to park a few feet from Joe.

"Can't give you a lot of style points," Joe said. "But you made it."

Kurt was glad of it. Now to find a way in. He climbed off the snowmobile and began shuffling through the snow. Joe did the same just off to his right.

They moved forward cautiously, shuffling side to side and kicking the snow off. At one point Kurt kicked an antenna housing. Moments later Joe got too close to the edge and found a sheet of ice that threatened to send him sliding down to the frozen lake again. But nearing the front of the aircraft they found what they were looking for: a depression in the snow, about where the open escape hatch should be.

Kurt kicked at the snow. It began to settle in the middle and was soon descending in equal measure from all four sides of the square-shaped opening of the unsealed escape hatch. When enough snow had gone through, the opening appeared.

"Like sands through the hourglass, so go—"

Kurt stopped Joe from finishing the line with a sharp look.

"I'll go get our gear," Joe said sheepishly.

Kurt brushed more snow from the edge and got down beside it. An escape ladder remained in place. Swinging his legs over the edge, he climbed down.

The darkened main deck was an eerie place. Silent and dormant.

The surfaces were gilded in frost; they glittered as the beam from Kurt's flashlight swept across them. With the exception of the copilot, who lay on the ground where Ridley had shot him, the dead members of the crew remained strapped in their seats, several slumped forward against their seat belts, one man slumped backward, his frozen face pointed upward, his unseeing eyes open and looking toward the ceiling.

They looked like wax figures without the slightest sign of decay. The computer terminals and control panels in front of them were undamaged, their stations were squared away.

Kurt had been in enough sunken ships that exploring one seemed almost normal to him. But the aircraft was different. It seemed more dormant than destroyed, as if it might come to life again at any moment.

The sound of Joe shuffling along on the top of the aircraft brought his attention back to the job at hand. Joe appeared in the opening and handed down a large tool case followed by a folder of schematic diagrams and then two saddlebags filled with explosives. As Kurt took the last bag, Joe climbed down the ladder.

Kurt pointed his flashlight aft. A door beckoned. "Weapons bay is back there. Think you can remove the components yourself?"

Joe feigned a hurt look. "Based on the schematics, I should be able to pull them in five minutes."

"I'll leave you to it," Kurt said. He picked up one of the saddlebags. "I'm going to start placing explosives and collecting dog tags."

Joe took the tools and the schematic diagram and went through the door. The weapons bay was a cylindrical compartment eight feet in diameter and fourteen feet high. The walls of the cylinder were clear Lucite, allowing the crew to see the working components inside.

Joe worked his way around the cylinder to the aft section of the cargo bay. Here the space was taken up by a twelve-pack of powerful generators capable of creating the huge surges of electricity to power the EAGL.

Joe knew enough about lasers to understand the basics of the system. Large amounts of electrical energy were pumped thorough fiber optics or crystals doped with exotic materials like ytterbium and neodymium. The crystals emitted intense beams of light that were focused and aligned by a unit called a waveguide. The laser's power was determined by how much energy went into it and how focused the beam was.

One-kilowatt lasers could be used for welding, or to cut through steel forms. Five-hundred-kilowatt lasers could be used to shoot down drones and small aircraft at a distance of several miles. At maximum power, the EAGL generated five thousand megawatts. A thousand times the power of those other systems. It did this via a combination of scientific tricks, including shortening the pulse and combining it with other pulses of different wavelengths, all of which could occupy the same space at the same time. It didn't burn through an object as much as it vaporized everything in its path and exploded out the other side. The key to creating and harnessing such devastating power came from the materials used in the diode and the advanced structure of the EAGL's waveguide. Once those were removed the rest was just a high-energy but relatively standard laser system.

Reaching the far side of the clear cylinder, Joe found the hatch that would allow him to step inside. Releasing three clamps unsealed the door. He slid it to the right, ducked his head, and stepped inside the cylinder.

From the tool kit, he pulled several work lights, setting them up around him in a way that blanketed the laser unit with light. Double-checking the schematic, he located the outer panel covering the waveguide unit. He climbed up two rungs on a ladder attached to the cylinder and took a powered screwdriver to the bolts holding the panel in place.

Twelve screws came out with machined precision. Out of habit, Joe tucked them in his pocket, even though he had no intention of replacing the panel. Putting the screwdriver back in his pocket, he placed both hands on the panel and pulled. It came loose with a click.

He laid it gently on the deck and then looked back inside the compartment. He found a wiring harness and heavy-duty electrical cables on one side. On the other side, an optical comb connected with a dozen bundles of fiber-optic cable could be seen. In the middle . . .

In the middle there was nothing.

Joe grabbed the schematic and looked over the cutaway diagram once more just to be sure. His shoulders sagged and he shook his head in disgust. Tapping the headset, he spoke his thoughts aloud. "Kurt, we have a problem."

Getting no response, he tried again. Then he remembered the entire weapons compartment was shielded from electromagnetic waves to prevent interference with the laser's functionality. That effect went both ways. Keeping signals out and others blocked in.

A quick check revealed more missing components, including the boxes that housed the diodes and the emitter partition. Every item they'd been told to retrieve was already gone.

Joe hopped off the ladder and landed on the deck. Ducking out of the clear cylindrical compartment, he ran forward, leaving the work lights and the toolbox behind, grabbing only the satchel containing the schematics. He needed to find Kurt so he could deliver the bad news in person.

CHAPTER 44

The dead captain remained strapped in his seat with a look of surprise on his frozen face. His eyes were open, his oxygen mask hanging loosely, his frozen skin untouched by any form of decay. Even the knife in his chest looked staged, covered as it was with bright red blood while glittering with a thin coating of frost.

The captain's death was not a surprise to Kurt. Based on the video of the hijacking they knew the copilot had killed or at least incapacitated him. But a short distance away lay a significant mystery.

The copilot was dead as well.

His body was crumpled in a heap at the bottom of another escape ladder. The hatch above remained closed. An upward-angled gunshot wound to his back suggested he'd been blasted off the ladder from behind before ever reaching it.

The discovery felt odd. To Kurt it seemed like a clue that didn't fit with the rest of the puzzle. All along they'd known there were two hijackers, Ridley and at least one of the pilots, since someone had to fly and land the plane. But if the captain had been stabbed while he was flying, it was presumably the copilot who'd done it. That would leave Ridley to put a bullet in the copilot's back after they'd landed on the frozen lake. All of which begged the question: Who, then, was left to shoot Ridley in the tavern five days later?

Kurt had assumed it was the copilot. But now . . .

He put the idea aside, pulled the dog tag of the murdered captain, and then climbed into the copilot's seat, looking for the electrical panel. If they were going to do a proper job destroying the plane, they needed to get the power on and enable the self-destruct units, which Ridley and the copilot had turned off.

"Let's see if this thing has any juice," Kurt said. Finding the battery switches, he tied them together so they would work as one. With the batteries linked on the main bus, he flipped the switches to the on position.

In the eerie and almost unfathomable quiet, he could hear the circuits and instruments energizing as the power came back on. The tones resembled the strange high-pitched notes one heard when the pressure in their ears equalized. Almost inaudible, but unmistakable.

The sound made him think about the impact signal that had led them astray. The fisherman's report of a large aircraft flying low over the fjord had made everyone forget about the erroneous signal. But it hadn't been a phantom, the NSA had picked it up on a highly sensitive network. With the aircraft being safely tucked away on the icy surface of the "fish-head" lake, the signal had to be a false flag, a red herring designed to lure everyone away from the true location. But who'd put it out? It wasn't the Chinese or the Russians; they'd been searching the ocean as well. And it couldn't have been Ridley or the copilot, as they'd been here on the plane. It meant there had to be another conspirator, someone who was never part of the crew.

The more Kurt thought about it, the more it seemed like they were being led on. Little by little. Inch by inch. Not just NUMA, but the Chinese and Russians as a well. But why and by whom?

The lights on the panel flickered. The myriad circuit breakers and glowing switches came to life around him. They bathed the cockpit in a soft glow, far warmer than the beam of Kurt's flashlight. Directly ahead of him, the glass panel screens that dominated the cockpits of modern aircraft lit up one by one. But instead of maps or systems readouts or virtual versions of the instrument panel, they displayed the image of a man sitting in a dark room, posed as if he were ready to recite a poem. The face was instantly recognizable.

The image grinned with joy and malevolence. It gave Kurt the answer to all his questions at once. "Welcome to my parlor," the man's gravelly voice announced.

"Ahab," Kurt whispered.

There was no response, and Kurt realized he was looking at a recording.

"I must admit," Ahab said, "I expected you to die at sea, going down with your ship like an old captain should. But here you are, still chasing the rabbit I put in front of you. Your determination astounds even me. For the record, this trap was supposed to be the fate of your Chinese friend, Gushan, but don't worry, he will suffer in due time. He will suffer along with his country, side by side with yours.

"As I'm sure you've already realized," Ahab continued. "The important parts of the laser are gone. I'm almost saddened that you won't get to see what I do with it next, but this is where you come to your end. One step too far, a mile across the border into Russian territory. I was tempted to let them capture you and take you to a gulag somewhere, but on the off chance they might let you go, it seemed better to have them surround you in the aircraft, where they could watch me bury you in it.

"I offer you a choice," Ahab said. "Go face the Russians. Or stay where you are and warm up nicely. You have . . . two minutes to decide."

With that a number of lights on the panel flashed yellow and began blinking. A timer started counting down from a hundred and twenty seconds. The self-destruct system had been initiated.

Kurt jumped out of the seat, ignoring Ahab's continued pontification. He rushed toward the cockpit door and nearly slammed into Joe in the process.

"No laser," Joe said, breathing hard in the frigid air. "Someone already pulled it."

"I know," Kurt said.

"How could you know?"

Kurt nodded toward the screens. "Someone's been bragging about it."

Joe's eyes grew wide at the sight of a man they all thought was dead. "You've got to be kidding me. How is he alive?"

"We'll have to figure that out later," Kurt said. "Right now, we've got to get out of here."

A sudden brightening of the cockpit told him it was too late. A stark white glow reached them through the blanket of snow covering the windows, courtesy of spotlights being aimed their way.

Kurt rushed to the ladder that the copilot had died trying to climb. He went up to the hatch, unlocked it, and pulled it open. A foot of snow dropped in on him, coating him in white. He was fine with that. It would be camouflage.

Climbing another step and poking his head above the snow, he looked around. A hodgepodge of vehicles had come in from the Russian side of the lake. Kurt saw a couple of trucks, a pair of snowcats, and three snowmobiles. They were taking up positions around the plane. Some of them had turned their headlights on, others aimed articulated spotlights at the jet. The pristine snow sparkled with the illumination. The tracks Kurt and Joe had made with the snowmobiles stood out in contrast.

A number of men emerged from the nearest truck, armed with guns and ladders. Additional men were spreading out to various points around the plane in order to prevent any escape.

"What's the word?"

"Fifteen to one," Kurt said.

"But there's two of us."

"And thirty of them."

"Math," Joe said. "Got ya. What do you want to do?"

"I'd like to invite them in, show them Ahab's video, and explain that we've all been tricked, but we don't have the time."

He pointed to the self-destruct timer, which was ticking down and closing in on ninety seconds.

Joe took a deep breath and held up one of the charges. "Don't really need these if the whole plane is going to blow up. We could use them like grenades."

"Now you're talking," Kurt said. "I'll distract them. You get to your machine."

"You'll end up stuck here," Joe said, not happy with the plan.

"Are you kidding?" Kurt said. "I'm taking the easy route. I'll stroll off this thing while they're all chasing you."

"Okay," Joe said. "That sounds more like it."

As Joe left, Kurt twisted the timers on three of his four charges. He set them for ten, twenty, and thirty seconds. He would have preferred five, ten, and fifteen, but the safety protocol would not allow a shorter fuse.

Pressing the start buttons, he waited calmly as thirty pounds of C-4 ticked down to detonation. When enough time had passed, he heaved the charges out one after another.

The first charges crashed into the snow, perhaps ten feet from the point man of the approaching group. He shouted a warning to the others and ran. The group scattered, dropping their ladders and rushing clumsily through the snow for safety.

It detonated as they cleared the area, blasting a thirty-foot crater in the snow and sending a number of them flying. Unknown to anyone at the time, the blast cracked the ice below in a spiderweb-like pattern.

The second charge went off to a similarly spectacular effect, blasting so much snow into the air that it cleared half the hidden wing, while spearing a fog of sparkling ice crystals across the snowy plain.

By now the startled Russians took cover. Some of them responded by leveling their rifles at the cockpit and firing away.

Kurt slid back down the ladder as bullets tore into the upper half of the cockpit. He dropped to the deck and scrambled aft as the incoming shells tore the small space apart. He was out of the cockpit and into the control bay when the third charge went off, thudding the plane like a nearby thunderclap.

He reached the control bay ladder. Looking up, he saw Joe's feet disappear through the opening. He raced up after him. A vague clock in his head telling him the bigger bang of the self-destruct system was not far off.

Poking his head out, Kurt saw clouds of ice particles drifting through the air, the Russians trying to regroup, and Joe burrowing through the snow on top of the plane like an Arctic fox. It kept him out of sight until he reached his snow machine.

Pulling himself aboard, Joe twisted the throttle. The electric machine accelerated instantly, and Joe was soon racing along the fuselage and down the side. The Russians saw him, but held their fire. No doubt they had orders not to shoot up the section of the plane holding the laser.

That amnesty ended the moment Joe hit the frozen surface of the lake. But he had already hit top speed by then. He whipped past the tail, cut to the left to avoid a snowcat, and sped off into the dark. A few tracers followed him, but the gunfire stopped as all three of the Russian snowmobiles went after him.

Kurt followed Joe's path along the fuselage and reached his own chariot. He climbed on board and grabbed the throttle. His more awkward ascent meant he had to turn around before he accelerated. He let the motor surge once as he spun around. Then put the power on smoothly.

As the belt dug into the snow, he picked up speed briskly. Instead of going for the tail as Joe had, Kurt used the wing as an off-ramp. Halfway down he turned sharply to the left. He was just going off the edge as the self-destruct timer hit zero.

Three successive explosions erupted behind him. The cockpit first, then the control compartment aft of it, and then a larger, hotter detonation as the weapons bay erupted from within.

A white ball of flame accompanied the blast, blinding everyone who had been caught looking.

The immediate effect of the explosions was the complete dismantling of the plane. The top of the fuselage blew upward and out. Geysers of flame jetted skyward, while jagged sections of aluminum pirouetted as they flew out into the night.

A secondary effect was the shock wave. The blasts were channeled upward for the most part, but shock fronts expand in all directions like a bubble. This one hit Kurt with a powerful off-center shove, which forced the machine onto one rail. Kurt was thrown off the side and went face-first into the snow. The last he saw of the snowmobile, it was careening onward, curving back toward the inferno.

CHAPTER 45

Joe heard and felt the explosion, but was already half a mile away. He wanted to come about and check on Kurt, but he had more pressing issues. The three Russian snowmobiles were chasing him. They were big and loud, but mostly they were fast. And, he had to admit, well driven.

The Russian drivers worked together, hounding him like a pack of border collies. One led the chase, with the other two keeping formation a little way back. If Joe turned right, the main pursuer tracked him, while the machine on the right turned hard to cut him off. If he turned left, the same thing happened. So far, Joe hadn't been able to get out of their headlights.

He would have been fine with that except for one other issue. To avoid the snowcat and pair of commandos with Kalashnikovs, he'd made a hard turn to the left as he sped away from the C-17. He hadn't had much choice, but as a result, he'd ended up heading toward Russia instead of Norway. With the group of hounds keeping him on track he was getting farther and farther from safety, not closer to it.

He needed a smoke screen, or a mine-deploying system, or a

rearward-firing machine gun. "Where are all the cool James Bond switches when you need them?" he muttered.

Remembering Kurt's rooster tail as he topped the aircraft, Joe realized he could make a smoke screen of his own, or a snow screen at least.

He whipped the snowmobile into a turn, slowed, and then gunned the engine as it began to sink into the powder. A spray of snow and ice crystals surged into the night air behind him. He turned the other way and repeated the procedure, going back and forth.

After a few practice rounds, he went all out, creating a huge curtain of ice crystals behind him and then turning hard and racing back toward his pursuers. The suspended crystals shimmered as the lights of the snowmobiles converged on it, becoming more opaque as it brightened, the way fog becomes harder to see through when it's lit up at night.

The first Russian snowmobile burst through the curtain like a train coming the opposite direction on a high-speed track. It passed on Joe's right, vanishing in a blink.

The second sled passed by wide to the left. But the third appeared almost directly in front of him.

Joe flicked his sled to the left, trying to avoid a head-on collision.

The other driver turned harder, lacking Joe's finesse and failing to shift his weight. As his runners turned, he caught an edge and the sled tumbled hard, catapulting the driver out into the night.

"One down, two to go."

He held the throttle wide open and looked back. The remaining sleds had made the turn and were spreading out, widening their formation to prevent Joe from performing the same trick again.

Still, Joe had bought himself some time and space, and he was no longer heading for the Russian coast. Instead he was charging toward the cliff and the drop-off on the other side, where the lake tumbled in a series of frozen waterfalls toward the fjord, a thousand feet below.

In the daylight it would have been no problem, but at night he would not see where the lake ended and the thousand-foot drop began until his headlight stopped reflecting off the snow. That would not leave enough time to turn.

Still, he charged toward it like a man possessed. The Russians chased him with no less determination.

He glanced over his shoulder toward the dim, orange glow of the burning plane. It looked to be a long way back. *Miles back*, Joe thought. But as the only point of light it was impossible to really tell. He squinted, trying to see out beyond the headlights. For another moment he continued to speed into the darkness. Then all at once, he decided against it.

He carved another sharp turn, kicking up a wave of snow as he cut hard to the left. Much of the snow fell quickly, some of it lingered. Other flakes dropped over the edge of the cliff, floating gently down toward the waters of the fjord far below.

Joe would never know what instinct caused his nerve to fail at just the right moment, but he was glad of it. He was now racing along the edge of the cliff, heading toward the Norwegian border.

Looking back, he saw the Russians making the same turn. They closed in once again, this time flanking him to the inside and pinning him against the cliff's edge.

Joe bent his course inward, but at the same moment the nearest Russian sled pulled even and blocked him. The two machines crashed together and then veered apart.

Joe sped up, cut the throttle, then sped up again, trying to create some space. But the Russian driver was too good. He matched Joe's pace changes almost instantly. With Joe effectively blocked, the Russian inched closer, far too smart to swerve foolishly toward Joe and risk overshooting and flying off the cliff himself. No, it seemed this would be a slow, firm shove.

The front cowlings hit and bounced apart. The skids scraped against each other, locked for a second, and then freed themselves.

Joe held his ground with only a few yards to spare. But that allowed the second Russian snowmobile to close in behind him. Together they tried to run Joe toward his doom.

A bump from the back pushed him forward. A bump from the side sent him to the right. He had maybe thirty feet to play with. Then it was twenty.

The first sled hit him again, knocking him closer to the edge of the world. The second one slammed him from behind.

Joe felt a sudden lack of control and a dearth of power as he tried to accelerate. A vibration through the machine told him the track had been damaged. Most likely the tread was unraveling. He cut his speed to conserve what was left. But that was just blood in the water for these sharks. The lead sled hit him once more.

This time the two machines locked together. The Russian sled leaning into his. Joe shoving back against it. Joe pushed the runners as hard as they would go, but he was losing the battle. Glancing to his right, he saw the edge and the void and a smattering of lights miles off and far below.

The tread suddenly unraveled. It flew off the back end, soaring directly into the chest of the rider trailing behind. Joe lost all control of the machine. In desperation, he leapt from his snowmobile onto the Russian one beside him.

The move surprised the Russian driver so much that he leaned and twisted, lifting one hand off the controls and swinging it backward in hopes of swatting Joe away.

Joe grabbed his arm, pushed it upward, and twisted, wrenching the driver out of position and forcing him off the machine. He fell sideways, hitting the snow and tumbling like an acrobat. At the same time, Joe lunged for the handlebars and took control of the speeding machine.

With a new horse under him, Joe watched the NUMA snowmobile nosedive off the cliff. It was followed by the trailing Russian snowmobile, whose driver had reacted late after being struck by the flying tread and had plummeted over the edge. Joe turned away, gunning the throttle on the machine and leaving the last of the pursuers behind him.

Kurt found himself in a far different predicament than Joe. Instead of moving too fast, he wasn't moving at all. Having been catapulted off the snowmobile and into a drift, he'd burrowed downward, covering his face as a wave of flame washed over his back.

Snowmelt poured over him as the heat turned the water to liquid once more. Kurt crawled forward, escaping the flames by staying in the drift and emerging on the far side.

Looking back, he saw a mushroom cloud of smoke and flame rising into the sky. The body of the C-17 was a shattered hulk; the fuselage and wings engulfed in the unmistakable cloud of orange and black that only a fuel-fed fire produced.

The heat from the fire had cleared the snow from the plane. What was left sat as he suspected, with only the top half visible. The Russians were scattered about. Some of them scrambling to get back to their vehicles, others just running from the plane.

A sudden shift of the ground told Kurt why: the explosions had cracked the ice. The fire was weakening it further. With the weight of the aircraft pressing downward, it wouldn't be long before it broke through.

With the snow around his feet turning to slush, Kurt looked for the snowmobile. It had run on after he was unhorsed, speeding and turning back toward the plane. It lay on its side near the tail, a few hundred feet from him.

It had been pushing full speed when the explosion launched Kurt off of it. Without any weight on the seat, the automatic kill switch had shut it down, but momentum and speed had carried it to where it now rested. Kurt just hoped it was still operational.

He trudged toward it, pushing through the soft snow and shielding his face from the waves of heat. As he neared the tail, one of the Russian commandos lumbered after him.

The man had been near the plane when it blew. His coat had been ripped open. His arm and shoulder were on fire; his face was singed. His rifle was nowhere to be seen. Staggering forward in the orange light, he looked like a member of the walking dead, but when he saw Kurt, he drew a knife and charged.

Kurt took a half step back as he blocked the stabbing motion. With a twist of the man's arm Kurt separated the elbow. The knife went free, the man grunted, and Kurt leaned hard, throwing the man over his shoulder and down into the slush.

Kurt landed on the man and put a knee on his chest. He raised his fist for a knockout blow, but instead of hammering the Russian in the face, Kurt shoved his arm and shoulder down into the slushy mix. The flames went out, the burning clothes flaked off, revealing red, charred skin.

The Russian stared upward, squirming. Obviously in some kind of shock. Kurt lifted him to his feet.

"Get out of here," he shouted. "*Idti!*" he added, using the Russian word for "go" or "run."

The Russian stared blankly. In addition to the shock, he might have been deaf from the explosion. Kurt pointed him away from the aircraft and shoved him forward. He stumbled onward toward safety, never even looking back as Kurt turned for the snowmobile.

Kurt's method of escape was no more than sixty feet away, but the journey to get there was a surprisingly difficult one. The snow was now twenty inches of deep mush. Not firm enough to walk on, not watery enough to wade through with ease. The slush gripped Kurt's legs with a tremendous amount of suction. Each step requiring a herculean effort.

He trudged forward as waves of heat baked his face and kerosene fumes stung his eyes and irritated his lungs. Halfway there the ice shuddered and tilted as a heavy section of the C-17 broke through, settling a few feet deeper. The tremor knocked Kurt down on one knee. He got up and pushed forward, slogging his way toward the tail end of the aircraft.

A secondary explosion went off as he reached the snowmobile. A new fissure emerged in the ice, snaking its way almost directly beneath the snowmobile. Water shot up from it and spread out, mixing with the slush.

As the gap widened, Kurt righted the snowmobile, jumped aboard, and pressed the start switch. The lights came on instantly.

Moving was another story. The tread churned in the slush, blasting a slurry of material out behind him. It was a slow, fitful process, with Kurt backing off the throttle and then pumping it again like a man trying not to spin his tires in a Chicago blizzard.

Just as he slithered out of the muck, one of the Russian snowcats appeared.

"Not today," Kurt said. He turned hard and went back the other way. The heavy tracked machine followed until it hit a fissure and went down at the front end.

The last Kurt saw of it, the men were abandoning it and running for safety.

On his own now, he sped past the ruined nose of the aircraft. Somewhere inside he imagined Ahab still talking, no doubt congratulating himself on his own greatness. The idea was both revolting and laughable.

Clearing the plane and leaving the Russians behind, Kurt attempted to call Joe on the small radio attached to the console. Without the helmets and their built-in speakers he had to lean close to the snow machine's console with its built-in microphone. He shouted, hoping Joe had his volume up.

Three tries brought no response.

Kurt scanned the open snowfield in front of him. There was no sign of Joe. But a headlight blazing through the night was racing toward him from the Russian side. It was a warm yellow beam, as opposed to the cool, blue-white glow the NUMA headlights made.

Apparently, the Russians weren't done yet.

Kurt turned hard, making sure to stay out of reasonable firing range. But instead of going after him, the Russian snowmobile raced on by, heading directly for Norway. Either a lone Russian had decided to invade Europe all on his own, or it was Joe.

Kurt turned to follow and put on the speed. He pulled alongside Joe and the noisy machine.

"I see you have a new ride," Kurt shouted.

Joe nodded at his friend. "I jumped at the chance to get it."

Kurt had a feeling Joe meant that literally. "You get much on your trade-in?"

"Not really," Joe shouted. "It wasn't going to be in drivable condition much longer."

Kurt looked back. They were unfollowed and home free at this point. The Norwegian border was no more than a mile away, with the safety of the tree line a few miles beyond that.

As they reached it, the euphoria of escape gave way to the reality of the situation.

They'd survived Ahab's trap, escaping both the plane and the Russians, but they had little else to show for it. The laser was gone, the C-17 was destroyed, and the hijackers were dead. Any link they could forge to Ahab, or any hint regarding his ultimate plans, had vanished as well.

"Now what?" Joe shouted, a hint of dejection evident in his voice.

There was only one answer. "Now we go find Ahab," Kurt said. "And stop whatever he's planning to do."

CHAPTER 46

The ride back to the *Lyra* was done in both radio and personal silence.

Kurt kept his eyes on the snow ahead, tracking back toward the harbor on the same grooves he and Joe had come out on. Not much had changed, but everything had changed. The biggest question was also the most inscrutable one: If he didn't want to sell the laser, what on earth could Ahab possibly want with it? Without more information there was simply no way to know. But Ahab would have an endgame in mind beyond getting revenge on Kurt and Gushan. Otherwise, he could have simply left the laser in place and blown the plane to confetti as soon as Kurt or Gushan stepped on board.

Kurt let the question be and allowed his mind to go quiet. It had been working overtime for a week, along with his body. Both needed to rest before he made another major decision.

Nearing the outer edges of Tromsø, he eased up on the throttle and straightened in the saddle. The outer layer of his clothing creaked and cracked; it had frozen solid from the slush. His hair was a shell of ice, whiter than its normal silver-gray. Remarkably, his core remained toasty warm, thanks to the heated seat and handlebars.

They dumped the Russian snowmobile at the edge of town and rode together on the surviving NUMA machine. There was a bit of fire in the sky. It almost passed for the coming of dawn, but was actually the glow of the northern lights. The Vikings believed the auroras to be the shimmer of light reflecting off the armor of the Valkyries, the divine female warriors that carried fallen heroes to the afterlife in Valhalla. Perhaps they'd been expecting Kurt to join them. If so, they'd have to wait, he still had things to do.

Easing their way around the outskirts of town, they rounded the clusters of small buildings, bringing the harbor into view once again. Both the Chinese icebreaker and the Russian spy trawler were gone.

Reaching the *Lyra*, he could see the repairs coming along. The ship would need a few more days before it could safely risk oceanic travel, but it was nearly seaworthy.

Parking beside the gangway, Kurt and Joe eased off the sled, stiff from the ride and the cold. An enlisted member of the crew came down to greet them. Kurt handed him the keys. "You can park it around back. We're not going to need it again today."

The baffled crewman took the keys and nodded, then got on his radio to get the cargo hatch opened so he could pull it inside.

Climbing the gangway, Kurt shook the last of the ice from his clothing.

The captain met them as they stepped aboard. He searched their eyes. "Well . . . ?"

Kurt shook his head.

"Damn," the captain said. "So, who ended up with it? The Chinese or the Russians?"

"It's more complicated than that."

"Way more complicated," Joe added.

Kurt motioned toward the empty berths across the harbor. "When did the Chinese leave?"

"About ten minutes after our helicopter got back," the captain said. "I guess they realized they'd lost."

The ruse had worked, not that it had made any difference in the long run. "And the Russians?"

"About an hour ago. They hightailed it out of here."

That sounded about right.

Kurt pulled off his coat and tossed it into a garbage bin. It was singed in places and smelled of jet fuel. "I need a cup of coffee, and a secure line to Washington."

"Why don't you two get some rest first?"

"We'll sleep on the plane," Kurt said.

"Plane?"

"Once I tell them what happened, they're going to want to see us in person."

CHAPTER 47

The NUMA helicopter took Kurt, Joe, and the Trouts over the mountains from Tromsø to the town of Vadso, where an airport large enough to handle big jets waited. A Norwegian air force C-130, dispatched at the request of the U.S. government, picked them up. It flew them to Oslo, where an extended-range Gulfstream G650 dressed up in NUMA colors collected them for the long ride back to Washington.

True to his word Kurt slept most of the flight. He woke up an hour before they began their descent into Reagan National, had a snack, and remained in the world of his thoughts, saying little to the others. After a brief check-in at NUMA headquarters all four of them went home. Twelve hours later Kurt was at the White House, where he briefed Sandecker, the President, the chief of staff, and the director of the CIA on the events of the past week.

He'd already written an exhaustive report, but they asked enough questions to make him wonder if anyone had read it in depth.

To his surprise, none of the four seemed nearly as glum as he was.

"You should be congratulated for what you accomplished," the President began. "You frustrated the Chinese so badly that they're plowing through the Arctic ice on their way back to China as fast as they can go. You destroyed the C-17, and most importantly you kept the weapon out of Russian hands."

Kurt cringed at what he was hearing. He'd never been a fan of moral victories, and he didn't like credit or a pat on the back when he hadn't done a thing to deserve it.

"With all due respect, Mr. President, I didn't keep the weapon out of Russian hands, Ahab did. It was him all along. He lured NUMA up to Norway with faked artifacts from the U-boat we had been looking for. He brought the Chinese in, promised them an easy score, and then strung them out. I'm guessing he pulled the Russians in at the last minute as some kind of wild card. And while our adversaries may not have the weapon now, Ahab does. That cannot be a good thing for anyone."

With the President's permission the director of the CIA chimed in. "It's a valid point, Kurt, but our sources tell us the Chinese and the Russians both believe the EAGL components were destroyed when the C-17 exploded. They think you and Zavala were behind the self-destruct code, which makes sense when viewed from the outside. Given your combined reputation as something of an unstoppable force, they have no reason to believe otherwise. We want to keep it that way."

Something bad was coming. Something he wouldn't like. Kurt could feel it. Otherwise they wouldn't be laying the praise on so thickly.

Sandecker spoke next. In his own inimitable way, the Vice President added a few more cards to the stacked deck. "I know it sticks in your craw, but you're going to be feted for this. Privately, of course, but in a way that will confirm to the Chinese and Russians that you're being rewarded for a job well done. That will keep them thinking: *Close, but no cigar.* Which reminds me, as part of your reward I'm sending you a box of cigars. You can share them with anyone at NUMA—except Al Giordano."

"He seems to have his own," Kurt noted, then turned back to the issue at hand. "And what if Ahab decides to sell the laser to the Russians or Chinese now?"

"We don't believe he will," the CIA director said.

The chief of staff chimed in next. "If he wanted to turn the laser over to them he missed his best chance. At this point he'd have to convince them you didn't destroy the laser, and that what he has is real, and then he'd have to explain how he got it and why he didn't give it to them before. A tall order all around."

"Which means he's not going to sell it to them," the CIA director added, closing the loop.

"So what is he going to do with it?" Kurt asked.

The question landed like a lead ballon and sat there. No one had an answer. If they possessed even a clue, they were keeping it to themselves.

"I'm not going to ask you if we're looking for him, because it would be pure insanity not to," Kurt began, "but why don't you let Joe and I help? We're very motivated to find him and bring him back to justice."

The President looked at his silent team. They would have kept silent until the end of time if he didn't give them permission to talk. Finally, he nodded toward the CIA director.

"We don't think Ahab is going to be a problem for very long," the director said.

Kurt narrowed his gaze.

"We have verified intelligence that suggests he's dying," the DCI elaborated. "The bodies of his conspirators that were pulled from the sea around that freighter two years ago were contaminated with radioactive materials. It was in their skin, in their blood, in their organs. The boat itself was virtually glowing. Ahab was on that boat, covered in his own toxins. That he's still alive is honestly surprising, but he won't be for long."

There was a smug certainty to the statement, the kind Kurt hated to hear from government officials. "Even if that's true, it just makes him more dangerous. A man with nothing left to lose."

The confidence that Ahab was not a problem continued. "Ahab is a smuggler, a terrorist, a murderer, and a traitor to at least three countries," the DCI said. "What he's not is an engineer, a scientist, or a specialist at fabricating high-tech devices. He would need significant technical help and a substantial amount of time to turn the parts he's stolen into a working weapon. With the Chinese and Russians out of the running we don't see anywhere he can get his hands on the expertise, and in any case, we don't think he has the time."

Kurt wasn't sure he agreed with the assessment. Ahab had proven to be incredibly resourceful. He was not a man who did things halfway. "He has plans for this weapon," Kurt insisted. "And if we don't find him first, we're only going to learn what those plans are when things start blowing up."

"Of course we're looking for him. But we think he's likely to run out of time before we find him. Either way," the DCI insisted, "we'll handle it from here."

The room fell quiet once again. The hum of the air filters in the background the only sound.

Kurt let it go. They'd given him more than he expected, he appreciated that, but the final words were the type that didn't allow for another round of questions.

"Sorry, Kurt," Sandecker chimed in. "As usual you've done a hell of a job. Time for you to rest up. You and your whole team are going on extended paid vacations. I've already cleared it with Dirk and Rudi. They agree that you've earned it."

And that was that. An hour later Kurt was back at his townhouse on the banks of the Potomac, sitting on his deck overlooking the river. It was a crisp November afternoon. The trees had lost all their leaves. Thanksgiving was a week away. From his vantage point, the river looked like a painting, a silver path running through a land of gray and brown. He put his feet up, tipped back a glass of whiskey, and watched as a formation of Canada geese flew overhead, honking loudly as they got a late start for warmer climates.

The silence that followed was deafening.

"Forget this," he said, getting to his feet.

He stormed back into his house, nearly pulling the door off the track as he threw it open. Heading to his study, he sat down at the glass-topped computer table, and after another sip of the whiskey, he opened his laptop.

After logging into his NUMA account, he opened a folder called NUMA FILES CLAS X-1. It was the classified reports he'd filed when chasing Ahab two years prior. He read through everything he'd written, supplemented by information developed and attached by other sources. Finally, he went over the information shared by Gushan and the Chinese. It was almost hard to believe how much things had changed since that brief moment of cooperation.

He switched from whiskey to coffee and was brewing a second pot when the doorbell rang. A check of the security camera revealed Joe's smiling face. "Avon calling."

Kurt laughed and pressed a button to unlock the door remotely.

Joe came in, shut the door behind him, and walked through the townhouse and up the steps to the top level. He was surprised to see Kurt's desk covered in papers, photos, and Post-its. The computer screen had at least nine different windows open. "You look like a detective trying to solve a crime on late-night TV."

"I am trying to track someone down," Kurt said.

Joe looked down at one of the printed photos. It was of Ahab and an accomplice, loading weapons into a shipping container. It had been taken a couple of months before they caught him on the freighter.

"Oh no," Joe groaned. "Tell me you're not . . ."

"I was ordered to take a vacation," Kurt replied. "No one specified where I should go or what I should do while I was on that vacation."

The glee in Kurt's voice was a combination of caffeine, sugar, and the always uplifting feeling of being productive.

Joe looked down in the dumps about it. "I'm pretty sure this isn't what they had in mind."

"Who knows what they had in mind?" Kurt said. "This might have been their plan all along. I mean, do they not know us by now?"

"Us?" Joe asked.

"You don't have to join me," Kurt said. "But you will."

"You sound awfully confident," Joe replied.

"You don't like to be alone," Kurt said. "You have pathological FOMO, and you won't want me to have all the fun. And most importantly, after everything Ahab put us through, you want to see him locked up just as badly as I do."

With a sigh of exasperation, Joe grabbed a mug from Kurt's cabinet and poured himself a cup of coffee. He didn't bother with the sugar or milk. "What have you found?"

Kurt gestured to different parts of the evidence board he'd created. "Nothing, nothing, nothing, and nothing," he said. "Except for this." He pointed to a photo showing Ahab standing next to a tall man with ginger hair and a scruffy beard. "His name is Rand; he's a South African expat who worked with Ahab on a few things, but ultimately didn't want anything to do with dumping radioactive waste."

"Even smugglers have to have standards," Joe said.

Kurt laughed. "I think his objections came from a place of self-preservation more than morality. He's something of a germaphobe and that tends to include fear of other invisible things that might hurt you like toxic waste and radioactive material."

"I like him already," Joe said, swigging the coffee. "How does he help us?"

"He's the one who ended up selling Ahab out to the Chinese. Under a significant level of pressure, Gushan was able to pry a few details out of Rand. Including the name of the freighter Ahab was using to haul the toxins. True to his word, Gushan kept it quiet. Rand stayed free. And as far as I know, Ahab never put the puzzle together."

"So, he's still out there?"

Kurt nodded. "And I think I know where."

"Please tell me it's somewhere warm."

Kurt tapped the computer screen and clicked on one of the open tabs. An image showing a beautiful white-sand beach, dotted with palm trees and fronting a turquoise bay, filled the screen. A large house with several floors and multiple verandas sat back from the beach. It was partially hidden by the tall palm trees, but several cars could be seen in the looping circular driveway, including the latest version of the Hummer H3 and what appeared to be a pair of matching Ferraris. Several speedboats with fast profiles sat on the beach as if waiting for tourists to come and ask for a ride. An outbuilding that looked like an airplane hangar offered a partially closed roof and a tantalizing glimpse at something white and shimmery inside.

"Is that our hotel?" Joe asked hopefully.

"It's Rand's house in the Philippines."

Joe grumbled at this revelation. "Once again, I find myself in the wrong business."

"At least with our jobs we don't have to worry about being shot, blown up, or dragged off to some far-flung prison colony by a hostile government."

Joe offered a withering stare.

"Yeah," Kurt said. "You're right. We're obviously nuts. Are you ready to go?"

"To the beach house in the Philippines?" Joe said. "Sure. When do we leave?"

"As soon as you're packed," Kurt said. "I figure all you need are shorts and a couple of T-shirts."

"I have an image to uphold," Joe said. "Besides, if this guy Rand happens to be looking for a partner, I'm going to want some sharper attire to interview in. What about Paul and Gamay?"

Kurt expected the situation would end up with some form of direct combat, more like what they'd been through the last time they dealt with Ahab than the dangers the Trouts were used to facing. He shook his head. "It's not their fight."

Joe nodded. "All right. Let's go."

CHAPTER 48

Despite Joe's quip about bringing something to interview in, he was happily soaking up the sun in full beach mode within thirty minutes of stepping off the plane.

Kurt had arranged a ride to the marina and the rental of a boat. As they pulled away from shore in a V-hulled boat made for deep sea fishing, Joe was wearing swim trunks, flip-flops, and a faded T-shirt that complemented his quickly darkening tan. A ragged straw hat he'd bought from a vendor on the side of the road kept the sun out of his eyes, while giving him the look of a local, or perhaps a beach-combing surfer hunting for the perfect wave.

As Kurt drove the boat, Joe studied the shoreline through a set of binoculars. Two hours into their journey, he finally laid eyes on Rand's palatial estate. It appeared even larger when viewed from the sea.

"What do you think?" Kurt said.

"His air-conditioning bill alone would put me out of business," Joe said.

They were cruising slowly along the coast about a mile offshore. As the bay in front of Rand's place opened up, Joe watched the waves curl in from the south. They twisted toward the caramel-colored stretch of sand after rounding an extended point in the rocks, and then broke across a low reef, about two hundred feet from the beach. From there they flattened out, surging forward with far less power until they washed gently up onto the sand.

Joe spotted a man fishing from the rocks. He had a long pole and a cooler beside him, and a hat like Joe's. Closer in, a pair of men worked on the engine compartment of one of the speedboats. Farther up the beach he spotted an attractive woman lying on the sand under a shade of a palm tree. Despite her beauty, it was the waves that interested him the most.

"There's definitely a reef in our way. Looks like there's a gap we could shoot through to get in, but we're going to have an audience."

Kurt stood at the controls in the shade of the Bimini top. He was dressed much like Joe, though instead of a faded T-shirt and straw hat he wore a loose-fitting, long-sleeved linen shirt. It had buttons and a pocket and a casual wrinkled look that went with Kurt's cargo shorts.

"Pretty sure we've been under surveillance since we rounded Delgado Point," Kurt said, referencing a jutting stretch of land two miles behind them. "Five will get you ten the guy with the fishing pole hasn't caught a thing all day. And the girl on the beach probably has a radio in that tote bag somewhere."

Rand was a smuggler ensconced on an out-of-the-way little island, but he didn't exactly live inconspicuously. According to Kurt, he made hefty donations to the local constabulary and other government officials. The kind that allowed for an ostentatious lifestyle. But there were other things to watch for: competitors, angry customers, not to mention agents of foreign governments who might have a bone to pick with his delivery schedule.

Joe offered some options. "We could race in through the gap and make it obvious, or continue on and come back tonight?"

"Don't have time to wait for nightfall," Kurt said. "But check the gap once more. I have a feeling it's not as open as it looks."

Joe raised the binoculars again and focused on the one spot where the waves tucked in close and then continued on toward the beach unimpeded. He stared for a while, focusing and refocusing as the lenses steamed up in the humid environment. Finally, he saw what Kurt was referring to. A thick rusty chain had been stretched across the gap. It was anchored to unseen concrete pylons hidden in the coral. A miniature version of the "Great Chain" that had been stretched across the Hudson to keep the British ships from sailing upriver during the American Revolution.

"That could be a problem," Joe admitted. "Don't want to rip the bottom of the hull out or tear the prop off."

"Think we can crest it with the surf?"

Joe considered the draft of the boat they'd borrowed, the height of the waves, and the effect of traveling in at high speed, which would lift the boat up, but also make an impact far worse if it occurred. "Fifty-fifty."

"Good enough for me," Kurt said.

"What if I'd said thirty-seventy?"

"I'd still try it."

"Ninety-ten that we crash and get thrown from the boat?"

"That long shot has to hit at some point." Kurt laughed. "Might as well be now."

Joe shook his head. He was not surprised. "What if I said I was one hundred percent sure this would end in disaster?"

"I'd figure your math was wrong and try it anyway," Kurt joked. "Hold on. Here we go."

Kurt turned the boat away from the beach as he began to pick up speed. Looping around to the south he guided the craft back toward the reef and pushed the throttle up farther. Speed mattered, but hitting the gap with the crest of one of the waves mattered more.

Joe grabbed the gunwale of the boat with one hand and held the straw hat down with the other as Kurt let the engines roar.

The sound caught the attention of the fisherman on the rocks, who dropped his pole and grabbed what looked like a walkie-talkie off the cooler.

The men working on the outboard stopped what they were doing and looked up, but otherwise they didn't react. The woman propped herself up on her elbows. Eyes hidden behind dark sunglasses as she watched them approach. She was too far away for Joe to detect a smile, but she seemed more curious than afraid.

With Kurt constantly adjusting the throttle, they caught up to the swells and began speeding over them. A smooth ride up, and then down, and then back up again. Because of the peculiar way fluids move, the waves actually picked up speed as they entered the narrow gap, surging through, and then spreading out on the other side.

Aiming to hit the gap with a particular swell ahead of him, Kurt pushed the throttle harder. The twenty-foot Boston Whaler caught up to the back end of the next swell just as it surged into the gap between the corals. The boat rose up onto the hump, threatened to overshoot the crest, and then settled a bit as Kurt feathered the throttle.

The chain in front of them appeared and then vanished beneath the water as the crest of the wave rode over it. A scraping sound raked across the bottom of the hull, passing behind them as they shot the gap.

They were in, the prop was still attached, the hull seemed intact. Joe marveled once again at Kurt's luck.

Then a jarring impact almost threw him out of the boat. They'd hit a second obstacle: a submerged concrete bollard placed in the water to prevent someone from doing what they'd just done. It punched a hole in the underside of the boat, splintering the fiberglass and throwing the entire craft upward. Joe was airborne for a brief moment, his hat vanishing in the wind. He came down on the deck hard enough to bite a chunk out of his lip.

Holding onto the controls, Kurt managed to remain where he was. He yanked the wheel to the right, pushed the power level to full, and caught the energy of the following wave. It pushed them toward the beach.

Hitting the sand, the boat lurched to a stop. Joe slid into the open bow, slamming against a locker that doubled as a front seating area.

Grunting in discomfort and dabbing his bleeding lip, he looked back at Kurt. "At least we didn't hit a mine," he muttered.

Kurt was still standing at the pedestal, but was slowly raising his hands.

Joe looked up. The tanned face of the woman on the beach appeared above him. She was even more attractive close up than she'd been from a distance. He smiled at her. There wasn't much else to do at this point.

"That was impressively stupid," she said in a South African accent. "It's not every day you witness such foolishness."

Joe continued to smile. "All I hear is that you were impressed."

"American," she said, shaking her head.

Joe sat up, taking sudden notice of the MP5K machine pistol in her hand. He dialed back the charm offensive and surrendered to reality.

The two men who'd been working on the outboard ran toward them, along with three armed men from the lower level of the big house. They were outnumbered and surrounded.

Joe put his hands up, though he noticed Kurt seemed oddly pleased.

The woman glared at Joe. "Give me one good reason we shouldn't shoot you right now."

Joe deferred to Kurt. "Ask him. It was his idea."

The woman looked Kurt's way.

With one hand still in the air, Kurt reached slowly toward the breast pocket of his shirt with the other. He unbuttoned the pocket and removed a double-folded envelope with two fingers. He handed the envelope carefully to the woman. "Give this to Rand," he said. "If he still wants to shoot us after reading it, I won't even run for it."

The woman eyed Kurt suspiciously and rubbed the envelope with her fingers as if trying to determine what was inside.

"Keep your guns on them," she ordered as she turned toward the house and strode purposefully up the sand bank. "If they do anything foolish, shoot them and dump their bodies out in the sea."

CHAPTER 49

Kurt remained in the boat with his hands up. The crash had been unexpected, but other than that everything was going according to plan. A couple of minutes went by, enough time to make him ponder the need for a backup plan, and then the double glass doors to the lower level of the house opened. Four people came out. The young woman who'd threatened them, two members of the house staff, and a tall, redheaded man with a ruddy complexion, whom Kurt recognized as Rand. He was wearing a silk robe and oversized sunglasses. His hair was much longer than it had been two years ago, and he had the aura of a fading, hungover rock star.

They marched down to the wrecked boat at the waterline.

"Well, well, well," Rand said, taking a look at Kurt, Joe, and the wrecked boat. "You've really done a number on your whaler. Afraid that's not going to make it out of here."

"Yeah," Kurt said. "I owe someone a boat. Maybe you can give him one of yours."

Rand laughed. The fierce woman at his side did not. "Why would I do that?"

"To make amends for your wicked ways," Kurt suggested.

"I'll consider it," Rand said. "Now out with it. Are you here as interlopers, investigators, or friends? Or did you hear about the party I'm throwing tonight and decide you just couldn't miss it?"

"Party sounds interesting," Joe said.

"None of the above," Kurt insisted. "Mind if I put my hands down? Shoulder is a little sore from some swimming I did in the Arctic."

"Argh, man," Rand exclaimed. "What would make you want to swim in the Arctic?"

"You'd be surprised," Kurt said.

Rand waved his men off and told the woman to put her weapon away. She protested, to which he said. "Pru, please, what are they going to do?"

Kurt lowered his hands. Joe did the same, the smile returning to his face as things took a turn for the better. *Pru*, he thought. *I like that.*

"We should probably speak in private," Kurt suggested, nodding toward the woman.

"There's nothing you can say in front of me that my sister can't handle," Rand said.

"Sister," Joe said. Things were really looking up in his opinion. Though based on her scowl, she didn't seem to feel the same.

"How about lunch and a beer in the shade?" Kurt said. "Wrecking boats always works up an appetite."

Rand grinned and waved for them to follow. With his angry sister at his side, he led them back to the house. They went up a small flight of stone steps and then past a shimmering blue pool and into the great room on the lower level. The room was a marble-walled museum of a space, with a grand piano, animal skin rugs on the floor, and built-in couches clad in exotic leathers around the walls.

"This is where the party will take place," Rand told them.

"The two of you will be long gone by then," his sister insisted, glaring at Kurt and Joe.

"Hopefully," Kurt said.

"But if it works out, and we're still here . . ." Joe began.

They went up a spiral staircase designed to look like a huge strand of DNA. The steps were wide enough to accommodate three or four people side by side.

At the top of the staircase they emerged into a slightly less ostentatious room. Comfortable couches were set up in front of an ultra-high-definition television so massive it took up an entire wall. In dizzying fashion, it was displaying the qualifying rounds of the Formula 1 race in Abu Dhabi.

"I was supposed to be there," Rand told them, sounding disappointed. "I was supposed to be there right now. A friend with a very large yacht invited me to spend the week, surrounded by very beautiful women drinking absurdly expensive champagne. But I couldn't go. You know why?"

Before Kurt could hazard a guess, Rand's sister replied.

"It's not safe," she reminded him. "You haven't been given amnesty . . . yet."

"Amnesty," Kurt said. "Really?"

"We're working on it," Rand insisted. "Pru is, anyway. I don't hold out much hope."

"Maybe we can help," Kurt insisted.

"Not getting me killed before it's granted would be a start," Rand said, showing the first bit of irritation at Kurt and Joe's presence.

They passed the wall-sized screen and settled onto the couches. Kurt could not recall sitting on a more comfortable piece of furniture.

Rand touched a button. The television went dark. The wall slid back and a view of the beach and the turquoise bay appeared. It was a million-dollar view in a ten-million-dollar house, but Rand continued to fidget like a hunted rabbit.

"Heavy lies the head that wears the smuggler's crown," Kurt said.

"Occupational hazard," Rand said. "And then there's your letter, which has thrown me off a bit."

"Help me and you won't ever have to worry about what's in that letter," Kurt said.

"This is all wrong," Pru snapped, standing up. "Who are these people to come in here and talk to us like this? If they mix you up in something new, we'll never be free of this life."

It suddenly occurred to Kurt that Rand's sister was his protector, as serious and determined as he was flighty and boisterous. It sounded as if she were trying to help him escape the life of crime he'd built for himself. She thought Kurt and Joe were fellow criminals.

"Why do we even have to talk to them?" she continued.

Rand sighed. "Because, darling, I once did a very stupid thing and let my conscience make a decision for us. These men know about it. And in this letter, they detail who else will learn about my poor choice, should they not return unharmed to the streets of Washington, D.C."

She looked confused.

"Maybe I can help," Kurt said. "We work for the United States government. We're not smugglers or weapons dealers. Two years ago, your brother gave us some information that helped us stop an incredibly dangerous man from dumping radioactive waste into the sea. That secret remained hidden, as we promised him it would. But as I detailed in the letter, if Rand wants it to continue that way he needs to help me one more time."

"Ahab," she said grimly.

Rand nodded. "Ahab."

"This is extortion," she insisted.

"That's one word for it," Kurt said. "But let me put it to you this way. Ahab is on a revenge tour. He tried to kill Joe, me, and Gushan. If I don't find him and stop him, that tour is going to continue. At some point it will probably make a visit to your neighborhood. But if I get my hands on him, that's one less thing you'll have to worry about. And if you're actually closing in on some form of international amnesty, then a good word from friends of mine—who are far more prestigious than I—could be entered on your behalf."

The look on Pru's face softened, though a sense of suspicion remained. "How can we trust you?"

Rand began laughing. "Oh, darling, these are the fools who still believe the world is a good place. They're more than willing to shoot down anyone who challenges them to prove it. But their word, I have found, is plated in gold."

Kurt sat back, sinking into the bolster on the comfortable couch. Rand was in. His sister would be in, too. Now to convince him to risk everything one more time. "I need to know where Ahab is hiding. And I need a way to get there."

"What makes you think I have that information?" Rand asked.

"Because you're the first person I've encountered in two years who didn't think he was dead. If you did, my letter wouldn't have bothered you in the least. Which means you know he's alive, and you've probably done some work for him along the way."

Rand bit his lip and looked around, irritated at himself. "Never was a good poker player."

"Are you still working with him?"

"No," Rand said.

"We don't smuggle the things he deals in," Pru insisted.

"What does a smuggler named Prudence deal in?" Kurt asked.

She looked at Rand.

"Go ahead," he said. "What difference can it make at this point?"

As she spoke, Rand pressed an intercom button and ordered a spread of lunch to be brought up.

"We smuggle high-tech chips and other items into China," she said. "Things your government has banned them from purchasing. And then we smuggle out rare earths and specialized magnets that their government has stopped shipping to the West."

"It's been a beautiful setup," Rand boasted. "Everyone loves us now."

"I can see why that would help you," Joe said. "As a user of powerful magnets, I thank you."

Kurt wondered how hard Joe had hit his head when the boat crashed. He'd never heard him quite like this. He was either smitten or concussed. Maybe a little bit of both. "Back to Ahab. Where can we find him?"

"He doesn't exactly keep me apprised of his whereabouts," Rand insisted.

An elevator door opened at the back of the room. A small wheeled robot carrying two trays of food maneuvered through the room toward them. The aroma was delectable. Kurt saw perfectly prepared sashimi and freshly sliced mangoes. Glasses of beer in frosted mugs looked undeniably thirst-quenching.

"He's hiding now," Kurt said, returning to the subject of Ahab. "Waiting to make his next move. Does he have a favorite place to hole up?"

"What makes you think I would know?"

"Because you rescued him from the freighter," Kurt said.

Rand stared.

"I shot Ahab and his boat to shreds," Kurt said, recounting the basics. "We found it drifting a mile from the ship. It was swamped, half-submerged, and empty. His men were floating in the sea, but

Ahab was nowhere to be found. There were no other ships in the area. No helicopters for him to jump onto. No way for him to escape. Data points that led everyone to believe he was dead. But he's alive, which means someone had to pick him up in a submersible. Otherwise, we would have spotted his rescuer. I'm guessing it was you."

Rand passed the trays of food out with great pride and precision. After taking a bite, he dabbed his mouth and then looked at Kurt. He shrugged. "You know, I always thought you NUMA guys would figure that out. Who else would understand the utility of a long-range submersible?"

"Shame on us," Kurt said. "We thought we'd won the day. Where did you take him?"

"Taipei first," Rand admitted. "He needed doctors. He needed to go somewhere the Chinese wouldn't be able to get to him. Taiwan fit the bill."

Kurt nodded. "And then?"

Rand hesitated once more and then rubbed his hair back and forth as if speaking the truth was causing him pain. "Siabat Island," he said finally. "It's a small atoll between here and Taiwan. There's an abandoned American air base there, left over from the Cold War. Ahab uses the old hangars as a workshop and staging area. If he's on the island, that's where he'll be. But he won't be alone."

Kurt raised his eyebrows and offered a sinister grin. "Neither will we."

CHAPTER 50

Outfitted in black fatigues borrowed from their hosts, Kurt and Joe climbed into the back of the pearl-white Humvee. Two packs filled with weaponry and tactical gear sat in the footwell between them. As Kurt unzipped the pack to check the contents, Rand climbed in behind the wheel, and his sister took the front passenger seat.

They drove out of the estate, passing two layers of walls and gates before turning onto a road that was a far cry from the smoothly paved driveway. As they rumbled down the uneven, crumbling pavement, Kurt wondered how Rand ever got to use either of the Ferraris. He doubted they could be driven at any speed without needing major suspension work by the time they returned.

The Humvee took the uneven surface with no problem, and they were soon cruising along the coast. Several miles from the estate they pulled into a small marina. A few fishing boats bobbed empty on the surface, but there were no fishermen to be seen. A small barge with rusted but operational-looking dredging gear sat anchored a hundred feet from the shore. The place was quiet. A waterside ghost town.

Rand parked the Humvee under the shade of several trees, climbed out, and led them down a path to a dilapidated building that stretched out over the water. Letting them into the building through a padlocked metal door, they found themselves in a large boathouse of questionable construction.

After clearing some cobwebs from a metal breaker box, Rand opened the panel and flipped a switch. A number of bare overhead lights flickered and came to life. They illuminated the space, revealing a concrete dock. Resting against the edge of the dock, held in place by several lines, was a tubular-shaped vessel. Kurt assumed it was Rand's submarine, but the oddly proportioned, algae-covered machine didn't inspire confidence.

Moving closer, Kurt stopped to examine the hull. It was short from nose to tail, but wide in circumference. It was covered in barnacles, tangles of seaweed, and beards of algae. The hull appeared—even on close inspection—to be made from rotting planks of swollen wood.

Joe spoke his shock aloud. "You've got to be kidding me."

"Not at all," Rand said. "This is my secret."

"You said it was a submarine."

"It is," Pru insisted. "And it's perfectly safe and highly seaworthy. All you're seeing is what I want you to see. Our disguise."

She climbed onto the wooden hull and picked her way forward to the only part of the hull that stuck upward; a rounded bump that was several feet in diameter. Reaching down, she lifted a hidden lever, which she turned counterclockwise a half dozen times as if she were stirring a cauldron. With the last turn complete, she leaned back, pulling the heavy hatch open. A soft hiss of air sounded from the inside as the pressure equalized.

Joe climbed onto the hull to get a better look. Reaching Pru's position, he peered down into the hatch. He saw a collar of green-painted steel, a short ladder attached to the side, and a sturdy, functional interior with heavy rubberized controls.

"Pretty good disguise," he admitted.

"Sitting on the surface, it looks like driftwood, a capsized wreck, or even a dead whale," she replied. "When we surface during the day we scatter anchovies about to attract the seagulls. It adds to the disguise."

There was a great tone of satisfaction in her voice, the complete opposite of her manner at the house.

"You built this," Joe guessed.

"We bought the hull from a friend in the Vietnamese government who was supposed to have it disassembled. It was an aging coastal sub they were discarding in favor of newer and larger boats. Used to carry a crew of twelve and eight torpedoes. We cut the stern off, ripped out the interior, and installed a fully electric engine that runs on lithium-ion batteries. Then we welded a new end cap on the stern, added an overlarge propeller with a shroud around it to keep the cavitation to a minimum, and called it a day."

"My sister is the mechanical genius of the family," Rand said proudly. "Our father sent her to trade school for a hands-on education, and then to engineering courses at university. I think he hoped she might build bridges and skyscrapers one day. Guess it didn't work out that way."

"It still could," Pru insisted.

Kurt had to admire her optimism. "How did you go from there to smuggling?"

"Our father's business went bankrupt," she said. "He was an exporter of precious metals. Apparently, he had been skimming from the shipments for a long time. People were angry. Jail terms were coming. Dad ended up having a terrible heart attack. He died before they could prosecute him, so they came for us. About that time, Rand found a shipment of gold and platinum Dad hadn't yet turned over to the government. It was worth eight million dollars on the free market."

Rand jumped in to add to the story. "My dear sister, Prudence, earned her name by suggesting we surrender it. I promised her I would and then put it on a ship and sold it to one of Dad's old partners in Malaysia at a discounted, tax-free price." He shrugged his shoulders as if it were all a happy accident. "Voilà, a new career was born."

"At that point it was either go to jail, or go on the run," Pru explained. "So I joined him. We moved around a lot. Malaysia, Thailand, Vietnam. Finally, we found a spot here where we could operate undisturbed."

Joe nodded and turned his attention back to the submarine and its unorthodox exterior. "How does the disguise affect your speed and range?"

"Not as badly as you might think," she replied. "The lines of the wooden planks create a slipstream of sorts, and we never let the algae growth get long enough to be a problem. It costs us maybe two or three knots, but we're not trying to set any speed records here."

Kurt had a question. "How good of a welder are you?"

"Good enough that this boat has never sprung a leak," she said, knocking on the wooden plank. "Besides, we never dive below eighty feet. Easy swim to the surface from there if something goes wrong. Shall we go inside?"

Joe nodded and Pru swung her legs over the opening and climbed down. The submersible wasn't large enough to need more than a three-rung ladder, and that was more useful for climbing out than getting in.

Joe went in after her, with Kurt and Rand following suit. With the lights on the interior felt like a throwback to an earlier era. Analog dials for everything from speed to depth to pressure; thick steel valves that required substantial muscle power to open, close, and adjust; mechanical linkages and levers to control and set rudder and dive planes. About the only modern touches were a keyboard and computer screen between the two seats, used primarily for navigation, and the fully electrical motor powered by long banks of lithium batteries that lined the sides and bottom of the vessel.

Kurt noticed brand names on the battery packs, quickly realizing they'd been repurposed from electric cars.

Near the front of the vessel were two seats arranged in a staggered formation. The rest of the hull was cargo space, flat, open, and dotted with anchors and attachment points to tie down and secure whatever was brought aboard.

"How much contraband can you haul in this thing?" Kurt asked.

"Almost three tons," Rand said. "But we run out of space before we run out of buoyancy. Computer chips don't weigh that much and refined earths are running five hundred dollars a pound these days. Million-dollar shipments each way. Our twenty percent adds up quickly."

"Did I mention being in the wrong business?" Joe said once again.

Kurt laughed. "Got to hand it to you, you've made yourself invaluable to Western governments, who want those rare earths, and the Chinese, each of whom should theoretically be trying to stop you. Are you certain you want to go straight?"

Rand's reply couldn't have been simpler. "What good is all the money if you can't enjoy spending it?"

Kurt could understand that. "Get us to Siabat Island unobserved and we'll do whatever we can to help you get clear."

CHAPTER 51

The journey north was a long one; even at eleven knots it took almost eight hours. That left plenty of time for thinking, resting, and talking. With the cargo compartment empty, there was plenty of room to stretch out. Kurt could even stand without banging his noggin on the overhead, something that was rare even in the largest of NUMA submersibles.

With Joe staying close to Pru for personal and professional reasons, Kurt ended up discussing Ahab with Rand, hoping to tease out what he might have been up to. He figured the best way to do that was to go back to the moment Ahab had disappeared.

"What happened after you rescued Ahab in this thing?"

"He was all shot up," Rand said. "He needed doctors and a place where the Chinese wouldn't look for him. I took him to Taiwan like I told you. I had contacts there. They found a hospital that would take him, no questions asked."

"I'm sure he appreciated that," Kurt said. "How long did he stay there?"

"A month or so," Rand said. "They had to patch him up. Get the toxins out of his system. I took him back to Siabat when he was ready. First thing he did was ask me to bring him some equipment."

"By that you mean weapons," Kurt assumed.

"No," Rand said. "We don't trade in weapons. He wanted tech stuff from me. Parts and machinery. Avionics gear. Computers. I must have made a dozen trips to the island hauling that stuff. The weirdest thing I brought him was a set of mirrors that came from this telescope-manufacturing company. They weighed a hundred pounds each. Ahab was insanely specific about how they were to be shipped and stored. He did not want them getting damaged or warped."

Kurt could see the picture forming. Ahab had an aircraft; he had the waveguide and the other important parts of the laser; he had technical information and design specs from Ridley; and now he had a pair of high-precision mirrors cast by some specialty optics company. He was building his own laser. But why?

"Who's he working with?" Kurt asked. "Most of his old crew are dead or in prison."

"He's gotten friendly with the Taiwanese," Rand said. "He linked up with them after his stay there. By the way they talk and all their tattoos, I'd say they're the Free Chinese types, the ones who intend to fight China to the death if they ever try to take over the island."

"You've seen these new friends personally?"

Rand nodded. "I've brought some of them over. Hard men. One of them was silent for eight solid hours. Made me really uncomfortable."

"What does Ahab want from these guys?"

"Your guess is as good as mine. Maybe he figures he owes them. Or maybe he hates the Chinese Communists as much as they do now."

Kurt considered the information. If there was any country in the world that might pay more for the laser system than Russia or China, it would be Taiwan. A hundred miles of water was all that separated them from an angry neighbor that wanted to conquer and control them. An angry neighbor with the world's largest army, a growing navy, and a lethal air force with thousands of combat aircraft and ten thousand cruise missiles in their arsenal.

Taiwan was also a technologically advanced country, one filled with scientists and engineers who could understand and reverse engineer what the Americans had done with the laser, allowing them to build copies on their own.

If Kurt understood it right, the Pentagon figured a fleet of thirty to fifty EAGL-equipped aircraft would be enough to put an impenetrable shield around the United States. A handful of such planes with overlapping fields of fire would make Taiwan untouchable. From high above the island, they could wipe out the Chinese air force as its jets took to the sky. They could fill the Taiwan Strait with spent and shattered cruise missiles.

The U.S. couldn't sell a weapon like that to Taiwan without starting World War III, but it might be worth it for the Taiwanese government to steal the design, even if it meant the loss of all future support of the United States.

The idea almost made sense. But something was off.

To begin with, the notion of Ahab playing the white knight to the people of Taiwan didn't quite fit. Helping others was not his way. Using them for his own ends was more on-brand.

And if Ahab was working for Taiwan, he wouldn't have risked all of the theatrics in the Arctic. He would have simply taken the laser, blown up the plane that carried it, and hightailed it back to Taipei. He'd also be living in unrivaled luxury in the hills around the capital, not holed up on a barren island that wasn't even Taiwanese property.

There was something more going on, but try as he might, Kurt couldn't decipher the riddle. Ahab's plan remained an enigma. But knowing the man's desire for revenge, Kurt didn't doubt that the end result would be carnage on some massive scale.

A voice from the forward part of the compartment broke his train of thought.

"We're coming up on the island now," Pru announced. "I'll raise the mast in a few minutes so we can all take a look."

CHAPTER 52

Pru took the submarine within a mile of the island and brought the vessel up to a depth of twelve feet. After aligning the sub with the current, she set the power to maintain directional control while letting the sub drift smoothly. Activating a hydraulic switch, she raised a twenty-foot metal post that was attached to the outside of the hull. It rose upward like a flagpole, extended out of the water, and locked into place. A pair of cameras mounted at the top of the mast acted like periscopes. One gave a wide-angle view; the other could be zoomed and directed. The images they captured appeared on a screen in between the two seats.

She and Joe had front-row seats. Kurt and Rand huddled around them to get a better view.

At first the images revealed nothing but darkness.

"Did you guys forget to take the lens cap off?" Kurt said.

"It's called nighttime," Pru snapped back.

It was two hours after midnight. The moon hadn't come up yet, but the thousands of stars created a slightly bluish backdrop in the night sky. As Pru adjusted the contrast, the island appeared like a dark curtain in front of them.

Tapping away at the keyboard, she enhanced the image further still. The image brightened, the sky turned green, the island remained black.

"We have night vision," she said, "or thermal imaging."

With the touch of another button the image changed once more. The sky went from green to black. The island changed from black to gray, with white tones where the rocky terrain radiated left-over heat.

"This works," Kurt said.

The image showed what they already knew to be true: Siabat Island was a mostly flat landmass, with only a single elevated section on the right side, which corresponded to the northeastern end. It looked dry and scrubby and appeared to be completely devoid of trees. As spartan and forsaken as Rand's estate was lush.

"Not much to it," Joe said.

"That's what enticed your country to build an air base on it fifty years ago," Pru said.

The air base was a relic from the Cold War. At this point it had been abandoned for twelve years.

"How do we approach it?" Kurt asked.

"There's a channel just before the promontory," Pru said. "It leads to a sheltered gap where we would off-load our deliveries."

"There's a road leading from the cove," Rand said, jumping in. "It's more of a trail really, hardscrabble and unfinished, but it leads from the water back overland to what's left of the air base. If Ahab's on the island, that's where he'll be. He's made himself a base of sorts in the old, rusted hangars."

Joe grinned. "Sounds like someone else we know. Any chance he has a classic car collection?"

Rand didn't get the reference. "As far as I know he's not into cars. But I heard a jet engine idling once when we were there."

Kurt checked the time, four hours till dawn. If they were going to get onto the island, this was the time to do it. He glanced down at Pru. "Can you get into the channel in the dark?"

She looked up at him and smiled. "Do you think we make our deliveries in broad daylight?"

Kurt laughed. "Good point. Let's go. I want to see what Ahab is up to before morning reveille."

Using a GPS position tracker and the thermal cameras, Pru was able to navigate toward the channel with meticulous precision. They entered the channel at periscope depth and then rose another five feet. Moving slowly and steadily, they sailed past a rocky outcropping that acted as a natural barrier to the waves and found themselves in a large V-shaped cove filled with calm waters. Halfway toward the narrow point of the cove, Pru brought the sub to a halt and released a pair of anchors. One fell from the bow, the other from the stern, the idea being they would keep the sub from twisting in the current.

Opening a manual valve and pressing one of the rubberized buttons, she switched on a pump. A low hiss of air followed, accompanied by soft rumbling as water was drawn quietly out of the ballast tanks and replaced with compressed air.

The submarine rose slowly. It broke the surface with the stealth of a crocodile emerging from a dark jungle river.

Shutting off the valve and switching off the pump, Pru sat back. The submarine went silent, the tension rose. "Now what?"

Kurt replied, "Joe and I will take some of those weapons you don't smuggle and go ashore to find Ahab."

Rand nodded. "Sounds good," he said. "Any chance you might be willing to leave us a nicely worded letter of reference, proving how helpful we've been? You know . . . just in case things don't quite go as planned."

Kurt laughed at him. "No," he said bluntly. "But I will allow you to come with us, so you can lend even more assistance to the cause. That way Joe and I can be sure this submarine will be here when we get back."

CHAPTER 53

After the briefest of discussions, everyone agreed that Rand was a terrible candidate to join the landing party. He was clumsy, nervous, and pathologically incapable of being quiet for any significant stretch of time.

Pru, on the other hand, had the focus of a soldier, knew her weapons well, and was determined to make sure Kurt and Joe returned safely so they could help free her from the gilded cage she and Rand had built on the wrong side of the law.

With that settled they opened the hatch and emerged into the tropical night air.

Leaving the submarine meant stripping down, putting their gear and clothes into plastic bags, and swimming two hundred yards to a small beach, where the sediment had gathered. Pru led the way in the same black bathing suit she'd been wearing when Kurt and Joe had crashed the beach.

Joe followed, stripped down to his shorts and towing his gear behind him.

Kurt remained behind for a moment, warning Rand not to do anything rash. "Just sit tight and read a book. We'll be back before daylight."

"Just take care of Pru," Rand said. "She's terribly earnest. She'll try to prove how worthy she is to you."

It was the first time Kurt had heard real emotion out of Rand. "All she has to do is get us to the air base and keep us from walking into a trap. Once I confirm that Ahab is on the island we'll come back so I can alert our government. If all goes well, he'll be scooped up in twenty-four hours and you guys will be heroes worthy of a new life."

Rand sighed. "Sounds great," he said, "but how often does everything go well?"

Kurt offered a knowing grin. "All I can tell you is we're due."

He made his way forward to the sloping prow of the submarine, avoiding the slippery spots of algae and the sharp barnacles. At the far end, he slipped quietly into the water and swam off.

Even though it was November, the tropical water in the protected cove was warm and silky. It felt like a bath in comparison to the frigid dip Kurt had taken in the Arctic north of Norway. He moved smoothly and calmly, feeling positively weightless without the bulky drysuit, heavy tanks, and thruster pod. If it wasn't for the dangerous reconnaissance mission ahead of them, he could have flipped over onto his back, closed his eyes, and drifted peacefully. His ancestors might have been Vikings, but he couldn't help but think the Polynesians had picked a better set of latitudes to inhabit.

Shaking the thought away, he refocused on the mission at hand. Nearing the beach, he found Joe and Pru toweling off underneath a small overhang of a rocky bluff. He swam over to the sheltered spot, reeled in the plastic bag containing his things, and carried it with him as he left the water. In a minute or so, the three of them were dressed in loose black fatigues and hiking boots.

Laces were tightened. Weapons were checked. Suppressors were screwed into the barrels.

Pru slung the strap of her weapon over her shoulder and slid it around behind her. "The road is off that way," she said, pointing to a barely visible trail worn by foot traffic and wheeled vehicles. "I don't know what sort of surveillance gear Ahab might have in place, but I figure it's best if we avoid the beaten path and go overland." She nodded toward the craggy face of the bluff. "Think you two can keep up?"

"Only one way to find out," Kurt said.

She took them to a gap in the rocks and went up, climbing with an athletic ease and flexibility that was hard to match. Kurt and Joe followed, moving a bit slower. Reaching the top, they stood sixty feet above the water.

As Kurt surveyed the route ahead, Joe tapped him on the shoulder, pointing back down the channel. They could just make out the top of the submarine. It grew smaller as they watched, disappearing completely as Rand took it back down to periscope depth.

"Hope he sticks around," Joe said.

Kurt doubted Rand would leave his sister, and honestly didn't think he knew how to pilot the sub. "I just hope he's awake when we get back and not snoring obliviously in the depths."

"We can always swim down to the sub and bang on the hull to get his attention," Joe suggested. "A solid rock always makes for a good door knocker."

Kurt imagined Rand waking suddenly to a visitor twenty feet below the surface. He turned to Pru. "Which way?"

She pointed to the north and took off across the rocky terrain, swinging wide to stay clear of the road and hugging the broken terrain. As they came out onto flatter ground, they found a mix of scrub brush and scraggly vegetation. It offered a modicum of cover.

They moved between the hardy bushes in spurts, watching for trouble and keeping low. Before long they'd crept right up to the edge of the airfield.

Kurt took in the view through unaided eyes. Off to one side, he could see the outline of the control tower against the dark sky. An administrative building was attached to its side. Dispersed around the field were three large hangars, designed to accommodate B-52 bombers.

Kurt noticed Joe looking through a night vision scope. "See anything interesting?"

"There's light coming from the gap beneath the hangar doors," Joe said. "The building connected to the tower isn't fully dark, either. They probably have curtains up or the windows painted over, but they're leaking enough illumination to pick it up."

As Joe spoke, the silence was broken by the rumble of an old diesel engine starting up.

Kurt dropped to the ground. Joe and Pru did likewise.

Off to their left, a narrow band of warm light spread across the apron. Moments later a heavy truck rumbled out from behind one of the hangars. Its partially hooded headlights casting a yellow glow.

The big truck labored trying to pick up speed. With a reverberating clunk it shifted gears, heading toward a second hangar off to their right.

"Fuel truck," Joe said, recognizing the long cylindrical tank on the back of the vehicle.

"Fully loaded based on the lack of acceleration," Kurt added.

It lumbered across the ramp, followed by a couple of men in a golf cart. A wedge-shaped tug like those seen at any major airport came in from the other direction. A second golf cart carrying a group of men came across the field from the control tower. It headed toward the nearest hangar. The doors opened slightly, and the cart slipped inside.

"Didn't expect so much late-night activity," Kurt said.

"Something's brewing," Joe said. "Maybe they're shipping out now that they have the laser."

"Or getting ready to use it," Kurt said. "Either way we need to get inside that hangar and find out what they're up to."

Joe turned the scope toward the aging metal construction. The fuel truck and the golf cart had taken up positions outside the main doors, which opened just enough to let the tug slip inside.

Light spilled out, overwhelming the optics of the scope. The image flared and then darkened as the scope adjusted. Joe got a brief look at the interior as the doors closed behind the tug.

"Large aircraft inside," he said. "Couldn't tell you what type, though. It does appear to be guarded. I see two men with guns. A third just ducked back inside. We could probably hit them from here if we needed to."

The guards out front were not exactly on high alert, but it wouldn't do much good to start a shooting match. Even with the suppressors dampening the sound, Kurt and Joe would just give themselves away once the first man fell.

"Rather not," Kurt said. "Can you think of some way we might get into the hangar that doesn't require making a frontal assault?"

"I don't see any doors on the side or back," Pru said, looking through her scope.

"Neither do I," Joe said. "But I've got an idea. All we have to do is find just the right spot . . ." He was scanning the metal wall. With a grin on his face, he lowered his scope. "Follow me."

CHAPTER 54

Kurt and Pru followed Joe along the edge of the crumbling tarmac until they were directly behind the second hangar. Joe crept in front of them as if he were looking for a secret door.

He paused several times to study the building before moving farther down. He finally stopped for good in front of a vertical support brace, which acted as a binder for two flat wall panels.

"This is it," he said, a look of pride on his face.

"This is what?" Kurt asked from a spot in the brush. "All I see is a rusty wall."

"Not just rusty," Joe said. "Corroded through and through. Water and condensation collect on the panel and trickle down the vertical support brace, pooling in tiny gaps and cracks near the bottom, causing rust. Over time the rust eats its way upward. If this is anything like the hangars I had to patch up when I was in the Navy, you're looking at a sheet of metal that's more like Swiss cheese on the inside. You could push your finger right through it."

In the light of Joe's explanation, Kurt studied the rust more closely. In the dark it was hard to see how extensive the oxidation was, but it had been sitting in the salt air for decades. Several portions at the bottom had crumbled completely away, leaving gaps that were now filled with dirt and debris. Weeds were growing up from another spot.

"So we make our own door," Pru said. "Ingenious."

Joe beamed at the compliment. Kurt sensed the flirting was about to begin again. Before he could head it off, Joe interjected, "As an added bonus, this will let us into the back section of the hangar, where people tend to store junk and trash and spare parts that aren't in high demand. As the only four-time hide-and-go-seek champion of PS 133 in New Mexico, I can assure you that cluttered areas make the best places to hide."

Kurt let Joe have his victory. It was well-earned. "All right," he said. "Let's burrow our way in."

With Kurt standing watch, Joe and Pru crawled forward until they reached the metal wall. They quickly cleared some of the accumulated dirt and then began picking at the wall from the bottom. The first sections crumbled in their hands. They worked their way higher, snapping off large flakes and putting them aside until they'd cleared a half circle of material nearly two feet in diameter. A faint glow could be seen on the ground as light spilled out of the hangar.

Joe poked his head inside. He could hear voices, the rumble of the tug, and the occasional sound of items being moved or repositioned, but as he expected the back wall was a storage area, and directly in front of him lay nothing but dust-covered equipment and junk.

Pulling back, he worked a few more pieces loose and bent one chunk back and forth until he was able to fold it upward. "That's as good as it's going to get."

It would be a tight fit, but Kurt figured they could squirm through.

"I'll go first," Pru said. "I'm the smallest."

Kurt appreciated her dedication, but he figured Joe should do the honors.

Joe got down on the ground and crawled inside. "Once more into the breach," he whispered, ". . . literally."

Kurt followed, hunching his broad shoulders together and then crawling forward on his elbows until he was able to pull his legs through. Pru squirmed through behind him.

A six-foot stack of crates, buttressed by discarded equipment and other items, acted like a wall, shielding them off from the rest of the hangar. But the sound of a stern male voice echoed from the other side of the wall.

The first words they picked out were ominous: ". . . of course," the voice announced in a mournful tone, ". . . the Americans will end up suffering thousands of dead and wounded."

CHAPTER 55

A solid-looking man in his fifties wearing a green flight suit covered in squadron patches stood in front of a large whiteboard in the rear corner of the cavernous, dimly lit hangar. Sitting rigidly in front of him, as if at attention, were two rows of younger men in similar clothing.

The older man was addressed by this group as the flight leader. He was the ranking member of the Yellow Tigers, a faction that had sworn to defend Taiwan's freedom to the end. They were considered a terrorist group within their own country, having been responsible for intimidation, sabotage, and assassinations of several politicians whom they considered complicit with the Chinese Communist Party. Despite their outlaw nature, they maintained a sort of mythical status among many of the island's residents. *Guardians of the flame. Warriors of the last hope.* Some members of the government, the military, and even the civilian security forces were sympathetic to their organization. The flight leader himself had once been a colonel in the Taiwanese air force.

The men sitting in front of him had been selected from among hundreds of recruits. They were the most intense and loyal of the Yellow Tigers.

Two pilots sat in the front row. Each of them roughly around forty years of age. The flight leader had known these men during his time in the military and had recruited them personally. They were lifelong patriots and former captains in their own right.

The rest of the group was younger. Made up of brash, idealistic men in their twenties hardened by the desire to keep their island nation free, tortured by the constant insistence from China that this singular desire would soon be destroyed.

They marked their bodies with tattoos including various symbols of freedom. They saluted and took their name from an old flag, which sported a stylized yellow tiger prowling on a blue background, which represented the sea. The flag had been flown during the brief existence of the Republic of Formosa before it became Taiwan.

These choices were the equivalent of burning their ships as they reached the shore. If the Chinese ever did take the island, these markings and possessions would lead to imprisonment or execution. It made things simple for these men. They would prevail and keep their country free or die trying, but they would never surrender.

Until recently, the group had only limited weapons, ones that would be of little use in a major battle. But thanks to Ahab they now had something more. A chance to strike first, to strike hard, and—if everything worked out right—a way to bring the United States into the war, by making China strike back against them.

"Can we quantify the American losses?" one of the pilots asked in response to the flight leader's ominous proclamation.

"The initial Chinese counter will almost certainly target the American aircraft carrier and its battle group that will begin sailing through the Taiwan Strait this morning. Chinese losses will be significant, but ultimately most of the American ships will be destroyed."

It pained the flight leader to bring death and destruction on men and women he would have otherwise considered allies. But American resolve to defend Taiwan was faltering. It had waned considerably over the years and at this point there was no guarantee that America would commit its most valuable assets to the battle, nor risk a Third World War to defend a tiny island on the other side of the world.

But . . . if American lives were lost first . . . If an American aircraft carrier was destroyed by the Chinese . . .

"Are we sure the Americans will respond in force?" one of the men asked.

Anything could go wrong, the flight leader thought, but there was no nation on earth that responded to naked aggression the way America did. From the Alamo, to Pearl Harbor, to the events of September 11, the American reaction to a surprise attack had always been mass destruction to its enemies wherever they hid in the world. If the Yellow Tigers met with success, that fire would be stoked to a raging inferno and pointed directly at the mainland Chinese. "They will come with fire and brimstone," he assured his men quietly. "But we must make the Chinese sting them first."

The group nodded in unison. Though it was the first they were hearing of the audacious plan, which had been kept hidden for obvious reasons, they understood it implicitly.

Stepping back to the board, the flight leader flipped it over to reveal the battle plan. A chart depicted Taiwan, the coast of mainland China, and the narrow strait in between. Target areas had been marked with coordinates beside them.

"The United States began a series of training exercises over and around our island yesterday," he began. "Those exercises will continue this morning and throughout the day. These war games are being handled in conjunction with our military and some units of the Japanese Self-Defense Force. In addition to the carrier battle group sailing through the Strait, there will be a hundred and twenty American aircraft in the sky. This collection of military force has obviously gained the attention of the Chinese, who are watching very closely. They will have their own aircraft flying and their own military on high alert. Into this powder keg we will toss a lit match."

Turning to the whiteboard, he pointed to various markings. The first was a bright red line that went north from Siabat Island into the strait and then turned toward the Chinese coast.

"Ahab and Saber One will travel to this point," he said, tapping a spot on the map. "At the first waypoint they will shoot down an American airborne tanker, take its place by using stolen transponder codes, and begin to create confusion. The changeover won't be seamless, and before long, the Americans will send fighters to investigate. Saber One will eliminate the approaching jets selectively and then turn for China.

"Not all things can be accounted for," he admitted, "but we have every reason to believe the Americans will scramble more aircraft in an attempt to intercept Saber One before it reaches Chinese airspace. The Chinese high command will be watching this on radar. To them it will appear as if Saber One is leading an American attack force directly for their shore. They will send up their own fighters to meet and intercept this approaching force. But the Chinese fighters will get no closer than the American jets did. Saber One will sweep them from the sky, an act that will only confirm to them that the Americans are attempting a massive airborne strike.

"As radio messages demanding answers fly back and forth, Saber One will turn north toward Shanghai, where the Chinese version of Air Force One should be found approaching the city. Saber One will lock onto it and knock it out of the sky at maximum range, killing the Chinese premier and a significant number of his staff."

"Won't the premier's aircraft turn back for Beijing as soon as the attack commences?" one of the men asked.

"Impossible to say," the flight leader admitted. "They'll be more than two hundred and fifty miles from the combat zone as they approach—more than three times the distance any American missile can cover. With good reason to believe they're outside lethal range, they may proceed to the nearest military base. Or they might wisely turn back toward Beijing. In which case they will most likely go at high altitude and maximum speed, preferring to get as far away from the danger as quickly as possible. In either case they will make a good target. At thirty-five thousand feet, Saber One can hit them at a range of three hundred miles. They will strike the premier's aircraft down before anyone knows what has happened."

The men in the group nodded approvingly. They believed the Chinese premier was planning to declare war against their country. An invasion would follow weeks of bombing and drone attacks in which thousands of their fellow citizens, family members, and friends would be killed. The idea of taking out the Chinese leadership before it could strike first filled them with a sense of justice.

But that was Saber One's job. The men in this group had another task. The flight leader explained this: "While Saber One tracks toward Shanghai, we will be in the C-141 Starlifter, denoted as Saber Two. Saber One will clear a path for us until we reach this point." He tapped the chart a second time, indicating another waypoint that was no more than ten miles off the Chinese coast, well within their territorial airspace.

"Our target is the new military control hub on Langqi Island in Fujian. Much of the PLA's high command will be gathered there to watch the American war games from afar. As soon as we're in range, the payload crew will open the aft door and begin deploying the missiles. They're programmed to open their wings upon attaining free fall. They will then glide down to an altitude of three hundred feet and ignite their boosters. Once active, they will self-guide to the targets, obliterating the command center with most of the Communist Party's generals and admirals inside."

"What's our final weapons count?" one of the crewmen asked.

"You'll be loading twenty-one missiles," the flight leader said. "Unfortunately, three of the weapons have failed prelaunch testing."

"Twenty-one cruise missiles hitting one target ought to get their attention," another crewman suggested.

The flight leader ignored the commentary and kept going. "All of this is a means to an end. It is secondary to the main objective. We must convince the Chinese that the Americans have made this preemptive attack. You will use only American-style English during your radio communications. You have been issued falsified American military documents and identifications. You will keep them on your person and discard your own. We hope, of course, to survive and return in order to continue the fight, but if we're shot down or captured, the ruse must be maintained until the end."

"What's our escape route?" one of the pilots asked. Even those on a suicide mission needed some hope of survival.

The flight leader acknowledged the question. "Once the missiles have been launched, we will turn directly toward Kadena Air Base in Okinawa. This will confirm for the Chinese that the Americans are behind the attack."

"The Chinese will come after us?" the pilot asked.

"They will," the flight leader told him. "Saber One will attempt to cover your retreat, but will itself be moving toward a position of safety. When you reach international waters, set the autopilot, arm the self-destruct switch, and bail out through the aft door. Rescue will be attempted, though it cannot be guaranteed."

The group turned sober and quiet, contemplating the likely end of this mission.

When they'd been quiet long enough, the flight leader snapped them back to attention. "Yellow Tigers!" he shouted. "This is your moment. Freedom for Taiwan! Freedom forever!"

"Yellow Tigers!" the men shouted in unison. "Freedom forever!"

Several rounds of call-and-response followed before the quiet finally returned.

The flight leader looked at his watch. "Go make peace with whatever god you believe in," he suggested. "Do it quickly. Saber One is nearly ready for takeoff. We'll be following as soon as the missiles are loaded."

CHAPTER 56

Kurt, Joe, and Pru sat in stunned silence as the airmen dispersed. When the area had emptied, Kurt risked a peek over the stack of equipment that stood between them and the rest of the building.

In the center of the hangar, he saw a C-141 cargo plane, painted in authentic U.S. Air Force colors. The large, four-engine jet, called a Starlifter in official Air Force lingo, was not as big and burly as the C-17, but it was still plenty capable. It could fly at nearly six hundred knots and had been designed to have outstanding maneuverability at low altitude, so it could dive, climb, and turn with the great agility required to get in and out of short runways near active war zones.

Off to one side of the plane, Kurt saw a baggage train made up of wheeled carts. Sleek-looking cruise missiles of a type he'd never seen before were being loaded onto them. The Starlifter, as the flight leader had said, was Saber Two. The laser-armed Saber One was nowhere to be seen. Kurt guessed it was in the other hangar on the far side of the ramp.

He dropped back down and whispered to Joe. "These men aren't just looking for a way to defend Taiwan. They're going to attack China, pretending to be part of our military."

"And kick off World War Three," Joe said. "I heard them."

No doubt the Yellow Tigers hoped it would be something less than Armageddon, but perhaps they didn't care. "At the very least they want to throw the first punch and ensure we're on their side as the brawl breaks out. It sounds insane, but there's a certain logic to it."

"Especially if they think war is inevitable," Joe said. "But what does this have to do with Ahab? What does he get out of it?"

"Revenge," Kurt said coldly. "On the recording in the C-17, he said he wanted to punish us for putting him out of business. Gushan as well. But that was only the first act, he also wanted revenge on our countries. What better way to do that than tricking them into fighting each other?"

"So the Yellow Tigers are just pawns," Joe suggested.

Kurt nodded. "Ahab needs men who are willing to fly a suicide mission into the heart of Chinese power. Where else is he going to get them?"

Pru spoke up for the first time. Her face was ashen. She knew Ahab as a dangerous, violent man. But she assumed he was at least selfishly rational. "Revenge is one thing," she said. "But if Ahab causes World War Three, the bombs will fall on him just like everyone else. He's not going to escape it."

"He doesn't want to," Kurt said. "He's dying. Those doctors your brother took him to couldn't pull all the toxins out of him. They've been killing him slowly. Looks like he wants to drag the whole world down with him if he can."

Joe clenched his teeth and looked at Kurt in grave seriousness. "Hate to say it. But we might have to reconsider that direct frontal assault." He held up the MP5. "We don't exactly have heavy weapons at our disposal, but if we shoot up the fuel tanks and engines, this thing will never get off the ground."

It was an idea worth considering, but they wouldn't live long after attacking the Starlifter, and their sacrifice would be nothing more than an inconvenience. "Even if we took this plane out, Saber One is the real problem. If it storms into Chinese airspace and blasts the premier's jet out of the sky, it'll be World War Three for sure."

"We need to warn Washington," Joe suggested. "Give our guys a chance to take out Ahab before he enters Chinese airspace."

Kurt had considered that, too. Not only wasn't there much time, but there wasn't much hope of that working. He felt like a man in a maze with no exit. "It won't do any good," he said bluntly. "Ahab will shoot down anything we send up against him. He'll do the same to the Chinese. Assuming his weapon works half as well as the original EAGL system, there's no aircraft in the world that can get within a hundred miles of him."

As Kurt spoke the words, he realized he was mistaken. He turned slowly toward the gleaming C-141 sitting in front of them. "No aircraft," he corrected. "Except this one."

Joe understood instantly. "We need to get aboard this plane before it takes off. It's our only chance to stop this."

Pru offered her services. "Do you want me to go with you?" Her normally defiant expression had returned. She was nothing if not brave.

"No," Kurt said. "I asked you to lead us here. Not join us on a suicide mission. Time for you to go back to the submarine and get out to sea. But I *will* ask you for one more favor."

"Which is?"

Kurt explained what he needed in detail, sent her on her way, and then turned back to Joe. “All right, amigo, you got us into this hangar. Any idea how we can get on that plane without buying a ticket?”

“One or two,” Joe said, glancing around. “But what are we going to do when we get there?”

“This whole thing started with a hijacking,” Kurt said. “I figure we can end it the same way.”

CHAPTER 57

While Kurt and Joe were trying to come up with a way to get on the Starlifter, Ahab was staring into a mirror and looking at a dying man.

The image told him more than any doctor's report could. His condition had worsened. His eyes were yellowing. His skin was gray and colorless, with a texture like old papier-mâché. His appetite had vanished. He tasted bile in his throat while feeling pain in parts of his body he didn't know had nerves.

The doctors had warned him it was coming. They'd told him all his major organs had been affected, but the liver, kidneys, and pancreas had absorbed more toxins than they could shed.

The sickness, combined with the rage he felt, produced the look of a madman, a human turning into a creature, a gargoyle.

Good, he thought, accepting his role, *they should see me as a monster when I turn their world to ash. They should remember me this way.*

With great difficulty he injected a pain-killing cocktail. It was followed by a mix of steroids and adrenaline. These tonics would bring him back to life as they flowed into his system, but the duration was getting shorter with each use.

A knock at the door caused him to cut his eyes toward the hall. "What is it?"

"The flight crews have been briefed," a voice told him through the door. "Saber One is out of the hangar. It's fueled and ready to go. Captain Chen is requesting permission to begin the start-up procedure."

"Is Saber Two ready?"

"It is being towed from the hangar now," the voice said. "Weapons loading will begin shortly."

Ahab looked at the clock. They were ahead of schedule. "Tell Saber One to start its engines and have the laser technicians run their systems checks one more time. I'll meet them shortly."

After the visitor confirmed the order and departed, Ahab gave himself one more injection. This one carried a mix of slowly dissolving amphetamines that would give him the strength and energy that his failing body could no longer produce on its own. He had a few hours of clear-mindedness ahead of him.

It was all he would need.

CHAPTER 58

With his cocktail of medications taking effect, Ahab walked toward a battleship-gray aircraft that the Yellow Tigers had boldly named Saber One. The plane had four wing-mounted engines, a narrow fuselage, and a vertical tail fin capped with a spear-like tube that stuck boldly forward. It was similar in ways to the Starlifter, but different. Every line, every curve, every point on this aircraft suggested the speed and style of a bygone era.

Like an art deco building or classic car, the aging 707 had once represented the zenith of modern design. It was the aircraft that had ushered in the jet age, the icon that spread the logos of Pan American and other airlines around the world. In its later years, the design had gone on to become the stalwart of the American military's aerial refueling fleet, using the designation KC-135.

This particular aircraft had been built and delivered to the United States Air Force in 1985. After years of service, it was sold to the Philippine military, where it performed admirably for another decade or so. It was finally retired to a boneyard after thirty-five years of loyal service.

Through his newfound allies in Taiwan, Ahab had purchased the old military bird. The Philippine government pulled it out of mothballs, brought it up to minimal flight standards, and flew it toward Taiwan, only for the plane to be "lost" en route.

An old plane vanishing over the sea with only two pilots on board did not make the headlines, not even in the Philippines. And no one, other than Ahab and the Yellow Tigers, had given it a second thought since.

Here on Siabat, the tanker had been repaired, refitted, and redesigned. It was now painted to match a KC-135 operating out of Japan. It carried matching registration numbers, correct squadron patches, and even the names of the crewmen displayed on the fuselage in red paint.

It matched the aircraft it was attempting to impersonate in every detail except two: instead of carrying large internal fuel tanks from which short-range fighters could draw jet fuel, it carried heavy electrical generators and Ahab's version of the laser system. The second distinction was a smoked-glass dome sitting on top of the fuselage thirty feet aft of the cockpit. The dome looked vaguely like an observation cupola, but was actually the port through which Ahab's laser would fire.

While the CIA had been correct about Ahab's own abilities, they'd discounted the possibility of him gathering technical personnel under his wing. The Yellow Tigers had taken care of that, finding pilots, mechanics, and weapons specialists, including men and women who'd worked with advanced laser systems on the island.

Between their expertise and stolen technical documents provided by Ridley, Ahab had been able to build his own version of the Enhanced Aerial Gunnery Laser in less than a year. All it lacked was the waveguide and other experimental parts that could only be found on the EAGL aircraft itself.

Knowing he was in a race against time, Ahab had pushed the Tigers to complete the work before he obtained those parts. Now after eight months of work refurbishing the plane and a few short test flights, the faux tanker was being prepared for its first—and almost certainly last—mission.

Ahab boarded the plane at the main door, turning forward and passing the bundles of cables and other electronics that would operate and guide the laser. The laser sat amidships, directly above the wingbox—the most stable part of the plane. The generators were behind it, making the plane into a tail-heavy machine that was cumbersome in takeoff and landing. They needed one good takeoff, Ahab thought. There would be no landing.

He reached the cockpit to find Captain Chen in the left seat. A copilot chosen by Chen sat in the right seat. Behind them was a control space, where a young weapons officer trained on radar and laser operations sat. Ahab took a seat beside him.

"Starting number three engine," Chen said, stretching for the controls and holding the switch down.

As the high-pitched wail of the jet engine rose up, the men pulled on their headsets. Ahab did the same, then pressed the intercom switch to speak. He figured one more rousing word couldn't hurt. "Today shall be a day the world never forgets."

The three men around Ahab nodded. The words meant something different to them than they did to him.

CHAPTER 59

As Saber One started up on the far side of the tarmac, Saber Two was pulled out of its hangar and into the night. The ramp outside the hangar remained dark, illuminated only by a smattering of flashlights and the glow of orange marshaling wands in the hands of the ground crew.

In the dark and tense moment—with their immediate duties and ultimate fates competing for attention—none of the crew took notice of two additional men in green coveralls and ear protection walking slowly behind the plane.

Kurt and Joe had found the rack of uniforms at the back of the hangar, not far from where the briefing had occurred. The coveralls were either actual American flight duty uniforms or extremely accurate copies.

The big aircraft came to a halt ninety feet from the hangar. An auxiliary power unit was started up, providing juice to the aircraft's lighting system. The tail ramp was lowered and tempered lighting came on inside the fuselage.

As Kurt and Joe walked casually toward the open ramp, the second tug came rumbling out of the hangar, towing the baggage train of cruise missiles. It approached the tail ramp and then climbed it slowly, pulling the cruise missiles into the plane link by link.

A group of crewmen checked the missiles as they were loaded, working diligently in the dim space to lock the carts down, ensuring that the missiles were properly held in place until they were needed.

Kurt saw no sign of an advanced launching system. He noticed that the tug remained on the aircraft. It seemed as if they planned on simply shoving the missiles out the back of the plane when the time came for launch, a crude but effective way to get a significant load of ordnance airborne in a short amount of time.

As ground and aircrew moved in and out of the aircraft, Kurt and Joe pretended to inspect the underside of the tail. When several members of the ground crew lumbered down the tail ramp on their way back to the hangar, Kurt spoke.

"This is our chance."

They eased toward the fuselage and walked calmly up the ramp and into the plane. They passed a trio of crewmen who were struggling to secure one of the bulky carts, and then a technician who was securing a new battery pack to one of the missiles. No one looked up.

A few seconds later they arrived near the front of the cargo compartment, where they hid in the darkness behind a stack of survival gear, including two large containers holding inflatable rafts.

From their hiding spot, Kurt and Joe heard the work progressing. Before long, the hydraulics kicked in, raising the tail ramp. The engines began to wail shortly after, and the Starlifter began to move.

Kurt had hoped they would be alone in the cargo compartment, but a group of four men in charge of the payload had remained on board, strapping themselves into a set of folding seats along the fuselage wall.

By now the plane was moving, rumbling, and juddering as it

rolled over the cracked, uneven pavement. It reached the far end of the runway, turned awkwardly, and then paused.

With the wheel brakes on, the engines wound up from a scream to a howl. With the brakes released, the jet began to move. It picked up speed slowly at first and then gained pace more rapidly. Finally, it tilted skyward and raced into the dark night.

It turned north toward China, leveling off at two hundred feet, where it could fly fast and low while remaining under radar until the rendezvous with Saber One.

CHAPTER 60

As the plane settled into the high-speed run, Kurt unzipped the top part of his flight suit, revealing the MP5 he'd smuggled onto the plane. Joe did the same. With the howl of the engines reverberating through the cabin, and the payload specialists strapped into their seats, it was time to move.

"We seem to be flying low to stay below radar," Joe said. "We won't have to worry about depressurization. But those missiles have solid rocket boosters and high-explosive warheads. Let's try not to hit any of them."

Kurt stood. "With a little luck we won't have to fire a shot. If you'll handle the lights, I'll deliver the surprise."

He clicked the safety off his weapon, and stepped out from behind the locker full of survival gear.

Joe moved to the control panel on the wall, which included the switches that operated the interior lighting. As Kurt stepped into the aisle, Joe switched off the lights. The cabin went pitch-dark. After counting to five, Joe flicked them back on.

The men seated against the wall of the plane were surprised by the sudden darkness, but not particularly alarmed. It was an old plane. Things happened. Maybe even the pilots pressing the wrong button.

Their sense of calm vanished when the lights came back on and they found a tall Caucasian man with a submachine gun standing directly in front of them.

Kurt looked over the group, aiming the weapon at the men, while raising a finger to his lips in the international symbol to keep quiet.

The crewmen, belted in and unarmed, froze in place. Kurt felt a tiny moment of euphoria. He had no desire to kill these men. In a different time and place they'd be allies, but he quickly realized a problem. One of the seats was empty.

He turned as the unaccounted-for crewman lunged at him from behind one of the stacked missiles. A blur was all he saw of a metal chain being swung at his head.

Kurt snapped his head back on instinct. The links of metal whipped past his skull, missing him by inches, but wrapping around the MP5 and tearing it from his grasp.

The gun flew across the deck as if thrown from a slingshot. Kurt didn't bother to go after it. He lunged for the attacker, slamming him against one of the carts and blocking him from swinging the chain with an arm bar.

With his right arm immobilized, the man slammed his left fist into Kurt's side, hitting him just above the kidneys. The impact was stunning, but Kurt ignored the pain. He twisted his body, wrenched the man's arm to the side, and flipped him into the fuselage wall.

The crewman pushed off the wall, lunging for Kurt with both hands, but Kurt grabbed him and slammed a knee into his gut. The man doubled over, but made a valiant attempt to get back into the fight. A right cross to the jaw knocked him woozy. He fell to the deck and stayed down.

With one man down, Kurt spun, expecting the others to have

unbuckled and jumped from their seats to mob him. To his great surprise they sat compliantly with their hands in the air. Held there by Joe's arrival and his own MP5.

Kurt was glad to see it. "Better late than never," he joked.

"I was adjusting the lights for the proper mood," Joe said.

Kurt found a roll of duct tape and quickly taped the hands, feet, and mouths of their prisoners. Then he retrieved his weapon, checking it for damage. It appeared to have only surface scratches.

"We've taken the cargo hold," Joe said. "But the cockpit isn't going to fall as easily."

"How many up there?"

"Two pilots and the flight leader," Joe said. "Maybe a navigator on this old bucket, but I didn't see one. Either way, we have to get through a closed door to get the drop on them. And while we didn't want to start shooting back here, we *really* don't want to open fire up there. Not if we need the plane to remain flyable."

It was a dilemma made particularly difficult by the fact that they were traveling along the deck at breakneck speed. The slightest forward push on the control column and they'd end up hitting the sea while going several hundred miles an hour.

"Let's be quick about it," Kurt said. "If everything is running on schedule, the shooting is about to begin."

CHAPTER 61

The flight leader sat behind the captain and the copilot, feeling an odd sense of calm, as if all other thoughts had been swept away. All his life he'd trained to fight the Chinese. Every envisioned scenario had been a defensive battle, a war of attrition, and if they were honest with themselves, all of them ended the same way, with Taiwan's air force spent and a Chinese landing fleet on the way. It felt good to be going on the attack.

"How long until we link up with Saber One?" he asked the pilot.

"Ten minutes," the pilot said.

The flight leader nodded. Holding a headset to one ear, he pressed the intercom button. "We're ten minutes from Saber One," he said. "Sixteen minutes from the launch point. Be ready."

Receiving no reply, he checked the headset connection and then repeated the message. "Payload, do you copy?"

All he heard was static.

He put the headset down in frustration. "Intercom must be out. I'm going to check on the missiles."

He unbuckled his harness, stood up, and stepped toward the cockpit door. A knock sounded as he grew near. He opened the door, expecting the payload chief, and was instead confronted by two men with guns.

Knowing that if they got shot down in China, he wasn't going to go quietly or allow himself to be captured, the flight leader had exercised his prerogative to arm himself.

Reaching for his sidearm, he tried to shout a warning. Before the words left his mouth, Kurt struck him with the rifle stock of his MP5. The blow cracked the flight leader's jaw, the sound barely audible over the engine noise and the rushing wind.

He crumpled backward, landing on the deck as the two men rushed past him to get the drop on the pilots. The two pilots turned at the commotion, twisting in their seats, but strapped in by their harnesses and unable to do much more than look at their attackers in astonishment.

Kurt had entered the cockpit first and leveled his gun at the pilot, while Joe leaned around him to cover the copilot. For the moment both pilots held still, their hands rising off the controls and held up in an instinctive surrender position. The plane remained straight and level, the dark sea and whitecaps whipping past below them.

"Easy," Kurt said. "Nobody move. Joe, how are we doing?"

Joe looked over the panel. "The autopilot appears to be on."

Kurt found that to be a relief, but much like cruise control in a car, it could be disabled by the slightest movement of the controls. He kept his eyes on the pilot's raised hands. If they flinched he would fire.

"Who are you?" the pilot demanded.

"We're Americans," Kurt said. "And we're here to stop you from causing a war."

"You're too late," the pilot replied. "Saber One will begin taking down your aircraft any minute now."

Kurt figured it was a good time to engage in a conversation. The longer the plane flew on autopilot, the closer it would get to Saber One. "How far are we from the rendezvous?"

No one answered.

Kurt pushed the barrel of the gun toward the pilot.

"Nine minutes," the pilot said finally.

Kurt tried to remember the details of the briefing. Saber One's first attack would come against an American tanker. That would be happening in a few minutes.

"Out of the seat," he demanded. He needed access to the radio.

The pilot looked at Kurt and then glanced at the copilot. He put a hand on the harness buckle and released it. Before he could stand, he shouted a command in Mandarin.

Both pilots moved instantly, one lunging for Kurt, the other grabbing for the control stick. The pilot managed to knock the muzzle of Kurt's gun aside as he rushed him. Hesitant to fire inside the cockpit, Kurt released his grip on the gun and grabbed the pilot's lapels as he bulled into him. He used the pilot's momentum to fling him out of the cockpit, both men falling backward into the rear cabin and tumbling over the unconscious flight leader.

The pilot landed on top, grabbing Kurt in a clinch and trying to headbutt him in the face. Kurt managed to turn away at the last instant, feeling a metallic object poking into his lower back. It was the holstered pistol of the flight leader, whose limp body was beneath his. The pilot lunged again with the crown of his head, striking Kurt on the cheek. Kurt brushed off the pain, bucking the pilot enough to free his right arm and reach behind him. He grasped the pistol and swung it high, striking the pilot on the side of the neck with the weapon's handle. The pilot's eyes fluttered a moment and then he collapsed to the deck.

Kurt rose quickly and stepped to the cockpit. He felt his stomach rise as the plane suddenly tilted. Joe had dispatched the copilot with a well-aimed blow to the temple, but the man had fallen forward. Though he was restrained by the belts, his arm flopped onto the control yoke, twisting it to the side and causing the plane to roll.

The autopilot disengaged, the copilot fell backward in his seat, and the yoke came up. As a result, the Starlifter went into a steep, climbing turn.

Both Kurt and Joe fell backward, nearly pulled out of the cockpit by the sudden application of gravity.

CHAPTER 62

Kurt grasped the doorframe to keep himself from tumbling backward. Joe latched onto the arm of the jump seat and held tight.

The nose of the C-141 continued to tilt upward. It was losing speed and rolling. At any moment, it would either stall and fall out of the sky or roll over and nosedive.

Wedging his foot against a notch on the deck, Kurt lunged toward the pilot's seat. He grabbed the backrest and pulled himself forward, struggling to slip into the seat. The plane was pointing upward as if climbing a steep hill. It started to shudder.

"Push the yoke forward," Joe shouted. "Hurry."

Kurt slammed his hand into the control column, shoving it hard. Instinctively, he turned the wheel back to the center. The aircraft nosed over, preventing a stall, and then picked up speed, rapidly transitioning from a climb to a dive.

Kurt was suddenly weightless, thrown upward, along with everything else that wasn't tied down. He slammed into the top of the cockpit and saw the horizon give way to the sea through the windshield.

He grasped the control stick with both hands and pulled firmly back. The g-forces mounted quickly, and Kurt pulled back too hard. The aircraft dipped to within fifty feet of the waves before pitching up and climbing sharply once again.

Joe rushed in, grabbing the controls and stabilizing the roller-coaster motion caused by Kurt's heavy hand. After a few small up-and-down oscillations he had the jet flying smoothly again.

"Okay, we're straight and level."

"Tell me you know how to fly this plane?" Kurt asked.

"Fly it, yes," Joe said. "Land it . . . not so sure."

Kurt figured they'd cross that bridge if they were lucky enough to get to it. He looked over the instrument panel. "We've gone off course. We were heading oh-four-nine. Get us back to our old heading in case anyone's watching."

Joe dropped into the copilot's seat and soon had the plane pointed back in the direction it had been going. With that done, he reactivated the autopilot.

"Assuming the flight plan is still programmed into the computer, this should take us to the rendezvous point. What's your plan once we get there?"

"First we call the Pentagon and warn them," Kurt said, searching the radio stack for a transmitter that would be compatible with NUMA's worldwide network, but wouldn't blow their cover. The only system he found that wouldn't give them away was a data link, the equivalent of an aeronautical text message. He hoped his typing skills were up to par.

"And after that?"

"We knock Ahab and Saber One out of the sky—even if we have to ram them."

CHAPTER 63

Five o'clock in the morning, north of Taiwan, was four p.m. in Washington, D.C. Things were winding down in the city. Half of Congress had already left for the weekend, while staff members of every agency were getting ready to wrap things up.

At the White House it was a different story, a strange message relayed through the National Underwater and Marine Agency had created a sense of confusion. The President was now in the Situation Room along with Vice President Sandecker, the chief of staff, and a dozen members of the military.

They sat dumbfounded, listening in shock as Rudi Gunn, NUMA's second-in-command, read the message aloud over a video link.

"Ahab in possession of the EAGL laser system," Rudi announced. He sounded like a man reading a telegram in a previous century. "Weapon is mounted on an old KC-135 painted in USAF colors and using authentic Air Force transponder codes. His intent is to cause a war between the U.S. and China by attacking them with this aircraft and passing blame to us. First target is actual KC-135 out of Japan now stationed for refueling. We will be in position to stop him shortly, but we cannot do anything about the initial attack. Advise crew to abandon the plane immediately."

"This is astonishing," the chief of staff said.

"I know," Gunn said. "Austin and Zavala—"

"Are out of control," the chief said, cutting him off. "What kind of nonsense are they trying to pass off here?"

"This message is deadly serious," Rudi insisted. "They're obviously embedded in Ahab's operation somehow, but are unable to act until after this first attack. We need to give them the benefit of the doubt."

The President was incredulous. "You want the Air Force to have one of their crews abandon a fifty-million-dollar airplane mid-flight because of a text message? How do we even know this is authentic?"

"The message was sent using a code that only Kurt knows. It identifies him as the sender."

"Unless someone has captured him and is forcing him to transmit this false message," a member of the National Security Council suggested.

"There are red-word protocols in place for that," Rudi explained. "If Kurt was under duress he would have worked those words into the message."

The President turned to the ranking member of the Air Force, a three-star who was assigned to the general staff in D.C. only this week. "Is there a tanker flying the route this message suggests?"

"Condor One Five," the general said. "Part of the training exercise. My information shows it on station now."

The President ran his hands through his hair. The strands that weren't ash gray were tuning white. He admired Austin and Zavala. Hell, he admired the entire NUMA crew, but this . . .

"Do it," he said finally. "Give the order."

"Mr. President—"

"Give the order," the President snapped. "Get those men out of that plane."

CHAPTER 64

Cruising at thirty-five thousand feet, the crew of Condor One Five could just make out the first sliver of dawn on the horizon. The sky was a periwinkle blue up above the earth, melding with a streak of misty orange to the east.

Their orders had them flying a racetrack pattern for the next two hours, rendezvousing with a flight of F-16s, which would tank up on their way over from Japan, and then a flight of F-35s.

As the pilot banked the plane into the first turn of the eight-mile loop, the sun poked up above the horizon, its yellow rays finding the exterior of the tanker and bathing it in a warm glow. The surface of the sea down below remained pitch-dark.

The captain pulled his glasses on. "Sunrise comes early at flight level three-five-oh."

As the plane turned away from the rising sun, the copilot received a coded message on the priority satellite channel. It came directly from the aircraft's squadron commander back in Japan.

"Condor One Five," the commander said, "we have strong reason to believe your aircraft will fall under imminent and lethal attack. This is a direct order to egress the plane immediately. I repeat, entire crew to bail out immediately. You may have only minutes."

The captain froze for a split second. Bailing out of a tanker at thirty-five thousand feet was not the same thing as ejecting from a fighter. The plane had to be depressurized. The crew had to pull on parachutes and squirm through a small hatch in the floor behind the cockpit—an act none of them had really trained for, since parachutes had only recently been put back on board after being removed from most of the Air Force's heavy aircraft for decades.

The copilot looked at a loss for words. The captain responded. "With all due respect, sir, is this some kind of joke?"

"No joke," the squadron commander said. "This order comes directly from the Pentagon. Set that plane on autopilot and get your crew out. Now."

Shaking himself out of shock, the captain gave the order. "Okay, let's move," he snapped. "Dump the pressure. Grab your . . ."

As the captain spoke, a blinding flash outside the window caught his eye. As if the sun were coming up again. But they were heading west now, into darkness. "What the . . ."

The first shot missed the cockpit by a matter of feet, close enough that it dazzled the captain the way a laser pointer did when reflected into the eyes.

The second pulse did not miss. It punched through the fuselage and out the other side, vaporizing the aluminum in its path and causing an instant and catastrophic decompression. The fuselage buckled outward and broke at the bend. It was in the process of coming apart when another pulse sliced through the upraised wing, rupturing a fuel tank and igniting thousands of gallons of kerosene all at once.

Seen from the outside, the tanker appeared in a haze of orange fire. Driven by the heat and pressure, the sphere of burning fuel expanded like the sun and then darkened into a smoke cloud broken by arcs of curling flame. Parts of the aircraft and unrecognizable chunks of metal fell through this cloud, trailing smoke and fire. The plane raced toward the sea like a shower of meteors, destined for a final impact on the surface of the water.

At the military air traffic control center in Japan, the squadron commander who'd given the bailout order stood over the shoulder of a radar specialist monitoring the flight. They watched the aircraft vanish from the screen.

For a brief moment, a larger, more diffuse radar return appeared in its place. It was caused by the radar waves reflecting off the rapidly expanding cloud of fuel and debris. The ghostly return faded quickly, leaving nothing but darkness.

The enlisted air traffic controller knew the plane was gone. He asked the obvious question. "Did they get out?"

The squadron commander shook his head. There was no quick way to get out of a tanker filled with fuel. "No," he grunted. "Not enough time."

The news hit the Situation Room like a tornado. The chief of staff allowed his fury to show. Now, in direct contact with the theater commander, the President demanded action. "Where is the impostor aircraft now?"

"It's over the Strait," he was told. A brief delay followed. "Mr. President, it appears to be heading for China."

The President shook his head in dismay. He looked up at the chief of staff, then over at the director of the CIA, and then at the three-star general representing the Air Force. They were right back where they'd begun, with the stolen laser system heading toward enemy territory. But this time they had it on radar and they had significant forces in the air already. "I want that plane destroyed," he ordered. "Send everything you have after it."

"It will be in Chinese airspace in less than five minutes," he was warned.

"I don't give a damn about airspace," the President snapped. "I don't want it making landfall. Do you understand me?"

"Yes, Mr. President," the commander said. "We should alert the Chinese to the rogue aircraft condition."

The chief of staff leaned in. "If you do that, you'll be telling them that the weapon is there for the taking."

"We'll inform them after the fact," the President insisted. "Just knock that plane out of the sky."

CHAPTER 65

High above the Taiwan Strait, Ahab savored his moment of triumph. The fireball marking the destruction of the American tanker burned like a supernova in the dark sky. He watched it fade and then allowed himself to enjoy the satisfaction. He'd done everything he set out to do, with one final act left to unfold.

"We're being painted by multiple acquisition radars," the copilot announced.

"American fighter aircraft inbound from three directions," the laser technician said. "I count . . . forty-one targets in total."

Ahab looked at the computer display. It was marrying the radar image to the laser tracking system. Swarms of yellow triangles were coming from the north, south, and east. All of them converging on Saber One's course as it headed for the Chinese coast. It was almost too good to be true.

"By all means," he said. "Come and get us."

The weapons technician seemed less pleased. "Forty-one aircraft calculates to at least a hundred and sixty-four air-to-air missiles. We need to hit these fighters before they get in firing range."

"Where would the fun be in that?" Ahab said.

"We could be overwhelmed by a mass attack," the technician insisted.

Ahab had faith in the computer control system. It would pick the targets and vaporize them effectively. It had done so in countless simulations. "Bloody their noses a little bit," he said. "Pick out the nearest aircraft and set them on fire."

The technician chose eight targets and instructed the computer to take them out.

Ahab stayed his hand. "Not all at once," he insisted. "We need them to think they have a chance."

With a tense look on his face, the technician adjusted the program and chose an initial target. He picked the closest American fighter, a fourth-generation F-16. One of the jets that was supposed to refuel from the actual tanker. He pressed the initiate button. "Firing now."

The strange high-pitched whine that accompanied the laser—created by the generators and the power draw—penetrated their headphones. The tone was more like an electronic malfunction on a speaker than the report from a weapon of war. But thirty miles away the F-16 exploded upon contact.

Seconds later the laser fired again, obliterating the F-16's wingman. Before a full minute was up, five American aircraft were plummeting in flames toward the ocean.

Ahab chortled with glee. "They'll never turn back now."

CHAPTER 66

From the cockpit of the Starlifter, Kurt and Joe saw explosions in the dark. The massive fireball from the tanker came first. The others flashed moments later as Ahab's laser struck the F-16s and F-35s out of the sky.

"Our guys are trying to take him out before he gets to China," Joe said.

"Falling into his trap," Kurt replied. "How close are we to Saber One?"

The autopilot had followed a prearranged flight plan and brought them up to thirty-five thousand feet. The sky was brightening with each passing second.

"There," Joe said, pointing to a gray outline ahead of them.

"Go for him," Kurt said. "With everything we've got."

Joe took over from the autopilot and pushed the throttles to the fire wall. The engines went from cruise power to takeoff power. The big plane picked up speed and Joe eased the control stick to the left. "Here goes nothing."

Joe turned the plane to the left, putting a foot on the rudder to coax the nose around. The big plane rolled with surprising agility and nosed down a bit. It picked up speed in a shallow dive, toward Saber One's tail.

"Saber Two, continue your turn," a voice on the radio demanded. "Saber Two, do you copy?

Joe kept the nose down and kept his eye on the looming target as it grew larger with every passing second, and then with a suddenness that defied the size of the aircraft, the old KC-135 turned hard to the right and pulled up.

Joe pulled back on the yoke, but the Starlifter was carrying too much momentum to match its target. It thundered past, missing Saber One's tail by a hundred feet.

Joe grunted as the g-forces hit. "Damn," he said. "Sorry."

They'd missed what might have been their only chance.

Aboard Saber One, the sudden turn had almost thrown Ahab out of his seat. He cursed at Captain Chen. "What the hell are you doing?"

"Saber Two tried to ram us," Chen said. "It almost took our tail off."

"What?"

Chen pointed at the targeting radar. A bright orange line revealed Saber Two's sudden change in course and its near fatal pass just behind their tail.

"Why would they do that?"

"I have no idea."

"Where is it now?"

"Trying to get in behind us."

Ahab fumed at the disruption to his plan. He looked through the small windows in the cockpit's ceiling. From the angle they were flying he could see the Starlifter trailing them. It turned as they turned. Pushing hard as they pushed. These acts could not be a malfunction.

"The Chinese must have an agent embedded in your group," Ahab snapped. "Traitors in your midst."

"I don't think so," Chen replied. "I've known these men for years."

"Then what explains this madness?"

As Chen brought the aircraft around, Saber Two followed. It was stalking them. Ahab turned to the laser technician. "Shoot it down."

The technician didn't hesitate. He locked onto the Starlifter and engaged the laser. The generators squealed. The green lights lit up. But when he pressed the fire button nothing happened.

"What's wrong?" Ahab demanded.

"They've dropped below our tail. The computer won't allow us to fire."

Ahab looked out the skylight windows again, but the Starlifter was no longer in sight. It had widened its turn and gone below them. If they fired at it now, they'd slice off their own tail.

"Prove to me your worth," Ahab said to Chen. "Shake them loose."

Chen whipped the big plane around in the other direction, but just as the Starlifter came into view, it vanished again. It would be no easy task.

The two planes wheeled and turned, switching positions twice, then three times. Joe was sweating as he attempted to stay out of the firing line. His path wasn't as simple as it sounded. When Saber One turned to the right, he had to take the Starlifter to the left for a moment and then back to the right. It was the only way to stay behind and below, and out of the laser's deadly field of fire.

With each turn he lost some speed. With each loss of speed, it became more difficult to stay in the right spot.

"We're drifting back," he said. "Another couple of turns and he'll have us."

"We need to stay in the fight," Kurt said. "As long as he's tangling with us, he can't focus on our fighters or the premier's plane."

"I'm on it," Joe said.

He brought the Starlifter around for another pass, but Saber One had other ideas. It straightened up and turned due west. Heading toward China.

Joe had to dive to stay out of trouble, but the added speed helped him turn the corner and line up once more behind Ahab's deadly gunship.

A blur in the sky signaled more laser fire. It flashed repeatedly, but the beam wasn't aimed at Kurt and Joe this time. It fired diagonally across the Strait, pulse after pulse burning the air in the general direction of Taiwan.

A new line of explosions lit up the morning sky. The first batch were smaller flares. Like matches lit and thrown in the air, they burned out quickly. Kurt lost count of how many as Saber One eliminated a volley of air-to-air missiles. When the missiles were dealt with, it turned its wrath on the aircraft that had launched them.

Several larger explosions bloomed, each one marking the destruction of an F-16 or F-35 that had pressed close enough to get off a shot.

Just as promised, Saber One was clearing the sky of any threat. Based on Kurt's rough estimate it would have a chance at the premier's aircraft over Shanghai any moment.

"It's now or never," Kurt said. "Dive hard and come up from underneath him."

Joe pointed the nose down and dove as Kurt suggested. The old Starlifter picked up speed rapidly and was soon shaking as it approached its maximum safe airspeed.

"Come on, you bucket of bolts," Joe said. "Go."

Aboard Saber One the danger became patently clear. "They're going to hit us from below," the laser tech said.

"Shoot them down!"

"They're still underneath our firing plane."

Ahab's mind spun. There was only one answer. "Take us down," he shouted. "If they want to stay low, we will go lower."

Chen shoved the controls forward. Saber One pitched down, racing to stay ahead of the old Starlifter.

As the plane picked up speed, the weapons tech looked at his screen. The Starlifter was so close, it couldn't be seen on radar, but through an optical tracker it appeared near enough to block out most of the sky.

He held his breath. After all the sudden maneuvers, he was just trying hard not to throw up. Slowly, incrementally, the cargo plane drifted back. Saber One was winning, but only by trading altitude for speed.

A flashing icon and a beeping sound in his headset told him a new target had appeared on the screen. Not directly behind them or across the gap where the last American fighters were, but out in front of them at the very edge of radar range, nearly two hundred and forty miles away.

The computer soon marked the target based on the radar return.

It was identified as a 747-800. Its designation was denoted as Air China 3701: the Chinese premier's plane.

The specialist tapped the screen to lock on. The targeting system focused. The data was confirmed. He pressed the fire button, but nothing happened. To his surprise the target had vanished from the screen.

"What?"

The technician cycled the screen, but it didn't help. The premier's plane was gone.

Saber One had dropped too far from its perch to see over the curvature of the earth. With each thousand feet of altitude it lost, the maximum range of the laser shrank by miles. Air China 3701 was still out there, somewhere over Shanghai, but Saber One could no longer see it. And it couldn't hit what it couldn't see.

The weapons officer was gutted. Their chance had come and gone. And with the steep dive continuing at full speed, it wouldn't come around again.

CHAPTER 67

Joe kept the Starlifter's nose pointed down even as the plane threatened to shake apart. With Saber One diving as well, the two aircraft were now engaged in a massive game of chicken from which neither could safely exit.

If Joe pulled up first, Saber One would fry them from close range. If Saber One's pilot got cold feet and leveled off, Joe would have the speed to slingshot forward and rip into Saber One from below.

Glancing at the dials on the instrument panel, Joe saw the airspeed indicator above the redline, the engines hitting an overspeed condition, and the altimeter unwinding like a broken clock. Thirty thousand feet had already become twenty thousand, it would be fifteen thousand in less than a minute.

He pulled back on the throttles a fraction. He wasn't sure how much the old plane could take.

They crossed the Chinese coast in a pair of matching dives. Two huge planes streaking toward destruction at the steepest of angles.

They closed in on ten thousand feet. Alarms began to go off. Joe had no idea what they were, but they couldn't possibly mean anything good.

They passed eight thousand feet without either pilot letting up.

"Kurt?" Joe asked.

"He's going to pull up," Kurt insisted.

"How can you be sure?"

"Because if he doesn't, we win."

Win?

Joe guessed that was one way to look at it. If both planes went full lawn dart mode, the rest of Ahab's plot would be foiled. It was something, though Joe wouldn't necessarily call it a win.

As they passed through five thousand feet, another alarm went off, but neither Kurt nor Joe bothered to look for the source. With the aircraft shaking almost uncontrollably, they passed through four thousand and on down.

Saber One grew closer and closer until it filled the windshield. And then, with a suddenness that suggested the plane had been yanked skyward by a giant string, it vanished from sight. Its tail-heavy condition had allowed it to flip the nose skyward with surprising agility.

Its pilot had had enough.

Joe followed suit, figuring this was their chance. He grunted as he pulled back on the control column. The old plane shuddered, threatening to break apart. Its wings leveled quickly, but even then its momentum continued to carry it downward like a car hydroplaning toward a guardrail.

With agonizing sluggishness, the descent slowed and then stopped. They were flying at a height of two or three hundred feet now, and heading directly for the spine of a jagged hill, which threatened to cut the plane in half.

Joe rolled the wings to the right, flipping the plane onto its side for a brief second. The belly of the aircraft missed the mountaintops like a matador avoiding the horns of an angry bull. Joe snapped the wing back down and continued on, trying once more to cut under Ahab's plane.

Though it had pulled out of the crash dive, Saber One had still come down to the deck, just at a more controlled pace. It was now racing along at an absurdly low altitude.

Joe chased it once more, locking in behind it as both planes thundered across the undulating hills, heading overland across the Chinese countryside.

"No more room to get under him now," Joe said dejectedly. "Not sure we can catch him, either. At least we've brought him down from the stratosphere. At this altitude, the laser might have an unobstructed range of ten to twenty miles. And that's if a mountain doesn't pop up in the way. They can't hit the premier's plane from here."

"One small victory," Kurt said.

The data link chirped, a message popped up. It came from Rudi. **Our jets are turning back. Chinese forces mobilizing nationwide. No response to attempted contact. President asks that you do what you can.**

It was a second victory, Kurt thought. Or part of one. Though the Chinese mobilization could turn it all into a defeat, and they still had to prevent Ahab from wiping out the Chinese air force or pivoting to whatever alternate target he and the Yellow Tigers deemed worthy of destruction.

"Stay in behind him," Kurt said. "I'm going to rattle his cage."

CHAPTER 68

Aboard Saber One, Ahab fumed at the disruptions to his plan. He seethed at being thrown around the cockpit as the pilot whipped the big plane about. The near fatal nosedive had ended only as he'd ordered the pilot to pull up. The premier's plane was now out of range.

He wondered to himself how his plan had gone so far off the rails.

As if in an answer to his question the cockpit radio squawked for all of them to hear. A confident, cocky, and irritating voice came over the airwaves and through the speakers.

"That was a fun ride," Kurt Austin's unmistakable tone announced. "But it's over now. Time to get off the roller coaster."

Ahab was as shocked to hear Austin's voice as Kurt had been to hear and see Ahab on the video aboard the C-17.

"Despite wanting to shoot you out of the sky," Austin continued, "our Air Force turned back before they crossed into Chinese airspace. Which means your future is to die at the hands of the Chinese or end up as their prisoners."

Listening to Austin, Ahab slammed his fist on the panel in front of him. The screens around him flickered and blinked. "How could this be?"

The rage he felt was uncontrollable. Austin had found him again. Was hunting him again. And though Ahab was in possession of the most powerful weapon on earth, he still could not strike Austin down.

"To the Yellow Tigers," Austin continued. "I understand your desire to defend your island, but this will not help. You might as well turn around and head for Taipei, unless you prefer the idea of Chinese prison over one in Taiwan."

Chen looked at Ahab with an expression that suggested defeat. Finding no solace in Ahab's angry face, he looked past Ahab to the weapons specialist. "Any sign of the premier's aircraft?"

The specialist had been watching the radar. "It was there for a second. But we dove too quickly."

Chen looked at their benefactor. "The American is right," he said. "We've failed. We should turn back."

"No," Ahab snapped. The feeling of being trapped in his own scheme was almost too much to bear. He needed a way out. A way to reignite the fire.

"The premier may be out of our reach," he said, "but the high command will still be gathered at the control hub. If Saber Two won't take it out, we can. A thousand videos of an American aircraft destroying their station will be impossible to deny. The Chinese people will never believe it wasn't American treachery. Survivors in the high command will demand retribution. The premier will be afraid of looking weak. We can still light the fire."

"We can do great damage to the aboveground buildings," Chen said. "But the laser will not be effective against the hardened bunker."

“Did you really board this plane expecting to return home?” Ahab asked. “Fly the plane into the building. The impact will kill everyone inside.”

Chen nodded. They’d all expected to die. At this point it was preferable to a life in prison and disgrace. He gave the order to the copilot. “Plot a course. We’ll take out the high command.”

CHAPTER 69

In an office on the second floor of a building attached to the new command center, Major Gushan sat at the desk he'd been assigned to when they returned from the Arctic. It was a humiliating duty, only one step above house arrest, but at least he still had his rank.

This morning he'd arrived before dawn, intending to appear as the most earnest desk jockey in the nation. Settling in, he quickly began work on an endless list of mundane tasks.

But the nature of the morning changed rapidly. A buzz throughout the building grew into frenzied activity. Out a window, he saw escalating movement. Pilots were being shuttled out to their aircraft in a hurried fashion. Fuel trucks and vehicles carrying weapons were charging about wildly. Farther off, he saw mobile antiaircraft trucks raising their launchers and moving into defensive positions around the perimeter.

He put it off as a drill, timed to coincide with the American war games. A surprise drill to test readiness, perhaps, but a drill, nonetheless. Then the air-raid sirens began wailing and nonessential personnel were ordered to take shelter, and he began to think it might be something more.

In the midst of all this, his phone began to chirp. A call was coming in on an encrypted communications app. It was the kind of app most Chinese were banned from using, but one that had been approved for men like Gushan, who needed it to stay in touch with clandestine contacts.

Gushan picked up the phone and studied the alphanumeric code that populated the top half of the screen. Puzzled, he put an earpiece in and answered the call. A breathless voice spoke to him in a South African accent.

"This is Rand. I'm calling with a warning. Ahab is coming. Coming for you."

Between the activity on the base and the out-of-the-blue nature of the call, Gushan found himself momentarily frazzled. "Rand?" he said. "What are you talking about? Ahab? Ahab is dead."

"He's alive," Rand insisted. "He has a plane. Like the one you were trying to nick from the Americans in the Arctic. He's coming for you. He's coming for China. Austin says he's trying to cause a war."

"Austin?" Gushan said. "Is he behind this?"

"Listen to me, man," Rand insisted. "I'm trying to warn you. Ahab's dying. He's trying to wreck the world on his way out."

To Gushan's absolute shock, the antiaircraft batteries fired off three volleys of long-range missiles in rapid succession. The building shook, the windows rattled. Outside, the crimson tails of the rockets hustled skyward, trailing white smoke.

Gushan steadied, putting the warning and the events together. At the same time, Pru took over the call, relaying everything she knew. "You have to tell your leaders America is not attacking. You have to make them listen."

By now pandemonium had erupted across the base, reaching a crescendo as a squadron of supersonic J-20 jets raced into the sky with afterburners screaming. It seemed like war had already come.

Gushan finished the call and then rushed from his desk, heading out into the main part of the building. Pushing past several staff members coming in the other direction, he rushed down the nearby hallway. A short turn took him to the stairwell. Two flights led him thirty feet below ground level, where he came face-to-face with the guard at the command center door.

Gushan offered his badge, but was denied entry.

"Understood," he said casually, "but I have an urgent message."

He threw a gut punch into the guard as he spoke. The man dropped to one knee. With two additional moves, Gushan subdued the guard and rushed into the main room of the command center's hub.

The room was shaped like a shallow auditorium, with long flattish steps leading down. The combined group of generals and admirals known as the high command were gathered near the front, looking up at a big screen depicting everything that was happening off the coast.

Gushan saw yellow trail markers that charted the paths of American jets. They came toward the coast from multiple directions. He saw blue boxes that represented the American carrier group still off to the north. Flashing white indicators suggested inbound missiles from the American planes. Even from his perspective, it looked like an airstrike was underway.

Red indicators marked Chinese units. The sheer number of them revealed aircraft scrambling all over the country. Targets had been picked out. Ports and airfields in Taiwan, Japan, and the Philippines. The American carrier group heading into the Strait was target number one. Closer to home the main focus were the pair of American jets that had crossed the Strait, dropped down to treetop level, and were now racing across the countryside. At least two squadrons were being vectored to intercept.

Gushan ran toward the group, finding Admiral Li of all people. Li's was the only face he really knew. "Keep the planes on the ground," he shouted. "You're just sending those men to their deaths."

Li was shocked. "What are you doing in here, Major? We're under attack!"

"It's not the Americans," Gushan insisted. "It's Ahab."

No one knew what he was talking about.

The main door flew open. A mob of military police rushed in. On-screen, the recently launched fighters began to explode, one after another after another. Radio chatter confirmed the disaster.

"We've been hit . . ."

"Bail out . . ."

"No missile lock . . ."

"Ahab is a terrorist," Gushan shouted while moving to stay ahead of the security team. "He's working with the Yellow Tigers."

The name of the group was well-known. It stirred some interest, but by now the MPs had surrounded him. They tackled him to the floor.

Gushan didn't resist. He shouted to Admiral Li instead. "Ahab gave them the laser off the American plane. The one you and I were trying to recover. He's using it to stir up this fight. What else could be shooting our planes and missiles out of the sky?"

"Preposterous," someone shouted.

"Get him out of here," another member of the brass yelled.

Two hulking security men were now piled on top of Gushan. They held him down, pulling his arms back behind him and cuffing him. As they lifted him up, Gushan briefly caught sight of the board. The tracking lines showed the Chinese planes and missiles vanishing from radar long before they got into firing range. Farther off, the lines demarking the paths of at least two dozen American aircraft had ended mysteriously as well.

"Did our jets take out the American planes?" he grunted.

No answer.

The guards started hauling Gushan out of the room.

"If not us, then who?"

One of the guards jammed a baton into Gushan's stomach to silence him. Gushan buckled and gasped for air. Still, he didn't resist, keeping his focus on the generals. "What about the missiles?" he called out.

The men gathered in front of the large screen studied the things Gushan was referring to with new eyes. Chief among them was General Wei, Supreme Commander of the Eastern Theater for the PLAN.

As the man upon whom immediate decisions rested, Wei had felt particularly baffled by what he was seeing. The leading American planes were slow and performing oddly. Radar cross sections recognized them as "heavies." Big jets. Possibly B-52s, but more likely cargo transports or even airliners. They had been flying erratically, changing course multiple times a few miles offshore, almost crashing into one another and then diving maniacally toward the coast.

The flight plan made little sense. Leading an attack with big, slow planes made even less. It had been suggested they might be carrying paratroopers, but two platoons of airborne soldiers wouldn't last long in even the smallest Chinese hamlet.

The vanishing American interceptors were another mystery. They had been converging on the larger aircraft before disappearing from view.

"Super stealth," someone had suggested, using the name of a rumored American technology that could turn any aircraft invisible at will.

Wei thought the idea far-fetched. But even if the Americans had such a system, there would be no reason to wait until they were halfway across the Strait to turn it on.

Radar had also confirmed the Americans launching missiles, but not so much as a single bottle rocket had landed anywhere in China. So many things about the airstrike seemed off, yet it was undeniably heading their way.

The door at the back of the great room banged open as the guards reached it with Gushan.

Wait," the Supreme Commander ordered.

The guards stopped and propped Gushan up.

Wei turned to Admiral Li. "Is this laser weapon a reality? Could it do what we've seen here?"

Admiral Li nodded. "It was aboard the plane the Americans lost in the Arctic. It could very well be responsible for shooting down all these aircraft and missiles. But that doesn't mean it's not being flown by the Americans. If we sit back and let them eviscerate our forces . . ."

It was the same argument that had been going on for the last twenty minutes. Hundreds of aircraft were being readied to fly, missiles were being unlocked and prepared for launch, some at the invading aircraft, others at bigger targets.

The Supreme Commander faced a great dilemma. He almost had to retaliate at this point. But something felt off.

The voice of an aide called out an alert. "Remaining American aircraft turning back. Other than the two heavy jets, I detect no incursions into our airspace."

The announcement gave Wei some breathing room. He turned to the board once more. "Their fighters are turning around," he said. "But why, then, do these two jets push on?"

"Because one of them is being flown by the Yellow Tigers," Gushan insisted. "And the other is controlled by a pair of Americans who are attempting to stop the Tigers from causing World War Three."

Caught halfway between Gushan and the Supreme Commander, Admiral Li found himself in a unique position. He wasn't an expert at too many things, but reading a room was one of them. The situation had turned. He saw an opening and sidled up to General Wei.

"General," he said, whispering like a snake charmer. "There could be an opportunity here. One we shouldn't pass up so hastily."

CHAPTER 70

Thirty miles from where they'd come across the coast, the two aging jets charged across the landscape at shockingly low altitude. They rose to avoid jagged bluffs, dropped down on opposite sides, and weaved back and forth as they flew between peaks of higher elevation.

Animals and agricultural workers on a terraced field snapped their heads around as the big jets suddenly appeared, raced down the valley beside them, and disappeared beyond the next rise.

If not for the incredible skill of the two pilots, both aircraft would have already crashed into a hill or had a wing ripped off by cutting a corner too sharply.

At each passing moment, the laser in Saber One fired repeatedly. Not at the Starlifter, which remained locked in its shadow, but at other targets: Chinese targets.

Radio chatter suggested several top-of-the-line J-20 aircraft had been obliterated. A swarm of ground-to-air missiles were wiped out seconds later.

"Damned impressive system," Kurt said.

The idea that a single forty-year-old plane could hold off the combined efforts of the world's two most powerful militaries boggled the mind. A second wave of missiles was taken out at long range, and then suddenly, quite miraculously, they stopped coming.

"Is this good or bad?" Joe wondered.

"No idea," Kurt said. "But I think we're on our own."

A wide, muddy river appeared up ahead. Saber One crossed above a smattering of industrial buildings and broke hard to the right. It flew lower and lower, until it was skimming the surface.

Joe matched the turn, continuing the high-speed chase over the last row of hills and down to the river. His heart was pounding. Handling the unfamiliar plane demanded tremendous effort and intense concentration.

"Where are we heading?" Kurt asked.

Joe looked at the moving map display. "This is the Min River. It leads to Fuzhou and Langqi Island. They must be going for the Chinese command center."

As they raced along the channel, the laser flashed in multiple bursts, ripping into the industrial buildings along the banks. The buildings erupted in flames, as if they'd been hit with firebombs. A refinery was the next target. It became a hundred-acre inferno in a matter of seconds.

"And they're going to leave a trail of destruction along the way," Joe added. "We'd better do something quick."

"I have an idea," Kurt said, "but we've got to take the lead."

"They're flying on the deck. I can't get under them."

Kurt was heading toward the cargo compartment. "Find a way" was all he said as he disappeared through the door.

Joe had a vague idea what Kurt was planning, but he couldn't imagine how they were going to get in front of Saber One without getting shot down.

Racing along the river with no more than twenty feet of space between the underside of the aircraft and the water, Joe's attention alternated between the plane in front of them, the moving map display, and the jagged terrain on the sides of the river.

A set of barges appeared up ahead. Tied up, sitting empty and riding high, they might as well have been a ten-story building in the middle of the waterway.

Saber One avoided them to the right.

Joe banked left. Seconds later the two planes were tucked in together once again.

Apartment blocks and condo towers raced by on either side. Joe could only imagine what the people of the city thought waking up to see two giant American aircraft streaking past.

Looking farther ahead, Joe saw large towers made of metal latticework on both sides of the river. They held power lines.

Saber One rose up, climbing above them. Joe kept Starlifter's nose down and risked going underneath. The plane made it through without getting ensnared. It picked up a few hundred yards on its quarry. Maybe, just maybe, Joe had found his way.

A second set of power lines appeared. Joe repeated his daring maneuver as Saber One took the safe route. The gap closed even farther.

Glancing at the map, Joe could see a different issue up ahead. Two miles on, a bridge crossed the river, and then another and another. Strangely, Joe remembered someone calling Fozhou the city of bridges. A quick glance at the map had proven this to be true.

If he could dive under some of them, or skim the tops of the lower ones, while Saber One climbed to fly above them, each bridge would pull him closer to taking the lead. If he managed to gain the lead by even a hundred feet, it would give Kurt the opportunity to enact his plan.

He tapped the intercom button. “You're going to get a chance in a few minutes,” he said. “Whatever you have in mind, be ready.”

Kurt lowered the tail ramp at the back of the plane. A hurricane of noise and wind stormed in. Out beyond he saw the rushing water and the mottled landscape roar past.

The plane dipped. The ramp almost hit the water. The power lines flashed overhead, disappearing behind them.

Silently, Kurt marveled at Joe's flying ability. If he had joined the Air Force, he would have been a test pilot or a member of the Thunderbirds. With Joe at the controls, he knew they had a chance.

Ignoring the shuddering airframe and the howling wind, Kurt went from one cart to another, releasing the brakes and disconnecting the tie-down chains that held them in place.

The plane pitched again. This time pulling up. A low concrete bridge flashed past. A truck tumbled over on its side, lifted off its wheels by the Starlifter's wake turbulence. A second bridge was skimmed without incident. By the time they skipped over the third, Kurt had freed the entire baggage train.

He climbed on the tug that had been used to pull the missiles onto the plane and prepared to push them out.

Without warning, the jet banked to the right. And instead of a shallow bump upward and quick drop down, it climbed sharply as if trying to scale a mountain.

The baggage train pulled tight. The tug began to slide backward. Kurt stepped hard on the brake and the big tires gripped the deck and held firm.

Through the open door, Kurt saw the city of Fuzhou with all of its high-rise towers, condos, and factories. He saw a bridge pass beneath them, then four more, all packed together across a narrow gap where the river turned to the right.

The first bridge was a low concrete span. It was followed by a pair of suspension bridges boasting tall, white towers. Shimmering steel cables stretched from the towers to the bridge deck like the strings of a giant harp. A bullet train was forging its way across one bridge on a set of tracks.

Both bridges were high enough that Joe might have flown under them, but another pair of older and lower bridges blocked their path.

The area known as Five Bridges retreated rapidly behind the plane as Joe dove to the river once more. They were heading east now, directly toward the Chinese command center.

Joe's voice came over the intercom. "One more bridge up ahead. It's now or never."

Kurt revved the engine and then put the tug in gear.

CHAPTER 71

In the front of the plane, Joe watched a colorful palette of warning lights come on. The plane had been overstressed. There was an issue with the hydraulics. Worst of all the engines were overheating. A condition pilots called overtemp. The Starlifter had been going too fast, for too long, at too low an altitude. The engines were simply not designed to run at full power in the thick air for that length of time.

Saber One seemed to be dealing with the same problem. Thin trails of smoke now streamed from two of its four engines. It had slowed enough for Joe to think he could get past it at the next bridge. But with his own overtemp issue Joe had to reduce power.

It was a temporary fix. Damage had been done. Catastrophic failures were imminent. At the same time, they were only five miles from the control center. Less than two minutes at these speeds. One way or another that marked the end of the road.

The two jets roared along the water, whipping up the surface in a cloud of mist and spray that trailed them like a pair of water demons or angry specters.

They roared toward the Langqi Minjiang Bridge, one of the largest in China. The span between its great towers stretched over eighteen hundred feet. A gap of two hundred feet stood between the deck and the water. High enough and wide enough for the large jets to fly under with relative ease.

Joe could see the problem now. Saber One was going to stay along the deck. Their last chance to make up ground would never happen. The Chinese command hub lay on an island two miles beyond the bridge.

The planes thundered closer. Joe willed Saber One to climb, but it stubbornly clung to the river, blocking him. He had no choice. He shoved the throttles to full, gained what speed he could, and pulled back on the stick.

Aboard Saber One the laser technician saw the Starlifter rise. It suddenly appeared into the targeting field. He'd been focusing on the command center up ahead, but this was their chance to deal with the Americans. He tapped the screen, locked onto their pursuer, and activated the laser.

The mirrors changed their position and focused. The high-pitched squeal sounded once again. The laser fired.

But instead of a fuel-driven explosion, all he saw through the camera was a sudden wall of darkness followed by a small eruption of dust and debris.

Saber One had flown under the bridge and the six-lane concrete deck had come between the laser and its target. The powerful beam vaporized a section of the concrete, superheating it instantly and causing thousands of small fragments to eject outward in a thermal explosion. A section of steel girder took the second shot, melting as the laser burrowed through it. A third shot sliced one of the harp-string-like cables, while a fourth blasted the main tower.

The damage was significant, but the bridge stood. The Starlifter passed overhead, shielded by its bulk. When the technician reacquired the pursuing plane, it was directly above them. It dove downward and pulled in front.

In the cockpit of the Starlifter, Joe braced himself for the superheated beam that would rip the plane apart. It didn't come. On the far side of the bridge, he pushed the nose down, cutting in front of Saber One and hoping Kurt was ready.

Spotting Saber One beneath the bridge, Kurt stomped on the tug's accelerator and sent the baggage train of missiles down the ramp and out through the back of the plane.

The carts were torn from each other by the Starlifter's slipstream, and they tumbled in haphazard fashion as they went out the door. Kurt drove the tug right to the end, leaping off before it hit the ramp, and grabbing for anything he could find that might keep him from rolling out along with it.

With his arm hooked into a cargo net, he watched the trail of destruction unfold.

The missiles, carts, and the tug fell like a metal avalanche toward Saber One. One projectile hit the top of the plane, another hit the tail, a third hit the wing. One of the carts was sucked into an engine, causing it to flare like a Roman candle. The tug fell last and most true. It rolled over once, heading directly for the cockpit.

Inside Saber One, the weapons technician had reacquired the Starlifter after the planes emerged from opposite sides of the bridge, but he hesitated, considering what might result if they shot it down while it was above and directly in front of them.

Looking out the cockpit window, he was astonished by how large and close it appeared. He was even more surprised by the barrage of projectiles pouring out of it and into the sky before them.

Ahab stood in shock, eyes wide, mouth agape. The plane shook as it was hit in various places. One of the cruise missiles tumbled past them, missing by mere feet. A cart hit somewhere on top of the fuselage, gashing it. Something hit the right wing, jarring the plane.

Ahab focused on the next object. The squat angular tug flipped slowly as it grew closer.

"No!" he shouted.

The thousand-pound tug crashed unstoppably through the cockpit. It destroyed the control space, killing Ahab and the others instantly.

From Kurt's perspective they'd scored a direct hit. Five of them, in fact. But the strike to the front of the plane was a fatal blow. Saber One careened out of control, turning slowly to the left as it rose and wavered. The right wing caught fire as venting fuel was ignited by the burning engine.

To Kurt's astonishment, the old plane refused to come apart. Instead, it veered gracefully toward the rugged hills on the left side of the river, trailing smoke and fire, then plowed into them at three hundred miles an hour.

The plane folded up on impact, compressing accordion style and exploding in a reverberating thud.

One look told Kurt there would be nothing left of the laser, the crew, or Ahab. He made his way to the intercom, buzzed Joe, and gave him the good news.

"Take us home," he suggested, "before the Chinese decide we might be useful to them somehow."

"Sorry, amigo," Joe said. "No can do. Engines have been used up. We need to set this thing down before they come apart."

Kurt took that stoically. "I thought you said you didn't know how to land this plane."

Joe's reply was confident, but noncommittal. "I guess we're going to find out."

CHAPTER 72

Joe put the cargo plane down at a small airport five miles from where Saber One had crashed. The landing was a little rough, especially with two of the engines smoking, and he pulled onto the grass as soon as he could, rather than continuing on the pavement.

He hit every kill switch he could find as soon as the Starlifter came to a halt, cutting off all fuel from the engines, which were glowing red-hot.

Emergency vehicles reached them quickly, dousing the plane in foam as a precaution. Military vehicles followed, and Kurt, Joe, and the surviving Yellow Tigers were taken into custody.

After a day in some kind of military prison, Kurt and Joe were transferred to a local apartment on the eighth floor of high-rise building, not far from the Five Bridges area.

They were held under a sort of house arrest, with guards placed outside the doors, down the halls, and in the lobby. Aside from a few initial questions, they were neither interrogated nor harassed. They were even allowed to spend an hour per day in the small courtyard connected to the building, as long as the guards came with them.

After a week without even a phone call, Kurt figured they were going to be there for a while and decided he would start learning Mandarin. He was looking through a rack of DVDs containing Chinese movies with subtitles when he found a copy of *Casablanca*, in English.

He was studying it when a knock at the door took him by surprise.

"Since when do the guards knock?" Joe asked.

"Must be a new thing," Kurt said.

He went to the door and opened it, surprised to see a friendly face waiting on the other side.

"Major Gushan of the People's Liberation Army Navy," Kurt said. "I suppose I should invite you in. Although I have a feeling you know your way around."

"Technically, this is my home," the major admitted. "But as you and Joe are the ones staying here, why not?"

The major came inside; he carried a small shopping bag and little else. The three of them convened on the apartment's tiny balcony, sitting around a small table and admiring the view. If they leaned out far enough they could just see a portion of the Five Bridges area.

Gushan sighed as he looked at the two men. He seemed weary. He was at a loss for where to begin. "So . . ." he said finally. "Ahab."

"Yeah," Kurt said. "Ahab. He almost got us. He almost got us all."

Gushan looked away. His tiny part of China was beautiful. He suspected Kurt's little part of Washington was just as nice. As were most of the neighborhoods all across the globe. He could hardly stand to imagine them all being destroyed.

"You almost got me arrested by having Rand contact me," Gushan said. "I was already on thin ice after what happened in Norway."

"Sorry about that," Kurt said. "Rand and his sister took us to Ahab's base on Siabat Island. We couldn't have stopped the attack without their help. Rand has promised to go straight, and I intend to help clear his name. A word from your government would go a long way."

"I'll do what I can," Gushan said with a nod. "You saved my life once and I suppose he saved many more."

"I thought we were even," Kurt said, recalling the unspoken subtext of their conversation in Norway.

Gushan wrinkled his face. "Eh," he said. "Not quite. But we are now."

"Fair enough," Kurt said.

Gushan shifted in his seat.

"How'd you convince your superiors?" Kurt asked.

Gushan gave him the short version of things, wincing as he thought of his sore ribs, two of which had hairline fractures from the MP's nightstick. "I told them the truth. It wouldn't have mattered if your planes hadn't turned around. That gave the generals enough breathing room to hold off on an immediate counterstrike. They kept our planes on the ground. At that point, with only you and Ahab left in the sky, they decided to let it play out."

"We noticed the missiles stopped coming," Joe said.

"We didn't want to shoot you down by accident," Gushan insisted.

Kurt could believe that. He figured there were other reasons as well. "I'm guessing the high command wouldn't have been too sad if Ahab had ended up landing or crashing softly somewhere. In which case, they might have gotten their hands on the laser after all."

"I wouldn't put it past them," Gushan admitted. "Nor could I blame them. Whatever the reason was, it didn't get passed along to me."

"Admirals and generals are like that," Joe said. "Even in our country."

"The laser is gone," Kurt said. That was one thing he was sure of at this point.

"Your country has others in production," Gushan noted.

"And I'm sure China has something similar on the drawing board," Kurt replied. "Who knows, maybe one day we'll all have them. Hundreds of these planes flying around making it impossible for anyone to attack anyone. Might be nice."

"High walls," Gushan said. "In this city we prefer to build bridges."

"I noticed that," Joe said.

"I'm sure you did," Gushan replied, laughing. "You don't know this, but you've become quite a celebrity here. The Mad Bomber, they call you. More than a few of my countrymen would like to commend you on your flying ability, including a number of those admirals and generals."

Joe offered an appreciative nod. "I'll give them a demonstration, if it helps us get out of here."

Gushan smiled. "I'll see if there are any takers."

"So, what now?" Kurt said, getting back to business. "I mean this place is nice, but it's going to get crowded with the three of us living here."

"It's all been arranged," Gushan told him. "Your government. My government. They've been talking. Arguing mostly, and accusing each other of things, but at least they're talking."

"That's better than nothing," Joe said.

"And?" Kurt asked.

"Tomorrow, you and Joe will go home," Gushan said, sounding a bit wistful. "But tonight, we celebrate." He reached into the small bag and pulled out the bottle of baijiu he'd been trying to drink in the Arctic. "Ahab is gone—for good this time. The three of us are still alive. And the world has survived to see another day."

Kurt studied the ornate decanter. He remembered a similar bottle being put on hold to commemorate the joint mission that ended on the burning freighter. With Gushan's injuries it had gone unopened. This bottle, Gushan uncorked without further delay.

As the aroma diffused across the small balcony, Gushan pulled some glasses from a small cabinet underneath the table. He filled them one by one.

"Last time we shared a drink you were angry with me," he said, handing a glass to Kurt. "I can only hope your feelings have changed by now."

Kurt understood Gushan. He was a professional. He served his country, just as Kurt and Joe served the United States. But when given a chance to cause unnecessary death and destruction, he'd chosen a path of honor, one that repaid a debt to his friend while avoiding needless bloodshed. He'd then had the guts to go to the high command with the request that they stand down while all hell seemed to be breaking loose around them. Kurt couldn't imagine how bad things would have become if Gushan had chosen to stay on the sidelines.

And yet, unlike the ending of *Casablanca*, this would not be the beginning of a beautiful friendship. In a world where China and America were competing for everything under the sun, Kurt figured they would likely cross swords again in the future. But that didn't matter now. Today they were just soldiers, sharing a drink, happy to be done with their violent labors.

Kurt raised his glass. "To the Solitary Hill," he said, a play on Gushan's family name, which meant exactly that. "May it always stand tall."

Gushan looked as uncomfortable with being praised as Kurt and Joe were. He pivoted to a toast of his own. "To building bridges," he said. "Ones that are long enough to reach the other side no matter how far away."

"And," Joe added, "tall enough to fly under when you really need to."

Kurt laughed. Joe had lightened the moment, something all of them appreciated.

"Now that," Kurt said, "is an idea worth raising a glass to."

ABOUT THE AUTHORS

PHOTOGRAPH © ROB GREER

CLIVE CUSSLER was the author of more than eighty books in five bestselling series, including Dirk Pitt®, NUMA Files®, *Oregon* Files®, Isaac Bell®, and Sam and Remi Fargo®. His life nearly paralleled that of his hero Dirk Pitt. Whether searching for lost aircraft or leading expeditions to find famous shipwrecks, he and his NUMA crew of volunteers discovered and surveyed more than seventy-five lost ships of historic significance, including the long-lost Civil War submarine *Hunley*, which was raised in 2000 with much publicity. Cussler passed away in February 2020.

GRAHAM BROWN is the author of *Black Rain*, *Black Sun*, *Clive Cussler Condor's Fury*, and *Clive Cussler's Dark Vector*, and the coauthor with Cussler of *Devil's Gate*, *The Storm*, *Zero Hour*, *Ghost Ship*, *The Pharaoh's Secret*, *Nighthawk*, *The Rising Sea*, *Sea of Greed*, *Journey of the Pharaohs*, and *Fast Ice*. He is a pilot and an attorney.

VISIT CLIVE CUSSLER ONLINE

cusslerbooks.com

cusslermuseum.com

ClivecusslerAdventures

CliveCussler_

TheCliveCussler